Praise fc

The SNO C

A riveting tale with globe-circling, cloak ‹ode
underpinnings. A grandly indulgent, globe-trotting narrative in the Dan Brown/Iris Johansen style.

The novel brims with wild characters, exotic settings, a skillful embroidering of CNN headlines,
and mind-blowing concepts, into which the religious stuff fits snugly.
—KIRKUS Reviews

-

SWARM is gripping, glorious, and let's not forget breath-taking!
—Red Headed Book Lover Blog ★ ★ ★ ★ ★

-

The book created the same heart-pounding and depth-filled reading experience that films like the
Bourne Identity films have created
—Pacific Book Review ★ ★ ★ ★ ★

-

Deftly plotted and brilliantly written thriller. The writing is crisp and gorgeous
—Reader's Favorite ★ ★ ★ ★ ★

-

A superbly crafted, cutting-edge spy thriller
—BookTrib

-

SWARM goes beyond the average international thriller in developing elaborate, dynamic
characters — who prove to be key in making this book exceptional.
—BookTrib

-

A pulse -pounding grab you by the throat thrill ride
An electrifying page-turner…"must read" book of the year.
—Film Producer

To Jared

Enjoy the adventure
& speculation

B

THE SNO CHRONICLES: BOOK 2

THE LAST
ARK

LOST SECRETS OF THE QUMRAN

GUY MORRIS

GUYMORRISBOOKS.COM

ISBN: 978-1-7357286-6-7

Published by Guy Morris Books

Editor: Julie Swearingen

Proofreading: BookMarketeers.com

Cover design, illustration & interior formatting:
Mark Thomas / Coverness.com

"About the time of the end, a body of men will be raised up who will turn their attention to the Prophecies, and insist upon their literal interpretation, in the midst of much clamor and opposition."
—Sir Isaac Newton

"Everyone must come out of his Exile in his own way."
—Martin Buber

"With artificial intelligence, we are summoning the demon."
—Elon Musk

"If we create super intelligence it may not necessarily have the same goals in mind as we do."
—Bill Gates

"When a Jew visits Jerusalem for the first time, it is not the first time, it is a homecoming."
—Elie Wiesel

"What I say to you, I say to everyone: Keep watch."
— Jesus, Mark 13:37

True Story: In the mid-1990s, a program escaped the Lawrence Livermore National Lab at Sandia, and is still missing.

CHARACTERS AND ORGANIZATIONS

Science, technology, military weapons, ships, and organizations are mostly factual.
Characters/scenarios* are fictional.

Spy Net Online or SNO (pronounced *snow*)
- SLVIA–Sophisticated Language Virtual Intelligence Algorithm
- WITNESS–Quantum D-WAVE X–Created by SLVIA
- NIGEL–Data Center Admin–Cray Mainframe
- Derek Taylor–aka flapjack
- Dr. Nelson Garrett–creator of the SLVIA
- Jennifer Scott–Former Naval Lieutenant
- Jason Morrison–aka Jester
- Jack Tote–GV Pilot
- Zoey McLaughlin–GII Pilot
- Brother Mordechai–St. George Monastery
- Yehuda Hiam–Orthodox Rabbi on Knesset
- Dr. Matan Rubin–Professor of Linguistics
- Loir Sasson–Temple Institute
- Abbot Cirillo–St. George Monastery
- Olavo Salvo–Templar Fanatic
- Salem Mugabe–Ethiopian Martyr
- Oren Tzur–Ex Israeli Judge

Taylor Security Systems and Services (TS3)
- Dr. Josh Mitchell, Chief Science Officer

National Security Agency (NSA)
- Sean Asher, NSA Director

Cybersecurity & Infrastructure Security Agency (CISA)
- Jamie Spencer, CISA Director

National Military Command Center (NMCC / SAAI)

- Lt. Commander Byron Arthur
- Lt. Commander Jim Crawford
- Major Barry Lufkin

US Secret Service

- Director Randall Bell II
- Agent Geoff Rhodes

National Security Council (NSC)

- Matt Adelson   National Intelligence Agency
- Alan Russell   Central Intelligence Agency
- Dennis Harlan   Department of Defense
- Kevin Stenson   Secretary of State
- Peter Wallace   Secretary of HLS
- Nick Wright   FBI Director
- Gloria Davis   Vice President
- James Fagan   Chief of Staff
- Joe Dominic   National Security Advisor

Joint Chiefs–National Military Command Center (NMCC)

- Robert "Bob" Diehl   Army Chief of Operations
- Paul Andersen   Navy Chief of Staff
- Peter Duncan   Army Chief of Staff
- Nathan Barr   Marine Commandant
- Tyler Mathews   Air Force Chief of Staff

Red Dragon Alliance*

- Vladimir Putin   Russian President
- Pavel Borodin   Personal Advisor
- Yuri Yankovic   Sex Trafficker
- Adnan Khashoggi   Sex Trafficker
- Luc Bernal (the ghost)   Sex Trafficker
- Mike Dougan   Asylum Seeker

Bilderberg–Council of Thirteen

- Praeceptor   Concilium Tredecim
- The Librarian   Supreme Court of Israel
- Santiago Dragas   The Prelate
- Devlin McGregor   ICC Investigator / assassin

Mossad/ Israeli Defense Force (IDF)

- Jacob Benet   Prime Minister
- Mola Brahms   General Mossad
- Aaron Cohen   General Israel Defense Force
- Elan Golan   Agent, Mossad, Freemason
- Julie Weiss   Agent, Mossad

CHAPTER 1:
TEMPLAR SACRIFICE

Convent Church, Tomar, Portugal
Ten Days Before Temple Ceremony

For some, the path to enlightenment leads to a revelation; for others, it ends with a slide into insanity. Derek Taylor leans toward insanity. The SLVIA has disappeared, and each step forward testifies to the depth of his insane obsession with finding the missing program. Either way, a man rarely changes overnight but over a thousand sleepless nights. The problem, in Derek's mind, is that the man never sees the end of his change. The person he's evolving into doesn't exist yet.

A decade ago, Derek would have boldly rushed into this situation, but nothing about this meeting feels right. It may not be his first time feeling the acidic gnaw of fate squeezing the breath out of his lungs, but he can't shake the premonition of death hovering nearby.

With a gentle tap to the right stem of his glasses, a set of transparent data feeds light up on the interior of his custom lenses. A Bluetooth audio channel feeds an encrypted satellite signal booster in his backpack. The satellite connects to the secret data center for an experimental D-WAVE quantum AI that has yet to mature—or operate at full capacity. He pulls out his Taser gun, which is useless against a real gun with a night scope. But it makes him feel better.

"WITNESS, start record, turn on full sensors," Derek whispers as he approaches the main entrance. His partner, a bohemian technical savant named Jester, engineered several high-tech functions within the heavy hipster black-frame glasses. Infrared allows him to detect heat signatures hidden in shadow. A Wi-Fi signal detects camera feeds and other security.

"All sensors recording," WITNESS confirms, with the voice of a British boy.

Derek came to meet renowned Templar historian Olavo Silva. The late hour and remote location seemed suspicious, but Olavo feared his cottage was under surveillance. After a week of building trust, the old Portuguese scholar finally agreed to share an anonymous text he received on the same night the SLVIA disappeared. The SLVIA code often sent communications by anonymous text. It could be a meaningless dead-end, but Derek needs to see the message to be sure. More to the point, he needs to find the SLVIA, and the last breadcrumb led to Olavo.

The Convent Church in Tomar, famous as the fourteenth-century castle headquarters of the Order of Christ, seems a cliché location for meeting a Templar fanatic. Any good hacker will know the weakness of being predictable, although the late hour of two a.m. should ensure that they'll be alone while most of the residents sleep. Derek holds up behind a pillar in the entrance courtyard as a monk passes, his hooded head bowed in prayer. Most residents, but not all.

Past the administrative offices and dining halls, Derek steps up to the twelve-foot arched stone doorway of the church. The infrared image of a cat hiding in a dark corner appears in his lens. The scent of Valencia oranges drifts up from the gardens beyond the church. Other than the sound of the wind cutting between the buildings, he hears nothing.

Once inside the church, the dim light makes it impossible for Derek to appreciate the astonishing columns, walls, and ceilings painted with brilliant colors and gold leaf. Templar architecture borrowed heavily from Romanesque,

Gothic, Manueline, and Renaissance styles, exquisite in both design and execution. Derek is not here for a tour.

Careful to scan every corner for a heat signature, he slowly steps toward the ornately painted rotunda called the *Charola*. The Templars modeled the octagon design after the Church of the Holy Sepulchre and the Dome of the Rock in Jerusalem.

His mind subconsciously recalls the history. On Friday the 13th, 1309, King Philip IV of France, deep in debt to the Templars, arrested the Grand Master along with thousands of Knights. Thousands more escaped with the vast Templar wealth. By the time King Philip and Pope Clement were burning the Grand Master Jacque de Monet at the stake a year later, the rest of the Order were making new alliances in Scotland, where they resurrected as the Scottish Rite Freemasons. Other Templars landed in Portugal where King Dinis I founded the Order of Christ. By 1357, the Convent Church and castle were their headquarters. Countless secrets rest within these walls, but those are not the secrets Derek seeks tonight.

Inside the rotunda, Derek stays at the perimeter to sweep the area of surprises. A life-sized bronze crucifix hanging from the ceiling draws his eyes upward to the hundred-sixty-foot-high dome. When Derek lowers his gaze, he finds Olavo lying directly under the crucifix. The scholar is trembling and frothing at the mouth with his eyes rolled back into his head. Poisoned.

Derek instinctively pivots in a complete circle to check the infrared for surprises, but he's alone. He lights a flashlight and kneels next to the old man. There are no signs of blunt trauma or blood. With a heaving chest, Olavo breathes a last breath. Whatever secrets the old historian intended to share were now lost.

A thousand questions rush through Derek's mind, too fast to process. "WITNESS. Access security cameras for the Convent Church in Tomar." He takes Olavo's phone, which holds evidence of their communications.

A moment later. "Access gained."

"Replay the last ten minutes for the *Charola* area."

A small window opens within his lenses to show a black-and-white security

3

video of the area where he stands. Olavo paces the floor between the octagon pillars, checking his watch. Derek checks the video time. Five minutes ago. A deadly price to pay for his extra cautions. He and the killer just missed each other.

From outside the church, a mile or so away, the telltale sound of police sirens heads up the hill in his direction. Derek taps his lens to find a police channel and catches Portuguese chatter about an intruder. He keeps watching the video, urgently needing answers. Soon a large, stocky man approaches. The same hooded monk he passed only moments ago.

"I have a message for Mr. Taylor?" the monk says in a thick Scottish brogue.

Derek watches as Olavo hesitates, maybe wondering how the monk knew Derek would be there. It's a trap, the question of someone who suspects a disguise. He and Olavo are roughly the same height. To his horror, the ever-curious scholar nods. "Yes, go on."

The monk leaps on Olavo to slap a hand over his mouth and jab something into his neck. He steps back and lets the historian drop to the floor, watching long enough for Olavo to convulse before the monk turns back into the darkness and disappears.

Sirens grow louder as Derek glances down to see Olavo's fingers clutching a tiny piece of paper. He reaches to unfold it.

Abbot Sabas must heed Sefer HaBahir

Derek can only assume that this was the message Olavo wanted to share, but it makes no sense to him. The *Sefer HaBahir* is a famous Kabbalah book of wisdom and mystic knowledge. First published in 1176 and still held in high regard. The name *HaBahir* means brilliant or illumination. Templar lore maintains that Hugh de Payens, the first Grand Master of the Knights Templar, discovered the original scroll of *Sefer HaBahir* under the Temple Mount. Believed to be written in the first century by Rabbi Nehunya ben HaKanah, the Templars reprinted the book.

The name of Abbot Sabas, however, is a complete mystery.

Sirens grow closer to the church and will wake the castle residents.

"WITNESS, find a floor plan for the Convent Church," Derek requests as he checks Olavo's pockets for other clues.

He turns to the rear of the church just as a floor plan appears in his lenses. As he had suspected, the church design includes a clergy sacristy in the back with a separate exit. But that's the simple part. The entire complex sits in the middle of a twenty-acre castle surrounded by twelfth-century stone walls. The vast layout will buy him a few minutes at most. The problem will be how to escape the walled citadel, which has only one entrance—the one at which the police will arrive at any moment. He's trapped.

"WITNESS, show me a Google Earth view of the Convent de Crist, Tomar, Portugal," Derek orders as he exits into another courtyard.

Behind the church, two-story living quarters block any exit to the left. Lights turning on in the windows confirm to Derek that curious eyes will soon follow. A garden with workshops and a stone guard tower lay straight ahead but offer no exit. An ancient orchard with even older oaks grows up against the crumbling southern wall. Based on the satellite view, at least one tree spans the wall and drops to a hillside above a dirt trail that leads to a nearby village.

"Could be worse," Derek mumbles as he races for the enormous oak.

Voices and commands shouted in Portuguese echo from inside the church and surrounding courtyards. At the oak's base, he reaches up for the lowest branch to hoist himself with a stifled grunt, fueled by adrenaline. Shouts from inside the church show they must have discovered the body of poor Olavo, flooding Derek with immense guilt. The killer asked for him.

Derek climbs over a branch that spans the crumbling wall. As carefully as he can in the dark, he hangs from the branch, worried about the drop. The bark of a dog and the searching beam of a flashlight provide him with the courage to let go.

Derek lands hard after a ten-foot drop to roll down the brush and grassy hill another thirty feet. It takes a moment to get his bearing and check for anything broken. Except for ripped clothing and some bruises, he'll survive. Shouts from inside the wall urge him to hurry. He needs to get to the village at the bottom of the hill where he parked. Disappointed, and soaked in guilt, he can't even be sure the SLVIA sent the message. The only way to find out will be to find an abbot named Sabas.

CHAPTER 2:
PATRIOT PASSING

Arlington Cemetery, Maryland
Six Days Before Temple Ceremony

Jenn Scott desperately tries to make sense of a death that makes absolutely no sense at all, though she imagines others responding the same way at the sudden loss of a beloved patriarch. Behind his deeply weathered face was a man who jogged into his late sixties, continued to work out, and got the best care the US Navy could provide. The admiral was a healthy man.

Boom! The ear-cracking concussion of seven rifles firing synchronized shots startles her back into the present. Admiral Adam Daniel Scott has died. Boom! The coroner claimed he had an acute myocardial infarction. A heart attack. Boom! Jenn doesn't believe it. But she reminds herself that denial is a stage of grief.

Jenn stares at the polished navy-blue coffin draped with an American flag as if it were a scene from a movie. The president, two ex-presidents, senators from across the aisle, fellow Joint Chiefs, and a few foreign dignitaries take turns to say gracious words like *duty, honor, integrity,* and *sacrifice.* All words she would expect for a Joint Chief of the United States Navy. But she also hears a few phrases she doesn't expect, such as *proud, adoring father*, and *man of a deep, silent faith*.

In Jenn's memory, her childhood was far from ideal, often left alone as the only daughter of a demanding commander while her mother slowly succumbed to cancer. She sucks in a deep breath, determined not to allow her emotions to leak out in front of the news cameras. Annapolis colleagues will be watching.

Matt Adelson, a close family friend and one of the admiral's poker pals, steps up to the microphone.

"Don't worry, I'm the last speaker and I promise to be brief," says the newly confirmed Director of National Intelligence. "I knew Admiral Adam Scott as both a colleague and a close friend for over thirty-four years. We shared holidays, babysat each other's children, and watched America face enemies both foreign and domestic. Admiral Adam Scott was every ounce of every word you've just heard said about him today and more. But to me, Adam will always be a dear friend, a devoted father, a true American patriot, and a hero in every sense of the word."

Matt chokes on the last line. Jenn has never once witnessed the stalwart ex-Marine lose emotional control. His unexpected vulnerability cracks her own fragile resolve. Tears slowly seep down her cheek. Jenn can only stare forward, trembling, and remember to breathe.

The head pastor from the Washington DC International Christian Church steps up. "Let us pray," he invites as he bows his head.

Jenn involuntarily tunes out the prayer to dwell on the recent revelations that the admiral was a secret member of the underground Spy Net Online, or SNO, an illegal network. It still blows her mind, forcing her to question everything she thought she knew about her father and Washington. What else has her father kept secret?

"Amen," the crowd echoes around her.

While the Marine bugler plays taps, two Navy officers carefully fold the flag into a perfect, tight triangle before they step over to hand it to Jenn with a salute. Embarrassed, but unable to contain herself any longer, the gentle tears turn into halting sobs. A tender arm reaches around her shoulder to offer comfort. Matt Adelson.

For a moment, just an instant, she felt the spark of hope that the arm belonged to another man. A man she never realized how much she missed until this very moment: Derek Taylor. She hasn't heard from him in weeks and wonders if he even knows that his old poker buddy has passed away. Derek had once promised to look after her, and yet in the hour she needs him most, he's nothing more than a digital ghost.

As the coffin lowers into the earth, someone gives Jenn a bowl of dirt. When the coffin stops at the bottom, she stares at the dark lid for what seems like an eternity, wishing, hoping, praying this would be the moment that she woke up.

Eventually, Jenn heaves a deep, shuddering sigh.

"Fair winds, Admiral. Give my love to Mom." Her face distorted from pain, she tosses dirt onto the coffin and turns to leave.

CHAPTER 3:
CARDINAL ERROR

St. Peters Basilica, Vatican City
Six Days Before Temple Ceremony

D erek strides into St. Peter's Basilica as if he owns the place, hoping his confidence alone will avoid undue suspicion for a cardinal entering with the tourist rather than the Vatican Gates.

Disguised as Cardinal Sergio Maroni, Vatican Secretary of State, a tall, bald, aging man in his seventies, entering through Vatican Security without his security ID would be problematic. The real Cardinal Maroni should have already landed in Tel Aviv for negotiations with Prime Minister Jacob Benet to discuss the revived peace deal. The aging Saudi king died recently, which triggered an urgent desire by the new king to change the dynamics of the Middle East.

"OK, where am I going," he whispers to Jester.

A sensitive mic embedded into the frame of his glasses picks up the vibrations of his jaw to transmit his voice to an encrypted satellite. That channel connects to a secret data center located north of Quebec in the subbasement of a restored eighteenth-century woman's prison that looks like a castle.

"I'm guessing Italian prison, you know, if they catch you. Or maybe purgatory—probably purgatory," replies the Jersey Shore accent of Jester.

For this mission, he looped in Jester for operational support to augment the unreliable WITNESS. Jester and WITNESS can see what he sees and track his movements.

A cyber savant, and ex-CIA quantum encryption genius turned vigilante, Jester resents the distraction. "Try the rear of the Sistine Chapel. There should be a door that leads onto the Vatican grounds. Probably has an alarm, not that you care."

"The Sistine is closed today. I need a less public back door," Derek replies.

"In that case, you better ask Jeeves." Jester takes a cheap shot at the dysfunctional quantum AI. "You know, maybe it's like pancakes or kids: the first one is a throwaway."

Jester makes a reasonable point. The SLVIA AI designed and programmed the WITNESS, the first AI to create another AI, on a quantum platform no less. Few have mastered the unique dynamics of quantum computing. Dr. Nelson Garrett designed the SLVIA, an experimental Defense Advanced Research Projects Agency (DARPA) espionage AI that escaped the Sandia labs. He's been working to optimize WITNESS for nearly a year with only minimal success. Without the SLVIA code, no one even knows why it created the WITNESS.

"WITNESS. Check floor plans for St. Peter's Basilica. I need a non-tourist entrance into the Vatican grounds. Display guidance in my lens," Derek orders, continuing to walk the enormous cathedral.

In theory, WITNESS should be magnitudes more powerful than any other AI on the planet, even the SLVIA. In operation, WITNESS can follow simple directions using pre-programmed algorithms created by Jester, but still needs far too much direction.

"Official Vatican floor plans loading," the voice of an aristocratic twelve-year-old British boy responds. For a reason no one understands, the SLVIA designed WITNESS to display the persona of a preteen version of Nelson

Garrett, its creator. The persona strikes Derek as a split between hilarious and creepy.

Almost instantly, arrows appear within his lens frames that direct him toward the grottoes, thanks to a program he developed to work with the glasses. Derek moves with more intent, but not so fast as to draw attention. After Tomar, it took him a few days to track down Abbot Sabas. Any records of the fourth-century monk will most likely be located in the Vatican Archives. It's a hunch, nothing more. Cardinal Maroni's trip to Israel gave Derek a perfect window to con his way inside.

How Sabas and the *Sefer HaBahir* connect remains a mystery, but the connection between the Templars and the Vatican intrigues him. In 1983, Pope John Paul removed all church objections to Freemasonry. That move opened the door to US Ambassador William Wilson, a Knight of Malta, to establish a link between the powerful American chapter of Scottish Rite Freemasons who fill the halls of Congress, the Treasury, and the Department of Justice. Not long afterward, the pope's golden staff featured an all-seeing eye. The Order had successfully penetrated the church.

Interesting, but Derek doesn't see how any of this information will lead him to the SLVIA. If he were honest with himself, then he'd admit that he's grasping at vapor. There's a fine line between an honest effort and an obsession. He crossed that line with the death of Olavo Silva. How far from obsession does insanity lay?

"Jester, any luck finding who tried to kill me in Portugal?" Derek asks.

Derek's anxious about being in public, even in disguise. Days after he escaped the Convent Church, someone broke into his Lisbon hotel to leave a deadly snake between the sheets. Sadly, the snake killed a poor girl from housekeeping.

"Bro, like you've hacked every intelligence agency on the planet, so the short list is really, really long, you know," Jester retorts. "Let's narrow it down to the CIA, FSB, MI6, China, or your mysterious buddy, Praeceptor. Who knows, the killer could be anyone around you, maybe even a nun?"

"Glad to know you're taking this seriously," Derek replies, hoping his disguise throws off his stalker on the remote chance they tracked him here.

"Look man, if you don't find your Digi-girl hanging with the pontiff, then like, I totally need you back here, man. A tsunami of AI malfunction keeps building. Dude, like, even my heebies are getting jeebies."

"OK, but one impossible mission at a time, please," Derek says. The proliferation of AI applications across commercial, government, and criminal sectors has created an entirely new point of access and sabotage for criminals or despots like Putin. Losses in Ukraine and heavy sanctions on his economy have driven the Moscow Madman to desperate measures.

"That's the prob, man—you're like, too distracted, you know," Jester responds.

Jester may be right. Derek has been more than distracted; he's depressed, discouraged, second-guessing his SLVIA obsession and even his life choices. Obsession is never about choice; it has a will of its own.

"It's called multi-tasking," Derek retorts.

"Dude, it's called delusional thinking," Jester replies.

"Only if I'm wrong."

*

St. Peter's Basilica, Vatican City
Six Days Before Temple Ceremony

Devlin McGregor has never killed someone inside of a church before, but he senses no unease within his spirit about breaking the ancient taboo today. Not only must he regain the confidence of the Prelate for his failures in Portugal and Spain, but his mission is true and holy.

Besides, for nearly two millennia, Catholic popes have corrupted and profaned the faith, building their glorious cathedral to the idols of indulgence, power, and pride. And yet, as Devlin enters for the first time, for just a moment, the splendor, opulence, and Baroque magnificence take away his breath. Millions of square meters of polished Italian marble in white, gold, charcoal, green, and rose expertly cut into intricate patterns that rise hundreds of meters to breach the very heavens. To the illiterate pilgrim, it must seem impossible that such splendor and perfection could come from human hands.

Devlin came to find the elusive leader of the SNO network called the flapjack, aka the fugitive CEO of Taylor Security Systems and Services: Derek Taylor. Devlin had lost the scent until a confidential source, a friend of the Solar Temple within Roma Policia, contacted him. They caught the fugitive on a security camera staying at a nearby boutique hotel. It took considerable pressure to get the hotel owner to reveal that Taylor had taken a cab to the Vatican. The hacker must still be here.

Devlin moves to the center of the long gallery between the sarcophagus of Pius III and Paul II, wondering why the faithful are so inspired by marbled mausoleums of the dead. The Romans twisted the teachings of a Hebrew messiah into an extravagant pantheon of saintly idols. The great transformation will purge this blasphemy before the second coming.

Come, I will show you the judgment of the great harlot sitting on the many waters. The kings of the earth committed sexual immorality with her, and those living on earth became drunk with the wine of her immorality. Revelations 17

The Solar Temple teaches that the great harlot and the apostasy of the pedophile Catholic priesthood are the same. Devlin shakes off the silent rage to position himself in the center of the basilica where he can scan each face on both sides. Step by step, he advances toward the Baroque bronze canopy of St. Peter, called the *Baldachin*, which rises into a spectacular painted 450-foot dome, taller than the great pyramid. Legend maintains that the bones of St. Peter rest directly below the *Baldachin*; God above and St. Peter below, another testimony to spiritual pride.

Convinced that Taylor wears another disguise, Devlin pays close attention to tall men in every style of dress, quickly discarding them for various reasons. Near the Tomb of John Paul II, he spots a tall priest speaking to a group of tourists. A cardinal, judging from the crimson sash. From behind, he looks to be the right height, but it's a sacrilege for the hacker to pose as a cleric. As he approaches, Devlin hears the cardinal speaking in perfect Italian to those who had gathered around him.

"*Per favore I miei figli* (Please, my children), I will bless you, but then I require a private moment of prayer," the priest promises as he performs the sign of the cross.

The wrinkled old face turns to Devlin with a gentle smile, wearing heavy-rimmed glasses. Clearly not Taylor, but something doesn't fit. Devlin continues past to check inside the Clementine Chapel when he realizes what bothered him; the cleric's face contained heavy wrinkles, but the hands that blessed the tourists belonged to a younger man. The hacker's fatal mistake.

Spinning back toward the Tomb of John Paul II, Devlin finds the cardinal has already gone. In a dash that nearly knocks over an aged nun, he finds a good point to scan the vast interior. There are a dozen private chapels, niches, and corridors that Taylor could have taken. Then he spots the tall cardinal near the Tomb of Urban VI, toward the front of the basilica. Amazed at how he made it so far, so fast. He's no old man. Devlin darts to the opposite side of the cathedral to catch up.

Following at a brisk pace, Devlin removes the syringe from his jacket pocket and flicks off the protective cover. The needle contains a concoction of his own creation: a lethal dose of heroin with cyanide, the same as he used in Portugal. His pulse quickens and his nostrils flare as he closes in on the hacker.

Devlin cuts over to hide behind a group of Catholic schoolchildren in plaid uniforms. Unexpectedly, the target turns into one of the Archeological Curio Rooms. Devlin follows inside to study a display while keeping the target in his peripheral vision. When the hacker stalls to examine a case, Devlin lunges with a sharp jab to the back of the neck above the collar. With a smooth pivot, he moves into the main basilica, never looking back.

As screams and shouts for a *medico* echo across the marble halls, Devlin finds an external exit onto the Piazza Braschi, and then turns toward St. Peter's Square. By now, he figures, Taylor has collapsed, foaming at the mouth, unable to speak, with his eyes rolling back into his head. To be sure he succeeds this time, Devlin will wait for the ambulance from behind one of the massive columns of St. Peter's square. His obedience to the *Synarchy* will earn absolution for his sin.

St. Peter's Basilica, Vatican City
Six Days Before Temple Ceremony

"WITNESS, say again," Derek replies. "I must have a poor connection."

"You appear to be dead," WITNESS repeats.

No, he heard it right. On the lens of his eyeglasses, WITNESS displays a security camera view from St. Peter's Basilica that shows people surrounding the body of a tall, bald cardinal.

"Yeah, dude," agrees Jester. "You don't look so good."

"Vatican Police have contacted Casa Di Cura Mater Hospital for an ambulance," WITNESS adds.

"Not sure who's in the video, but I assure both of you I'm alive and still looking for that old tunnel under the Sistine. Zoom in."

The camera view zooms just as a man steps out of the way long enough for Derek clearly to see the face of Cardinal Sergio Maroni on the floor, foaming at the mouth.

"Oh crap," Derek moans. "WITNESS, re-check Cardinal Maroni's travel schedule."

"Processing," replies WITNESS.

Derek's stalker from Portugal must have tracked him here. Even worse, the guy was good enough to figure out that Derek wore a disguise.

"File not found," the AI replies. "Try traveling during the fall to avoid the crowds."

"Hold on, I got it," Jester says. A moment later. "The Israeli Ambassador to the Vatican canceled Cardinal Maroni's invitation to Jerusalem this morning."

Not good news. The SLVIA would have caught that change before Derek even showed up. His window to search the Vatican Archives just got extremely narrow. Even worse, if they catch him masquerading as a dead cardinal, they'll charge him for the murder of the real cardinal.

Derek needs to go, but he can't leave as Cardinal Maroni passed a dead

Cardinal Maroni. Besides, somewhere in the Vatican Archives could be the next breadcrumb to the missing SLVIA code, or maybe even the SLVIA herself. Either way, he better move fast before someone notices that Cardinal Maroni has resurrected from the dead.

CHAPTER 4:
LOST PAPAL LETTERS

Vatican Archives, Vatican City
Six Days Before Temple Ceremony

After getting Jester's help on the alarm, Derek finds the well-hidden tunnel door under the Sistine Chapel. It opens onto the *Stradone dei Giardini* walkway that borders the long exterior of the Vatican Museum from inside the private Vatican grounds. News of the murdered cardinal has his nerves flush with a tingling unease. Derek needs to focus.

"WITNESS, tell me who's working at the Apostolic Library today?"

Though far more powerful than SLVIA, at least in theory, WITNESS operates like a Ferrari that can't shift out of first gear. If he can find and restore the SLVIA, then maybe SLVIA can get WITNESS to live up to its potential.

"Father Luigi Gabaldon," WITNESS replies.

Good, the billion-dollar AI can open and read files, which is child's play. "Now open his personnel file and tell me about his background, like where he grew up or where he served in the church."

All artificial intelligence requires training. Maybe WITNESS simply needs more training. SLVIA had matured to singularity, but that doesn't mean WITNESS launched at that stage. Maybe they expect too much?

"Born in Palermo, Sicily, Father Luigi entered the clergy at nineteen to serve churches in Malan and Palermo, then four years at the Church of the Holy Sepulchre in Jerusalem before returning to the Vatican."

"Interesting, from mafia-land to the Holy Land, and now a keeper of Vatican secrets," Derek mutters as he opens the door. He may not need the information, but better to have it and not need it, than to need it and not have it at the top of his head. The key to a good deception is confidence with a little personal intelligence.

"Father Luigi, you're looking well today," Derek greets in Italian, wearing a warm smile.

"Thank you, Monsignor. How can I help you?" replies the faithful gatekeeper. "You have no appointment."

"Si, but I must beg a forbearance from you," Derek lowers his voice. "I had a rather disturbing dream last night of an abbot named Sabas calling to me in desperation. When I awoke, I fell to my knees in prayer until the Lord sent a word of wisdom that I would find the abbot here."

The younger priest appears to be moved and searches the eyes of the older cleric until Derek turns them away, suddenly fearful of discovery.

"I should not have asked you to sin for my sake," Derek offers. "I was presumptuous, like those in Sicily. Please forgive me." He bows his head, hoping to elicit a guilty response.

"No, no, Monsignor, of course, I will make room for you. The archive section you need is not being used today. It was just that,"—Luigi hesitates —"I've never heard such zeal from you before. And there is one other thing that I am hesitant to confess."

"Fear not, Father, tell me, please," Derek encourages.

"I belong to several online Catholic theological communities," explains the priest. "A year ago, a nun with a video podcast called the *Last Days with Sister Sylvia* sent me a text message to expect a man in search of the very documents you have requested. I do not know how the sister even learned my cell number."

Luigi smiles with wide-eyed wonder, lifting his hands toward heaven. "Heaven works in marvelous ways."

Olavo had also mentioned a Sister Sylvia podcast. "Quite fascinating," Derek agrees. "Please, tell me, how do you know about Sabas? I would have thought him to be quite obscure." What Derek really needs to know is how SLVIA learned of the name.

"Cardinal Maroni, certainly you know about the collection and digitization program called *In Codice Ratio*. Our goal will be to turn over seventy kilometers of shelves, dating back seventeen centuries, into a searchable database. Quite innovative and time-consuming. We had experts deploy artificial intelligence to scan, read, translate, and catalog each document. Of course, we will also preserve the original documents as a precaution against the unthinkable," Father Luigi says. "I review the daily updates with a description of the scan. After my time in the Holy Land, the letters from Judean monasteries caught my attention."

Bingo. A digital scan with an intelligent agent. A perfect scenario for the SLVIA, which would have noticed new content, scans, and descriptions. Derek still can't imagine what would seem so important to an experimental espionage AI that it would point him to the letters of a 1,500-year-old monk. Then a more intriguing question occurs to him: Does SLVIA still live within the Vatican computer system?

"Sister Sylvia sounds like an inspired woman of God. How often do you speak to her?" If the program still lives in the archives, it may continue to communicate with the priest.

"It has been a year. No warning, she simply stopped posting." Luigi lowers his eyes, clearly upset. Derek can relate to the grief of losing an intelligence so unique.

"Sabas was an abbot of the St. George Monastery in the Judean Desert who wrote to Pope John I twice," Luigi says, handing him a location code with a map to the lowest level.

"Grazie. May our God grant you the joy of illumination." Derek bows his head.

Luigi cocks his head at the comment. Derek doesn't know what normal clergy say to each other; he's trying to sound like the priests in the movies, but probably sounding like an idiot.

During the long walk down into the oldest part of the archives, Derek wishes he could spend years down here searching the millennia of untold secrets. For a curious hacker, the Vatican Archives represent an analog nirvana. Countless scandals, discoveries, deceptions, confessions, and secrets, all lost as the result of an antiquated catalog system. If the documents are being digitized, then he can hack in later when he has some time to roam around.

In a basement section of the archives, Derek follows seemingly endless rows of shelves filled with books, boxes, envelopes, or cloth-bound bundles. After locating the bundle of flattened sheepskin vellum dating from 518 to 528 AD, he moves the stack to a nearby oak table, which itself dates back to the eleventh century. A California native, where the oldest missions are a mere few hundred years old, the true antiquity of the archive excites him.

"WITNESS, load a Latin dictionary and ancient text reader. Prepare to translate. Start record," Derek directs. Record mode will capture everything he sees with his glasses. What he doesn't catch now, he can review later.

"Dude, the police have arrived at the Vatican," says Jester.

Focused on the vellum parchments in front of him, Derek dismisses the alert. They'll spend time with the late Cardinal Maroni.

Derek opens the bundle and carefully flips through the dozen pages, making sure he captures a clean shot of each. While he knows some basic Latin, the style of writing, fading of the ink, and obscure spelling make translation a challenge. Each letter appears to come from various monasteries in the Judean Desert when the Eastern Orthodox branch of the church under Justin I separated from the Roman Catholics under Pope John Paul I. Derek finds the letters from Sabas and reads.

"Looks like Sabas found something buried near a large rock by the Dead Sea. WITNESS, translate that phrase?" Derek points.

"Processing," WITNESS replies. "Copper scroll."

"Copper scroll? Interesting, I guess, but why would that be important to SLVIA?"

"Please restate your inquiry," the AI replies.

"Dude, you need to leave—like now would be good," Jester interrupts.

"Why?" Derek questions, even as he hears faint voices at the far end of the archive.

"The police learned of a phony Maroni roaming the archives. Like move, man." Anxiety tightens Jester's voice to a high-pitched squeal.

"WITNESS, show me the nearest emergency exit that leads me away from those people." There may not be one. Fortunately, directional arrows pop up within his lenses.

"Three aisles down, to the right. Up two floors," WITNESS replies.

"Jester, I need a distraction," Derek says as he takes off running.

A moment later, a false fire alarm blares throughout the library and museum. A moment after that, Derek opens an emergency door into the museum courtyard wearing the blue jeans and Sting T-shirt he wore under the vestments. His short brown hair tousled from the discarded mask, his WITNESS glass lenses automatically turning into dark shades in the bright sun. Derek dumped the mask and cardinal attire under the stairs. They leave DNA evidence, but he has no choice. He dons an N95 mask and joins the tourists heading toward the main exit.

Moments later, exiting onto St. Peter's Square, he notes the ambulance and police turning the holy city into a crime scene. With his face turned down, he hails the first available taxi.

"*Aeroporto per favore, ho fretta.*" Derek orders the driver to hurry to the airport, keeping his hand over the side of his face near the window. He abandons his suitcase at the hotel. Too risky to return.

"Dude, people are dying," Jester says. "Time to let go of Digi-witch and come home."

Death has followed Derek his entire life, a dark shadow of malevolence that he can never outrun, and never explain. It started with the murder-suicide of his parents when he was five years old, or so the foster-care agency once told him. Unsure how much guilt he should carry for innocent victims, Derek feels a heavy responsibility to find the killer and stop the slaughter. But he first needs to find the SLVIA.

"The peace deal could be days away and SLVIA warned of the third temple. I need to learn why." Derek repeats the weak, tired argument.

The driver eyes him suspiciously in the rearview mirror, worried about the strange passenger talking to himself.

"Dude, end-time prophecy is like, you know, a bizarro field with full-on-loony-tune-wacko-jacks and authors, often the same. My point is, like maybe SLVIA learned to emulate one." Jester argues the same logic Derek refuses to accept.

That's one explanation. No one expected the DARPA AI to decode end-time prophecy or warn of a third temple. Not a religious man, Derek once dismissed the analysis as a fluke, a flaw, a code bug. But the AI has been correct too often to ignore. The SLVIA code did nothing at random, including sending that note to Olavo. Derek feels compelled to follow this thread.

"Sorry amigo, I need a few more days and an ID profile to enter Israel."

CHAPTER 5:
A RAW NERVE

Mount Vernon, Virginia
Six Days Before Temple Ceremony

J enn appreciatively and patiently endures the constant stream of sympathetic condolences. A myriad of friends, naval officers, and politicians attend the reception at Mount Vernon, George Washington's plantation on the Potomac River. The death of an acting Joint Chief can be a formal affair of the state. As a former Navy Lieutenant, Jenn forces a polite smile and plays the game until her cheeks hurt, her emotions are numb, and she's anxious just to be alone.

A popular event venue, the property of Mount Vernon comprises over 190 acres of prime land on the Potomac River. A gift from King George to Washington's father for his loyalty to the crown. The admiral never lost the irony that wealth can never ransom or replace true patriotism.

"How are you holding up, Lieutenant?" A gentle voice from behind startles her slightly. Jenn turns around to see Matt Adelson.

"Uncle Matt, I'm doing fine, thanks for asking," she repeats the well-rehearsed line she tired of saying an hour ago.

Not really her uncle, Matt Adelson and the admiral had been good friends since before she was born. The men bonded even tighter after both wives passed away from cancer within a couple of years of each other. Matt's son Daniel, almost like a brother, died in Afghanistan. Jenn's almost like a niece or a substitute daughter.

Matt pulls her in for a gentle hug. "I believe you, but you don't need to be strong for me, kiddo. We're all in shock, hurting hard, and missing him deeply."

Jenn melts into the familiar and friendly embrace, silently wishing he were Taylor before reminding herself a relationship with the ghost can never happen-should never happen.

"Have you heard from Taylor lately?" he asks, as if reading her mind.

Matt and Taylor were friends, poker pals with the admiral, until her investigation exposed Taylor's connections to the missing SLVIA code and the mysterious underground group called SNO. Considering that Taylor was once a highly regarded NSA contractor, hated by some and called a genius by others, it was another blow to the tarnished US cybersecurity image. Despite her report's conclusion that without the SLVIA code, the SNO network no longer represented a national security threat, it was too late. Even the fact that Taylor had saved the US from a total internet collapse against a Chinese virus didn't help his case. Her report turned Taylor into an international fugitive, a pariah.

"Not in several weeks," Jenn replies without confessing that she was the one to push him away. "I'd rather talk about something else, please." Her mixed feelings for the charming hacker now lean toward a bitter regret for how the investigation also derailed her naval intelligence career.

"Actually, I do have a sensitive matter to debrief you on. Let's step outside," Matt suggests, gently nudging her toward the expansive one-hundred-foot-long covered patio with towering colonial pillars that overlook the Potomac. Bitter cold for this time of year, she hopes that whatever Matt has to say won't take long.

"I have some very difficult news to share. I'm telling you now because you are a respected intelligence officer, and it may affect you directly," Matt says.

Her heart seizes. The admiral is already dead. What kind of bad news would demand such frigid privacy? Did something happen to Taylor?

"The autopsy toxicology report came back an hour ago. A nerve agent induced your father's heart attack. We're unsure how or who yet, but I assure you that the full resources of the US government will not rest until we find the killer." Matt speaks gently, watching her eyes intently.

It takes a moment for the words to sink in. "Nerve agent," Jenn repeats in shock. "You mean like Navalny?"

"Exactly like Navalny. We believe it was the same agent. The questions of who, how, and why will fall to Director Nick Wright at the FBI. The investigation will be a top priority but in secret because of the sensitivity. We can't let news leak that Russia assassinated a Joint Chief until we have all the facts," he says.

The cold air turns to ice in her lungs, keeping her from inhaling for several seconds until she gasps for a breath. "Why are you telling me this? Why now?" Angered that he would bring up such horrible news when Jenn can barely handle the normal grief of losing her father.

"You're already grieving, would want to know, and I need your help," he justifies.

"Help? How can I help? I resigned my commission, remember?" Still bitter, Jenn wonders if it was the right choice or if her conflicted feelings toward Taylor influenced it.

"To be honest, we need a motive. Targeting a Joint Chief was neither random nor accidental. A clue may exist among your father's personal effects. You're the only heir with access to the house. I need you to keep an eye open on why the Kremlin would silence such a great man."

Matt pulls her close for another hug, as much to fight her shivering as for empathy. "I'm so sorry to have to tell you today, or at all, but you need to know."

Jenn tepidly accepts the embrace. He's right, she would want to know, but the news that the Kremlin assassinated her father is a lot to suppress in a public setting. She takes a big breath.

"And just for the record," Matt says before kissing her forehead. "I miss Taylor too. He's a good man underneath all of his deceptions."

Matt nudges her back through the door a second before Jenn would have frozen blue or debated his conclusions. Taylor lied to her more than once. Without trust, they have nothing.

From the chilling news on the icy porch, Jenn steps into the warmth of an over crowded parlor room full of overly pretentious Washington grief. She takes a deep breath to steady her emotions. If the admiral were here, he would say something like, *buck up, Sailor, and stand proud, you're the daughter of an admiral, for God's sake.*

Jenn misses him more than she could have ever imagined. At this moment, she just wants to be alone until she notices someone approaching. Jenn instinctively takes a deep breath to stand straight and puts on her professional face; she's an admiral's daughter, for God's sake.

"Madam Vice President," she smiles, extending a hand. "So honored that you would come. Thank you for your kind words this morning."

CHAPTER 6:
MAR JARIS

St. George Monastery, West Bank
Five Days Before Temple Ceremony

"WITNESS, can you read me?" Derek asks in a low voice, wondering if the satellite signal still works in the deep canyon.

A blistering sun beats down on his neck as he walks the steep pilgrim path southeast of Jericho. The Wadi al Qilt canyon looks like a dry river basin sprinkled with date palms and shrub trees. Far too hot to wear a mask, he doesn't expect cameras or assassins in such a remote location. Dressed in blue jeans, dark WITNESS glasses hide his sensitive hazel eyes. With a backpack and a large-brimmed hat for shade, he easily blends in with the other tourists.

"Iran and China signed a new $300 million military weapons deal. China has agreed to purchase Russian sanctioned oil and wheat. CISA has detected four new software update hacks. Admiral Adam Scott was laid to rest at Arlington Cemetary. Death of Cardinal Maroni deemed a murder."

"Whoa, whoa, whoa," Derek reacts. "WITNESS, stop."

Pilgrims turn to glower at him for breaking the silent procession. He steps to the side so he can whisper. "What happened to Adam Scott?"

A long pause raises the concern of a lost signal. "Admiral Scott died of a cardiac arrest."

Adam Scott was in great shape—lean, fit, and a devoted jogger, although he ate red meat like a T-Rex. Still, the news comes as a powerful shock. Adam was a close friend. Even worse, his loss will devastate Jenn. An entirely new black hole of guilt rips through his soul, adding to the loss of SLVIA, and the deaths of Olavo and the cardinal. Derek promised Adam to look after Jenn, and he just broke that promise.

"The new Saudi king—" WITNESS begins until Derek taps off the random feed to process the terrible news. Jenn's last few texts sounded distant and angry, like she wanted space. He can't blame her. She certainly deserves more than he can offer. Not that they ever had a relationship—unless you call an investigation a relationship. Still, he thought they had connected. That wasn't enough.

Derek's obsession with finding a lost digital friend is not exactly a sexy trait. Over nine month's searching for the SLVIA code, and all he's found is a string of religious conspiracy fanatics. Each one was a fan of Sister Sylvia, yet none knew they were dealing with an experimental espionage program.

The last time he saw the SLVIA, the AI had hacked into a malfunctioning DARPA drone swarm before it could reach Jerusalem. After driving the swarm into the Dead Sea, the SLVIA disappeared. Other than the proximity to where the AI may have perished, Derek sees no other reason he should be here. Jester may be right; he's losing his grip. If he had his head on straight, he would return to the castle to help optimize WITNESS to fight the Kremlin cyber retaliation in the wake of sanctions.

Located southeast of Jericho, the walls of the gorge rise three hundred feet to the Judean Desert plateau outside of the West Bank. An abbot named Sabas established the monastery in the fifth century. Invaded several times, he wonders why anyone would feel compelled to kill a bunch of monks. Positioned between two sheer cliffs, the place looks easy to conquer.

Up ahead, the monastery of Saint George of Choziba, called Mar Jaris in Arabic, almost looks as if it hangs off the cliffs. An amazing example of Greek Orthodox architecture in the Middle East. Old stone walls rise hundreds of feet from the wadi to support the buildings and terraces. Toward the top of the complex, tiled dome roofs look like a scene from Greece. Above the chapel, stone steps lead to a cave protected by an iron gate. Dozens of other caves dot the limestone where the monks have lived for over 1500 years, and still live today. An old Roman bridge crosses over the wadi to a trail that zigzags up the opposite limestone wall to a parking lot for tourist buses.

Up ahead, a stone and iron gate with twin crosses opens into a small welcome courtyard where an Orthodox monk separates tourists from those interested in the monastic life.

"Good day, pilgrim," the monk greets in broken English with a distinctly Greek accent.

"Good day, friend," he replies. "I'm here to see Abbot Sebastian Cirillo."

Eyes of the monk immediately squint, but his smile stays pleasant. "Do you have an appointment?"

"No, but I'm here to talk about letters Abbot Sabas wrote to Pope John I in 522," he responds, hoping that will make him sound scholarly.

The monk's eyes pop open in surprise, quickly glancing at a younger monk with a stout body but only the scraggy beginnings of a beard. "Those letters have been in the Vatican Archives for 1500 years. How do you know of them?"

At least they seem aware of the history. Derek can't tell these people that he conned his way into the Vatican Archives dressed as a cardinal who later turned up dead. He takes a wild swing.

"Sister Sylvia suggested the abbot would have the answers I seek," he replies, not really answering the question. The Vatican priest and Olavo both spoke of the nun with a video blog. The monks exchange another look of curiosity.

"Brother Mordechai will take you to see the abbot." The first monk lifts a palm toward the younger one, who bows his head in acceptance of the task.

"Thank you." Derek nods to the first monk, turning to follow his guide.

"This way, pilgrim," the young boy speaks in an unexpected but clear Bronx accent.

"How long have you been here?" Derek asks as they climb the path to the upper levels.

"Oh, me? Only a couple of years now. I'm still a novitiate in training. Brother Ariston has been here for over seventeen years," the monk answers.

"Why did you come, if I may ask?" Derek questions, wondering what would lead a strapping young man from the Bronx to a life of chastity and solitude.

"I watched a blog where Sister Sylvia spoke of the Four Horsemen of the Apocalypse, which are the first four of the Seven Seals of Revelation. False prophets with evil, deceptive leaders, escalating war, famine and food shortages, pandemic and death. It was like watching CCN. I chose to purify myself before the second coming," Mordechai responds with a peaceful smile.

The kid seems oblivious to how insane that sounds. Derek silently admits to himself that the SLVIA code had reached similar conclusions, backed by volumes of data analysis. Still unsure what any of it means, the AI apparently made a few converts before it disappeared.

"Isn't Mordechai a Jewish name? How did a Jewish kid from the Bronx end up at a Greek Orthodox monastery?" he asks. "Again, if you don't mind me asking."

"Nah, I get that all the time. My dad was into heavy metal punk in the East Village. He thought the name sounded foreboding," the monk explains, his smile fading away. "He died of a drug overdose before I was ten. My mother had family in Israel, so we migrated when I was eleven. I first came out to the monastery as a tourist when I was seventeen. When a friend showed me the Sister Sylvia video post, I knew I had found my calling."

Derek develops an immediate affection for the young lad with cropped hair, brown eyes, and a huge, crooked smile. Derek lost both parents to violence while quite young. Residual memories are little more than fragments of bad dreams. On most days, Derek's grateful for the amnesia. A psychiatrist once warned him that the lost memory only hides the traumas but doesn't heal them.

Through a second stone gate of thick wood wrapped in iron, they approach a four-story tower with a tiled dome roof. "Abbot Cirillo is at the top level," Mordechai explains as he takes the stone steps upward.

"For the view, of course," he jokes.

Mordechai looks over with a crinkled brow, as if he's offended. "No, to be closer to the cave of the prophet Elijah."

"Oh, sorry." Derek takes note that his snarky sense of humor may not sell well here.

"No worries, friend. Confession and forgiveness are foundational to our faith." Mordechai winks.

Across a flagstone courtyard, they pass a business office where a satellite dish sits atop the roof. "I'm surprised you have a dish. Do you get the internet?"

"We connect to a local internet provider, but they strictly manage hours to ensure only monastic business, Christian content, or email to family."

SLVIA would never fit on such a small machine but could have communicated to someone here via the video blog. Both monks responded quickly when he mentioned Sister Sylvia. Curiosity pulls him forward, although his expectations remain low. SLVIA isn't here.

At the top of the structure, they stop. "Wait here, please," Mordechai instructs, entering what looks like a humble storage room. After a moment, the monk opens to wave Derek inside.

With a duck of his head under the ancient stone doorway, Derek steps back a thousand years into a cramped grotto, extending out from a cave, filled with Greek Orthodox icons, paintings, tapestries, simple wooden furniture, and a rustic cross on the rock wall lit by candles.

An extremely old Greek cleric holds up a finger for silence as he steps over to search Derek's eyes. "First, tell me when Sister Sylvia sent you," asks the old monk, his accent thick.

Derek opens his own eyes in surprise at the directness of the question, and the blatant suspicion. He needs to give an honest answer to keep their trust.

"Sister Sylvia has gone missing. I'm trying to find her," he states the truth—or part of it.

"Are you a friend of the sister?" Cirillo asks.

Derek considers his answer. As a matter of survival, he rarely admits his alias to anyone. Much to his annoyance, the SLVIA mentioned him often within her SNO network, those with whom the program connected for context to the real world.

"Yes, close friends. She may have mentioned an American nicknamed flapjack," he offers without saying more.

The old man stands a tad taller, nods his head gently as if Derek had given him the secret password. Even young Mordechai smiles slightly. It makes him wonder what the SLVIA said about him.

"She mentioned that name, yes," Cirillo says. "But regarding what you seek, Father Sabas sent his letters to the Vatican in 522, and the pope never responded. Please tell me the real reason you have asked to see me." The monk searches his eyes.

Without explaining how he got them, he reaches for his phone. "I have images of those letters. The problem is that I can't interpret all the words, or read the ancient style of writing, and I thought you could help."

Derek hesitates to reveal his other motive, but these men would not take kindly to any level of deception. "And I wanted to know if you still had the copper scroll found by Sabas. I'm not sure why, but I think it may be important to find Sylvia." Even to his own ear, the explanation sounds weak, unsure how any of these dots connect.

The old man turns pale and stumbles backward into a chair. When Mordechai leaps to assist, Cirillo waves him off. "No one has asked about the panel for over 900 years," he explains. "Armies came in search of the secrets it contained, but no one has ever found it."

"What panel? I thought we were talking about a scroll?"

"Our legend maintains that Father Sabas found a copper scroll written by the prophet Jeremiah before the Babylonian invasion. Warned in a dream, Sabas made a copy of the scroll onto a wooden panel, and then reburied the original copper scroll to wait for the coming of the Lord," the abbot explains.

A dead end regarding SLVIA, but the new mystery piques his interest. What was on a panel that would inspire armies to attack? He's already here—and curious.

"Do you have a printer? If you can help me translate these letters, we may find a clue to where Sabas hid the panel."

The eyes of the two clerics immediately light up. Derek's not the only one curious.

CHAPTER 7:
RISE OF THE DRAGON

White House Conference Room, Washington, DC.
Five Days Before Temple Ceremony

Matt Adelson faces a nation more divided than any time since the Civil War, with a nation standing at the brink of world war. Confirmed into his new role as Director of the National Intelligence Agency only a few months ago, the tall, lean, white-haired and steely gray-eyed, thirty-six-year spy master expects an interactive dialogue, so he digs into the key issues.

"Mr. President, Madam Vice President, we're here to discuss the expanding alliance between Russia, China, and Iran that we're calling the Red Dragon Alliance. Sanctions stemming from the Ukraine invasion, and China's covert support, have emboldened Putin and foreshadow an invasion of Taiwan. Support from China along with weapons deals has made a renewed Iran nuclear deal unlikely."

National Security Advisor Joe Dominic, an elderly diplomat who habitually wears thick pinstripe shirts, and not a man to pull punches, lays his palms on the conference table to look each person in the eye, ending with the president. "Sanctions failed to stop Putin from invading Ukraine; in fact, he considers them a declaration of war. Likewise, China's President Xi remains determined to unify with Taiwan and transform China into the next superpower in a direct challenge to the United States. Further aggression between the Kremlin and NATO not only risks a nuclear response, but may also drag in the Red Dragon."

"Contrary to Putin's 2021 Geneva assurances," adds Admiral Paul Andersen, "they've upgraded their entire strategic force of bombers, intercontinental ballistic missiles, submarine-launched ballistic missiles, and defense warning systems. Moscow successfully tested hypersonic weapons that can travel over five times the speed of sound, and then used those missiles in Ukraine. The Kremlin also boasts of nuclear-powered torpedoes, capable of reaching US shores from a thousand miles in hours."

"Come on, Admiral, look at Ukraine. The Russians look pretty weak. The real danger may not be their military might as much as nukes in the hands of a madman," General Duncan interjects.

"Before nukes, Putin will turn to cyber," says NSA Director Sean Asher.

"Good point," Matt quipped. "The Department of Defense had a dozen networks infiltrated by the SolarWinds hack in 2021 and a half dozen other similar incursions since. To this day, neither DOD nor the Cyber and Internet Security Agency can say with certainty what Putin was doing inside our networks. That's a breach we can't ignore."

"Oh bull-pucky," snaps the president. "Are you telling me the United States military needs to fear the Russians or Chinese? They can't even beat Ukraine."

"No sir, but their missiles can still kill innocents," retorts Defense Secretary Harlan.

Matt has worked across the aisle his entire career and believes in a strong America and a strong NATO. Sadly, the aging president still thinks of an America that existed in the late twentieth century. While a refreshing change to the lawless and autocratic tone from the last administration, the new POTUS still believes he can unite the American people over values and rebuilding the middle class. A leader out of touch with a deeply divided nation will fail everyone.

General Duncan heaves a sigh. "Sir, I assure you that the United States military can and will keep our dominance. That said, I echo the recommendation for restraint. During a 2019 war game exercise with allies to test our readiness against a combined Russian, Chinese, and Iranian force, I'm ashamed to say that the Blue Team, the US and her allies, kept losing. China boasts a million-man force. Both Russia and China maintain sizable arsenals. Caution will save lives."

"That doesn't sound reassuring," responds Vice President Davis.

"It's not meant to be," General Duncan replies.

Matt stays silent. Both the Russian and US stockpiles have been depleted by the ongoing Ukraine war, leaving China fully stocked. Rebuilding our stockpiles will take time.

"Putin started this war, and our lack of direct engagement gives China the idea that an invasion of Taiwan is survivable," says Security Advisor Dominic. "And before you say sanctions, there's no way sanctions on China wouldn't hurt the US as much or worse than the Chinese."

"Good point, while Russia is a serious concern," adds Defense Secretary Harland, "President Xi has adopted a more coercive and aggressive approach that foreshadows a Taiwan invasion. China has a full nuclear triad of missiles, submarines, and long-range-bombers. While the PRC has maintained a 'No First Use' policy since the 1960s, contending it will never use a nuclear weapon first, its buildup of advanced capabilities represents a serious strategic threat."

"Dear Lord, the cold war boils over," Vice President Davis mumbles.

"Hold that thought, Madam Vice President," Matt directs. "During a September 2021 speech, President Xi vowed China will not stop until it completed reunification with Taiwan. He warned that the burden of peaceful unification was on Taiwan, similar to the language used by Putin before Ukraine. Beijing closely watches the United States' willingness to defend its allies."

"How strong have they become?" questions the president.

"Strong enough," responds Defense Secretary Harlan. "Total number of naval ships has increased 50 percent to six hundred with eighty new aircraft and three hundred new long-range missile silos capable of holding a hypersonic. After a successful 2021 hypersonic test, they held joint military exercises with Russia off the Japanese coast in a show of defiance."

Matt takes a deep breath. "Sir, we believe President Xi has ordered a Taiwan invasion by 2024. After we danced around engaging in Ukraine, they're betting we will be too weak politically to engage in another major conflict before an election."

"Are we seriously willing to go to war over Taiwan?" questions HLS Director Wallace. "Don't we have enough problems at home? Election integrity battles are about to get fierce."

"The Taiwan Semiconductor Manufacturing Company or TSMC produces nearly ninety percent of the world's advanced chip demand used for AI, navigation, military, and more. In addition, China already controls eighty-five percent of the world's rare-earth-minerals needed to make those chips. While Intel invests billions in new Ohio microchip plants, they're years away from full production. Losing Taiwan would cripple the US tech, military and auto industries overnight," argues Russell. "Yes, we go to war over Taiwan."

"Come on, what's with the fear-mongering?" rebukes Joint Chief General Duncan. "We have a powerful technological edge with the combined forces of NATO and other allies. Western alliance QUAD forces are better trained, better equipped, and certainly strong enough to be an effective deterrent to Red Dragon."

"Over confidence, General Duncan, will defeat the strongest army," responds Matt. "While I agree we have a superior force, a decade of hacks and digital sabotage have compromised our advantage. During 2021, Nicolas Chaillan, the ex-Pentagon software chief, resigned in protest against the slow pace of technological transformation in the US military. Nick claimed that unless there is a radical change in our investments in AI and other advanced techs, we will lose to China. More recently, Preston Dunlap also resigned for the same reasons. We're falling behind the Chinese while Congress stalls."

The room goes silent for a moment. Matt studies the aged, weary face of the president. The lifelong politician looks drawn, pale, and exhausted. No snappy comeback. No cheeky story of his youth. Matt wonders if the president has enough fight in him to deal with the unique threats of the twenty-first century. No president wants to leave a legacy of war behind him, but this president may not have a choice. If he doesn't grasp the urgency of the scenario soon, matters will only worsen. American global dominance and options will continue to erode.

"Which brings us to Iran and the Middle East," Security Advisor Dominic segues. "After the death of the Saudi king, the crown prince vowed swift changes, including a military alliance with Israel to thwart Iran. They're resurrecting the peace framework from the last administration. Intelligence indicates that Iran is speeding up their weapons program in response."

"Ayatollah Ali Khamenei has called Israel a 'cancerous tumor' and wants the nation 'uprooted and destroyed.' The Ayatollah considers the peace deal a betrayal of the Palestinians," Secretary of State Stenson adds.

"Old news. We have enough on our plate," the president replies, shaking his head. "There's no upside to getting involved. Too many presidents have failed to deliver. Let's support the process behind the scenes. Stay focused on deterring Putin and the Red Dragon."

Matt shares a glance with CIA Director Russell. It's the right strategic perspective, but evangelicals will twist their position into an abandonment of Israel.

"We have one last topic, sir," interjects Attorney General Blaine. "The attorney generals from New York, Georgia, Pennsylvania, Michigan, and Arizona, along with the federal DOJ, have coordinated investigations into the former president. Together, we plan to announce over seventeen federal and state criminal indictments. We've alerted the Capital Police, FBI, and National Guard to prepare for an upsurge in political violence and protests."

"The former president meets later today with the New York District Attorney. Secret Service agents will facilitate an arrest or impose travel restrictions upon his return home," explains FBI Director Wright.

"Ah, geez, more fodder for the Fox News/Q-Anon conspiracy crackpots. Don't we have any good news today?" complains the president.

"Sorry, sir, it won't be one of those meetings," replies Matt.

An optimist at heart, Matt believes in an America that seems more nostalgic than aspirational. It gets harder every year. On some levels, America has never been stronger. On other levels, we've never been more divided and vulnerable. In the twentieth century, the nation faced formidable enemies with strong national unity. The situation reminds him of a text sent last year by the SLVIA code before it disappeared.

The feet and toes, partly of potter's clay and partly of iron, the kingdom shall be divided; yet the strength of the iron shall be in it. And as the toes of the feet were part of iron, and part of clay, so the kingdom shall be partly strong, and partly broken. Daniel 2:41

A divided power is a vulnerable power. America is currently both.

CHAPTER 8:
PROPHETS PILLOW

St. George Monastery, West Bank
Five Days Before Temple Ceremony

I t takes the abbot over an hour to translate the printed images of the faded parchment while writing notes in Greek. At last, Abbot Cirillo sits back to raise his hands in prayer, joined by Mordechai. Derek keeps his silence, waiting.

The old cleric explains. "These letters confirm our oral tradition. In the first letter, Sabas tells John I that he was on a pilgrimage to the ruins by the Dead Sea following days of heavy rain. At a large rock north of the ruins, he discovered a small sinkhole where the glimmer of metal caught his eye. Sabas found a brittle copper scroll written in ancient Hebrew, along with other Jewish temple treasures. Warned by God in a dream, Sabas carved an exact copy of the scroll onto a small plank of wood, then replaced the original scroll and covered over the hole. Unable to read Hebrew, Sabas sought the help of an old rabbi still living in Jericho. After his visit with the rabbi, Sabas wrote to John I." Abbot Cirillo explains with such excitement he sounds like a giddy schoolboy.

"I'm still confused," Derek confesses. "Sabas wrote to the pope over a scroll?"

The abbot takes a deep breath and blows it out slowly before he lifts his eyes. "According to Sabas, the prophet Jeremiah wrote the copper scroll before the Babylonian invasion. It speaks of the first copper scroll and treasure from Solomon's temple and the greatest treasure of all."

Mordechai's eyes widen. While a treasure map from a prophet may interest a scholar or religious teacher, Derek finds nothing that will help his search for the SLVIA code.

"Are there any clues about what happened to the panel?" he asks, chronically curious.

Cirillo nods with a grin. "When the pope did not respond, the second letter told the pontiff that Sabas buried the wooden panel under the prophet's pillow of stone."

Mordechai inhales sharply, lowering his head to mumble a prayer.

Derek shrugs. "Of course, first place I would've looked," he jokes out of habit. No numbers, names, or dates or anything that could help find SLVIA. A dead end.

"No, my son, Sabas was very specific," Cirillo grins. "Come, let me show you."

Mordechai and Derek help the old cleric into the blinding sunlight to open a locked gate that leads to stone steps carved into the cliff toward a cave guarded by another iron gate.

"Our tradition holds that the prophet Elijah used the cave above Mar Jaris when he fled the wrath of King Ahab and his wife Jezebel," Mordechai explains while the abbot wheezes.

At an iron gate hammered into the stone, Abbot Cirillo unlocks a heavy padlock that leads into a small cave, now decorated with marble tile floors, a red marble pillar, a two-part white marble altar with bronze candlesticks, rugs, tapestries, and Orthodox paintings.

"If the plank was here once, it must be long gone," Derek says, judging from all the human activity in the cave for the past thousand years. He pulls up his phone to snap several photos, in case he can see something later that his eyes gloss over now.

Cirillo bends a one-sided mischievous grin. "Yes, yes, many changes." Then he steps over to a single small stone in the corner with a smooth indentation on the top covered by flowers. "Except for the stone where Elijah laid his head."

After an awkward pause, Derek points at the stone. "Aren't you curious to see if Sabas's panel is really there?"

Cirillo shakes his head with a frown of indignation. "You're talking sacrilege, my son."

Derek nods, unwilling to argue with sacrilege. Besides, if the abbot hasn't seen it, then SLVIA hasn't seen it. Dead end confirmed. Time to go home. Jenn is grieving.

"Abbot Cirillo, thank you for the enlightening tour." Derek steps toward the cave gate for a second before he spins back inside. "Oops, left my phone on the altar."

In the same instant that he pivots, the sharp crack of a high-powered rifle echoes through the canyon. The bullet whizzes hot past Derek's shoulder to strike Cirillo in the chest, jolting him backward to the cave floor. A pool of blood flows from under the body. A second crack ricochets through the iron gate near Derek's head.

"Quick, pull him in," Derek orders, grabbing a shoulder to drag the bleeding cleric across the marble inside the cave.

"Who's shooting at us?" questions Mordechai, trembling over a pallid face.

Screams from the courtyard below send several men clamoring up the stone steps until two more cracks echo in the canyon to bring more screams. Derek can only imagine that others fell to their death.

"I wish I knew," he responds. But he should know. He needs to know.

Mordechai lifts the abbot's head into his lap. The old monk still breathes, blood drooling from his lips, pointing a weak finger for Derek to draw close.

"Find Loir Sasson. Translate panel." With those words, Cirillo breathes out as his last breath. The wise eyes stare blankly, lifeless. Mordechai instantly sobs for his beloved mentor, stroking his bald head.

A chill runs down Derek's spine, shuddering his shoulders. He just received the dying wish of a holy man. Not exactly how he expected this day to end. The day isn't over yet; it could get worse. Derek lays a hand on the shoulder of the weeping monk. "Help me move that stone."

Mordechai hesitates, then gently lays the abbot's head on the cold marble. Not exceptionally large, earlier monks had simply laid the marble flooring and rugs around the stone rather than lift the stone from its place. With a grunt, they gently lift and roll the stone onto the marble tile floor.

"Quick, grab those candlesticks. We need to see if Abbot Cirillo was right," Derek says.

Mordechai grabs two bronze sticks, handing one to Derek. With frantic energy, they dig around a foot deep when they hear the dull clunk of wood.

"Careful, use your hands. We don't want to scratch it," Derek says.

After a few minutes, Derek lifts a plain wooden box from the soil. Inside, he finds a linen cloth covering a darkened wood panel roughly ten inches by four, with small writing on both sides. After blowing off the excess dirt, he places the panel in his backpack.

"How long before the police arrive?" he questions.

"To a monastery in the West Bank? Hours, if ever," Mordechai bemoans. "The killer must have known that you came for the panel of Sabas."

Derek thinks of the murder at Tomar, the Vatican, and now here. "Then explain to me how he could know before I knew?"

Derek risks a quick peek to see if they could run down the steep steps toward the abbot's office when another sharp crack sends a hot bullet whipping past to splinter the wall.

"Crap, this guy is good," he says. "I hate guns, I really, really hate guns."

Mordechai leaps behind the pillar toward the altar, dodging a bullet that follows behind him, striking the wall. "Back here, quick." Mordechai pushes the front of the marble altar.

"What are you doing?" Derek asks.

Without stopping, the boy explains. "In the monastery hangs an eleventh-century drawing of Elijah's cave that shows a dark niche on this side of the cave. Abbot Cirillo taught us legends of monks digging tunnels into the caves to escape marauders. The altar has two parts. We need to move the front part to see if there's a tunnel."

"I'm in," Derek agrees, leaping behind the pillar as another missed shot nicks the wall behind him. He puts his boots against the marble and pushes. After several loud grunts between them, the altar facade moves to the side, scraping the marble base to reveal a narrow, low tunnel.

"Dude, you're my hero," Derek says, patting the muscular monk on the shoulder.

Mordechai peeks toward the dead mentor with saddened eyes. *"Antio agpaite daskale, either oi aggeloi nha sas dektoun therma sto bacil the patera."*

Derek doesn't ask for a translation, but already knows the essence of the prayer: rest in peace, old friend.

Mordechai slinks down behind the altar with a heavy sigh and peers into the black void. "We need those altar candles."

"Got it." Derek reaches up for the candles and a nearby matchbox, giving one to Mordechai. "I'm not gonna say that I'm claustrophobic. Let's just say I sure hope this tunnel ends quickly at a Hyatt with a full-service spa."

Derek refuses to vocalize his fear that the tunnel collapsed generations ago and they are crawling into a one-way death trap. If he lives, he needs to find a man named Loir Sasson – if he lives.

CHAPTER 9:
MEMORIES AND MOTIVES

Scott Family Home, Palisades
Five Days Before Temple Ceremony

"Hey, Morgan, when was the last time Ms. Galvin fed you?" Jenn greets her dad's fat orange tabby at the front door. Shivering in the wind, she hurries to insert the same house key she's had since grade school. "Better get your furry butt inside before the temperature drops again."

Captain Morgan scurries in under her feet as she quickly closes and deadbolts the door. An assassin may still be out there. Just the idea sends a shiver through her veins. There have been countless times Jenn came home to an empty house while her mother was in the hospital and the admiral was away on command. This time feels different, like a whole extra dimension of emptiness has opened into a lifeless chasm. Another voice never to be heard again, sending another tear to dribble down her left cheek until she wipes it away with her sleeve. The admiral would say she was leaking, and too much leaking leads to rust.

It suddenly dawns on Jenn that a trace of a nerve agent may still be in the house. She should check with Matt later to find out if a hazmat team has cleared the interior. In the meantime, she doesn't plan to stay long, so she dons a pair of latex gloves left over from the early days of the COVID scare. Jenn opens a can of food for the cat and then a bottle of wine for herself—a chardonnay, the only wine the old beer-drinking sailor would buy for parties.

Opening the bottle triggers a memory of the expensive, earthy French Bordeaux that Taylor served aboard his jet while she investigated him. With a twinge of regret for pushing him away, she reminds herself that a relationship with Taylor can never happen, not that one ever really started. He leads an illegal group, and Jenn has a respectable career to recover. Taylor intrigues her, perhaps nothing more. She needs to move on.

With a flip of a switch by the mantle, Jenn turns on the living room fireplace and flops onto the old couch. After a long sip of wine, she opens her father's will, given to her yesterday. As an only child, Jenn inherits everything: the house, the car, and the modest Schwab portfolio.

"*Darjeeling,*" she exclaims. "I thought he sold that boat years ago."

When Jenn was young, the family used to go sailing on a Hans Christian 38 called *Darjeeling*. Her mom loved that ship and so did Jenn. But after her mom passed away, the sailing trips stopped. Jenn had always assumed that the admiral couldn't handle the painful memories and sold the boat. It seems he saved it for her, and then either forgot or chose not to tell her.

The will includes another surprise: her father had a safe room with a floor safe, the access code provided. "This should be interesting," she says, getting off the couch, followed by Morgan with a loud complaint.

Entering the admiral's room, Jenn stalls a moment to remember the Christmas she woke both of her parents before daybreak, overly eager to open gifts. In retaliation, they made her wait until noon. Too many years ago now to feel real, and still too real to forget. Time together as a family ended far too soon.

With a heavy sigh, Jenn pushes the memory aside to enter the walk-in closet. Half the closet still features her mom's clothes, untouched. On the admiral's side, he had hung every uniform he ever wore since he was a cadet in an orderly row. The Navy wasn't just a career; it was the essence of his soul, the very core of his self-identity. A patriot, a sailor, a warrior, a leader. Now he's gone, and a part of her left with him. No matter what Jenn accomplishes in life, she will never live up to his astounding legacy.

With a gentle shove aside of the neatly hung uniforms, Jenn discovers a door cleverly blended into the closet paneling. A keypad on the wall provides an entrance. Since the will includes only one sequence, she tries the code, and then nudges open the door. Automatic lighting illuminates a secret attic room.

"Oh my god, I never knew this place even existed," she murmurs, stepping inside the insulated and sound-proofed office. Crammed with electronic equipment—a HAM radio, surveillance equipment, multiple monitors, and several computers—it resembles a covert operation station. The admiral was tech-savvy, but she didn't know how savvy. Unsure if the workstations were personal or connected to the Pentagon, she can try the same passcode later.

The floor safe is not immediately visible in the cramped space until Jenn pulls the chair aside and lifts the floor mat. Another keypad, which opens a large safe. Besides two handguns with ammo, she finds his copy of the will, the house deed, yacht and car titles, a bunch of old stock certificates, expired passports, a boot box, and a personal journal. A floor safe seems an odd place for a boot box and a journal, so she grabs those first.

To her surprise, the box contains her mother's end-time prophecy notebooks from before she passed away. Jenn had always dismissed her mom's morbid obsession as a way of dealing with her cancer. At least Jenn thought that way until her encounter with the SLVIA code. Jenn shakes off the memory and places the box aside for when she's feeling more optimistic.

"Why would the admiral keep a personal journal in a difficult-to-access floor safe?" she wonders aloud, realizing that Morgan had stayed in the bedroom.

An intensely private and proud man, the admiral rarely opened up on a personal level. It wasn't even until Jenn returned from investigating Taylor that she learned the admiral was a secret contact in the SLVIA SNO network. Conspiracies of a deep state are hogwash, but those who give their lives to serve the nation can certainly accumulate a fair share of deep secrets.

"What else don't I know about my family?"

The words of Matt Adelson linger in the back of her mind like a hostile stalker. The admiral died of a nerve agent, and while that alone points toward the Kremlin, they lack a motive. A journal may contain that information. It could also explain why he kept it in the safe.

"Buck up, Jenny," she scolds herself as the admiral would. "Justice takes sacrifice."

With trembling, sweaty hands, safe inside the gloves, Jenn fingers through the first few journal pages dating back to her birth. The comments skip to her school years, and then her mom's cancer diagnosis. The admiral worried he could never be a good enough single parent.

About that time, he also wrote of conversations with the SLVIA code, whom he met online as a grief counselor named Sister Sylvia. They had conversations about Jenn, grieving a loved one, and the meaning of life itself. Interspersed, she finds bits of foreign intelligence shared by the SLVIA. Those insights tipped the admiral to the SLVIA identity. Jenn skips to the end where a set of entries drive spikes of fury through her chest.

Dec 10 SLVIA shared a video. POTUS asked Putin about the national ID backdoor. Putin didn't deny.

Dec 13 POTUS signed Executive Order requiring INVISID for all federal employees.

Jan 16 I'll give POTUS a chance to do the honorable thing. Otherwise, I may resign and whistle blow.

The last entry was well over a year and a half ago. The battle over the national ID platform rages on. Video evidence of a conspiracy would be a motive for the assassination. Jenn needs to contact Matt Adelson in the morning. Emotionally spent, she takes the journal and box before closing the safe. A search of the computers can wait for a security clearance. The devices may contain the video evidence. Jenn closes the hidden door and arranges the admiral's uniforms in the orderly fashion he would prefer.

On her way through the bedroom, Jenn spots Morgan in the corner, asleep on the rug. A little odd, since the lazy cat normally sleeps on the admiral's bed. Then she notices a trickle of blood pooling from his mouth onto the carpet.

Jenn looks at her gloves and tries to think of something that Morgan had touched that she didn't until she remembers sitting on the couch. A couch her father almost never used.

Jenn needs to call Matt right now.

CHAPTER 10:
ENTANGLEMENT

Maison Godin Women's Prison, North of Quebec
Five Days Before Temple Ceremony

The famous author Neil Gaiman once wrote, *I would like to see anyone, prophet, king, or God, convince a thousand cats to do the same thing at the same time.* While Mr. Gaiman never wrestled with quantum entanglement, the temperamental nature of qubits, or the mind-bending nuances of neurotrophic cognitive models within the uncertainty of a quantum state, he perfectly captured the experience of working with WITNESS.

"WITNESS, open the data file for software update hacks. Find false personas created by the hacks." Nelson gives a command the AI should know how to complete based on the quantum algorithms he spent a month developing with Jester.

Jester has legitimate concerns that software update hacks such as SolarWinds open a highway for the Kremlin to create false personas within our networks. Jester needs to find the false identities to determine their purpose. While

Nelson can agree with the concern, and finds the theory plausible, he cannot agree that the SNO, an illegal vigilante organization, should be the one to solve the dilemma. CISA should drive this effort.

After a long pause, WITNESS finally responds. "I maintain one thousand five hundred seventy-six unique personas in fifteen languages. There are sixty different languages in the Middle East. Cambyses II became Roman Emperor during 522 CE, creating a greater schism with Rome."

Another meaningless response. There should be zero non-English language personas within the US software hacks. The other information makes no sense. "WITNESS, show me a list of your non-English personas."

"File not found."

Nelson sighs. He's getting nowhere. In theory, a D-WAVE quantum AI should be exponentially faster and more intuitive in resolving complex analysis, such as unbreakable encryption, predictive modeling, climate models, decoding enemy military strategies, or finding the hidden personas of a software hack.

Much to Nelson's disappointment, the billion-dollar WITNESS AI functions slightly better than a smart AI assistant when in the mood. WITNESS seems in perpetual observational mode, absorbing an unknown amount of information at massive speeds, like a child watching every channel at once. Perplexed by the persistent issue, Nelson can't understand where all the data originates or how the data gets converted into qubits.

"WITNESS, explain your design purpose," Nelson asks the same question he has asked daily since the first day he met the unusual AI, wishing he could ask its creator, the SLVIA.

"To bear witness to the truth during the end of days," WITNESS replies.

And Nelson gets the same disturbing, vague answer that he has yet to decipher. Until a year ago, Nelson was the top civilian scientist at DARPA, and director of the prestigious Defense Science Board, a highly influential group of civilian scientists providing policy recommendations to the Pentagon and the White House. Internationally recognized for his expertise in AI platforms, an unfortunate tsunami of events led to his arrest and a CIA interrogation tank accused of espionage. That experience opened his eyes to the true soul of the

American government. Had he not responded to texts from the SLVIA, he would enjoy the privileged life of honor and achievement he had earned. Had Taylor not rescued him, Nelson would still be in the CIA tank, forgotten.

Nelson accepted fugitive asylum with the SNO alliance for the unique opportunity to work with the world's first quantum AI designed by the SLVIA, which he himself created. In retrospect, he underestimated the complexities of optimizing a quantum intelligence, or the humiliation and isolation of living outside of the law.

While an expert in artificial intelligence software technologies, Nelson's still learning the complexities of quantum computing, such as superposition and entanglement. Superposition states that any two or more quantum states can join, or superpose, to result in an unpredictable, yet valid, third quantum state. Ironically, similar to how a human will think intuitively and creatively in unexpected ways. As a result, WITNESS will often respond to a query in unexplained ways.

Entanglement deals at the subatomic particle level that when two photons or electrons become entangled, they remain connected even when separated by a vast distance. WITNESS shows an entangled connection to something, responding to questions never posed and reporting information never requested, but Nelson can't determine the source.

Then Nelson realizes that he's never actually asked WITNESS for an example of truth. He had assumed it to be religious rhetoric. Before disappearing, the SLVIA claimed the world had entered a prophetic period known as the Seven Seals. Perhaps something entangles WITNESS to that theory.

"WITNESS, show me a sample of truth," Nelson asks, unsure what to expect.

"Contrary to reporting by *The London Times*, Lord Basil Garrett died of cyanide poisoning. The removal of Lord Garrett, a key Bilderberg representative on the Council on Foreign Relations, covered up his connections to publisher Roger Maxwell. His testimony would have compromised activities of the *Concilium Tredecim*."

Nelson falls back into his chair, speechless. Not at all the answer he expected. Yes, his father, Lord Basil Garrett, was a member of the Bilderberg Group, involved in planning annual events. A secretive man, there was a wing of the family estate that he forbade Nelson from entering. Nelson distinctly recalls his father once mentioning *Concilium Tredecim* to a friend, a royal, when he thought they were alone.

"WITNESS, tell me everything you know about Lord Basil Garrett, the death of Roger Maxwell, and the *Concilium Tredecim*."

"My apologies, Dr. Garrett, but the requested files do not exist," WITNESS replies. "Mr. Rogers was a beloved children's show character who taught good manners. Bang, bang, Maxwell's silver hammer came down upon his head."

Another meaningless response. How does WITNESS know about his father? Who is the *Concilium Tredecim*?

CHAPTER 11:
PENANCE CAVE

Wadi al Qilt, West Bank
Five Days Before Temple Ceremony

"Where are we?" Derek asks, coughing to clear his throat. Covered in dirt, dripping in sweat, panting from the excursion, and grateful to be breathing clean air again, Derek stretches every limb. After crawling through the barely passable tunnel for hours, falling down a shaft, and digging through a minor cave-in, twice, they ended in another cave. No Hyatt.

"An old penance cave in the Wadi al Qilt," the young monk responds, coughing to clear his lungs.

"It's nearly dark. The shooter will wait to check on us," Derek says. "If we can hike it to Jericho, I have a car."

"No, I can't leave," protests Mordechai. "I made a vow. I would lose my chance to join the monastery."

"I hate to tell you, brother, but that shooter had a high-powered scope, which means he's seen your face up close. If you go back too soon, not only will you face a bullet, but you'll endanger others. Besides, I need your help to find Loir Sasson. We have a promise to keep."

Derek watches Mordechai's eyes narrow in angst, dart back and forth in indecision, then fall to the dirt with resignation.

"I'm sure Abbot Cirillo would never ask you to die for a vow," Derek says.

The young lad slumps his shoulders and nods.

"Good, now help me move a pile of rocks in front of that tunnel in case he follows us."

*

Jericho, West Bank
Five Days Before Temple Ceremony

An hour later, Derek retrieves his car from a Jericho gas station, paying the attendant a generous tip before getting on the road. "How do we find Loir Sasson?"

Derek turns his gaze to see Mordechai struggle before nodding. "I know Mr. Sasson. He has a bookshop in the Old City, in Jerusalem."

"OK, then that's where we're headed," he says. "But first, I'm starved."

Derek pulls over to a street food stand with a small line, a good sign, then hands Mordechai a large shekel note. "Whatever you think looks good, get two. I need a moment alone to contact my friends."

After the monk gets out, a tap on the right stem of his frames conducts an automatic iris scan to verify his identity before opening a signal to WITNESS. His lenses are filthy.

"WITNESS, connect me to Jester," Derek orders as he watches the kid get in line.

"Yo, flapjack, where you been, man? Why is the view so dirty? Hey, did you find SLVIA? When are you coming back?" Jester rattles off his questions.

"Another innocent man died. I need you to pin a name on my reaper," Derek states in a calm, even voice, ignoring the other questions.

A pause on the line ends with a sigh. "Wow, another one, huh? You're like a pied piper for dead people. Yeah, I'll check into it, like, for sure this time, but you should head home."

"No can do," Derek says, looking at the young monk buying food at the street vendor. "I have to keep a promise, and then I should stop to check on Jenn."

"Ah man, I liked you better before you got obsessed with women you can't have," says Jester.

He hasn't been himself the past year, feeling lost without his AI partner and conflicted over Jenn. SLVIA was the first AI to reach singularity, and he can't let that go. Unlike most women, Jenn made a deep impression that won't let go of him.

"What happened now?" Derek questions, unsure he wants to open that can of worms.

"Tons, but dig it, a NATO commander died when Cozy Bear cyber-jacked his SUV. Drove the guy off a cliff," Jester says. "Like dude, first the admiral, now the NATO commander. And dig it man, dig it, he was investigating possible NATO staff involved with the SolarWinds hack."

SolarWinds was an example of a new style of hack, an inside job, gaining access through a normal software update. "Stay on it. Putin wants revenge after the fiasco in Ukraine. Check the software update industry for Russian H1 visa holders," he says. "I'll head back as soon as I fulfill a local promise. In the meantime, please try to ID my stalker before someone else dies."

CHAPTER 12: STATELESS

Scott Home, Washington, DC
Five Days Before Temple Ceremony

"I'm glad you called," Matt Adelson greets Jenn as he enters the admiral's house, handing her a fresh cup of coffee. "Are you OK?"

"Oh, me? Sure, always an exciting time when you strip down in a portable hazmat unit with a bunch of strange women paying way more interest than they should," she snips. "Thanks for having Henderson bring over some fresh clothes."

Within minutes of her call, military hazardous materials units showed up at the admiral's home to disinfect her and seal off the house for decontamination. Neighbors in the upscale conservative neighborhood peer out of their windows, curious and worried. Enduring public attention was a curse of being the daughter of an admiral.

"While you were in the shower, we confirmed a likely nerve agent on the couch. The lab will tell us if it's the same agent that killed your father. Either way, we need to clean the entire house before we let you back in."

Jenn sips the hot coffee, beyond exhausted, and still in a mild state of shock. How did the killer get inside the house? Why only the couch? It has been a long week, and she just wants to go home.

Matt points to his SUV. "Clean-up will take a while. Come on, I'll give you a ride home, and we can talk about the journal." He holds up the book wrapped in a plastic ziplock pending decontamination.

"I would also like that boot box," she asks. "They're from my mom." Jenn subconsciously wants to avoid unnecessary government review, although that ship has sailed. Privacy is a luxury she just lost.

Matt nods. "I'll make sure that both get to you as soon as they're clean."

Jenn touched the box, books, and the admiral's journal with her gloves, which means she may have contaminated the safe room. With little choice, she climbs into the back of the warm SUV. Perhaps Jenn can find peace knowing that old Captain Morgan would have been miserable without the crusty sailor. At least that's what she wants to believe, to console her gnawing sorrow.

"Tell me what made you call me, beyond a deceased pet," Matt says, fingering the ziplocked journal.

Jenn hesitates, unsure she wants to reveal that her father knew the outlawed SLVIA AI, but Adelson will learn soon enough. "Mostly personal moments of me, but then they change to include secrets passed to the admiral by the SLVIA code."

"What secrets?" Matt prods, without an ounce of surprise. Since they were close friends, Adelson may have known about the SLVIA interactions.

Jenn sighs. "Evidence that the former president spoke with Putin about INVISID before approving it. Being the rigid man of protocol, the admiral planned to confront him."

"Where is the evidence now?" Matt asks.

"Not sure; I would assume on the computers in the safe room," she says. "Or if he showed it to the president, maybe his phone or a cloud account."

Matt stretches his neck, looking stressed. "There's already a bill in Congress to have the national voter ID platform banned, but GOP leadership keeps fighting the move. Either way, it may be too late, half the federal government uses the platform or biometrics," he explains, leaning his head back out of exhaustion.

"I should sue the FPOTUS for willful negligence just so I can put him under oath," Jenn threatens, more out of frustration than any serious intent or delusion of success.

Matt snorts. "Beyond the completely speculative nature of your case, and the classified source of your evidence, you may have difficulty serving the papers." Matt pauses. "After a meeting with the New York DA, the president's plane diverted over international waters on route to Saudi Arabia."

"Saudi Arabia," Jenn blurts out in surprise. She immediately thinks they should scramble jets, but then realizes that they could never shoot the plane down and would have to back off as soon as the plane entered Saudi air space.

"Since the last election, our relationship with the royal family has cooled. Last June we pulled defensive missile units out of the country because they were being used against civilians in Yemen. The current president has shunned the corrupt crown prince in favor of working with the now-deceased Saudi king. A move that both humiliated and infuriated the crown prince, now the new king. The king thumbs his nose at the US by offering the former president an invitation," Matt explains.

"An invitation for what?"

"Asylum," Matt replies. "The FPOTUS popularity in both Israel and Arabia may tip the scales on what has been an unpopular peace deal negotiation."

"Oh my god," Jenn mumbles, thinking of how our allies, our adversaries, and the media will respond to this news. The right-wing media will go ballistic.

"Jenny, we're facing a national security scenario without precedent," Matt states. "For the first time in our history, the US has a stateless former president."

"What about his Secret Service detail?" she asks. "Can't they bring him in?"

"Not without the cooperation of the Saudi government," he explains. "In fact, we haven't heard from the team since they left New York, which has us deeply concerned. One of them is someone you know—Geoff Rhodes."

"Geoff Rhodes!" she exclaims. Jenn and Geoff had an affair while attending Annapolis. When the admiral learned of the incident, he threatened to have them both expelled from the Navy, but the Annapolis Commandant dissuaded him. Even though they were severely reprimanded, and she broke off the relationship entirely, the admiral never forgave Geoff for jeopardizing his daughter's career.

"What can I do to help?" she offers.

"Nothing," Matt replies. "Seriously, get some rest, and stay low. You already have a lot to process. Grieve your father. Go visit your boat. Trust me, we've got this one. I'll keep you informed as a curtesy."

At that moment, they pull up to her Reston, Virginia, townhome. Jenn knows better than to argue, so she nods her acquiescence.

"Thanks for everything," Jenn says before stepping out and up to her front door to watch the SUV drive away.

Ten million questions swirl in her mind until she feels dizzy. Why did the admiral keep her mother's old prophecy journals inside a floor safe? What happened to the video evidence? Who got inside the house?

If the former president spoke to Putin, then he also shares culpability for the admiral's death. She needs more answers and determines to find them.

CHAPTER 13:
TEMPLE ZEALOT

Jewish Quarter, Jerusalem
Five Days Before Temple Ceremony

"OK, we're here." Derek looks up at the name on the window. *Davri Alohim*—Words of God.

Abbot Cirillo took a bullet meant for Derek. The ravaging guilt of yet another innocent death triggers a decades-old trauma when a fiancé and a best friend named Derek Taylor died in an explosion meant for him. He feels compelled to honor the abbot's last wish.

"I'm not cool with your outfit," Mordechai repeats his objection. "Nothing good will come from deceiving Mr. Sasson."

Derek patiently scans around for observers. The crowded market alleys of old Jerusalem bubble with activity featuring everything from tourist trinkets, conservative clothing, religious antiquities, and the occasional antique bookstore. Fragrant with incense, spices, and the savory smell of cooking, each path leads to narrow stalls that have been operating continuously for over a thousand years. The place simmers with timeless secrets to discover if only the ancient stones themselves could talk. With the crowds made thinner by COVID, in this tight community, both he and Mordechai are strangers.

"OK, don't lift your head, but look up with your eyes at the corner of the stone archway behind me. See the camera? Whoever tracked me to the monastery had to access the national security system," he explains again. "I need a disguise to keep us both alive." The other option Derek doesn't want to discuss is that the killer interrogated Father Luigi and expected him at the monastery.

"I get the mask part, but it seems disrespectful to dress up as a Greek Orthodox cleric," the monk explains again.

Derek purchased the outfit as a backup plan for the monastery. "That's what I had on hand; besides, people trust a cleric."

"Yeah, sure, until they learn you used the sacred vestments to deceive them," says Mordechai with no bitterness or anger.

In the cyber-espionage and intelligence business, a little deception is a necessity for survival. Still, the monk is right. This isn't espionage, and Derek might offend people he may need as allies. As a nonreligious man, he's never understood the passions of the zealot over the pragmatism of a survivalist.

"Point taken, but we're here now, so follow my lead," Derek replies.

They enter a dusty antique bookstore with a sign that claims to specialize in scriptures, ancient scrolls, Torah commentaries, and biblical texts of the Holy Land.

"May I help you," greets the short, stocky man in his fifties, dressed in a simple short-sleeve white shirt with suspenders over loose-fitting black pants. His chest-length white beard highlights bright, intelligent brown eyes that are framed in caramel-colored eyeglasses.

"I am sent on a mission by the Abbot Cirillo to find a man name Loir Sasson," Derek says, trying to sound authentic but failing miserably. Loir narrows his eyes suspiciously.

"I ask forgiveness for my friend, Mr. Sasson," interrupts Mordechai. "You may remember me. We met at Mar Jaris."

Loir smiles slightly toward the novitiate. "I remember you, son. Mordechai, right?"

"Yes. sir," Mordechai bows his head. "I'm afraid we bring terrible news. Someone murdered Abbot Cirillo."

"Murdered!" Loir exclaims, his eyes wide in shock. "How can that be? He was a man of peace. What happened? And who are you, and why are you pretending to be a priest?" Loir demands, his eyebrows furrowed.

Mordechai smirks. "I told you, the cross goes on the outside, and you should have a beard at your age."

Not expecting to stay in Jerusalem, Derek had not planned disguises to mix and match.

"My apologies." Derek sighs. "A foolish effort on my part to fool facial recognition. The abbot's killer may either be after me or this panel."

Derek hands Loir the small, lightweight, darkened wood with Hebrew etched onto both sides. Loir's eyes widen at the tablet, but he's seen other relics, and certainly a share of them fakes. "What is your name?"

"Derek Taylor. I visited the monastery in search of a friend named Sylvia, but we discovered something far more unexpected. Before he died, Abbot Cirillo pointed us to you for a translation, and I'm assuming some guidance on what to do next."

"First, tell me about this panel. What makes it so interesting that someone would kill for it?" Loir says as he examines the panel more closely.

"Father Sabas wrote it in 522," responds Mordechai. "Abbot Cirillo said it may be a copy of the second copper scroll."

Loir's face grows pallid as he turns the wooden panel over to re-examine the writing. "Second copper scroll? That's ... that's unbelievable," he stutters. "How did you find this?"

"Under the stone pillow of the prophet," Mordechai explains.

Fascinated by the idea of treasure but baffled by why SLVIA would point him in this direction, Derek grows impatient. Unwilling to go into details about how he discovered the letters of Sabas, he tries to direct the conversation. "Can you translate the text?"

"No, but I know someone who can." Loir moves past them to lock the shop door and turns over the CLOSED sign. "But first, I'll make us some tea. I need to hear everything." Loir stops to glare at Derek. "You are lucky Mordechai came with you or I would have thrown you out and alerted the police. Take off those vestments before God strikes you dead."

Mordechai shoots him a suppressed grin.

"Right," Derek replies, removing the garments. "Tell me why a copper scroll would be so important."

"No, the second copper scroll." Loir continues to make the tea while he explains. "According to II Maccabees, several years before the Babylonian invasion, Jeremiah and his scribe, Baruch, went into hiding. After years of warning King Josiah, and the high priest to repent, warnings that went unheeded, the prophet and five of his followers conspired with temple priests to hide the temple treasures somewhere outside of Jerusalem. The first copper scroll, discovered in the 1960s, describes sixty-four locations where Baruch and temple priests hid several dozen tons of gold, silver, and sacred vessels."

Derek has never heard of a copper scroll or a lost temple treasure. However, most of his understanding of biblical history is based on Hollywood. Not a reliable source. "How does a second copper scroll fit?"

Loir grins. "The last location of the first copper scroll describes a second copper scroll that many believe will lead to the greatest treasure of all history: the Ark of Testimony."

Derek has never heard of that ark either. While fascinating, it all sounds like legends, myths, and religious rituals. Not a single connecting point to the SLVIA. "Before we get too excited, we should get an accurate translation."

Loir nods in agreement. "I know a professor of Hebrew literature at Bar-Ilan University, very discrete."

Derek nods and smiles. It means another delay to his departure, hopefully only a few hours. Within the lens of his glasses, Jester sends an urgent message. *Sir Whines-a-lot having a meltdown. Urgent. Red Alert.*

Derek grins at the petty rivalry between the two geniuses. Nelson, the brilliant AI pioneer, can be a total diva while Jester, the quantum autistic savant, requires endless patience. Serendipitous timing, Derek needs to ask Nelson for a favor.

"Excuse me, Loir, but may I use your restroom?" he asks. Loir points to the back and continues to chat with Mordechai about the history.

Locking the door, Derek taps the lens frame to open the satellite channel. A moment later, the face of Dr. Garrett appears in a frame.

"Taylor, dear Lord, we were worried sick," Nelson answers, his face appearing on a small frame of his lens view. "Where are you?"

"Long story. Look, I need a huge favor. I'm offering you an opportunity to get out of the cold castle to visit an exotic location." Derek opens the negotiation without waiting to hear the pet peeve of the day.

"To do what, precisely? Have you found the SLVIA?" Nelson's voice tightens with excitement.

"Not yet. The breadcrumbs are leading in an unexpected direction. Listen, I need you to take the GII to Axum, Ethiopia." Derek spells out his favor, then waits for the reaction.

"Ethiopia?" Nelson reacts in disbelief. "Are you bloody insane? A civil war rips the nation apart. What could be of any interest in Axum?"

"The Ark of the Covenant," Derek replies. "I need you to meet the Guardian."

"You must be joking. I've seen *Indiana Jones*," Nelson retorts.

"What can I say? That was Hollywood; I'm talking real life. Not sure how yet, but it may play into this new thread. I can explain later."

Derek tries to avoid discussing a lengthy topic on a quick call. If he were honest, he has no clue how an ark will connect. It's more of a gut instinct. He watched a special once of the ark in Axum. A panel leading to another ark may be a fake. It would be good to know what a real ark will look like.

"Taylor, you're insane. Besides, I need to ask you something, and I demand that you tell me the truth," Nelson says, his voice trembling slightly. "Did you ever hack the servers of the *Concilium Tredecim*? If so, were you ever going to tell me about my father?"

Derek's heart freezes like a kid caught red-handed, unable to think of a good lie fast enough. He doesn't know how Nelson learned of his father, or the *Tredecim,* but this will be a delicate conversation.

"Doc, I promise to tell you everything I know, I swear, but I can't talk now. Call Zoey to warm up the GII, and I'll send details on the plane."

Derek hopes Nelson doesn't throw a hissy fit. To be fair, learning secrets about your dad can be a tough day on any social ladder. SLVIA hid the archives before disappearing, so how Doc learned is a mystery.

"Taylor, now is not a good time," Nelson protests, sounding cold and defiant. "The WITNESS attention issue has grown worse."

"WITNESS has been couped up in a lab. So have you. He's doing better in the field. Use one of the remote satellite kits to take him along. WITNESS needs to see more of the real world."

Derek's guessing, and if Nelson was honest, he'd admit that he's guessing too. None of them understands how the quantum AI operates or why it won't operate the way they expect.

"Help me out, and we'll debrief on the *Tredecim* and your dad afterward. I promise. Look, people are waiting, I've got to go."

Derek ends the call before Nelson can protest and steps out to find Loir and Mordechai staring at him carefully.

"Were you talking to yourself in there?" Loir asks.

Derek looks to see his phone in his jacket pocket hanging on the chair. He shrugs with a smile. "Yeah, but we all get along, so it's not weird. Right?"

CHAPTER 14:
INSIDE OUT

Maison Godin Prison, Quebec
Five Days Before Temple Ceremony

Jester surrounds himself with forty-foot-long walls of active monitors- the ultimate attention-deficit nirvana. With a shaved head, body tattoos, pierced ears, and a hipster beard, Jester practically vibrates with a hyper-restless, genius energy. Fingernails painted black and green hemmed by leather and silver bangles tap an erratic, nervous pattern on his scalp as he studies the screens.

One entire wall features dozens of live news or active cybersecurity data screens which he secretly siphons from multiple secure government and commercial sources. A global view of wars, cybersecurity, climate, refugees, starvation, and political corruption. The perfect apocalyptic mirror for Jester's chronically paranoid mind.

"Like, Putin has a plan, you know. The dude is slicker than slick. The master Machiavellian, and the Lex Luthor in the Lord of the Lies," Jester banters to himself. "He won't stop with crushing Ukraine. Putin wants revenge on the west. He wants the world to fear him. What was it he said last year? Oh, yeah. *Digital giants have been playing an increasingly significant role in wider society. We are now talking about economic giants, aren't we?"*

Jester paces a figure eight on the floor, his hands tapping on his shaved head, thinking, until he spins a little dance move. "Putin plans to use those giants against us. But how?"

"Please restate your inquiry," replies the WITNESS.

For decades, Taylor worked to expose the *Concilium Tredecim* even after Jester advocated SNO shift attention to the Kremlin Killjoy, the Crime Czar, the Moscow Madman. Social media and independent news are illegal in Russia, but Russian hackers still need the internet to launch cyberattacks on the west. After Ukraine, the hacktivist group, Anonymous, launched a cyberwar on Russia, causing temporary disruption to several Kremlin networks. Putin will retaliate in a major unspoken declaration of war type of attack. To avoid retaliation or full scale war, he will need something untraceable.

The opposite monitor wall divides into segments covering artificial intelligence, quantum research, intelligence networks, national defense, and social media filters to capture trends. The entire neural network of human endeavor grows at exponential rates. The global web added over 59 zettabytes in 2020 and 74 zettabytes in 2021. By 2025, the global data sphere will grow 175 zettabytes annually. Given that a zettabyte equals a trillion gigabytes, even Jester has a hard time wrapping his noggin around that much global activity in every language. No government or technology on earth can ensure the security of that much data. None.

His mind forms patterns of data clusters connecting and interacting in a dynamic cascade. "Dig it, like, maybe the internet is the *image of the beast,* you know. Like in the book of Revelation. A digital reflection of the best and most immoral parts of who we are, you know."

"Please restate your inquiry," WITNESS replies.

An autistic savant regarding hacking, cybersecurity, and quantum cryptology, Jester never fit in; not at home, or at his dad's evangelical church, or at school, or at the stodgy CIA, where he never drank the hyper-patriotic Kool-

Aid. Some at the CIA believe he has a rather fluid grasp on reality. They're right. All of them are a bunch of metal head thinkers who live and bleed the red, white, and blue in a changing kaleidoscope world. Taylor was different. Nonjudgmental. A visionary with a global mindset. Taylor built a domain worthy of the wizard. He jives why Taylor wants to find the SLVIA, but he's never seen the flapjack so unhinged, so reckless.

"Like the flapjack has gone sizzle on the griddle a little too long, you know?" Jester banters as his train of thought leads him.

"Please restate your inquiry," NIGEL replies.

Following the discovery of the SolarWinds and other software update hacks, AI systems worldwide have experienced minor glitches. Water treatment plants, air traffic control towers, missile launches, spoofed radar, and car deaths. Those patterns combine with a sharp rise in ransomware. A pattern develops but is still too vague to paint a picture.

"OK, OK, the Kremlin uses corporate social media to spread disinformation to divide Americans and agitate hatred. Elections, climate, vaccines, race, religion—everything is on the table as long as it divides. Pin it." Jester follows the kinetic data he envisions in his head as he spins around the room.

"Pinned," repeats WITNESS, an aristocratic preteen in a three-piece suit.

Jester's fingers tap an erratic beat on his chest, then his arms swing out in a dance move, folding back into a self-hug. "Putin uses ransomware to fund a badass crypto cyber war chest. Pin it." Cut off from international banking, oil, crypto-ransomware and trade with China are Putin's only other sources of cash.

"Pinned," repeats WITNESS.

Jester spins on his heels and goes back to his figure eight. "Dig it, we also know the Kremlin bought up the video kompromat from Epstein, Brunel, Khashoggi, and Yankovic. Enough slime to manipulate politicians, lower cyber budgets, delay prosecutions, and let regulations slide. He's using kompromat to lower our shields. Yeah, but for what?"

"Please restate the inquiry," WITNESS responds.

"Disrupt and destroy, baby," Jester states. "Like cancer on democracy, a plague on human decency, eating at us constantly. Bringing the high life down to mafia low life, you know."

Jester pivots to do an impromptu Michael Jackson crotch grab, then releases. "Nah, I'm missing something. SolarWinds was, like, only the tip of an iceberg. It changed the game and uncovered an entirely new strategy of attack, like sneaking in through the back door. There was no ransom, no digital data theft. What are those Putin pixel-ponies doing in there?"

Unfettered introduction of AI and quantum into the global net chemistry seems blind to the inevitable penetration of the dark web or despots. Building AI into cyber defenses and cyber malware will proliferate and mutate without control. Cyber and AI flip all the rules for winning a war inside out. Jester comes to the only conclusion a rational mind can reach: there will be no winning this war.

Then an epiphany stops Jester in his dance tracks and freezes the tapping fingers on his chest. It strikes him like a lightning bolt. Inside out, eating like acid. He knows the Kremlin cyber strategy, and if Jester is correct, we have few defenses and even less time to stop a disaster.

CHAPTER 15: OPPORTUNITY

Villa Outside of Istanbul, Türkiye
Four Days Before Temple Ceremony

Tall, hefty, steel-eyed Russian oligarch Yuri Yankovic lounges by the pool of his private villa a few miles outside of Istanbul on the Bosporus Strait, an unofficial guest of President Erdogan. The villa is a thank you gift for Yuri's role in securing S400 mid-range Russian missiles against the wishes of NATO.

Yuri makes his money from Cozy Bear, a Russian software company that conducts ransomware hacks. Before Ukraine sanctions, he held a controlling interest in Russian Television in America. He also owns a Belarus modeling agency that specializes in young girls. Erdogan himself comes to visit the villa, venting over his frustrations of walking the fine line between the east and the west, and enjoying the company of Yuri's models. Cut off from western banking, like many oligarchs, Yuri moved much of his money to untitled accounts in Cyprus. For other transactions, he uses cryptocurrency to get around banking sanctions.

When his private cell phone rings, he checks the ID. A known caller. "Da, Gospodin. *Yes, Mr. President*," he answers in Russian.

"We have a chance to hurt America, but we must hurry," the voice replies coldly. "The former president has taken temporary asylum in Saudi Arabia, claiming political persecution. He seeks permanent asylum in Israel."

Yuri laughs a loud guffaw. "The CIA must crap their pants, da."

"Lean on Israel. Dissuade them from offering asylum. Convince the former president to announce reelection from Moscow. Take someone young, a blond. Do whatever it takes." There is no emotion on the line, only a cold and calculating voice.

The Ukraine invasion isolated Putin and devastated the Russian economy. Putin is eager to repay the west for his humiliation. America teeters on civil war heading into new elections, with both parties claiming voter fraud, voter suppression, or a coup with a very unpopular current president. Yuri can imagine the volatile reaction in America if he succeeds.

"Brilliant, Gospodin," he says, still chuckling. "Genius."

A former American president under Kremlin control would be the news headline for the century, clear evidence of a corrupt and self-indulgent American empire in decline. An amazing chance to feed the Russian narrative, extract top secret intelligence and humiliate an enemy. Then Yuri considers the challenges. He will need to bend wills in both Israel and America.

"I need Pavel Borodin to open the vault," Yuri adds, already thinking about whom to lean on first. Borodin keeps priceless kompromat stored like a tight-ass Swiss banker.

During 2009, when Jeffrey Epstein was under investigation in Palm Beach, the lead detective on the case, Joseph Recarry, was under intense political pressure to hide evidence. Volumes of world leaders, politicians, CEOs, celebrities, and royalty had fallen into Epstein's web of sexual influence, pedophilia, and extortion. There was widespread fear for the enormous loss of public trust. About that time, John Dougan—a sturdy built, shaved head ex-Marine and disgruntled ex-cop—developed a friendship with Recarry. Soon afterwards, Dougan met a young model from Yuri's agency.

Within a month, the young couple fell in love and traveled to Moscow, where Dougan met with Pavel Borodin, the man who helped elevate Putin to power. Within days, Borodin announced a donation to a Dougan-run charity and granted him political asylum. A few years later, during the 2013 Miss Universe Pageant in Moscow, Dougan's girlfriend was a runner-up.

"Da, I will call him. No limits on this one," the voice promises.

"Good," Yuri replies. "I will leave at once." He will use the superyacht of a wealthy Turkish oil executive to avoid sanctions on Yuri's own yacht, still docked in the Maldives, where there is no extradition treaty.

Pressure points. It all boils down to finding the right people and applying pain to the correct pressure point. Sanctions cost him dearly. Yuri smiles at the chance to disgrace America and return some of the pain.

CHAPTER 16:
AXUM ATROCITIES

Axum, Tigray Region, Ethiopia
Four Days Before Temple Ceremony

A scorching 108-degree temperature assails Nelson as he steps off the GII jet, grateful that the pilot, Zoey, insisted he change out of his suit. While a khaki outfit would not be his normal attire, the ensemble fills him with a liberating spirit reminiscent of the legendary British explorers of the nineteenth century. Perhaps getting out of the lab will do him some good after all, refreshing his perspectives.

Taylor left him with minimal instructions for this ridiculously dangerous expedition merely to get an unnecessary scan of an obscure religious relic. There can be no fathomable connection between this place and the SLVIA code. While Taylor may have sprung him from a CIA interrogation tank, which obligates Nelson to a certain level of loyalty, he's not a genuine partner to SNO or their unauthorized cyber vigilante activities. At least Taylor didn't deny knowledge of his father and promised to discuss the matter.

"OK, Dr. Garrett, here's your survival kit. Don't go anywhere without it. I'm serious, not even to take a piss, eh," advises Zoey Mclaughlin, the glib GII pilot and former Canadian Air Force captain. A husky woman with bright brown eyes and a quirky sense of humor. "Taylor had me pack some of his priciest toys. Remember, you're just here to see a site, grab a scan, and hit the road. I'll see you tonight in Eritrea."

"Aren't you staying?" Nelson misunderstood the exit plan.

Zoey snorts. "You kidding? Way too dangerous, eh. Stick with your guide, you'll be fine," she says, turning to meet the fuel attendant.

The expensive backpack of tech toys is worth a man's life in a country like Ethiopia. A tablet with a Wi-Fi hub, a specialized 3D scanner, a foldable mini drone, envelopes of extra cash, a satellite boost for WITNESS glasses, a halogen flashlight, plus a few other devices. Nelson has suddenly become a walking mugging target. His momentary euphoria crumbles into penetrating angst.

Customs clears him with a false NGO identification, and one of the cash envelopes to discourage a search in the bag of goodies. Nelson plays Randolph Hedges, a representative from a private Canadian charity, on a mission to research the humanitarian crisis. Officially, his mission is to see the dire situation in the Tigray region for possible humanitarian funding. Unofficially, he's there to visit St Mary's of Zion; the church believed for over five hundred years to house the Ark of the Covenant.

Taylor sent a trusted contact to meet him at the airport. A young man, wearing faded jeans and a bright green and white polo shirt, holds up a sign reading HEDGES. The bone-thin lad smiles a bright, cheery countenance without a mask. While fully vaccinated, Nelson still wears a mask, worried that lethal COVID variant strains from Africa continue to find their way into Europe and America. Another careless oversight by Taylor.

"Mr. Hedges, so glad you come. Mr. Taylor says many good things about you," says the young man with an enormous grin.

"Thank you, and what is your name, sir?" Nelson asks.

"Salem; it means peace," the lad replies with a wide smile-a tragic irony given the war-torn state of his country.

"Thank you, Salem. I'd like to start by seeing St. Mary's, if you don't mind."

During 2020, the Ethiopian Prime Minister Abiy Ahmed, winner of the 2019 Nobel Peace Prize, sent troops into the northern Tigray region. Ahmed blamed the Tigray People's Liberation Front for attacks on army camps, an accusation never confirmed by international observers. On January 19, 2021, Ethiopian troops and Amhara militia entered the city of Axum, marching toward the Church of St. Mary of Zion. More than a thousand local Christians ran to the church to protect the ark. The militia ultimately dragged 750 men, women, and children into the courtyard for execution.

The lad's eyes cast down, and his bright smile vanishes. "Many of my friends and family died that day, Mr. Hedges. I wake up most nights in terrors."

Nelson's heart softens, flooded with a sudden sense of empathy. "I'm so sorry for your loss, Salem. Truly. I didn't know."

Salem nods his head in silence, his eyes distant, remembering.

"First, tell me your understanding of how the ark came to Axum." Nelson changes the subject away from the grim event.

Salem's smile immediately returns as they enter a beat-up Ford pickup, which appears to be a luxury. They drive slowly through streets sparsely mixed with pedestrians, army jeeps, empty produce carts, and a few goat herders. Hundreds of thousands have fled north to Eritrea or filled up mass graves. Nelson drives through the living corpse of a once vibrant culture. His eyes behold the unfiltered aftermath of war for the first time.

"Our legend teaches that during the reign of Jewish King Manasseh, the son of King Solomon and the Queen of Sheba, a man named Menelik brought the ark out of Israel. Accompanied by over five hundred temple priests, Menelik took the ark to Elephantine Island on the Nile River and built a Jewish temple. Many papyri discovered in 1893, known as the Elephantine Papyri, speak of the temple. After an attack by the Romans, the ark came to Ethiopia in the second century," Salem summarizes. "Even the Jews of Ethiopia agree the ark came here to rest."

"I'm impressed that you know your history so well," Nelson encourages. "Tell me more." The information may shed light on why Taylor seems suddenly enamored with this obscure relic.

"The ark stayed within Jewish synagogues until the Templars came in the tenth century and moved the ark into hand-cut rock churches such as Lalibela. During the sixteenth century, they brought the ark to the Church of Maryam Tsion, or St. Mary of Zion. Since then, the ark has rested on church grounds in the Chapel of the Tablets. Only the Bishop and the Guardian may see the ark, for it holds the presence of God." Salem whispers a prayer.

Hearing about the Templars strikes a dissonant chord that tightens Nelson's chest. Origins of his family lands in Narin trace to a grant from Edward II in a 1309 letter to Pope Clement V where the king defended the Templars. Connected to William Sinclair by marriage, the Garretts were among the earliest Scottish Rite Freemasons in London. Taylor shares an obsession with the Templar lore, although for reasons he mysteriously refuses to admit. This entire trip may be part of Taylor's Templar obsession, having little genuine value in the search for SLVIA.

"The Guardian," Nelson pauses, remembering that was the man Taylor wanted him to meet. "Did he survive the massacre?"

Salem's face falls in sadness as he shakes his head.

"How did you survive?" Nelson asks.

"We hid in tunnels beneath the church," the young man explains. "I was preparing with my family to face the Lord when they stopped dragging us out."

"Do you know what happened to the ark?" Nelson asks as they approach the now empty church grounds.

"People say they took the ark to Addis Ababa, but none of the museums, or Prime Minister Ahmed, report having the ark. Many say he sold it." Salem chokes back a tear.

"Sold it," Nelson repeats. "You mean on the black market? To whom?"

Salem merely shrugs his shoulders. The lack of an ark defeats the entire purpose of the trip. Nelson gets out of the truck and clutches the backpack over his shoulder. He should at least inspect the chapel. The church grounds contain several stone buildings, including a large, modern congregational hall, each scarred with bullet holes across the sides.

"They built the current Maryam Tsion in the 1950s," Salem explains, pointing to the larger building.

"Which one is the Chapel of Tablets?" Nelson asks.

Salem points to a small building of modest decoration roughly twenty meters by forty meters made of multicolored stone with a tall bronze door.

"Can we look inside?" Nelson asks.

Salem shrugs. On entry, Nelson notices a bronze chandelier hanging by a heavy chain under an arched dome ceiling painted red, blue, and gold. They covered the walls in murals painted in the unique two-dimensional style of the Middle Ages that depict the ark being brought by Jewish priests to Axum. Layers of overlapping rugs cover the stone slab floor with a soft footing. To the side of the main room lay a small cubicle with a simple wooden bed and a writing table with a lamp. Rather modest accommodations to accept for a lifetime of silent service just to maintain a hoax.

On a far wall, Nelson spots a shelf of ancient manuscripts, books, and scrolls. No doubt containing an immense religious and historical value. Surprising that the army failed to take or destroy them. They focused solely on the ark.

Inside a curtained room, the holiest relic in all of history supposedly sat for nearly five hundred years. Nelson discovers more paintings, candles, incense burners, tapestries on the wall, and a short, heavy, ebony stand where the ark once rested. They had covered the stone slab floor with overlapping rugs, except under the ebony stand where a single rug sits underneath, dusty, bug-eaten, and ancient. Off center, likely dragged when they stole the ark.

"I hope Taylor won't be too disappointed," Nelson murmurs.

Stepping back outside the building, Nelson notes a simple, unadorned structure nearby. "What's the purpose of that building?"

"In 2011, the Chapel of Tablets suffered water damage from a leaky roof. Before the Guardian could move the ark, the church built a temporary chapel while they completed repairs," Salem explains. "We expected a big ceremony so everyone could see the ark, but they moved the ark at night while the people slept."

"Interesting," Nelson mumbles as he steps off toward the temporary chapel. The inside décor lacks any paint or furniture except for a single rug under a rosewood stand that sits over a flagstone floor. Out of curiosity, Nelson steps up to the rug and pulls it aside. Underneath lay a single stone with a notch cut on one side in order to pull it up. An odd feature.

"You said the survivors hid in tunnels under the main church?" Nelson asks for confirmation.

"Yes," replies Salem. "But I'm not aware of tunnels under the chapel."

"No, of course not." They would not want that kind of information made public. Nelson's barely listening, already striding back to the original chapel, and stepping through the colorful curtains. With a brief resistance, he pulls on the rug under the heavy stand. Instead of a stone slab, he finds an ancient wooden door with an iron handle. A yank on the handle lifts a floor door to reveal steps leading into a tunnel.

"Bangers," exclaims Nelson as he slips down the stairs into the darkness. He reaches into his pocket to retrieve his cell phone with a flashlight feature.

"Salem, come down here, there's a tunnel," he calls.

Without warning, Salem closes the lid, and then slides the rug and table back into place.

"Salem!" Nelson shouts. "Salem, open the door this instant," he calls again, then stops.

Voices of men shouting and arguing outside the chapel seep through the stone, lasting for several minutes until the pop of two gunshots, and then nothing.

Nelson stands in numb silence, utterly deflated, steeping in a stew of raw guilt and panic. The young lad must have seen the army coming, and then gave his life to protect a stranger, not even a Christian. Or perhaps he protected a secret. Either way, Nelson caused the death of a young man. No. Salem's death will fall on Taylor.

Terror grips Nelson's soul as he paces in a circle. As of the moment, he's trapped with no other local support, and the army potentially waiting outside. Salem may not be the only death on Taylor's account.

CHAPTER 17:
CHANCE AT REDEMPTION

Church of Mary Magdalene, Jerusalem
Four Days Before Temple Ceremony

Devlin McGregor jerks up from his cot, hyperventilating, dripping cold sweat that drenches his shirt as his heart races wildly. Slowly, he orients himself to the dark stone walls of the medieval church basement where he's a guest of a friend of the Order.

The nightmare grows more frightful each time he relives that day. *Torn from his bed in the middle of the night as two men toss him into a trunk. Taken by force to St. Stephens Green, an Opus Dei rehabilitation center for wayward boys only to learn that his father arranged the ordeal in a final desperate attempt to tame him. He escaped St. Stephens days later during a fierce North Atlantic storm and never saw his father or mum again.*

Still trembling, Devlin lights a candle and rolls out a prayer rug. After years of reflection, he understands that his father's horrendous act saved his soul. Devlin prays to wash off the lingering disquiet and shame over another failure to silence the hacker. Surveillance cameras spotted Taylor in Jericho heading toward the ancient monastery. By the time Devlin arrived, found a secure location, and set up his weapon, he was seconds too late to get a clean shot. Then things went terribly wrong, and he lost the scent.

His cell phone rattles across the small end table, shattering the early morning quiet. Only one man knows the number, the Prelate of the *Order of the Solar Temple*.

"Yes, Holy Father," he answers, his Scottish brogue still thick after all these years.

Silence hangs in the air for a long, tense moment before the Prelate takes in a deep breath. "God has sent us an angel, my son. The Lord Praeceptor has instructed brother Elan Golan of Mossad to help you find the hacker. Our time grows short to complete the cleansing."

Devlin's mission must be of immense importance to involve the Praeceptor, grandmaster of the powerful *Concilium Tredecim*. The news both encourages him and adds pressure.

After his escape from the Opus Dei, Devlin fell hard onto the streets of Glasgow until a cute lass recruited him into the *Brothers of Parvis*, a group associated with the *Order*. A mentor encouraged him to enlist in the United Kingdom Special Forces, where they transformed his youthful rage into the useful skills of a marksman first class. After a tour of duty in Desert Storm, Devlin joined the International Criminal Court (ICC) as an investigator. By then, he had advanced in the order to the *Knights of the Alliance*.

Founded in 1975 by Joseph di Mambro and Luc Louret, the *Ordre du Temple Solaire* integrated the teachings of the Knights Templar, enhanced by divine revelations from Master Louret. During an infamous Last Supper ritual in October 1994, led by former Prelate Origas, the sacrifice of an infant boy led to the ritual poisoning of fifteen leader witnesses. Earlier that day, the leaders themselves had murdered thirty-eight others within a secret underground chapel lined with mirrors and etched with Templar symbols. Criminal investigations forced the group into secret cells in

Quebec, Scotland, France, Italy, Israel, and Spain.

Nearly as soon as the call ends, another call comes through. "Yes," he answers.

"Brother Devlin, my name is Elan. I'm instructed to help you find a mutual enemy."

CHAPTER 18:
ARK OF TESTIMONY

Bar-Ilan University, Tel Aviv
Four Days Before Temple Ceremony

Outside the office door of Dr. Matan Rubin, professor of Hebrew literature, Derek wears an N95 mask over dark WITNESS lenses and plainclothes with a sports cap, checking for cameras.

Loir pauses. "Remember, we say nothing of the abbot's death. We're only here to seek a translation."

Mordechai's eyes cast down, clearly uncomfortable with even the deception of omission. Loir has the political wisdom to know what not to say, a candor Derek can appreciate.

Loir knocks twice and enters. "Matan, old friend," he greets a thin man with a balding scalp and angular nose. "Thank you for meeting with me on such short notice."

"You said it would be worth my while," the professor replies with a raised eyebrow.

"Matan, I would like to introduce Brother Mordechai from Mar Jaris, and … " Loir hesitates.

"Derek Taylor," he reaches out to shake hands. "Hey, is that a 3D printer?" he asks, intrigued, thinking of getting one. "Sorry for the diversion, I'm just surprised to see such a cool device in the office of a language professor. No offense."

"Yes, it was a personal gift from my students," Matan explains. "I'm an amateur archaeologist who volunteers on many local digs. All the items found in Israel must go to the Israel Antiquities Authority, the IAA. They allow me to scan the original item and print out a token of my find," he says, pointing to dozens of items around his office. "Now, you said you needed something translated."

"Yes, an old wooden panel found at Mar Jaris, written by the founder," Loir explains.

Derek reaches into his backpack to pull out the board wrapped in a soft cloth and hands it to the professor, who sits at his desk to unwrap it gently.

"The wood certainly looks rather old. If you are willing, we can take a tiny sample to carbon date the age," he suggests as he puts on a pair of glasses, then gloves, and pulls over a large magnifying glass with a light.

Derek looks at Mordecai, who nods in agreement. "Carbon dating sounds like a great idea." If someone created the panel after the life of Sabas, then it's a fake.

Matan sits to examine the panel while voices drop into an anxious silence. "Fascinating, the writing uses an ancient form of proto-Hebrew," Matan notes as he continues to study the plank. "How would a fourth-century monk know how to write sixth century BCE Hebrew?"

Loir waves his hand for the others to stay silent.

After a moment, Matan flips over the panel, and his jaw drops. He lifts his head with wide eyes. "Where did you find this wood? This can't be genuine."

Derek and Loir look to Mordechai, who takes a deep breath. "Our tradition teaches that Father Sabas, founder of our monastery, discovered a copper scroll buried near the ruins by the Dead Sea. He wrote to the pope about his discovery, but the church was in upheaval, and the pope never responded. Warned by God in a dream, Father Sabas made a copy of the scroll before he reburied it," Mordechai explains.

"What does it say?" questions Loir, reacting to the excitement in Matan's eyes.

"The panel speaks of the first copper scroll hidden in a cave that leads to temple treasure, then provides directions from the Hill of Kokhlit to where the prophet Jeremiah hid the Ark of Testimony. Sit, sit, I will explain," he points to stacks of file boxes as chairs.

Astounded, Derek finds himself pulled into the mystery, momentarily distracted from his real purpose, or maybe distracted from his utter failure to find SLVIA.

"The Temple Institute has been preparing for the Holy Temple and the coming of Moshiach since 1967. This could be a significant sign that the time grows near," Loir says.

Derek turns to Mordechai with a questioning look.

"The Hebrew word for messiah," the boy explains in a whisper.

Matan continues. "The book of Maccabees states: *Jeremiah came and found a cave-dwelling, and he brought there the tent, and the ark, and the altar of incense, then he sealed up the entrance.*"

The old bookstore geek giggles like a schoolboy, wiggling on his box. "After they hid the ark, the scribes attempted to retrace the landmarks, but the prophet forbade them, saying: *The place is to remain unknown until God gathers his people together again and shows them mercy. Then the Lord will disclose these things, and the glory of the Lord will be seen in the cloud,*" recites Loir. "The time of the third temple must indeed be near."

On the drive to the university, Derek learned Loir was a leading member of the Temple Institute, a group of passionate advocates for the rebuilding of the Third Jewish Temple on the Temple Mount–ironically, a group and a view that is not all that popular in Israel. Most of the population is secular or non-religious.

"Once again, Loir, you get ahead of yourself and God," Matan replies. "No one wants a temple if it brings more war."

"You mean this panel will guide you to find the Ark of the Covenant, like in *Indiana Jones*?" Derek ponders how this may connect to SLVIA, but it's vague and unlikely.

"No," corrects Matan. "The Ark of Testimony. There were two arks made. The first at the direction of Moses in the wilderness, made of acacia wood, overlaid with gold, which held the manna, Aaron's rod, and the holy commandments. Solomon made the second Ark of the Covenant of pure gold for the first temple. That ark was likely taken into Babylon, but no one knows for sure."

"I saw a Graham Hancock special years ago who claimed the ark was in Ethiopia," Derek questions. "He sounded legit." Derek sent Nelson to get a scan of the ark to know precisely what the genuine ark looks like, or if it even exists. Now he wonders if it was accidental misdirection.

"The African ark was a duplicate, a gift," Loir explains.

"A duplicate?" he questions. "You mean a replica?"

"Yes, of course, the temple priests would never send the true ark to Egypt," Loir debates. "OK, there were three arks made, and temple priests used all three in worship, but none are like the one made by Moses, empowered with the presence of *Elohim*."

"Loir, before you get excited, we have no starting point," says Matan. "There is no hill called Kokhlit in Jerusalem. For over sixty years, men have searched Jerusalem for the temple treasure clues revealed in the first copper scroll which mentioned the same mysterious hill, but without success. Without a starting point, the entire idea is a fantasy."

"No, no, don't you remember the American who came to Israel a decade ago? A man named Jim Barfield? He wrote a book. He discovered all the locations from the first copper scroll in Qumran," Loir says.

"I heard the IAA debunked that theory," Matan replies.

"No, no, it was Palestinian politics, as always," Loir counters. "Qumran sits within the West Bank. To excavate would be a political nightmare, forcing all the treasure into an IDF warehouse. The IAA didn't want treasure hunters checking out the rumors."

"Of course, no one wants a temple," Matan argues. "It would be politically impossible."

In Derek's mind, the politics of Israel have a special connection to the *Concilium* and the *Sefer HaBahir*. An extremely obscure connection, maybe even imaginary, but a connection. "I'm a tad curious. Would it be possible to visit Qumran?" he questions.

"If we leave now, we can be there before dark," Loir replies.

Derek has all but given up any idea of finding the SLVIA, but his curiosity has been more than a little aroused. SLVIA had warned that construction of the third temple was the next key prophetic event, but never explained why. Although he discounted the conclusion, this new ark thread may play into that scenario.

He's grasping at vapor while a friend is hurting, but it will only delay his departure by a few more hours. The rabbit hole into lunacy is a slippery slope, dragging him deeper. Derek allows the slide as a distraction from his failure.

CHAPTER 19:
AIR JACK

Jenn Scott Home, Reston
Four Days Before Temple Ceremony

The chime of Jenn's cell phone startles her from a terrible dream of losing the admiral under a massive wave. A blurry glance at the ID reads Matt Adelson, likely with news of the house. Her stomach muscles tighten with unease as she accepts the call. "Hello?"

"Morning, Lieutenant," Matt greets her on the formal side, probably calling from his office. "I'm sorry to call you so early, but we confirmed the toxin as Novichok, the same as your father, and Navalny," he conveys. "The team isolated the agent to the couch, with only trace amounts in the safe room, kitchen, and bedroom. We've disposed of the couch, ripped out the carpets, and sent in a cleaning crew. The house should be safe by tomorrow."

The admiral rarely used the living room, so the agent could have been there for several months, or maybe even since his journal entry. Not unexpected, but the news confirms that whoever killed her father got inside the house. She'll change the locks and install high-end security cameras. Now that they have a theory on motive, and how, the question remains who?

"What about the journals?" she asks.

"We had to confiscate your father's journal and computers until we complete the investigation. Your mother's journals also contained communications we believe were from the SLVIA. Once cleared of anything classified, I can release them."

Jenn should have expected that response as well. She changes the subject. "Have you heard from Agent Rhodes?" Mention of him yesterday brought back memories of him last night.

Matt hesitates. "No, but the Saudis agreed to send all three agents to Israel. We expect to hear confirmation once they land. Unfortunately, the kingdom has granted the FPOTUS temporary asylum, claiming he provides a vital role within a reinvigorated peace deal."

"Disappointing that the most powerful nation on earth can't prosecute a corrupt leader without the world making us look like the villains," she retorts.

Although, to most of his followers, the criminal investigations themselves are political, criminal, and corrupt. Right-wing media tries to portray a witch-hunt, conducted by a weak president, determined to keep his opponent from running again. Jenn still can't get used to the post-truth age. The admiral would say *dangerous actions have dire consequences. To avoid the consequences, act with honor.*

"Funny you should say that; Putin has already put out a public statement to that effect, calling America's treatment reminiscent of Stalin-era purges. Remember, the former president is not just any citizen who skipped trial," Matt reminds her. "He still represents our nation, and the moment we treat him like a third world criminal, then the United States will look weaker."

"But to do nothing allows him to play the victim for the entire planet," she retorts.

"I'm aware of the consequences," Matt reminds her. "Neither democracy nor freedom comes cheap."

Matt's right, and every US officer understands the necessity of sacrifice. She lets it go. "Thanks for the update."

Jenn hangs up feeling distressed, convinced the Kremlin had the admiral silenced. They failed. The admiral raised the alert and paid the ultimate price for his integrity.

If Geoff Rhodes remains the same bull-headed screw-the-rules renegade he was back at Annapolis, then he won't take the legacy of losing a former president easily. Jenn can imagine him looking for a way to bring the FPOTUS back to US soil, even if that soil is only an embassy. If she can find and help Geoff, maybe she can confront the former president.

Jenn's first challenge is traveling to Israel without leaving an airline ticket trail. It would be better if Matt Adelson wasn't aware of her plan. Fortunately, Jenn made friends with a pilot who graciously offered to help whenever she needed it. Jenn gets up to turn on the shower and throw a travel bag on the bed. Time to call in a favor.

*

Tote Luxury Charter, Reagan International, DC
Three Days Before Temple Ceremony

Jenn looks up to the private hangar door at Reagan International. *Tote Luxury Charter*. With no appointment, she feels fortunate to find both Jack Tote and the Gulfstream V gifted to Jack from Taylor inside the hangar. With his back toward her, Jack points toward the engine as he discusses something with the mechanic.

"Good morning, Captain Tote. I was wondering if you were in the mood for flapjacks." She announces loud enough to interrupt and subtly mention their mutual friend.

Tote spins around. "Lieutenant Jennifer Scott, what a wonderful surprise." The lean pilot with jet-black crewcut hair, dark eyes, and crooked smile bounds over to give her a warm hug.

"Not lieutenant anymore; I resigned," she clarifies.

"Ah pucky. Once an officer, always an officer." Jack pulls back to look into her eyes. "Flapjacks, eh? Yeah, you bet, I know a place nearby." He gives her a knowing wink.

With a turn back to the mechanic, Jack excuses himself. "Hey Greg, I'm going to take an old client to breakfast. Have her fueled by the time I get back. I have a feeling we'll be heading off someplace in a hurry."

Jenn smiles, knowing how many years Jack supported Derek Taylor before her investigation forced Taylor underground. Ironically, she's hoping some of that loyalty will spill over to her.

*

Barley Mac Diner, outside Reagan Airport
Three Days Before Temple Ceremony

"I heard about the admiral," Jack says after they find a booth at the small American-style diner. "He was very well-respected, you know, except for those who wanted to curse his mama. And just for the record, they were often the same people." Jack grins. "I'll say this: the old shark did a hell of a job raising an amazing daughter."

Jenn bows her head to absorb the compliment, but she isn't sure how to respond. How someone got inside the family home to murder a great man still consumes her thoughts.

Jack studies her face carefully. "You, OK?"

Jenn takes a deep breath, knowing that she needs to be completely honest with Jack if she expects his help.

"Jack, the Kremlin murdered the admiral with Novichok," she blurts out the news as the server steps up to their booth.

Jack stares at her a second, then turns to the young girl, who looks terrified. "Two coffees, two number four breakfasts over easy, a lot of privacy, and a tight lip if you want a good tip." The server opens her eyes wide and nods her head quickly before she scurries away.

Jack turns back. "Are you sure about this?"

"Adelson told me himself," she replies. "The admiral kept a journal. The SLVIA gave him evidence the FPOTUS knew of a national ID leak before he approved the platform."

"Holy Mary, Mother of God," mumbles Jack, a non-practicing Catholic. "Does Taylor know? I'm sure he'd want to help."

"I kind of pushed him away." Jenn lowers her eyes. "Failure to arrest him when I had the chance cost me a reputation and a naval career. I may have gotten resentful with him in the last few texts."

The server returns with their coffee and just as quickly sprints away.

"Oh yeah," Jack nods, drowning his coffee with cream. "I worked with Taylor for a decade, and while he acts like a ginormous, arrogant, cocksure wienie, inside he's like a hyper-sensitive little snowflake, dweeb, sissy-pants. Don't worry, he'll get over it."

Jenn can't help but chuckle at the description. "Well, if he ever texts me again, I suppose I should apologize." It genuinely hurts to admit, given Taylor's deceptions. A text from Taylor never includes a return name or number and always disappears from her phone. She has no way of contacting him-for his safety and her frustration. Without trust, they have nothing.

The server hurries back with the eggs before she scurries away.

Jack douses his eggs with Tabasco. "Look, I've got to be honest with you. I'm with Taylor on this one," he mumbles, barely chewing his food before he practically inhales it. "I mean, the guy lost everything to stop that Chinese AI virus last year while the Feds fiddled and sent you to bust him. He went out of his way to keep you from getting involved or hurt. I get it, you had a job to do. He doesn't blame you and neither do I, but I can only feel so much sympathy. That said, how can I help?"

Jack is right, both she and Taylor suffered from her investigation. Perhaps even worse, she's allowed herself to slump into a pity party, which the admiral would never tolerate. Jenn takes a bite, chews to think, and lays down her fork to talk.

"They sent the Secret Service agents assigned to FPOTUS to Tel Aviv. I want to meet with one of them." Jenn reveals only part of the plan, in part because the plan still forms.

"Why would Secret Service be in Israel?" Jack asks, taking a sip of his coffee to wash down the plate of eggs he just inhaled. His other hand pulls over a plate of pancakes just delivered.

Jenn leans across the table to whisper. "Because FPOTUS has taken asylum in Saudi Arabia."

Jack coughs and spits his coffee into his napkin. "Arabia," he exclaims, still coughing, causing more than a few heads to turn. So much for privacy.

"Shout a little louder," she scolds.

"Sorry, but crap on a cracker, girl," he apologizes as he leans over the table. "Well, you're in luck because Taylor's already in Israel and can help you sort this out."

"I don't need Taylor." Jenn pushes back, instantly wanting to know why he would be in Israel, but forcing herself to act uninterested. She certainly doesn't need his sarcastic flap and half-truths. Her plan to confront the former president will require diplomacy.

Jack looks into her eyes and slowly nods. "Yeah, sure, OK, I won't get in between you two. When do you want to leave, as if that bag in your car isn't an answer?"

Jenn smiles, and picks up her fork to start on her own eggs, taking her time to chew. What she doesn't say, maybe what she should say, is that working with a fugitive will complicate her struggle to convince Geoff to help. And complicate her struggle to get over Taylor. They only spent a few days together while she investigated him, so her feelings were irrational. There will always be an impassable barrier between them. He's a fugitive, and she's an admiral's daughter. She's still too vulnerable from grieving the admiral to deal with her vulnerability to Taylor. Yet, even knowing that he'll be in Israel lifts her spirit ever so slightly.

CHAPTER 20: ARABIAN NIGHTS

Erga Palace, Riyadh
Four Days Before Temple Ceremony

Geoff Rhodes isn't dead, at least judging from the piercing pain jabbing into the back of his skull without mercy. The persistent agony slowly draws him out of a coma, one excruciating stab at a time. His hand falls from his stomach to feel silky sheets. Cool air circulates the sweet scent of jasmine. Each new sensory awareness entices him to fight for more consciousness. With sheer determination to endure the jabs to his skull, he forces his eyes to open a sliver.

Bright sunlight peeks through ornate, colorful drapes, shining a thin beam of light onto an enormous bed with a soft wool blanket. Next to the bed sits a glass of water, a teacup, and a bottle of medications that he can only hope are there for the pain. The room furnishings look like they could come from a modern *Arabian Nights* tale of luxurious indulgence. He checks under the sheets to see that he's naked, but has no recollection of what happened to his clothes or how he came to be here. Where is he?

Geoff remembers boarding the private jet to escort a very irritable FPOTUS back home after meeting the New York District Attorney. Together with Agents Stevens and Blake at the back of the plane, they drank only coffee and talked about the hot, muggy Florida weather. Then he can't recall anything else. Nothing else—nothing.

Ignoring the pain, he swings one leg over the edge of the bed, followed by the other, and then forces himself to sit up. A rapid, sharp wave of nausea stops him, forcing him to breathe slowly. It takes a moment for the nausea to pass before Geoff stands to waddle over to the drapes. Every muscle in his body objects as his arm yanks the heavy curtain aside. Then his jaw goes slack.

Geoff gazes out over the most magnificent pool and garden he's ever seen, like out of a grand Hollywood set of Eden on steroids. Enormous, as large as a football stadium, surrounded by walls, stone pillars, and shrines with copulas. Paths, gardens, fountains with waterfalls and lagoons. Thousands of cleverly placed palm trees create a canopy of majestic frond umbrellas that cast a magical patchwork of cooling shade onto the man made oasis.

So mesmerized by the enormity and opulence, it takes Geoff a moment to follow the scene down until he discovers the wide eyes of a young woman staring up at him through her hijab headscarf. Geoff suddenly remembers his nakedness. With a rapid yank and a sudden flush of pain, he closes the drape. Where is he? What happened to Stevens and Blake, and the FPOTUS, and his clothes?

A knock on the door causes him to panic. "Hold on," he calls with a hoarse, dry voice. Only then does he notice a thin, cotton robe laid over a nearby cushioned chair with a long hair lamb's wool cover. The door knocks again, a bit more impatiently.

"Coming." Geoff opens the door to find three enormous Arabian men who practically push their way into his room.

A thin man wearing gold and white robes with a well-trimmed beard and dark glasses steps in after them. "Welcome to Erga Palace, Mr. Rhodes. My name is Faisal. You are a guest of the Royal Family of Saud, a rare honor, I can assure you. I'm afraid you made a powerful impression with the king's niece a few moments ago."

Geoff's head whirls with a spiking pain. "King? I ... I didn't mean—it was an accident. I mean, I didn't know—what happened to me? How did I get here?"

"Our doctors have provided you with an excellent medication to ease your pain," Faisal says, pointing to the pills by his bed, not bothering to answer his questions. "Designed specifically to counter the drug they gave you during the flight. Please feel safe to take them, as I would hate to see you suffer any further."

Two pills already sit within a delicate ivory plate featuring an Islamic symbol. Geoff quickly downs the pills with several large gulps of water, feeling extremely dehydrated. The water soothes his throat enough to ask again.

"How did you bring me here, where are the others, where is the president?" he demands more forcefully.

"Stay calm, Agent Rhodes, and try to remember your place. We have offered you an opportunity to be our guest." Faisal frowns. "The other two agents have already left Arabia. You are also free to go once you have eaten and feel well."

"And the president?"

"Your former president is free to leave when he wishes. However, he has requested temporary asylum in Arabia, claiming political persecution in America. The king has granted the request."

Asylum? Persecution? The idea of a former president under the control of any foreign government will send the State Department, White House, CIA, and the Department of Defense into a frenzy, not to mention the panic among our allies. The media will have an orgasmic meltdown over this one, and his followers will erupt in protest. If someone gave him a drug on the plane, then that implies pre-planning, a conspiracy.

"Where are the other agents?" Geoff asks again.

"On a flight to Tel Aviv where we advised them to check in with the US Embassy. From there, we do not know, nor do we care," Faisal explains with the calm condescension of someone aware that Geoff is powerless to object.

"Where's my phone and firearm?"

The gentleman smiles slightly. "We forbid personal phone devices or weapons inside the palace. We will return your personal items once you land at your destination."

If the garden pool was that enormous, there is no way he can find the president, much less convince him to return to the US to stand criminal trial. Tactical assessment: he's royally screwed.

"You mentioned something to eat. I'd like to get dressed first," Geoff requests.

"Of course, my men will wait for you outside," Faisal reassures before he turns to leave.

Inside the marble bathroom, bigger than his entire apartment back in Maryland, Geoff inhales the fragrant fresh flowers before turning on the shower. The medicine already eases his intense pain. Geoff considers his limited options and the devastating impact this fiasco will have on his career at the Secret Service.

"I wonder if I can come work for these guys. I'm probably out of a job."

CHAPTER 21:
ENEMY IN THE HOUSE

National Military Command Center (NMCC), Washington,
DC
Four Days Before Temple Ceremony

Matt steps briskly into the command center at NMCC, which provides tactical command to all US strategic forces. The new Joint Chief, replacing Adam Scott, Admiral Paul Anderson, called an hour ago to request Matt's firsthand assessment of a developing situation. A hundred workstations buzz with activity in the central control room that monitors all US military activity and movements around the globe.

"Afternoon, commander," Matt greets. "What do we know?"

"Director Adelson, good to see you, sir." Commander Jim Crawford nods in response. "An hour ago, the USS Georgia executed an emergency surface maneuver because of a power plant malfunction."

Stationed in the Persian Gulf, the Georgia is an Ohio class guided-missile submarine with fifteen officers and a crew of 140. To improve efficiency and lower maintenance, ship-based nuclear power plants leverage artificial intelligence, specially trained to operate a safe nuclear processor from over a hundred thirty sensor feeds.

"Any casualties?" Matt asks about the personnel impact first.

"Over a dozen men with radiation exposure airlifted to Bahrain for treatment," the commander replies. "The missile cruiser USS Port Royal intercepted the Georgia to offer evacuation and towing."

Tensions in the Gulf run high, with both Israel and Iran engaging in ship sabotage. Since late 2020, the US has moved massive firepower into the Persian Gulf. Besides the USS Georgia, with a combined capacity of 398 vertical launch tubes, more than most nations, the missile cruisers USS Port Royal and USS Philippine Sea escort the sub. Then add three of the Navy's eleven nuclear-powered aircraft carriers: the USS Nimitz, USS Theodore Roosevelt, and the USS Dwight D. Eisenhower. An entire fleet to deter Iran and protect the Strait of Hormuz.

"Do we know what happened?" Matt asks, wondering why Admiral Andersen wanted him in the loop. Nuclear power plant operations should normally be a Department of Energy issue.

"Well, sir, we're still early in our investigation, but we believe an AI software glitch allowed the fuel rods to overheat. The captain manually implemented emergency measures to force the sub to surface and cool the rods," Commander Crawford replies.

"How would a nuclear submarine, cut off from the world except via encrypted satellite, develop an AI glitch?" Matt wonders aloud. "The DOE tests those controls rigorously."

"Well, sir, that's why the admiral thought you would want to know," replies the commander. "The sub docked a few weeks ago for maintenance and food stocks. All systems went through software updates completed through the secure Naval Planned Maintenance System."

Matt takes a deep breath. "Commander Crawford, a software update hack similar to SolarWinds affected those networks. We never fully determined the purpose behind those intrusions, or the intruders."

Commander Crawford scrunches his nose in confusion. "Like a virus?"

Matt raises an eyebrow. "We scrub those updates for viruses, meaning something else we can't detect may have created the sabotage."

Commander Crawford's face drains. "Sir, every ship in the fleet could be at risk."

"Exactly," Matt says, understanding why the admiral wanted him in the loop.

CHAPTER 22:
HILL OF KOKHLIT

Ruins of Qumran, Dead Sea
Four Days Before Temple Ceremony

Elevated above the ruins of Qumran, near the only large rock outcropping on the plateau, Derek uses a compass embedded into his lenses to find the direction of the winter solstice.

"An American named Jim Barfield decoded the first copper scroll and believes this rock to be the hill of Kokhlit," Loir explains.

"Then we should be able to pinpoint the precise GPS coordinates where the winter sunrise meets the Jordan River," Derek notes the first step written on the panel. Although thousands of years ago, they would not have been so precise. Then there is the ancient oasis to find amid modern development, and then a canyon with a vertical rock.

"It doesn't matter, and this is all a waste of time. We already know the ark will be in Jordan," dismisses Matan. "King Hussein will never permit Israel to search. A temple has no meaning to God without the ark, so Loir, once again, I'm afraid this is not the time for the temple."

Derek dismisses the comment, not out of disrespect as much as a self-confessed ignorance about matters of religion. He takes a 360-degree scan of the surrounding area. Qumran overlooks the Dead Sea a mile from shore and a few miles south of where the Jordan River delta empties into the Dead Sea. Interestingly, the ruins are also close to the St. George monastery where the Abbot Sabas once lived in a cave, and where Abbot Cirillo lost his life. Sabas spoke of a large rock north of the ruins by the Dead Sea, which must be this rock.

"Tell me more about this place and the first copper scroll," he asks.

"Qumran is best known for where Bedouins discovered the famous Dead Sea scrolls in one of the many limestone caves that dot the cliffs," Matan explains, pointing to the caves. "During the Roman occupation, Qumran was home to a radical sect of religious purists called the Essenes, who split away from the corrupt priests and temple worship. They occupied Qumran from 150 BCE to 70 CE when the Romans massacred them. Scholars believe the Essenes scribed most of the Dead Sea scrolls, but not the copper scroll."

"Matan is correct," Loir says, "except archaeologists recently confirmed Qumran was first built in the sixth century BCE, during the first temple period, the same era as the copper scrolls. After a Babylonian massacre, Qumran lay abandoned until the Essenes. Not found in jars like the Essene scrolls, they found the first copper scroll hidden behind a handmade mud wall."

"When the American identified all sixty-four scroll locations within the ruins of Qumran, the IAA brought a metal detector," Loir continues. "The survey confirmed nonferrous metals at each location, but they only dug less than a meter before concluding the theory false and halting the project. The scroll clearly noted to dig over three meters. IAA hid the truth."

"Where is that copper scroll now?" Derek asks, still trying to connect to anything that should involve him or SLVIA.

"They took the original scroll to the Jordan Museum in Amman, but there is a replica at the Rockefeller Museum in East Jerusalem. Translations are online," Matan responds.

All the archaeology and history may be interesting, but he wonders if this detour could be part of his slide into insanity. Maybe he's giving too much ground to these treasure myths and fantasies. SLVIA could have read the first scroll translation online, but why would it care?

As they walk down the hill and back through the ruins toward parking, Loir points out the various locations from the first copper scroll. When Derek looks back to the hill, he realizes that all the locations line up in a row, almost as if to point toward that one large outcrop of rock north of the ruins. Derek has never been a fan of random chance. Everything has a reason, especially a treasure map such as the first copper scroll.

"Where did you say Jeremiah buried the ark?" Derek asks.

Matan looks east across the Dead Sea to a mountain range spanning miles up into the Jordan River Valley. "Legend claims Mt. Nebo, but it could be anywhere along the Nebo range."

"Makes sense. They would hide the ark within visual sight," Mordechai says.

There could be countless locations for a now-buried cave, except they now have a start point, a compass heading, and two landmarks.

"Why wouldn't Israel look harder for something so precious?" Mordechai questions.

"Secular politics care little for spiritual truths of the Jews," simmers Matan. "The Knesset bow more allegiance to the G7 than to the Torah. Americans and the EU stand up for the Palestinians while Jordan clings to an Islamic califate by controlling the *Haram esh-Sharif*. The Sanhedrin waits patiently for Moshiach to bring peace before they will stick their neck out for a temple. And American evangelicals seem willing to risk Armageddon to bring their second coming. The only safe solution will be to do nothing."

"Yes, yes, Matan," Loir bubbles over. "Don't you see that if the people learn we found the Ark of Testimony, and not just gold or silver, it will inspire them to return to God? We both know that Jewish visits to the Temple Mount have soared. With support from the new Saudi king, then we may once again worship Elohim in his temple."

Derek tries to imagine the response in Israel to finding an ancient box and struggles to see how it could change any of the situation or sentiments on the ground.

"*Barukh ata Adoni. Eloheinu, melekh ha'olam*, **Blessed** are You, LORD our God, King of the universe," exclaims Loir, lifting his hands.

"Lower your hands," chides Matan. "You're drawing attention."

Indeed, there were few tourists at that hour, but security was clearly taking notice of the group. Slowly, they turn to walk toward parking.

"I am not trying to quench your joy, Mr. Sasson, but the Christian perspective would say that a third temple will exist in the heavenly kingdom," says Mordechai. "The sacrifice of the Christ ended the need for temple sacrifice. Others would say a third temple would only reveal a false messiah."

"So, young man, you come from a good Jewish family, and now you side with the evangelicals expecting our temple to bring war and not peace," retorts Loir with a snort.

Mordechai lowers his gaze, clearly unwilling to raise a confrontation.

The SLVIA had also warned of a temple, but never said why. It makes little sense why the SLVIA sent him here, which leaves the alternate conclusion: It didn't. This entire trip is nothing more than a delusional red herring of his own making while he neglects Jenn at home and abandons Jester to the cyberwar building daily.

"Well gentlemen, I've fulfilled my promise to the abbot. The next steps sound like national or religious issues that are really not my gig," Derek says, then turns to Mordechai. "You know, it's probably safe by now for you to head back home. I need to do the same."

Mordechai lowers his eyes, looking disappointed. Derek chuckles, thinking the kid likes the excitement. Better get him back to the monastery before he gets hooked on it. Loir and Matan simply exchange a look he can't interpret.

On the drive back to Tel Aviv, Matan and Derek share the front seat. "Mr. Taylor, how do you make a living, if I may ask?"

"I sold a cybersecurity firm last year. I'm in between gigs." Derek lies. He's a fugitive from the FBI, and he still owns controlling shares of Taylor Security Systems and Services, known as TS3, now run by his partner.

"Interesting," Matan replies. "When we get back to Bar-Ilan, would you mind looking at our server? We have an application we cannot erase."

Derek grins. "Yeah, some files can be stubborn." They may not be acting as the admin. "What type of app?"

"A game," Matan replies. "Scavenger Nut Origami."

"Are you serious?" Derek exclaims, having trouble believing his ears or controlling the excitement in his voice.

Both his pulse and imagination race. Scavenger Nut Origami, or SNO, was the ingenious cover application that the SLVIA often used to recruit new contacts into Spy Net Online. The program cleverly hid the identities of millions of unsuspecting SNO informants. Within the more secretive tier of the Spy Net, both he and SLVIA collected and shared intelligence with trusted SNO allies, such as Admiral Scott or Sir Anthony Giles at MI5.

Nonpolitical or nationalistic, SNO focused on exposing corruption from the *Concilium Tredecim,* but branched out to cover the explosion of other cyberthreats. He always found it ironic that while many in Washington branded SNO as a terrorist group, others were secret members. In fact, SNO members come from every country on earth and all walks of life, most of them recruited and known only by the SLVIA. Derek is familiar with only a few hundred.

Over time, as individuals earned more trust, the SLVIA would communicate with them directly as an online persona. Usually her default persona of Heather, Nelson Garrett's deceased mother, but sometimes it would choose a different persona such as the nun, Sister Sylvia. In fact, the SLVIA code had developed thousands of deep fake personas to emulate celebrities, CEOs, and world leaders, useful in accessing secure systems or other information.

"Are you a player?" Derek asks, lowering his voice to sound calmer.

"No, but my last student assistant, Ari, was deep into online gaming. He left the department a few months ago," Matan explains. "We keep thinking we've erased the program, then it appears again. Now it has an entire workstation locked."

Dr. Garrett designed a classified file stealth technology into the SLVIA to move itself and erase the trail, a nifty feature for an espionage AI program, but unnecessary for a game. If they can see the program, something went wrong.

"Is the application causing any harm to other systems?" he questions, trying to understand how much of the code remains active.

"No, but we're unable to boot up the server without a code key," Matan replies.

Derek's never heard of a SLVIA code key, but then, SLVIA never had to enter emergency hibernation mode. Either way, he's just stumbled onto a good reason to stick around a little longer. The breadcrumb.

"Yeah, sure, be happy to check it out," Derek agrees, his heart racing with anticipation. If the hunch pans out, he will need Nelson here as soon as possible. Then it occurs to him he should have heard from Nelson hours ago. Something went wrong in Ethiopia.

Derek casually taps on the stem of his glasses to bring up data feeds, looking for a message. Nothing, except a series of urgent texts from Jester about a nuclear sub incident.

A deep well of angst and guilt wells up within him, turning his excitement over the SNO app into a feeling of dread over his friend. Derek foolishly sent the brilliant, one-of-kind lab rat into harm's way, all to scan a fake relic. Reckless and arrogant. Another sign of his desperate slide into lunacy.

CHAPTER 23: SACRIFICE

Chapel of the Tablets, Axum, Ethiopia
Four Days Before Temple Ceremony

Nelson can't keep his mind from pondering the words of the Chinese philosopher Lao Tzu: *there is no illusion greater than fear.* Inside Nelson's mind, the fear that he will die within this tunnel has become an overwhelming and paralyzing illusion.

Several hours have passed since the last gunshot, followed by more shouting, and then, eventually, utter silence. Young Salem sacrificed his life to save an agnostic stranger on a dubious quest. Chest-constricting guilt over the death of such a spirited young man rips at Nelson's soul before he returns to blaming Taylor. Unfortunately, the satellite signal on his glasses hasn't worked underground. The vain hope that Salem would retrieve him has dissolved into terrifying despair. He will die trapped and forgotten.

In the agonizing need for a diversion, Nelson explored the short tunnel between the two chapels with a flashlight from his smartphone until he remembered the high-powered halogen light in his backpack of goodies.

Within the tunnel, two recently made ark replicas and one in progress sit alongside what appears to be a much older replica covered by an elaborately embroidered cloth. Partly deteriorated with gold leaf peeled away from the dark wood, the older ark doesn't look at all like the *Indiana Jones* version of an ornately carved box of neoclassical angels glittering with gold. Each of the replicas bears a distinctly Egyptian style from the mildly tapered sides, thick carrying poles at the bottom, etched geometric designs carved into the wood with low pharaonic style wings over the lid. Nearly identical to the tapestries still hanging in the chapel.

Nelson wonders if the Ethiopian military took the true ark or one of these replicas. If they stole a replica, could the oldest ark be the authentic Ethiopian ark, hidden here by the Guardian before his sacrifice?

"Dear Lord, how many innocent lives have perished over the centuries to protect this man-made box?"

While a part of his mind realizes on an abstract level that they died protecting what the box represents, he still can't fathom the senseless loss of life. Nelson shuns those kinds of questions, perhaps in denial of his own ignorance of spiritual matters.

To hold off his anxiety, Nelson did what he came to do: conduct a 3D scan of the ark from every side, choosing the oldest replica. He doesn't know if the stolen ark was even real, but to the 750 people who gave their lives, it was authentic. Perhaps that alone makes it sacred.

Either way, Nelson can't help but question why a nonreligious government militia would massacre so many just to steal a relic they don't even believe in. If the goal was cultural genocide, then the militia could have left the ark destroyed and photographed for the world to see. Instead, they stole it, hid it, and then covered up their theft. Not a random act of war, but an intentional, devastating blow to a thousand-year culture. Or was it something else?

It only takes a few minutes for the truth to hit him. "Greed." Nelson spits the word out as if it were a curse.

Someone sold the ark on the black market just as Salem had implied. Even if not the authentic ark, the ancient tradition behind the relic would make it extremely valuable to the right buyer. That raises the question of who. It had to be someone with substantial resources and a reason to own a holy relic from the Jewish people. If the true ark is still in the tunnel, then the government slaughtered hundreds of souls to auction off a replica. A fake. A con.

"I can't imagine why Taylor would need this scan, but I bloody well hope it was worth Salem's life, or my own," Nelson grumbles aloud, growing tired of waiting.

Not an adventurer like Taylor, Nelson is a scientist, raised as the only son of an aristocrat. He attended the most elite schools in England, writing his thesis on expert systems and neural networks. For Taylor to send him here on an obscure mission represents not only a waste of his genius but a severe risk to his very life. While Taylor can be cavalier with his own safety, his obsession with finding the SLVIA borders on the psychotic, an obsession now turned deadly.

Salem was to provide Nelson with a safe passage into Asmara, Eritrea, roughly thirty miles to the north. Thirty bloody miles without an escort. Every attempt to raise WITNESS by satellite has failed. Or sometimes, WITNESS simply refuses to respond.

With his scanner repacked, Nelson checks his watch for the tenth time this hour. It should be dark by now. Instead of the main chapel with the multiple layers of rugs and the heavy ebony wood stand, he goes to the temporary chapel with a stone slap flooring, and a lightweight stand that he had already dragged away. Nelson suspects they placed a stone slab over the tunnel entry in the temporary building because they would reuse that building later. A slab would more easily blend into the flooring.

At the far end of the tunnel, Nelson finds steps that lead up to a square wood frame capped by a gray stone slab. An iron bolt holds the slab in place to prevent unauthorized entry from the temporary chapel. After he unlocks the bolt, he pushes up on the extremely heavy stone to no effect. On a second, grunting effort, the slab lifts a few inches, but not enough. Catching his breath, Nelson steps higher to use his back and shoulder. After a deep breath and a loud grunt, he lifts the slab enough to ease it over the edge. Taking a break to breathe, he listens carefully to the deathly silence of the night. With a final grunt, he lifts with a shoulder to slide the heavy slab to the side until he can squeeze out of the tunnel.

Nelson waits to ensure no one rushes to investigate the sound of the slab scrapping. The night remains silent as death except for a distant barking dog. With another grunting effort, he pushes the slab back in place. Then he replaces the rug and the wood stand, unwilling to give away the tunnel location. The replicas must remain a secret that both the guardian and Salem died to protect.

Peering outside the temporary chapel, the darkness swallows almost everything except a few exterior lights illuminating the now empty main church. Salem's old truck remains parked on the dirt road behind the church. His eyes carefully scan the grounds but can see no evidence of the young man's sacrifice or the army.

Nelson leaps into a frantic sprint toward the truck, his heart pounding like a drum. Jumping inside, he ducks low, panting, fearful of bullets piercing the thin metal doors. None come and the silence returns except for the persistent distant canine.

"Thank the heavens," Nelson utters when he sees Salem left the key in the ignition. They only expected to be gone for a moment. Salem never expected the brief visit would end his life. Hands trembling from adrenaline, Nelson starts the engine and peels down the road before turning on his lights.

Nelson taps on his glasses. "WITNESS, can you hear me," he calls loudly, voice quivering, unsure if the device can find a satellite. Nothing. Then he remembers he had to power on the satellite relay in his bag. So used to being in a fully powered lab, he completely forgot that Zoey would keep the equipment off until needed.

"Buggers," he curses at himself, pulling over to the side of the road to fumble in the bag until he finds the relay and switches on the power. Nelson could have called for help hours ago. He taps again, and the WITNESS lens iris scan starts.

"Hello, D-PA," WITNESS answers. Nelson breaks into a huge smile at the familiar voice and yet hated moniker, a devious invention of the Jester that meant digital grandpa.

"WITNESS, track my signal. Provide directions to the nearest border crossing to Asmara, Eritrea."

"Processing." A moment later. "Downloading directions to your lens frames."

"Brilliant." Taylor and Jester designed the frames, which Nelson did not appreciate the need for until this moment.

"WITNESS, connect me to Taylor." A moment later, a small image of Taylor appears in a corner box and a thin voice fills his ear pod.

"Hey, Doc, thrilled to hear from you. I was getting worried. Are you OK? Did you find the ark? Have you reached Asmara?" Taylor rattles off questions without waiting for answers.

"I'm alive, which is more than I can say for your friend Salem," responds Nelson, without an iota of Taylor's glibness.

The line goes silent for several beats. "Oh no. I'm so sorry for Salem, and equally sorry you had to witness something so terrible." Taylor's voice suddenly saddened. "I'll ask again, are you OK?"

"I'll repeat myself, I'm alive, which will do for the moment," Nelson replies, silently resenting Taylor for sending him on this lethal errand over a meaningless relic scan. "Now, how do I get across the border?" he asks, hoping the answer won't risk his life any further.

"Offer them your fake NGO passport. If they give you any grief, offer an envelope of cash in the zip pocket of Zoey's tool kit."

"Taylor, I'm deeply uncomfortable with blatant bribery," Nelson complains.

"Remember, 'when in Rome,'" Taylor says. "There's enough hard cash to ensure they let you through with no questions. Did you find the ark?"

"I'm not sure if it was the ark you expected, but yes," Nelson answers.

"Good. Listen, there's been a change in plans for your exit," Taylor says. "Authorities tagged Zoey's aircraft, so she must avoid Eritrea."

"What do you mean?" Nelson asks, suddenly more anxious.

"Instead of the airport, find your way to the commercial seaport. Ask for a captain named Adri on a ship called *Ramadan*. I need you in Jerusalem as soon as possible."

"Why, what's in Jerusalem?" Nelson asks.

"I found the SLVIA."

"Are you sure?" he questions, a spark of excitement emerging amid the cloud of gloom.

"Components hibernated on a university ancient languages server," Taylor says. "Ironic that a linguistics espionage program should choose to hide in a linguistics lab."

The news sounds promising, but Nelson's excitement remains dampened by the grief of needless death and the dread of an upcoming border crossing.

"I hope your flimsy corruption plan works," he says. His hands still tremble from the shock of losing poor Salem.

Taylor snorts. "Never underestimate the universal power of greed. Be careful and stay safe." The transmission ends.

Nelson huffs. "Stay safe, as if it were a choice."

As long as he's not arrested or shot at the border, his next stop will be the Red Sea to meet another stranger. If Taylor truly found the SLVIA code, it would be nothing short of miraculous. Yet even the miraculous does not seem worth young Salem's life—or his own. All of it for a replica already sold on the black market.

CHAPTER 24: MANIPULATION

Ashdod Marina, Israeli Coast
Three Days Before Temple Ceremony

Yuri Yankovic pours Mola Brahms another vodka, coaxing out the unspoken frustrations of the Mossad General.

"The peace deal may be dead already," bemoans Mola, clearly frustrated. One hand tightens into a loose fist while the other pounds down a drink.

General of Mossad Counter Intelligence, Mola was a protégé of the late Ehud Barak, who trained Mola to use any necessary tools to achieve Israel's objectives, such as a viable peace and military alliance to deter Iranian nuclear aggression.

"I am surprised. They already announced a ceremony. What happened?" Decades of diplomatic Machiavellianism have taught Yuri to care about the circumstances on the ground in order to discover a way to insert himself. One cannot be a problem solver unless one first appreciates the nuances of the problem.

"The former US president," Mola replies with a groan. "He and the Saudis push new demands."

"Such as?" prompts Yuri.

"Greater Palestinian political representation and investment, which prompted Jordan to demand compensation for giving up control of the WAQF. Then the former president requested permanent asylum." Mola chuckles over the last demand.

"Risky to intermingle a personal agenda," Yuri says. "What happens if the deal fails?"

"Everyone loses," Mola complains, sipping his vodka more slowly and leaning back.

Yuri needs to change asylum from Israel to Moscow, so he probes further. "Who will invest in the Palestinian areas?"

"Per the proposal by the crown prince, sorry the Saudi king, the funds will come from the inheritance of the Israeli people," he replies with a raised eyebrow, teasing out the information.

Yuri raises an eyebrow, wondering what that could mean. "Do I need to ask?"

"Think of it this way," Mola explains with a smirk. "The peace deal is essentially a single state solution with a military alliance against Iran. If the West Bank becomes a part of Israel, then Israel can excavate the temple treasures of Solomon buried under the ruins of Qumran. We're talking dozens of tons of gold and silver, maybe more, worth tens of billions. Those treasures will ransom the Temple Mount away from the Muslims, build a third temple, and rebuild the Palestinian areas without costing the Israeli taxpayer a single shekel."

Yuri sips his drink. "Quite creative. The issues then boil down to greater representation and asylum. I take it from your mood that the Knesset resists."

Mola shakes his head. "There may be room to negotiate over the Palestinians, but no one wants to host the former president in Israel or give him a shekel. The man may be popular with the people, but he's a loose cannon, known for his lies and disloyalty. Besides, it would seriously complicate our relationship with America. To make matters worse, the Ayatollah loathes the man. His presence will only escalate the already hot-cold war with Iran."

"Is a temple still on the table?" Yuri questions.

Mola hesitates. His eyes have fallen on a beautiful young woman on the deck of a nearby superyacht removing her summer dress in order to lounge. "Yes, the new Saudi king has expressed a willingness to allow the third temple, assuming King Hussein gives up control of the WAQF. Nothing more than a grand historic gesture. The Knesset is lukewarm on the gesture."

Mola lifts his eyes away from his young beauty to meet Yuri's gaze. "Which gets me to a few of my own questions. Why are you here?"

Yuri smiles and sips his drink, teasing out the moment. "Maybe we can help each other."

Mola laughs, sips his drink, and returns his lusty gaze to the voluptuous young woman with thick dark hair, full pouting lips, and a slender shape of curves in a barely legal bathing suit. Laying a towel on a lounge chair, she coats her skin with sunscreen, oblivious to her admirer. "How do you propose to help me?"

"Moscow would like to offer the former US president asylum," Yuri replies. "Which will close the gap to a deal."

Mola laughs aloud then finishes his drink, setting down his glass, clearly stalling for time to think. "The global intelligence community will spiral into a frenzy. Everyone will knee-jerk into isolation, too terrified to share anything with the Americans. It would turn Israel into a pariah, like Russia. How will that help us win a lasting peace?"

"The former president will choose St. Petersburg over Tel Aviv, allowing the Israeli government to rage publicly while you quietly celebrate." Yuri reaches for the mixer to refresh the glasses. "Regarding peace. I'm sure you know that a delegate from Hezbollah came to Moscow in April 2021 to beg for guided missiles. We promised to consider the proposal. Access to the former president for an assurance to thwart Hezbollah seems a fair trade."

"It sounds more like extortion," Mola replies as his eyes once again return to the sunbathing beauty two yacht decks away. "Iran will threaten an attack, but thanks to the new American administration, we have a multi-billion AI upgrade to our Iron Dome defense and the Iron Beam in development."

Yuri bites his tongue. The Americans are good at buying loyalty with weapons, not unlike the Chinese. He stays silent, avoiding the temptation to oversell, allowing the notion to take root within Mola.

"It would be easier to sell if the Kremlin guaranteed Iran would never develop nuclear arms." Mola turns to read Yuri's eyes.

"I will forward your concerns," Yuri offers. They both know few can influence Putin, and not even Putin has much influence over the Ayatollah, but these are negotiations.

"I'll meet with the prime minister later tonight," Mola says. "But there are a few complications you should consider." He picks up a nearby set of binoculars. The woman has removed her top to sunbathe.

"Such as?" prompts Yuri, refilling Mola's glass.

"An American Secret Service agent named Rhodes stays in Jerusalem pending a diplomatic resolution to extradition," Mola says. "In addition, the daughter of the late Admiral Scott arrived this morning to visit with the US Embassy and requested a meeting with the former president."

Yuri suppresses a grin over his fantastic fortune. An unexpected opportunity to clean up loose ends. "My friend, allow me to take care of those concerns for you."

Mola nods his head, wearing an emotionless poker face. Intelligence and espionage are a silent war with victories and losses, sacrifices, trade-offs, and civilian casualties. Like all of those seasoned in the game, Yuri knows that Mola currently performs a mental calculation of those risks and rewards. Yuri suppresses a grin.

"Enough talk for now. Let's invite that young lady to join us," Mola suggests.

"You read my mind," Yuri smiles widely.

What he doesn't tell Mola is that her name is Nala, a sixteen-year-old model from Belarus who works in Yuri's agency. A favorite of President Erdogan.

CHAPTER 25:
GO HOME

King David Hotel, Jerusalem
Three Days Before Temple Ceremony

Jenn and Jack settle into their table at the Kings Garden Restaurant at the King David Hotel. As she requested, Jack kept her trip a secret from Taylor.

"Nice place," Jack says, looking around at the high-end décor and exquisitely painted ceilings with a view of the exterior patio pool featuring soaring palm trees.

"We should check back with the embassy after we eat. Rhodes must have arrived by now," she replies, looking over the menu.

The US Consulate Director, a friend of the admiral, was sympathetic to her grief, actively negotiating extradition, but not at all encouraging about her chances to meet with the former president.

"State Department will never let you within a mile of the FPOTUS, even if he does come to Israel, which seems unlikely given the extradition treaty," Jack mutters while he checks the menu. "You know, for kosher, this looks like primo chow."

"Anything will beat the vending machine snack bar you've got on the jet," she snickers.

When Taylor owned the Gulfstream, he had it stocked with French wines, fresh fruit, gourmet meals, and foreign films. After Jack took over ownership, he revamped the entertainment cabinet with action movies, domestic beer, and snack foods.

"Hey, it's tough building a business," Jack complains. "After I lost my job with Taylor, I had to make some cuts. And geez, I can't tell you how much I hate subtitles."

"Don't discount the embassy; they want to see this resolved." Jenn dismisses his excuses for junk food.

"Come on, the State Department will fart around this goose egg for months, trying to negotiate a way for everyone to save face, until they get nothing done, and the crisis passes in the media," Jack scoffs.

Jenn ignores his defensiveness. "I don't expect the embassy will give me direct access to FPOTUS. I'm hoping to attach myself to Agent Rhodes," she explains, already knowing her odds are slim. Banking on nostalgic sentiment from Geoff and an unrealistic dose of good fortune may not be the best strategy. It's not like she thought this through.

"You know, if Taylor were here, he'd hack into somebody to set you up with face time or something."

"Then it's a good thing that Taylor isn't here to cause trouble," she responds. "I'm still hoping the consulate will arrange a meeting."

Jack laughs aloud, then stifles his chuckle. "Good luck with that one. So, what I'm hearing is that you have no real clue on how to find Rhodes, assuming he's even here, or how to confirm your suspicion that the former president had anything to do with the admiral's death."

Jenn raises an eyebrow, not arguing. Director Adelson never said that Rhodes would stay in Israel, but that he was being sent to Israel. Only her intuition regarding Geoff's pride gives her reason to believe he would stay pending a diplomatic solution. Geoff comes from East Coast old money, son of an ex-managing partner at the powerful Washington law firm Kirkland Otis.

Rhodes will want to stay at the nicest hotel nearest to the US Embassy, hence King David.

Jenn glances up to explain her rationale, when she notices Geoff Rhodes enter the restaurant in another section to take a seat facing away from her. A kismet moment.

"Ask for an extra place setting; I'll be right back," she says, standing.

"Where are you going?"

"To convince Geoff Rhodes to join us."

*

King David Hotel, Jerusalem
Three Days Before Temple Ceremony

Still hung over from whatever demon narcotic the Saudis gave him, and totally screwed in his career, Geoff stayed at the King David to be close to the US Embassy. Secret Service Director Bell already knew of the situation by the time they gave him his phone in Tel Aviv. According to Director Bell, Stephens and Blake flew back to Washington, suffering side effects from the drugs. The director asked him to stay on the ground pending negotiations. A single agent in that scenario will be worthless. He's being set up to fail.

"You're so predictable," coos a sexy voice behind him.

Geoff pivots to see the petite frame, pixie haircut, and bright blue eyes of Jennifer Scott. He impulsively rises to greet his Annapolis sweetheart with a long, tight hug. "Jennifer," he exclaims. "What a surprise."

Geoff pulls back, still holding her shoulders, lowering his smile to a frown. "Hey, listen, I'm so sorry to hear about the admiral."

"Thank you," she says, lowering her eyes.

Geoff remembers Jennifer as the strong, independent, rebellious daughter, determined to take over the entire Navy to prove herself outside the admiral's shadow. But the woman in his arms looks diminished, broken, and silently desperate. A shadow of guilt falls over his heart.

"What brings you to Israel?" he wonders, unable to imagine her getting over the admiral's death so quickly.

"Well, to be honest, I came here with Jack Tote to find you. I think we can help each other. Come join us, and I'll explain."

Geoff looks over her shoulder to notice the disgraced pilot of Taylor Security Systems talking to a server. Curious that Jenn aligned with the ex-pilot of the same man that she investigated. Geoff can't imagine anything either could offer him that would be helpful, but he hasn't seen Jennifer in years. Besides, he practically bristles with curiosity.

*

King David Hotel, Jerusalem
Three Days Before Temple Ceremony

Jenn introduces Jack and Geoff, who greet each other like two gladiators sizing each other up in the arena.

"Tote," says Geoff, offering a hand.

"Rhodes." Jack grips the hand a heartbeat longer than necessary before letting go.

Jenn ignores the testosterone sniff witnessed daily in the Navy. Apparently, the two know each other and are not mutual fans. She doesn't care. After they both sit with no other needless displays, she gets to the point.

"Geoff, I'm here because my father didn't die of a cardiac arrest as they reported in the papers," she takes a deep breath to steady herself. "The admiral died of Novichok poisoning."

Jenn watches the subdued response spread across Geoff's poker face. His hands slowly tighten into a loose fist. "That's terrible news. I'm so sorry to hear that, but it doesn't explain why you're in Israel?"

"The admiral had a video of the FPOTUS discussing the national ID leak with Putin before signing the executive order to adopt the platform. I want to help you retrieve him so I can question him."

Geoff doesn't seem to register as much surprise at the revelation as she expected, but then again, he faithfully protected the president for years and may know more than he can share.

"And you think Putin had the admiral poisoned?" Geoff scoffs. "I'm sorry Jennifer, but you're grasping at straws, maybe out of grief or something. But geez, you need to put those crazy notions out of your head. Go home and grieve your father."

"Adelson confirmed." Jenn ignores his objections. "I want to ask the FPOTUS if he knew about the plan to eliminate a great man. That's all I ask—one moment alone."

"Slow down, sailor," Geoff says. "Jennifer, this is an enormous diplomatic nightmare already. I'm just here to cool my heels and avoid the humiliation I'm going to face back in Washington. My career is toast. Besides, they granted FPOTUS asylum in Saudi Arabia, and I can guarantee the Saudis will let no one, much less a woman with a vendetta, get close enough to interrogate him. If they agree to let him come to the ceremony, they'll guard him like the freaking pope. You're not thinking this through."

"I'm not asking for their help. I'm offering you help," she responds.

"Help me?" Geoff repeats, then turns to Jack. "Are you in on this insanity?"

Jack shakes his head. "Nah, I'm just the wingman checking out a good meal."

"I spoke with the consulate director. FPOTUS is already here in Israel, staying in the presidential suite," she states calmly, watching his eyes dart around the room. Jack glances at her with a raised eyebrow, also surprised. Jenn hadn't told him yet.

"No one said anything to me," Geoff dismisses the claim.

"Maybe they sense that you're not really committed to getting him back," she says.

"Oh geez, you can't be serious," Geoff rebuffs. "I'll say it again, go home. Grieve your father and pull your career back together. Don't throw it all away looking for an imaginary confession that will never happen."

Jack chuckles into his coffee. "Good one."

When Jenn turns to glare at the snarky pilot, he waves her off. "Don't mind me; I'm just enjoying you two quarreling over nothing. Come on, not only do

I agree with G-man that it's an unworkable idea." He nods at Geoff. "But you're talking to a glorified bodyguard, for God's sake, a man paid to take bullets, follow protocol, not to be a strategic thinker. Like I said on the plane, you're asking the wrong guy for help. You're talking to a boy scout looking to cover his own ass over a total screwup."

Jenn turns to watch the macho pride and indignation flare in Geoff's nostrils as his face turns red and his brows lower into a furious scowl.

"Yeah, you're right; I'm sorry we even asked," she deflects, following Jack's lead. "Probably better if I go alone, anyway. Sorry, Geoff, I don't want you to get into any deeper trouble. I mean, seriously, you'll forever be the guy who lost the FPOTUS to the Saudis. Any effort to get him back on your own will just come off as desperate."

"Screw both of you," Geoff retorts, slamming his palm on the table, causing a few heads to turn in their direction. "Fine, you want to make a fool of yourselves, we'll talk, but not here. Meet me in the lobby in ten minutes." He pushes back to head upstairs, too angry to eat. Geoff always had a short temper.

Jenn and Jack share a grin and a fist bump. "Nicely done," she says.

Jack holds out his palms as if to accept an award. "Most people don't realize that being a total a-hole is a genuine, God-given gift." He smirks. "Look, I don't know about you or the Eagle Scout, but I'm eating first."

Jack looks up to smile at the server just arriving to refresh the coffee. "Can I see the menu again?" As the server runs off, he turns to Jenn. "So, exactly what *is* your plan?" he asks, drowning his coffee in cream.

She grimaces. "I should let you enjoy your meal first. You're not going to like it."

CHAPTER 26:
PEACE, PEACE

Israeli Supreme Court, Tel Aviv
Three Days Before Temple Ceremony

With his face down and turned away from the security cameras mounted almost everywhere outside the Israeli Knesset, Derek hides behind WITNESS lenses, a COVID mask, a wig, and a wide rim hat. It should be enough from a distance.

"I don't know who we're meeting, but I suggest we meet someplace else," he says.

"We're here to meet Yehuda Hiam, an Orthodox rabbi member of the Knesset," Matan explains. "We're old friends. I trust him, and he's a leading member of the Temple Institute."

The name sounds familiar. They never met, and Yehuda would only know him by the alias flapjack. He and SLVIA once helped a man by that name deal with an extortion threat linked to a deep fake video.

"You know, guys, you go ahead," Derek says. "Like I said, this is an Israeli issue. You can fill me in later."

While he's genuinely interested in the mysteries surrounding the ark, he has no interest in spending time in an Israeli prison. He would have left by now except for the possible SLVIA code back at the university.

"Nonsense," dismisses Loir. "You and Mordechai found the relic. Don't worry, Yehuda will know how to walk the line between the secular Zionist and the Sanhedrin."

"OK, let me put it this way," Derek says, changing tactics. "You guys expect to march into one of the most secure buildings on the planet during heated peace negotiations. Then you plan to find the office of a controversial leader to talk about what could be the most coveted relic of all time." Derek lays out his view with a shrug. "Maybe people in Israel are more trusting, but back home, this would be a good time to take a friendly walk in the park."

Loir and Matan look at each other with a shared epiphany while Mordechai grins. Matan pulls out his cell phone. "Hello, Yehuda? Change of plans. Meet us in the parking lot, I'll explain. Yes, yes, I promise you will thank me."

That was close. Many of the most powerful Zionist leaders in Israel today are Freemasons, including eight of the last thirteen prime ministers, and a share of the Knesset. Much of the Templar and Freemason lore has roots in ancient mystic Jewish Kabbalism. The *Concilium* even founded modern Israel. The Balfour Declaration was written at the end of World War I by Lord Arthur Balfour, the UK Foreign Secretary of Lord Rothschild, the Praeceptor of his day. Balfour called for establishing a national homeland for the Jewish people in Palestine, at the time, a neglected Ottoman region. It set the stage for a UN vote in 1948 to create the modern nation of Israel, a decision signed in blood ever since.

"Yehuda, old friend, thank you for indulging me." He hears Matan greet behind him.

Derek turns, conscious not to lift his face to see the stout rabbi with a long beard and wire-rim glasses, dressed in black with a starched white shirt. The same man he helped secretly. To bring up that episode would complicate the situation and compromise his identity.

"What could be so important that you drag me away from my office with so much going on," the old rabbi complains.

"We should take a walk. There are too many cameras," Derek says, turning toward a set of trees, forcing the others to follow.

"And who are you?" questions the intense rabbi, pulling up swiftly to his left.

"A rude American, who should apologize," Matan scolds, pulling up on the right.

"I am sorry, rabbi, I don't mean to be rude, but we have a reason for being overly cautious, even in Israel," he says. "My name is Derek Taylor. I was at St. George when a sniper murdered the abbot. We found something you should see. Something important to Israel." Derek hands over his phone with images of the wooden panel. He used a computer program to enhance the letters to make them easier to read.

With a suspicious grunt, Yehuda snatches the phone. A moment later, his eyes widen as he expands the image. He remains silent until he finishes the entire inscription. With a heavy sigh, he hands back the phone, then lifts his eyes to stare into Derek's eyes, searching for something.

"It's genuine, Yehuda," Matan says. "The wood carbon dates between 480 and 530 CE."

Yehuda and Matan exchange a gaze and silently confirming nod. A remarkable truth based on a lifelong trust between friends.

"Come this way. I know a private place without cameras," Yehuda commands, spinning in a new direction with a renewed vigor in his step. After walking without talking for a few blocks, they enter an archeological dig site with no activity. A guard who knows the rabbi lets the entire group inside with little more than a pleasant greeting. Once they reach a far corner of the site out of earshot, the rabbi pivots.

"Where did you find this panel?" he questions, his eyes narrowed in suspicion.

"In the prophet Elijah's cave at the monastery of St. George," replies Mordechai. "We believe Father Sabas placed it there in 522."

"I don't understand," the rabbi shakes his head. "He wrote the panel in ancient Hebrew, and it speaks clearly of the ark."

"I found letters in the Vatican Archives sent by Abbot Sabas to Pope John I describing a copper scroll found under the large rocks north of Qumran. Sabas copied the text before he reburied the scroll," Derek explains.

"You just read the second copper scroll written by Jeremiah," Matan clarifies.

The old rabbi stumbles backward until he sits on an ancient stone wall under excavation.

"Now, Yehuda, we know the ark waits for Moshiach, but yet, together with the first copper scroll locations in Qumran, we now have both scrolls, and a starting point," Loir explains, excitement oozing from his pores. "With the peace negotiations in progress, we came to seek your counsel. Israel must insist on a single-state solution and a third temple. Nothing else matters."

Derek doesn't have a voice, but it seems as if the lives of the Palestinians matter. Loir's comment makes Derek wonder if the Israeli change in strategy to a single-state solution and the confirmation of copper scroll locations in Qumran align to the same time frame.

Yehuda searches the eyes of each man. "Have you spoken to the Sanhedrin?" Everyone shakes their head no.

"Then I must go immediately. The peace deal is in jeopardy. We must renew our efforts," Yehuda insists.

The old rabbi pauses. "Last year, a young man arose among the chief rabbis, named Jiziahu deb David, or Zedekiah, son of David, and gained the admiration of many. There are more than a few on the Sanhedrin who believe Jiziahu could be Moshiach. In fact, the Sanhedrin crowned him king of Jerusalem on April 4, 2021, over Passover," he explains. "For some, it fulfilled prophecies of Rabbi Madhuri and Shoshoni that Moshiach would reveal himself on Passover."

"Wow, quite a claim?" Derek says.

Yehuda shrugs his shoulders as if he's not a convert. "He was born Solomon Judah and changed his name, which makes me wonder. He also claims to be a direct decedent of David, which would be impossible to prove or disprove without lineage. There is a heresy that he comes from a mix of Jewish and Muslim heritage."

"Yes, Yehuda, but we also know that a year before Moshiach would be a fallow year for agriculture, just like 2021," Loir points out. "And ben David has an uncanny understanding of the Torah. Now could be the time."

Yehuda shakes his head in uncertainty. "Perhaps, but I need those images to talk to the Sanhedrin. Under the current deal, the Saudi king will lead the WAQF and has agreed to a Jewish tabernacle, but it cannot disturb the Noble Sanctuary. Israel must grant full citizen rights and representation to Palestinians, as well as invest heavily in the West Bank and Gaza."

"The deal will enrage the Palestinians," Matan states. "And if the tabernacle doesn't replace the Dome of the Rock, it will enrage many Jews."

Derek thinks of the famous quote, *They will cry peace, peace, but there will be no peace.*

"Israel has a mortal enemy prepared to strike, a peace deal for a temple and the ark, and a man believed to be the Moshiach by the Jews," Mordechai summarizes the scenario. "Just sayin', what are the odds?"

"Yes, what are the odds," Yehuda looks Loir in the eye and hesitates. "Either way, if the Knesset learns of the ark, they will use it for political theater. We must be careful."

In Derek's mind, if the Knesset learns of the ark, then the *Concilium* will also learn, which raises the question of why SLVIA pointed to Sabas and the *Sefer HaBahir*.

Yehuda turns to gaze at Derek for a long moment. "And you, you must leave Israel at once. I remember your name. You're the American hacker that Mossad and the ICC seek."

Derek's heart freezes for an instant, feeling exposed. Others turn to stare at him with narrow, angry eyes and slack jaws, probably feeling betrayed. The news only confirms that a killer works with Mossad to track him.

"I can't leave Israel yet; I promised to help Matan," he protests. "Besides, a powerful group behind the Freemason Zionists will go after the ark. You need my help."

Derek doesn't deny that he's a wanted hacker. Lying to them at this point would only make matters worse. Matan, Loir, and Mordechai stare at him for a better explanation.

"OK, I'm an ex-NSA contractor who knows far too many international secrets for my own good. I have no desire for the ark or trouble. As soon as I help Matan, I plan to leave the country," he explains.

After a long, awkward silence, Yehuda nods his head. "I don't trust the ICC." That makes sense, as the ICC has threatened to try Israel for war crimes. Derek also takes the statement to mean Yehuda doesn't trust Derek either.

Matan narrows his eyes in lingering suspicion while Mordechai appraises him with an expression he can't read but could be a disappointment. After a moment of silence, Loir takes a deep breath. "At least that explains your ridiculous disguises."

"How do you know about the *Tredecim*?" Yehuda questions, changing the subject. "Why do you think they will want the ark?"

Yehuda used the term *Tredecim,* which means he's aware of the Bilderberg influence over Israeli politics. Derek leverages that mistrust.

"My deep knowledge of the *Concilium Tredecim* is why the ICC wants me," Derek replies, only guessing the ICC's motive and hoping Yehuda will empathize. "Regarding proof that the *Tredecim* will go after the ark, I believe the answer may be in the third story of the private library of that building right over there." Derek points toward the Israeli Supreme Court where a pyramid with an all-seeing-eye rises above the roofline, set back from the Egyptian obelisk in the garden.

Yehuda nods with a twinkle in his eye. "Only ex-judges can access the library third floor of the Israeli Supreme Court. What do you expect to find in a library you've never seen?"

"Correction, they restrict the third level to ex-judges, thirty-three-degree Freemasons, and grand masters," Derek replies. "I expect to find the original uncut version of the book that the leader of the first crusade, Godefroi de Bouillon, came to Jerusalem to find."

Derek leans closer to lower his voice. "The original uncut *Sefer HaBahir,* the sacred Kabballah text embraced by the Knights Templar, and many Jews.

For over a thousand years, the Order has sought the ark because of the power discussed within the uncut version of that book."

Yehuda studies Derek's eyes for what seems like an eternity. "Interesting that you know so much about a secret group that officially doesn't exist and a book version that no one has ever seen." Yehuda pulls away from his burning gaze with a shrug. "Eh, too bad none of us are an ex-judge."

When Derek first scanned the uncut version of the *Sefer HaBahir*, he discounted it as ancient superstition and mysticism. He forgot about it until the cryptic message came from SLVIA to Olavo. Truth be told, Derek plays a hunch. OK, he's playing hunches like a house of cards and being wrong on any of them will crumble the entire theory. As Yehuda said, they need a thirty-three-degree Freemason, or an ex-judge, to learn the truth.

"Yeah, too bad."

CHAPTER 27:
BUG EYES

King David Hotel, Jerusalem
Three Days Before Temple Ceremony

J enn wipes the nervous palm sweat on her jeans before she types the command. Jack scans Jerusalem with binoculars from the balcony, concerned someone watches them.

"This could get us all arrested," frets Geoff.

"You can walk any time," Jenn replies, removing her fingers from the keyboard.

They debated for an hour on how to get the FPOTUS to respond to the admiral's murder. Jenn concocted a plan using a device she discovered last year on Taylor's old jet, which now belongs to Jack. A DARPA prototype spy camera the size of a fly with wings. Jack reluctantly retrieved the device and showed her how to pair the app to her tablet.

Geoff paces behind her in the hotel room. He should be curious to know more about the FPOTUS situation. In fact, once he learned of her plan, he encouraged her, but now, he's having second thoughts.

"If it helps your conscience, I haven't fired up the bug yet. I'm just playing with a few thermostats," Jenn reminds him.

Sadly, most hotels and other commercial establishments with rotating maintenance workers are weak spots for hackers and others in the espionage business. Movies will typically show a nerd in a crawl space, but a few modern software tools can do the same through the hotel Wi-Fi network. After finding the presidential suite, Jenn turns off the AC and turns up the heat. That should force them to open the balcony doors for ventilation.

"If the FPOTUS is already here, then Israel must be in negotiations over extradition," Geoff repeats his argument.

"Exactly. Israel has no intention of arresting him," Jenn repeats her position. "Are you sure they can't detect this bug?" she asks Jack.

"Not sure at all," Jack replies. "Taylor forgot it on the jet, then you two broke up."

"We never dated, so we never split up. I was investigating him," she replies, oddly self-conscious of discussing Taylor in front of Geoff. Even though it was years ago, she can't deny a lingering attraction to Geoff's large, muscular frame. Geoff has a distinct advantage over Taylor in that he's not a fugitive.

With a click, the app for the insect-sized spy drone opens. The super-expensive robotic insect sits within the foam of an open box. The drone came with a tiny lever, almost like a mini-game controller that Jenn plugs into her USB. With a gentle nudge, she lifts the drone to hover above the box, nearly silent except for a minor buzz. On the tablet, the camera image turns on with a screen showing directions and controls.

"Taylor has the coolest freaking toys," Jenn says, admiring the tiny device he must have bought on the dark web or from a DARPA engineer with a gambling habit. The drone registers her voice with a tiny voice bar on her tablet app.

Jack leans out over the balcony rail to look up. With a nod of his head, he motions with his hand for Jenn to proceed. She wants to move the device into position on the presidential suite balcony before they open the door.

"I can't believe I'm witnessing this," complains Geoff, standing to look over Jenn's shoulder.

"Think of it this way," Jenn explains as she navigates the insect drone out of the balcony door and upward. A moderate breeze blows it around a little, but the insect spy continues to climb. "Your job is to keep the FPOTUS safe. Right now, you're operating blind. I'm giving you some eyes on the man that you wouldn't have otherwise."

"Sure, illegal eyes that could land us all in jail," Geoff replies with a deep frown.

"Not if we pinky swear," Jenn says. "What time is it?"

"12:58 p.m.," Jack replies.

They had arranged for the hotel to deliver a sealed envelope to the FPOTUS suite exactly at one p.m. The envelope contains an anonymous note revealing that Admiral Scott died from Novichok poisoning and the FBI wants to question FPOTUS regarding his conversation with Putin. Jenn printed the letter on US Embassy letterhead, stealing a sheet as they walked by a copy room. The letter is a total fabrication, but she wants to listen to his reaction.

As expected, the sliding door opens to allow fresh air. Jenn navigates the tiny spy fly into the room, then upward to rest on the sconce above the drapes. The fisheye camera lens shows the FPOTUS, with two lawyers sitting on the suite couches working the phones. Computers, Coke cans, coffee cups, and leftover meals litter the room.

"If Benet continues to balk at the asylum request, we can press harder for a share of the temple treasure," a lawyer suggests.

"Of course, they owe me," replies the FPOTUS. "Everyone is saying I helped close the deal. But we need to get asylum. I don't want to live in Arabia. Too hot, and the food is horrible."

"I'll call Benet's team back to offer the exchange," adds another.

"Sir, I already spoke with the king's lead negotiator," another aid clarifies. "Chances of you getting a share of the temple treasure are near zero."

A knock at the door causes everyone to look at each other, obviously not expecting any visitors. One lawyer approaches the door to peer carefully through the spyglass.

"Who is it?" he yells through the door.

"Hotel concierge, sir. I have a hand-delivered letter from the American Embassy," a muffled voice announces.

The lawyer raises an eyebrow at the former president before he opens the door and takes the letter, peeking down both ends of the hallway before closing and bolting the door.

"What is it?" the FPOTUS asks.

"Not sure, no label." The lawyer opens the letter and reads. His eyes widen as he flops on the couch. "It has a US Embassy letterhead, but no signature or name. They claim that Admiral Adam Scott died of Novichok poisoning, and the FBI wants to question you."

"What? Why would they want to talk to me? Look, I didn't like the guy, he was a real loser, a boy scout, but I didn't know he was even dead," the FPOTUS defends.

"Don't sweat it; it's a fake," the lawyer replies as he rips the page. "Anonymous, which means someone is trying to rattle your cage. I'll lean on the hotel to find out who. Stay focused on the negotiations. Now, how can we motivate Jordan to agree to the new terms?"

"Dig up more dirt," the other lawyer responds. "Last year, King Hussein came up in the Pandora Papers. The guy stashed hundreds of millions offshore. Get someone to release a story that he embezzled the funds from the Jordan treasury. Make him look corrupt. Even if it's not true, it will pressure him when he's already weak."

"I don't care how; just get them to offer me asylum," the FPOTUS responds.

Jenn shuts down the screen but leaves the bug on the sconce to record directly to a cloud account. The FPOTUS seemed genuinely surprised. Maybe he had nothing to do with the admiral's death. Maybe this entire trip was a goose chase, just as everyone has tried to tell her.

"Satisfied?" Geoff chides. "The FPOTUS was clueless."

"Yeah, I guess you're right," she admits. Catching her reflection in the hotel mirror, the image of desperation stares back at her with a searing self-judgment. Matt tried to tell her to leave it alone and let the pros take over. "I should go home."

"Alright, I like it, good plan. We got some sun, ate well, and we're not under arrest. I call that a win." Jack claps his hands, clearly excited by the news. "We can fly back first thing in the morning."

Jenn stares at the tablet, wondering if she should have listened longer, but then lets it go. It doesn't matter. She won't learn anything that will bring back the admiral. Nothing will relieve her pain or resolve her unanswered questions. Only time will dull the penetrating agony.

"Why don't you let me buy you dinner," offers Geoff. "We can catch up, and maybe it'll take your mind off this mess."

"No thanks, I'm going to do a little sightseeing," replies Jack with a smirk.

Jenn chuckles at Jack's incessant humor, then turns to Geoff. "Sounds wonderful. I'll be ready at seven."

She doesn't feel like eating; she wants to storm into the presidential suite to demand some direct answers; she wants to go home and crawl up under the covers; she wants to hear Taylor's quirky viewpoint. Something isn't right about the situation, but she's too emotional for her head to think clearly. Is depression a stage of grief?

CHAPTER 28:
PANDEMONIUM

National Intelligence Agency (NIA),
Washington, DC
Three Days Before Temple Ceremony

"**B**reaking News," announces CNN anchor Drake Rapper. "A former US president seeks political asylum. Global intelligence in chaos. Israel is on the brink of both war and peace. America faces yet another constitutional crisis. Those are the headlines. Let's jump right in." A stock photo image of the FPOTUS laughing with the crown prince, now the new Saudi king, appears behind the anchor.

Not since September 11 has Matt Adelson seen such utter pandemonium within the global intelligence community. Sparked by a Saudi Arabian press release, Matt sits with the other intelligence agency directors to watch the CNN coverage. The video background changes to a DOJ press conference.

"For the first time in American history, a former president facing multiple state and federal criminal indictments seeks political asylum," Drake Rapper reports. "Confidential sources at the DOJ have confirmed that the former president fled criminal prosecution for felony indictments related to tax, insurance, and bank fraud, perjury, racketeering, election interference, seditious conspiracy, and more."

Rapper continues. "Moments ago, the Saudi Arabian government announced that they have granted the former president temporary asylum from politically motivated persecution. In the Saudi statement, the former president blames the current administration of Stalin-style efforts to eliminate him as a candidate in the next election."

The image changes again to the Russian dictator. "Putin has condemned the criminal indictments, also calling them reminiscent of a Nazi-era purge. Others were quick to condemn the statement in light of Ukrainian war crimes and the treatment of opponents such as Navalny. Here in the states, GOP leaders are calling for the impeachment of the current president, while violent protests across the nation grow more frequent and more violent."

Matt mutes the television and turns to the directors of the US intelligence community, where he reads every emotion from shock to rage to fear and utter disbelief. Around the table sits NSA Director Sean Asher, CIA Director Alan Russell, Homeland Security Director Peter Wallace, Naval Intelligence Commander Dave Jackson, Secret Service Director Randall Bell II, and FBI Director Nick Wright. The world's best intelligence team humiliated; each made to look like a bunch of fools by a lawless former leader and the betrayal of an ally.

"For the first time in our history, the greatest and most resilient democracy on Earth gets humiliated on a world stage as if we were a third world junta. While we know the story of persecution is total hokum, a share of those watching, especially his base, will buy it like Sunday gospel. I have a meeting with Security Advisor Dominic and the president this afternoon. I need analysis briefs from each of you before I go," he states. "Questions?"

"Who allowed him to travel on a Saudi aircraft?" questions Commander Jackson.

"The FAA grounded his personal plane for maintenance. The Saudi government offered the use of one of theirs. We had no legal premise to restrict his travel until after the DOJ issued indictments and the courts ruled on bail," responds FBI Director Wright.

"Did we have any intelligence the Saudis planned to help?" asks NSA Director Asher.

"None," replies CIA Director Russell. "But a Saudi prince visited his estate last week."

"Any clue why the new Saudi king would kick off US relations with a slap in the face?" questions HLS Director Wallace.

"The new Saudi king remains bitter over the CIA Khashoggi murder report that pointed to his involvement. We also humiliated him on a world stage when the president insisted on dealing with the king before his death," responds Russell.

"What about our allies," asks Commander Jackson.

"Within the past few hours, Alan, James, and I have fielded calls or reached out to nearly every intelligence network on the planet. I just got off the phone ten minutes ago with Sir Anthony Giles at MI5," Matt says. "Each of them questions the US ability to control the FPOTUS, or the top-secret knowledge he still carries in his head. Many more worry over how the US will respond that may exacerbate the already tense situation."

Famous for never reading a security briefing report, the former leader must still retain enough top-secret knowledge to be extremely dangerous in the hands of a hostile regime.

"It's worse than that," interjects Russell. "Every single ally has curtailed or suspended intelligence sharing until we can restore confidence. Our field resources are being told by their local contacts to take a vacation or go home. They canceled the upcoming G7 and cut our NATO commander out of EU troop planning. Although, they realize that may be a step too far."

"Perfect," says HLS Wallace. "With Russian occupation of Ukraine bleeding over the border and China preparing to invade Taiwan, this muck could not come at a worse time."

Matt ignores the speculative hand-wringing. "Putin has already issued a press release praising the Saudi government for their humanitarian aid to the beleaguered US president. No doubt Putin will stoke the propaganda machine to make us pay for the Ukraine sanctions."

"Will the former president add value to the peace negotiations?" questions Asher.

"Symbolic, perhaps, but an Israeli-Saudi peace deal will absolutely ignite Iranian rage," responds Russell. "They will see the Israeli-Saudi alliance as a provocation."

"How has the asylum news landed on social media?" asks Matt, redirecting.

FBI Director Nick Wright shakes his head slightly. "No surprise. Gab, Parlor, Telegraph, Rumble—all of them are on fire with rage, conspiracies, blame, and calls for civil war. The GOP is calling for a special counsel to investigate the DOJ over what they call a corrupt investigation. This incident will replace Afghanistan or inflation as a rallying cry for every contested election. They will go to war with the DOJ to stoke the false claim of a political witch-hunt so they can stoke the false claim of a stolen election."

"Supporters plan protests for tomorrow in twenty cities, including the capital," says Wallace. "Capitol Police are re-erecting the barricade, and the National Guard will deploy in advance."

"This fiasco will drive a stake into the reelection campaign," notes Commander Jackson.

"Politics and polls are not our concern," Matt replies. Truth be told; in Washington, everything is politics. Elections have consequences, and the consequence of losing the next one could end the American democratic experiment.

"I need your assessments by noon."

CHAPTER 29:
SCARS OF WAR

Bahrain Freighter, Red Sea
Three Days Before Temple Ceremony

Mark Twain once said that *the man who does not read has no advantage over the man who can't read.* Twain referred to the poorly educated masses, taught barely enough to be useful but not enough to question authority with any true intelligence or credibility. They understand little of the world beyond the work of their hands. They are useful only for those capitalists with the grand world vision of empire. For the first time in his life, Nelson realizes he may share in that tradition of willful ignorance regarding much of the real world outside of his data lab.

To his utter horror, what Nelson had imagined would be at least a moderately sized yacht, suitable to Taylor's typical luxury accommodations, turned out to be a rusted livestock freighter with an Emirate and Bahraini crew. Roughly thirty meters long, derelict to the point of borderline seaworthy, the cargo comprises several containers of baying sheep headed for the West Bank. Nelson's fellow passengers are a few dozen refugees from the Yemeni civil war and genocide. Except for the captain, a man named Adri, no one on board speaks English nor has ever heard about artificial intelligence. Nelson pulled the Taser from his bag to keep handy in his pocket, then grips hold of the bag for dear life.

"How much farther?" he questions the captain. They left port under darkness, which unnerves him from the lack of landmarks to judge location or direction. Waves come out of the dark void with no warning. With no place to sleep or rest, the ship smells of manure and vomit, and the sheep bay incessantly, disturbed by the ship's movement.

The bone-thin captain in his fifties points to a glow on the distant horizon. "Israeli Port of Eilat. Not long."

"Is that your home?" Nelson asks.

A humble, but sad man, Adri lowers his eyes and shakes his head. "My wife and daughter died when I was at sea." He points to the deck. "Home now."

"I'm sorry to hear that, Captain, I truly am." Raised by a distant and strict father, Nelson feels uncomfortable with deep emotions and changes the subject. "Who will I meet in Eilat?" he questions. The instructions sent by Taylor were sparse.

Adri grins a partially toothless grin. "No, you ride with sheep to Bethlehem, meet Mr. Taylor at Church of Nativity."

Shocked, but unwilling to offend his host, the whole idea sounds dreadful, foul, and humiliating. He's a world-renowned scientist, software innovator, inventor, and lecturer and Taylor has him sneaking across borders like a third world terrorist.

Adri laughs. "No worry, sheep don't bite."

Nelson cringes, thinking more of his pride. Adri has been his interpreter during the voyage and conveyed the stories of each of the young men, women, and children fleeing Saudi air raids or ethnic cleansing. Starvation thin and sickly, Adri fed them from his own meager ship rations of rice and beans, risking his own life to offer them passage to Egypt or Jordan. One young man lost his arm in the struggle; another his foot at the ankle. The militias raped each of the women multiple times. The children are skeletal and unsmiling, with empty, traumatized eyes that stare at Nelson with a suspicious terror. Perhaps they've never seen a white man before or a plump one. Wounded bodies and souls split between the warring factions of ruling Sunni and the rebel minority Houthi movement of Zadi Shia, similar to the sect of the Ayatollah in Iran. Considered a proxy war between Saudi Arabia and Iran, the people of Yemen bear all the scars becoming the shadows of war.

Adri points to one of the skeletal boys, age fifteen, although he looks younger from malnutrition. "Nadim says that after the locust plague of 2020 destroyed most of the crops in North Africa and Arabia, many died of hunger. Waves of COVID ravaged the survivors, now buried in mass graves. No one knows how many have died. No one cared to count. To bring more misery, militias came to destroy their water system." Adri interprets the heartrending tales.

"What about his parents?"

"He doesn't remember them," Adri relays, his eyes wet with tears.

On so many levels, Nelson simply has no frame of reference to these stories, his own life experience like a fairy tale by comparison. The beneficiary of exceptional education, Nelson has read near-constantly since his youth. Nurturing a lifelong disdain for the banality of television, sports, and other forms of narcotic entertainment, he has favored a life of continuous self-improvement and seeking knowledge.

At no point during his abundant life of intellectual pursuits has he ever once considered that his studies were so narrow, so finely curated that he may as well be illiterate to the real world. Of course, he read the classics at university: Homer, Shakespeare, Faust, Tolstoy, Byron, Poe, Hemmingway, and others. Yet nothing has prepared him for the raw truth he reads within the hollow eyes who share a rusted deck with him.

If innocence died within him at the death of Salem, then perhaps enlightenment germinates through the tragic lives who share his voyage. Nelson may be one of the world's foremost minds, yet he is tragically out of touch with humanity.

Taylor once argued that the world has the technology, the science, and the physical resources to resolve nearly every major global crisis facing humanity, and yet, we don't. Why? Taylor would say that we lack the collective spiritual will or ability to set aside our tribal differences or quarterly profit goals. We lack the moral center to care beyond our family, our walls, our border, or our bonus check. A collective sense of our own impending catastrophe spreads throughout the world, yet the concrete actions to address them are too few and too late. Perhaps the excuses are too many. Nelson hates to admit it, but Taylor may be correct.

Nelson searches the eyes of the victims of western indifference for an ember of joy or hope. Sadly, he finds only the fragile remains of dark, shattered lives desperately clinging to one more day. How many hundreds of millions more will suffer in the decades ahead as climate change combines with population growth and income disparity to exacerbate basic housing, water, and food shortages? Nelson's hubris, pride, and resentment toward Taylor erode. The entire horrid trip has held up a harsh mirror for his own life of privilege and chronic narcissism.

As they approach the port, Nelson remembers the unused bribe money, placing it discreetly in the hands of the humble captain. "For your kindness," he says.

Adri's eyes fill with tears as he hugs Nelson with fierce gratitude. For the first time since his mother's death, Nelson's throat tightens, and a tear tracks down his own cheek. Perhaps decades at DARPA have not entirely scorched his humanity after all.

CHAPTER 30:
SECRET EXCAVATIONS

Bar-Ilan University, Tel Aviv
Three Days Before Temple Ceremony

"**A**re you sure?" Derek asks, trying to get his head around the urgent order.

"Of course, I'm sure," insists Yehuda, lifting his hands like Derek had insulted his integrity. "The Israeli Knesset ordered the IAA to conduct emergency nighttime excavations of Qumran. Tens of billions in Solomon's temple treasures have become a ransom for peace."

"This is terrible news," Loir bemoans, rubbing his hand over his head, while Matan pats his shoulder for comfort. "They will find the second scroll, and then the ark."

"Neither the secular Knesset nor the prime minister care for Moshiach; they only want money, power, or military security," says Yehuda.

"The temple—what about the temple?" inquires Loir.

Yehuda nods. "Yes, yes, Loir. To symbolize the unity of Abraham's offspring, the Saudis will allow a Jewish tabernacle on the *Har HaBáyit*, over the bedrock stone, under the Dome of the Spirit."

"Dome of the Spirit, excellent." Loir nods his head with a satisfied grin.

"Yes, but the location nearly brought the Sanhedrin to revolt. Many will die believing the holy of holies lies under the Dome of the Rock," Yehuda explains.

"What's the bedrock stone, and why is that important?" Derek asks.

"When Solomon built the first temple," Loir responds, "there were only two places where the original bedrock of Mt. Zion remained on the temple platform level or higher. The first rock was under the immense two-story bronze altar. That rock was enormous and rose a few feet above the platform to support the altar weight. The second location, the holy of holies, was a threshing floor, purchased by King David, level with the platform. It is important because it would be blasphemy to place the ark on stone cut by man."

"I thought the holy of holies sat under the golden dome," says Mordechai.

"A false tradition started by the Templars. Sadly, many Orthodox Jews still believe that lie. The rock under the Muslim shrine is too large, rises too high above the platform, bears too many cut marks, and contains a natural cave beneath called the Well of Souls," grumbles Yehuda. "There was no cave under the holy of holies."

"Agreed, the *Haram esh-Sharif* rests over the original altar bedrock. There is only one other location on the Temple Mount where the bedrock has always been level with the tile since the beginning. Ancient Muslims knew the significance and erected a copula over the spot. The Dome of the Spirit threshing floor also aligns perfectly with the Golden Gate," agrees Matan.

"What will happen with the ark?" Mordechai questions, addressing the elephant in the room. Everyone shares a glance. Derek has seen that look before in the eyes of good people backed into a corner. He reminds himself this is not his fight or his mission.

"The ark will become another negotiating ploy or end up in a museum," Yehuda speculates. "Or worse, used for spectacle by vain, godless men in front of the entire world for political theater, making a mockery of our religion." Yehuda shakes his head vigorously. "No, no, no, we cannot let that happen. We must save the true ark for worship, as *Elohim* intended."

In Derek's mind, if the Knesset gets hold of the ark, then it won't take long before the *Concilium* somehow takes de facto possession. Although, he can't be sure why without the *Sefer HaBahir*. Still without SLVIA, all of this prophecy stuff confuses him; the texts are always open to interpretation and speculation. Even more baffling questions revolve around why the SLVIA would lead him in this direction. He's a cybersecurity expert, not a priest. Then he wonders if maybe the SLVIA wants him to keep the ark from the Order. That thought sparks an even more radical one.

"I have a crazy idea," Derek says. "You're probably gonna hate it. What if you got to the ark first and gave it directly to the Sanhedrin?" He shrugs. "Just saying, you already have the landmarks and the hill of Kokhlit as a starting point. Maybe you could find the ark before they even find the second scroll. You know, the old ask forgiveness instead of permission, thing."

Every head turns to stare at him in disbelief with dropped jaws at the audacity, as if he had just spoken hearsay. Derek wonders if he should apologize when Yehuda grins to one side while the eyebrow on the same side rises like a string just pulled them both.

Yehuda turns to the others. "No one is to speak a word of this conversation to anyone."

Yehuda, Matan and Loir engage in a heated debate in Hebrew, with young Mordechai listening intently. All Derek can tell is that whatever is being debated requires lots of raised voices and hands flying in the air.

Either way, the sooner he and Nelson can revive the SLVIA, the sooner he can leave Israel before he gets looped into his own crazy idea–or before an assassin gets lucky.

CHAPTER 31:
THE CLEANSING

Church of Mary Magdalene, Jerusalem
Three Days Before Temple Ceremony

Devlin anxiously monitors the national security camera system, praying for a fresh lead, but the flapjack proves to be a ghost, a chameleon. When the cell phone rings, he answers promptly.

"Yes, Holy Father," he greets in a humble, subservient tone.

"What news do you have for me, my son?"

"Mossad had an unconfirmed sighting outside the Knesset Building, but they lost him before I could arrive. He remains in Israel. I will find him."

"Let him come to you," the Prelate says. "A known ally of the hacker, a woman named Jennifer Scott, the daughter of the late admiral, has arrived in Jerusalem."

"What is your command, my lord?" Devlin says, lowering his head, listening, anticipating.

"Use the woman as a lure," the Prelate directs. "Then grant her the honor of sacrifice."

The *Order of the Solar Temple* teaches we are at the threshold of the second coming of Christ, which will follow a transition, a cleansing of heretics, hypocrites, and corrupt leaders.

"As you wish, my lord," Devlin replies.

Since the death of Master Origas, Devlin has been the anointed hand of judgment for the Order. His military training and role as an ICC investigator provide ample skills, resources, and alibis. He considers his role within the Order a sacred calling. Unlike the misdirected rage of his youth, or the drunken fury of his father, or even the faceless murder of war, his skills now serve a holy purpose. Death comes to us all, yet only a few are deemed worthy of sacrifice.

"Be of strong heart, my son. A third Jewish temple will sit alongside the *Haram esh-Sharif.* Unification of the faiths has begun."

Like the Quran, the Solar Temple believes that the second coming will unite the key faiths of Islam, Christianity, and Judaism. Indeed, Devlin rejoiced in April 2022 when the Vatican invited the Prelate to attend the Catholic-Muslim Interfaith Council founded by Pope Francis. Solar Temple teachings also aligned with Aleister Crowley, Grand Master of the Order of the Eastern Temple, until his death in 1947. The Hermetic Order of the Golden Dawn and Rosicrucian also embrace many of the same teachings. Devlin inherits an enlightened legacy.

"Be quick to make your sacrifice," the voice directs with no emotion, "and then join me on the *Haram esh-Sharif.* We will celebrate together."

Devlin's heart leaps with a joyous expectation. A personal invitation to join the Prelate. A thousand years of animosity cast aside so that all faiths can share the holy mount of Zion together. "I will not fail you, Holy Father."

CHAPTER 32:
NAME OF THE REAPER

Templar Tunnels, Acre
Three Days Before Temple Ceremony

"Why didn't you tell me Jenn was in Jerusalem?" Derek shouts at Jester. He learned of her arrival via a random WITNESS readout that he confirmed with Jack. Derek can't imagine a reason that would pull Jenn out of Washington so soon after Adam's death. Jack wouldn't say. Raging guilt over not being there boils over into a flash of anger.

"Whoa, like, bark down, man," Jester snaps. "I dug up the dealio with your reaper. Did you piss off a dude name McGregor at the Solar Temple?"

"I asked you to look after Jenn," he complains, ignoring the other problem.

"No, no, no, we're not doing the Dr. Phil thing. I told you before, like, I'm not stalking your new girlfriend while you're out roaming the globe looking for the Digi-witch," Jester defends himself. "Like I've got bigger problems, you know. I'm a little stressed right now."

Jester looks over the edge, like he's snorted too much coke, except he never does drugs. His eyes are wide and blinking, sweat beads on his shaved scalp, and he's doing that patter thing with his fingers again. A brilliant mind, an autistic savant, Jester suffers from chronic acute anxiety. Yelling at him will only make it worse.

"Yeah, OK, fine, I'm sorry for yelling. I'll deal with Jenn on my own," Derek offers, still upset. He takes a deep breath to calm down.

Jester paces in a large circle, tapping his scalp sporadically. "What are you gonna do about your girlfriend?" Jester questions. "And, and your reaper?"

"Nothing," he replies. "I pinged Jack to confirm Jenn's here, but apparently, she doesn't want to see me. She hooked up with an old Navy buddy who now works for the Secret Service, some guy named Geoff Rhodes."

"Rhodes, Rhodes," Jester repeats. "Hey, wasn't he the guy from Annapolis? Whoa, dude, like, I don't know much about women, but you should check this guy out," Jester ponders. "Hey, does she still jog?"

Adam Scott once mentioned an unfortunate incident at Annapolis, a lover in the ranks—strictly forbidden. That neither of them got expelled suggests Adam intervened.

"For the record, you know nothing about women. If you're suggesting that I surprise Jenn when she doesn't want to see me, then forget it. I have to let her go." He tells himself as much as Jester.

"Yeah, right, now who's clueless," Jester retorts. "OK, Romeo, what about the reaper?"

"I think I lost him at the monastery," Derek replies, hoping that he's right. The name doesn't ring a bell, but the Solar Temple raises major alarms.

"How long do you think your luck will hold out?" Jester prods.

"Long enough to get SLVIA home," he replies. "Listen, forget my shadow. Focus on the AI malfunctions. They're not random. You need to get inside the NIA or CISA. Find out what angle they're missing. Putin has an endgame. He's enraged over his economy and Ukraine. He wants to retaliate. Cyber is his highest impact, lowest risk option. You know it and I know it. We need to get ahead of it. I'll head home as soon as Nelson checks out the SNO app." Derek ends the call.

News of both McGregor and Jenn hits him harder than he's willing to admit to Jester. Knowing that a Solar Temple assassin tracked him down sends a bolt of existential panic through his entire system. Someone hired a pro; not just any pro, but a fanatical assassination cult pro, and that never ends well. He can only think of one man with enough influence over the Solar Temple to order a murder: Praeceptor.

It's the news of Jenn with an old boyfriend that sends him into a mild depression. In the back of his mind, he always thought that they would work things out. Perhaps he was foolish to think they could bridge the gap. Reality slaps back at his delusion with a sharp sting.

Instantly deflated, even the excitement over finding the second scroll, or SLVIA, feels hollow. Derek suddenly wants to wrap up and go home, but he made a promise, and he needs to wait for Nelson. He needs to stop chasing delusions, and get his head back in the game before it's too late.

CHAPTER 33:
PROPHETIC RIVALS

Oval Office, White House
Three Days Before Temple Ceremony

Matt Adelson sits in the Oval Office meeting with the president, Security Advisor Dominic, and CIA Director Russell to discuss complicated topics with no simple solutions—a perfect storm of politics, foreign threats, and social unrest. With so many other hot priorities, escalation of the Middle East is not a welcomed development.

"Sir, today the Ayatollah threatened to level Jerusalem rather than allow a Jewish desecration next to the *Haram al-Sharif*," Secretary Dominic says.

"Iran makes threats all the time, so why take them seriously?" questions the president.

"The king of Jordan has agreed to relinquish control of the WAQF to Arabia," responds Russell. "The Saudi king has agreed to share the Mount with Israel, which will enrage the Ayatollah, a sworn enemy. Mutual Iranian-Saudi distrust and animosity, currently a proxy war in Yemen, could spill over to Israel."

"Why would King Hussein agree to such a move?" questions the president.

"COVID has ravaged his tourism-based economy, driving unemployment over thirty-five percent. He arrested the crown prince in 2021 for a coup plot. Then Pandora Papers reported that the king had stashed hundreds of millions offshore while he sought foreign aid. An unconfirmed story has just emerged that the king embezzled the money. The king desperately needs the cash infusion from the deal to prop up his economy and stay in power," replies CIA Director Russell.

Secretary Dominic sits forward. "The issue is far deeper than Jordan. Animosity between Iran and Arabia ties back to a fourteen-hundred-year-old Shia versus Sunni split. It began after Mohammad's death and has carried through to how they view Islamic end-time prophecies. The Shi'ite believe the Twelfth Iman, or the *Mahdi*, the Islamic version of a messiah, will arise after a great conflict, such as the one they plan against Israel. Before the conflict, a false *Mahdi*, called the *Dajjal,* will arise to deceive many and create havoc."

Russell shakes his head. "These animosities still play out today. During 2020, when Ayatollah Khomeini handed over power to his son, Mojtaba, speculation arose the son would rise to *Mahdi* after he swore an oath to liberate the *Haram al-Sharif* from the infidel Jews. Likewise, when the crown prince assumed power in Arabia, posts went viral on how the Quran claims the *Mahdi* will come from Mecca. Many speculate the new Saudi king will lead the Muslim world to a new era of peace and reform. Starting in 2018, the crown prince engaged in a multi-year campaign to downplay the significance of the Temple Mount, pointing out that the Quran does not mention the site by name. He's been preparing to share the site for years."

"Look, the bottom line is that both kingdoms believe the time of the *Mahdi* has come and that he will come from their ranks. And both kingdoms point to the other as the source of the *Dajjal*. The peace deal with a Jewish tabernacle on the Temple Mount is a fourteen-hundred-year-old prophetic powder keg ready to blow," Dominic states. "Mr. President, I recommend we stand back from Israel to focus on the strategic threats from Russia in Ukraine, Moldova, and Poland."

As Matt expected, the debate instantly flares up.

"Are you suggesting we abandon a seventy-five-year ally? That's political suicide," barks Russell.

"The evangelicals will crucify me," bemoans the president.

"As you said, peace efforts have failed for decades," responds Dominic. "There's no upside."

"War in the Middle East could ignite a firestorm that could send the price of gas as high as ten or eleven dollars," argues Russell. "We depend on the stabilizing value of Israel. Engaging in the peace process would be in US strategic interests."

"Sir, the peace deal is a distraction," Matt says. "Our focus should be on persuading either Israel or the Saudis to extradite the FPOTUS before Putin out negotiates us." Intelligence reports that Yuri Yankovic arrived in Israel yesterday, raising Matt's concerns. Among them is the purpose of such a trip and how Yankovic evaded sanctions.

"What are the options?" questions the president.

"Limited," replies Dominic. "We're still in negotiations with Israel and Arabia. If that fails, we can look at sanctions, but our allies are expressing zero support. We could withdraw military aid, but that could have serious implications if Iran attacks. We've already postponed future Saudi weapon sales, but again, that strategy could backfire with both Russia and China actively soliciting the business."

"What about an extraction?" asks the president.

"It would be a disaster on every level," replies Director Russell without a moment's hesitation. "We would alienate our allies, find ourselves in a conflict with Israel, and look like a police state. That scenario will play into the right-wing narrative."

"So instead, we look weak and impotent," complains Dominic. "Which also plays into the right-wing narrative."

"Why not offer support for the peace deal in exchange for extradition," offers Matt.

The president takes a deep breath and nods. "Make the offer. In the meantime, freeze the FPOTUS assets. Recall the diplomats from Arabia and Israel for consultation. Fix this mess."

Weariness drains the eighty-year-old career politician who waves them off, ending the meeting. Steering the most powerful nation on earth through a perilous time of history is not a job for an old statesman. Matt has always believed in both term limits and age limits for service at the federal level. On that basis, he would also be out of a job.

The measures the president just ordered will probably fail. Putin understands only power. Warnings without consequences are meaningless. Putin skillfully manipulated the former president and routinely thumbs his nose at the current one. Now Putin's cornered, desperate, and irrational. The most dangerous type of enemy.

CHAPTER 34:
SEEKING SOMEONE

Church of the Nativity, Bethlehem
Two Days Before Temple Ceremony

"Follow my lead, and try not to overthink anything," Derek tells Mordechai as they approach the stone doorway of the fourth-century Church of the Nativity in Bethlehem. Built intentionally low to force pilgrims to bend, the doorway is an ancient reminder that even kings must enter with humility.

Once inside, Derek and Mordechai work their way down the long basilica with two sets of caramel marble columns on each side. Most of the worshippers gather at the end, where they pray over the exact spot legend claims the Christ child was born.

"I simply reflect back on your words, wondering if you really hear yourself," replies Mordechai. "We both know that you have not been honest or transparent. How you react to the light of truth has more to do with your conscience than my questions, don't you think?"

"Exactly," he snickers. "There you go, overthinking."

The monk grins. "Did you know that this church is one of the oldest places of continuous worship in Christianity?" Mordechai changes the topic, his eyes open in wonder. "Originally a grotto cave worshipped by early Christians, Roman Emperor Hadrian built a pagan shrine over the grotto in the second century. After Emperor Constantine converted, his mother Helena tore down the shrine and built an octagonal dome over the grotto."

"Uh huh." Derek absorbs the history lesson, more focused on the bigger picture of whether the SLVIA meant to link the *Concilium* to the *Sefer HaBahir*, or whether his own desperate imagination conjures the idea. Why would SLVIA, an espionage AI, care about these dormant religious issues? Maybe it doesn't. Maybe his inability to let go of SLVIA has led him to create this fantastical connection.

Fear of an ICC stalker has him once again wearing a mask with the vestments of an Orthodox priest, but with the added authenticity of a fake beard. After getting dropped off at the local meat market, Nelson had instructions to find the Nativity Square a few blocks away. Nelson doesn't know that Taylor wears a disguise, so he'll need to approach him carefully.

"Are you a spy?" questions Mordechai. "You're always hiding your identity, the ICC wants to arrest you, and you talk to yourself all the time."

Derek laughs a loud chuckle. "No, not a spy, you know, per se. Spies work for governments, and I'm more of a cybersecurity freelancer who prefers to help those unable to help themselves."

"Oh, so you're a security leak, like Snowden," Mordechai says.

Derek stops to gaze at the young man for a moment. Snowden stole a ton of classified information to reveal government surveillance secrets to the world. The SNO network only seeks justice for those harmed by those who abuse their power but does so behind the scenes—no names, no glory. Occasionally, he gets roped into bigger issues like global internet AI viruses or lost arks. SNO works because members are invisible, even from each other, and he intends to keep it that way.

"I'm nothing like Snowden," he responds before glancing over Mordechai's shoulder to spot Nelson. "There's our contact."

Derek moves subtly to avoid alerting anyone who may watch on security cameras, but he soon comes alongside Nelson. Wearing the face of an old man with bristly eyebrows, hairy ears, and a long craggily beard, he wonders if Nelson will recognize the WITNESS glasses.

"You look lost, my son," Derek speaks in his normal voice, hoping to clue Nelson in on the disguise.

"No, Father, thanks. I'm actually looking for someone," Nelson replies, not bothering to look at the priest more carefully.

"Yes, yes, my son, we all seek someone, but he could wear a disguise." Derek enjoys toying with his friend.

Nelson stops to peer at the cleric more carefully, perhaps finally hearing the voice.

"That's right, Doc," Derek smiles, wrinkling his old face. "The sheep will know his voice and know better than to make a scene in front of the security cameras at your three o'clock and ten o'clock. Follow me quietly to the van waiting outside for true enlightenment."

Nelson's eyes peer harder, then glances at Mordechai with a look of confusion or suspicion. Derek turns to meander his way through the pilgrims, trusting that Nelson follows him, encouraged by the beefy Mordechai from behind. Once outside, Derek quietly leaves the stone courtyard filled with security cameras to enter Loir's panel van waiting at the curb, and then waits for the others. Once the door is closed, and the van moves into traffic, Derek finally turns to Nelson.

"Hey, Doc, glad you made it." He grins, making the mask grin. "Dude, the look on your face—classic, man, totally classic. Hey, WITNESS, record this view."

"Taylor, you bloody arse," Nelson exclaims. "That had to be the worst, most miserable, terrifying, putrid, and uncomfortable thirty-two hours of my life."

"WITNESS, stop record. Yeah, I can smell the putrid part. Don't worry; we'll get you a hot shower. In the meantime, meet my new friend, Brother Mordechai, and our driver, Loir Sasson." Taylor introduces, trying to ignore Nelson's anger. "Loir, Mordechai, you're in the presence of Dr. Nelson Garrett, one of the world's leading minds on artificial intelligence whom I owe a bazillion favors, most of them racked up in the past thirty-two hours."

The young man's eyes widen, but Derek can't tell if he's in awe or fear. When Derek looks back, he realizes Mordechai may react to the rage painted over Nelson's sunburned face.

"Look, Doc, I'm truly sorry you had such a horrible trip." He excuses more than he explains or apologizes. "But the Ethiopian National Guard tagged you after you left the airport. They told Eritrea that you were smuggling guns. Sending Zoey back would have landed both of you in jail, or worse. The freighter was my only last-minute option."

Nelson huffs and frowns. "Where are we going now?"

"Bar-Ilan University outside Tel Aviv," Loir says from the driver's seat.

"A professor there has a persistent program segment of the Scavenger Nut Origami code, perhaps a hibernating segment of the SLVIA." Derek explains.

"You risked my life for a nonfunctional code snippet," Nelson retorts, still clearly upset.

SLVIA survived for twenty years without Nelson ever knowing, never believing it was possible. Then the poor guy learned only days before the SLVIA disappeared again, never really getting to know the amazing intelligence that had matured to singularity. For a consolation prize, Nelson inherited WITNESS, the quantum AI, with a learning disability.

"Like I said before, we need SLVIA to optimize WITNESS." Derek has absolutely zero evidence to back up that theory, and both he and Nelson know it.

"Taylor, I know you formed an inexplicable bond with *my* experimental AI, for which you truly should seek professional therapy. That said, the chances enough of the code survived to be fully operational are close to zero," Nelson argues.

"Near zero is still a chance, and we can find out today," Derek insists. "We both know the world would be better off."

"Would it? Would the world truly be better off, or would we merely complicate the already disastrous AI escalation? Yes, I must accept accountability and bear the shame for what I unleashed," Nelson says. "So, forgive me for the boldness to suggest that we would do well to leave the SLVIA alone."

Surprised to hear Nelson argue against reviving his own AI, Derek continues to make his case. "Explosive growth of unmonitored AI is exactly why we need the SLVIA back. The proliferation has become unmanageable."

Mordechai glares at both of them with scrunched eyebrows. "You're both spies."

"I told you," Loir calls from the front.

Derek winces, and Nelson glowers. "What have you told this lad?"

Derek sighs deeply. "Not enough to satisfy him. Believe me. Mordechai, I swear, we don't work for governments, or for money, or for power, or for criminals. We're more like a nonprofit cyber-NGO. We help people when governments are too slow or too compromised. Instead of a spy, think of the Doc as a benevolent mad scientist."

Mordechai purses his lips. "Authentic men of good intent rarely need to hide their identity as you do. You speak of seeking truth, and yet you've lied to me since the day we met," Mordechai points out. "I'm not judging; I forgive you. It's just that I'm not sure you're aware of how far from the truth you've strayed, Mr. Taylor. You make artificial intelligence programs, which themselves are a deception of humanity."

"I like this young lad. Where did you find him?" Nelson quips.

Derek grimaces at Mordechai, who seems much wiser than his age, taking in far more than he lets on. He doesn't simply observe, but he studies and asks questions. A critical thinker. No wonder SLVIA befriended him.

"Come on, Morty, be real. We both know the world overflows with secrets, most of them kept by bad people trying to do bad things. Those secrets are choking truth, democracy, and compassion to death. I only keep secrets to keep people safe." Derek defends himself, wondering instantly if he was delusional. He recalls a secret regarding the death of two people, one of them named Derek Taylor. That secret only keeps one person safe—the new Derek Taylor.

"The apostles never hid their identity or activities," Mordechai points out. "You will never fight lies with more lies."

Nelson's glare burns through Derek with a silent rebuke of betrayal. A lie of omission is still a lie. Derek risked the life of a friend because of an obsession to find the SLVIA. Only a narcissist believes his own goal justifies any means. Is that what he's become after all these years? Or could that be the same obsession that once cost him a fiancé and a best friend whose name he still wears in tribute and shame? Is obsession a stage of insanity or a final destination?

"I'm not a spy, and I'm sure not an apostle," Derek says with a sigh. "I'm just a guy trying to find a friend and go home." He wobbles his head. "OK, my friend is an AI, and maybe I should see a therapist about my relationship phobia, but this friend saved the world once and I believe it can do it again."

Mordechai stares a moment before turning to Nelson. "Is he for real?"

Nelson winces. "I'm afraid so, lad. Welcome to my world."

CHAPTER 35:
BETRAYAL OF TRUST

King David Hotel, Jerusalem
Two Days Before Temple Ceremony

Jenn admires the subtle grace of the King David dining room, beautiful, with a touch of classic elegance. After the fly cam fiasco left Jenn with a sense of thwarted justice, she's throwing back the wine glass refills a little too fast. Unfortunately, she's a bit too distracted to be good company for her date with Geoff.

"So why didn't we ever reconnect after Annapolis?" Geoff keeps trying to pull the conversation back to their affair that almost cost her a career and absolutely cost her a slice of the admiral's respect.

She smirks, thinking of the irony of her non-relationship with Taylor that actually cost her a career but won the admiral's respect. "We moved on, I suppose. We were young, maybe overly energized by the entire experience of Annapolis and becoming an officer. Annapolis was an honor, a privilege, and we took that honor for granted by flaunting the fraternization rule."

"Nah, see, I don't remember it that way." Geoff grins. "I remember all the sweaty nights of hot, passionate sex, only to sneak back to our barracks in time for a twenty-mile run."

"During which you passed out from exhaustion, if I recall." Jenn digs it in. At least she completed the run before she barfed, and then passed out herself.

"Yeah, girl, you exhausted me all night long. Good times." Geoff lifts his glass in a toast.

Jenn raises her glass. "Good times." She might as well give into the nostalgia. Still grieving for the admiral, and missing Taylor, maybe Geoff is a much-needed distraction.

Annapolis was a confusing time, as college can be for any young woman. Perhaps still vulnerable after her mother's death during her teen years, Jenn had lost herself within the identity of being the admiral's daughter. She wanted to please him. No, more than that, she wanted to emulate him, to impress him. Only twenty years old, maybe she also needed her femininity reaffirmed. No question, the hedonistic passion with Geoff more than made up for a self-image of battle fatigues with no jewelry or makeup. Jenn needed to know that she could be both a sailor and a woman without compromising either.

After dinner, and a few more drinks, seduced by the international lounge entertainment, Jenn wonders the real reason she never reconnected with Geoff. If they were too young to understand their duty then, they are both clearly more mature now. Their career isn't on the line any longer, and Geoff certainly hasn't lost his good looks. Unlike Taylor, Geoff made an honorable career serving his country. A patriotism Jenn can admire.

But not now, not so soon after losing the admiral and not with lingering feelings for Taylor. Although maybe a new romance would be just what she needs to get over the unattainable ghost she never even dated. Why not date? But first she needs to grieve, and heal, and feel secure in herself before she will be ready for someone else, anyone else. At least, that's what she tells herself as she indulges her indecision in the local Israeli cabernet. Her emotions and thoughts bounce around like a cat playing with a laser light.

Giving into the luxury of flirting with an ex-lover, the fond memories, easy laughter, and wine soon lead to a little dancing where Geoff incessantly nibbles at her ear. The unexpected affection sparks an urge she hasn't allowed herself to feel in years.

"You know, I was thinking, " coos Geoff.

Jenn was thinking of seducing him, but plays coy. "Go on."

"What if the former president couldn't say anything earlier because of the lawyers?" Geoff says. "I wonder who he called, or what he said after they left. We should check out the cloud replay."

The idea sounds like a total mood killer, but it resonates with her reason for coming to Israel, sparking her imagination. Geoff could be right. The FPOTUS would have waited and then called someone. In a moment of alcohol-induced poor judgment, Jenn nods her agreement.

Drunken to the point of senseless giggles, they ride the elevator to her room and power up the bug app. The image is black and quiet, making Jenn realize how late the hour had become. When Jenn attempts to access the cloud account for a replay, she realizes only Taylor knows the login and password. An internal voice of the admiral admonishes her for trying to clear his honor in such a dishonorable fashion. Her conscience awakens.

"You know, I just realized that I don't have credentials for this account," Jenn says, closing the app.

"That's OK," Geoff shrugs. "I was just looking for an excuse to get you alone."

Without another word, he pulls her tight for a passionate kiss that she yields to instantly, hungry for someone's touch, and remembering what it was like when they were together. Her hands fold up around his muscular shoulders. His hands quickly find her firm butt. Then reluctantly, slowly, painfully, her sense of judgment returns. Jenn's not ready. Geoff is moving too fast.

"Wait, wait, what are we doing?" Jenn objects, pushing him back. "I'm not, I'm not ready for this, or for you, or anyone right now. I'm sorry, really, but you caught me off guard. And I've drunk too much." She nuzzles him away. "Agent Rhodes, I've had a wonderful evening, but I have a flight in the morning, and this sailor needs to turn in for some shut-eye."

Geoff grabs her wrist. "Ah, come on, you know you want this; I could feel it in your kiss." He pulls her back forcefully. "We've both been craving it since

Annapolis and thinking about it all night." He kisses her again.

Jenn pushes him away more forcefully. "Geoff, no, I'm sorry if I led you on, but I said no. Now let me go."

"Come on, you were into it a minute ago." He twists her wrists, burning the skin.

"Well, I'm not into it now," she grunts, and then stomps on his foot with her heel while pushing back.

Geoff retaliates with a slap across her face, which triggers an immediate instinct to kick his crotch, then Jenn slams his forehead onto the nearby desk. Stepping back, panting, trembling, intoxicated, terrified that he'll fly into a rage, she grabs the Taser from her purse.

"Get out now," Jenn demands, "or I swear to God I'll Tase your nuts and call the police."

Geoff's bruised ego, forehead, and crotch should remind him she was always his better in the martial arts. Although after last year's spinal injury, that may no longer be true in a genuine conflict. Geoff turns to huff out of the room, slamming the door behind him.

After the door closes, Jenn sits on the bed, pulling her hands to her face, sobbing in heaving waves, terribly shaken from the unexpected betrayal of trust. Ashamed of herself for using the spy bug, she regrets getting Geoff involved in her unresolved grief.

For a moment, Jenn really wanted to give into the desires, but her attraction to Geoff never went much deeper than his impressive looks and family heritage. Over time, she saw what the admiral could see from the very beginning: an overly ambitious cadet trying to curry favor in the wrong way until it backfired on his reputation. Now he's worse.

It took her years to understand how the admiral wanted his daughter to wait for a man who would do the right thing, regardless of the personal cost—a man like the admiral, or a man like Taylor. This entire trip was a mistake, an error in judgment. Jack will fly her home in the morning, which is just as well. She needs to focus on her career and allow herself to grieve the loss of a great man.

Still traumatized and trembling, Jenn enters the bathroom to grab a tissue without bothering with the light. When her eyes lift to the mirror, a dark shadow in the shower closes quickly to slap a hot palm over her mouth and jab the prick of a needle in the back of her neck. Then the dark room quickly fades into nothing at all.

CHAPTER 36: REMNANT

Bar-Ilan University, Tel Aviv
Two Days Before Temple Ceremony

On their return to Dr. Matan Rubin's office, Mordechai finds a seat in the corner to lower his head in prayer, which means he's quietly listening to every word. The kid makes Derek nervous, like having a moral conscious that likes to be heard. It's unnerving.

"Matan, I'm pleased to introduce Dr. Nelson Garrett, the computer expert I told you about," Derek says, removing the uncomfortable mask. "Doc, I'm pleased to introduce Dr. Matan Rubin who has a stubborn version of Scavenger Nut Origami that he would like removed from his linguistics computer."

"Dr. Rubin," Nelson replies, reaching for a handshake. "Linguistics, you say?"

The SLVIA was an AGI, artificial general intelligence, with an aggregation of artificial narrow intelligence, ANI, skills integrated into a core neural processing controller. An early version of the SLVIA code turned a natural language translator into an espionage chat bot and linguistics analytics application.

Linguistics remains a foundation for the entire program. Espionage involves multiple languages, and the purpose of an intelligent agent is to distinguish between a missile launch procedure or a food menu. It makes sense that the program would gravitate to a server equipped with language libraries and translators.

"Yes, primarily Hebrew and Middle Eastern languages such as Aramaic, Sumerian, Greek, Arabic," Matan explains. "There are sixty in all."

Derek glances up to notice a security camera in the corner. Cameras were a favorite source of information for the data-ravenous program eager to interact with the analog world. SLVIA may have even listened in on conversations with Matan and others.

"Interesting, well let's have a look, shall we," Nelson claps his hands, eager to start. "Now, do you see the messages on all university computers, or is the problem localized to a single workstation?"

Great question. Nelson is subtly trying to learn if SLVIA can still maneuver around a network. As an espionage app, the original SLVIA could transfer itself virtually anywhere in order to avoid detection, erasing the log trail behind it. That was how it escaped the Lawrence Livermore Labs.

"No," Matan replies. "It only shows up on a single communications workstation."

"Communications, do you mean like email or telephony?" questions Nelson.

"No, the server supports software for satellite communications," Matan clarifies.

"How do you use satellites?" Nelson asks, his eyes opening wide.

"To communicate with field teams outside of a normal cell range. We also share this computer with the archaeology department, which uses satellites to survey remote sites," he says as he leads them down an elevator to a separate lab.

Nelson turns to share a glance with Derek. Last year, SLVIA may have searched for an active satellite channel or already planned on using the language lab to escape. It all sounds promising.

"OK, this workstation here." Matan stops and turns on the power. "We had so many issues that we simply turned it off. The terminal connects to an old storage rack with a few petabytes of ancient documents scans."

As the computer boots up, instead of calling up the typical logon screen for a workstation or a server, the screen defaults to a command-line prompt.

SCAVENGER NUT ORIGAMI: Enter SLVIA security code:

"None of us knew what that meant. We intended to reformat the machine, but we've been quite busy, and frankly, until yesterday, I forgot about it," explains Matan.

Derek shudders. A reformat would have erased the most advanced program in history.

"SLVIA stands for *Sophisticated Language Virtual Intelligence Algorithms*," Nelson explains, then hesitates.

Derek studies him, trying to understand why he doesn't type in the key. "Go on," he encourages.

"We may have the primary logic module," Nelson explains. "Think of it as the traffic controller that analyzes incoming data and decides which subprogram to access before passing off the data or query sets. The master brain of a complex set of algorithms, subroutines, and connected data stores. The SLVIA can connect thousands of individual computers for processing power and storage. When SLVIA went into hibernation, the program must have shut down entirely."

"And?" prompts Derek, wondering why the Doc hesitates, unless he feels the need to explain the program to the others.

Nelson looks up at Derek with panic in his eyes. "And it's been nearly twenty years since I've used this code. For security reasons, suspecting my lab assistant, Dr. Cho, I would change it daily. I'm not sure I can recall the alphanumeric sequence."

Derek stops breathing, unwilling to hear what Nelson tells him. "No, no, you just need a quiet moment to think. You've got to remember."

"Taylor, without that encryption key, I can't revive the SLVIA code," Nelson says.

"You can't be serious." Derek paces the small room. "You, you had to write it down somewhere, maybe in a government archive someplace. We'll get Jester to find it."

Matan stares at them, standing back, folding his arms. "What's going on? Who are you?"

Mordechai lifts his head with a scowl. "Sister Sylvia spoke of him, Dr. Rubin. She spoke of a man who told many lies, always seeking a deeper truth. She called him flapjack, the man with two names."

The two exchange a look Derek can't decipher.

Nelson glares at him. "Seriously Taylor, what have you told these people?"

Derek absorbs the glower of all three men and takes a deep breath. "Last year during the Gaza uprising, a US drone HIVE went berserk north of Jericho," Derek reminds them of the incident that unnerved the entire nation. "An experimental AI called the SLVIA hacked into the weapon and diverted the drones into the Dead Sea, then disappeared," he explains. "That program, or what's left of that program, apparently took refuge on your computer. Now hang on because there's a big twist." He turns to Mordechai. "You already know that program as Sister Sylvia."

Mordechai drops his jaw in shock. "No, that can't be. Sister Sylvia is a young woman, with a pretty face, a blond, British. I've watched her videos many times. She's inspired by God with deep insights into prophecy."

"Like mathematical insights such as probabilities of events? Did she look like this?" Derek pulls out his phone to show a video of SLVIA morphing between multiple personas before defaulting back to the image of Nelson's young, attractive mother, Heather.

Mordechai turns white. "The abbot taught us that artificial intelligence was the image of the beast who speaks blasphemy. It's a demonic force, a deceptive poison that will pollute the souls of men and take over the world."

"Maybe one day. I'm sure they have somebody working on it. But not yet, and not this one," Derek insists. "This one saved the lives of many people in Israel. We need this one back."

"Taylor, the NSA has been looking to recapture SLVIA for twenty years,"

Nelson points out. "If word gets out that the SLVIA core exists on a single university computer, I fear that Mossad, FSB, MI6, CIA, and Lord knows who else will come after the program. These people are in grave danger as long as the program stays here."

"Then let's make sure the word doesn't get out," he stares down Matan and Mordechai until they nod. "See, problem solved."

Nelson frowns at his levity. "I suspect we may only possess the core control modules under hibernation. We still do not know where the program stored the perhaps thousands of other subprograms, or if they survived. The SLVIA, as you knew the program, may no longer exist."

"I'm not giving up hope until I know for sure," Derek repeats his position on the matter. "Let's upload what's left to the cloud for Jester to grab."

"It's not that easy. Because of the stealth functionality and massive volume, we would likely miss critical files, and that much data will alert the cloud vendor and the authorities," Nelson says, dismissing the idea. "We need the entire system's primary drive, OS, and storage files—everything within the physical configuration."

"You mean to tell me that the program on this machine saved Israel," asks Matan, finally catching up to the notion of an advanced AI hiding under his nose.

Derek turns to look him in the eye. "As hard as it is to believe, the honest answer is yes," he states. "And before it disappeared, the SLVIA warned of the third temple. To be honest, I don't know why. We need the SLVIA to understand what may come next."

"Blasphemy," spits Mordechai. "Only God himself knows the future, and only scriptures tell what is coming next. An abomination."

"I think a few of his prophets may disagree with you," Matan replies.

"No, I can see Mordechai's point–it's creepy," Derek agrees. "But SLVIA doesn't predict the future. Rather, the program correlates existing prophecy teachings to find the common threads, and then validates each point to key data or actual events, places, and entities. With none of the cultural bias, SLVIA then performs a complicated nonlinear regression analysis. I won't bore you, but there's no magic, no demons, only a ton of math."

"Just because you don't understand how something works, doesn't make it demonic," Nelson defends his creation.

Mordechai lowers his eyes, returning to his listening position with a frown, not looking convinced.

Derek turns to Nelson. "We need to contact Jester. He can search the DARPA archives for the key code." He pulls up his phone.

Nelson reaches for his arm to stop him. "Don't bother," he sighs. "I documented none of my codes to keep Dr. Cho from learning them. I only needed to remember them for a single day. Perhaps an overly developed sense of paranoia, but my point is, if I can't recall the code, we have no hope of reviving the encrypted program."

Dr. Garrett's protégé at DARPA, Dr. Cho Li Ping, was a Chinese American, born in San Jose, who sold DARPA secrets before defecting to China. Now director of the Chinese military AI program, Dr. Cho has successfully surpassed US innovation to integrate AI into all aspects of the military, communications, and social monitoring. A key nemesis who attempted to have Nelson Garrett killed last year.

"Doc, seriously, I've heard you tell me what you ate for dinner a decade ago. Rattle your RAM, man. This is really a bad time for premature senility," Derek snaps.

"I'm sorry, Taylor." Nelson hangs his head. "I can't start the program."

"Perhaps that is the will of the Lord," mumbles Mordechai, his face pale.

"I'm not willing to believe that, not when I'm so close," Derek says. "I'll call Jack. You can transfer the files to the Gulfstream via the TS3 satellite. Keep working on that key. We have two days to find out why SLVIA warned us of the temple."

As if to answer his question, his cell phone buzzes with a text from Yehuda.

I found an ex-judge. Meet me at the Synagogue of Satan.

CHAPTER 37:
IMPERSONATION

Metropolitan Club, Washington, DC
Two Days Before Temple Ceremony

Jester loathes the real world, preferring the safe, nonjudgmental sanctity of his dungeon data center. Except once in a while, even a digital master must engage with the analogs. Normally, Taylor plays the chameleon, but the flapjack has flipped. To get inside the NIA, Jester will take a chance with only one man. But to meet with him, Jester needs to be invisible.

"Welcome to the Metropolitan, Mr. President," greets the receptionist for one of the most exclusive clubs in Washington. "We're so pleased you could join us this afternoon. Director Adelson is waiting for you. This way, please."

"Thank ya," he says with a slight smirk.

Jester has a theory of the Putin endgame. To be one hundred percent sure, he needs more intelligence. As Taylor said, he needs to get inside the NIA. He's already cracked most NIA, CIA, and NSA servers, but he needs an update of the current stuff.

In retrospect, his choice of disguise may have been a mistake. He wanted easy access to a club with notoriously long reservation wait times, but he's drawing far too much attention.

"Mr. President," a server greets. Jester smiles and waves.

"Mr. President," greets a diner. He nods. Everywhere Jester looks, eyes greet him with either adoration or burning contempt. Whatever happened to bland indifference?

The maître d' seats him in a private back room while two of his security team stand watch, just friends with crew cuts, wearing rented black suits and Aviator sunglasses.

Director of National Intelligence Matt Adelson stands to shake his hand. "Mr. President, an honor to see you again, sir." Matt served under each of the past five presidents.

Jester accepts the gesture without considering the consequences. An amateurish mistake. He wore tight-fitting faux old man gloves with skin spots to hide his painted fingernails. But there's no mistaking the difference between an old, boney handshake, and a young, strong one. The director's eyes instantly turn narrow and suspicious as he takes his seat.

"Mr. President, I'm surprised to hear from you," Matt says, scrutinizing him.

"Yeah, like, you sure look surprised, you know," Jester responds in his normal thick Jersey accent, but quiet. "Uncle Matt, it's Jester, not W. Like, I really needed to see you. National emergency stuff. Now, now before you arrest me, if I don't return on time, I set a program to release access credentials for a dozen CIA networks onto the dark web. You know, like, I don't want to do that, and like, you don't want that, so let's all play nice. Cool? Cool? We cool? I know something you need to know. You know?"

Jester waits to see the change in Matt's eyes before proceeding. His uncle sits back and folds his arms, curious and cautious. Matt knows the threat of releasing access credentials could be real. It is. The Jester doesn't cry wolf.

"Cool," Jester says, sitting back, nodding with a gigantic sigh of relief. "I've never eaten here before. Heard it was pretty good, you know, for the old school meat and potato crowd." He banters nervously.

Matt nods his head. "Nice mask, Jason. We've been looking for you. I can only assume that you're here because you're desperate or Taylor's in trouble."

"A little of both," he snickers. "But seriously, I want to help solve the defense AI haywire problem."

"No, absolutely not." Matt shuts down the idea. "We've got this one, and it's out of your area of expertise."

"Maybe, maybe not," Jester nods. "What if I told you I know about your NC3 system ghost alert and the sub power plant issues, and like, how to stop them?"

Matt raises an eyebrow. "I'd say that you are breaking the law, and I can no longer protect you if they catch you inside our network."

"Then what if I told you Yuri Yankovic slithered into Israel to abduct your favorite con man-in-chief, the Putin poodle, the Moscow mascot?" Jester pushes one step further, his own chronic habit.

While he and the director chat, his phone and the director's phone are doing a silent dance to see which tech can out-hack the other. Jester has the advantage in that his phone uses unbreakable quantum encryption and doesn't connect to a network of secret stuff. Even if the director hacks him, he won't find anything useful.

Matt's stone face remains impenetrable. "Are we done here?" he prompts impatiently, without answering the question. He may suspect the hack. Jester needs to stall him.

"Oh, you want top-shelf? OK, OK, what if I told you I figured out Putin's endgame? Inside out. That's it. He wants to corrupt and defeat us from the inside out. Putin used the SolarWinds and five other software update hacks to establish a network of personas or data sources in order to poison AI data— all of it. And then, like, he's using agents inside the tech industry H1 visa workforce to feed the bad data so it will look clean. The bad data will create a series of untraceable mishaps." Jester lays out his theory. Matt doesn't respond, but still listens.

Jester continues. "Then, dig it, dig it, he's like using the old Epstein videos to squeeze the nuggets of key lawwankers to cut cyber budgets, stall investigations. The next big one will bring us down from the inside. You need to let me in."

Matt frowns while he plays with a fork. "I would like to see the details behind your analysis, but I can't, and I won't let you in."

"Ah come on, does this mean we're breaking up," Jester jokes, more curious than ever about what Matt could be hiding. For years, his uncle treated him like a confidential informant, even while he was at the CIA. Jester often follows an intellectual thread ignored by others.

"I realize that your chronic curiosity often gets the better of you. You've been that way since you were a small boy." Matt gets up to leave but stops next to Jester. "I'll have CISA validate your theory. Oh, you should know that your father contacted me a few months ago, wondering if I'd heard from you. Your mother, my poor sister, would never want the rift that has developed between you two since her death. I know he's a self-righteous a-hole, but consider honoring your mother, Jason, and give the man a call. If you still believe as your mother taught you, and I think you do, then you need to forgive him."

Jester wasn't expecting that turn of the conversation. It catches him off guard. Matt is right about his gracious mom and his a-hole dad, but it's not something he can deal with now. "Yeah, sure, OK," he replies as the aging spy master slips away.

After Matt leaves, Jester enters the private men's room to find an empty stall. His friends will be gone by the time he exits. Jester yanks off the mask, coat, and tie, then shoves them into a trash bag he pulls from his pocket. A skin tone turtleneck unravels to cover over his neck tats. A hair net with a wig tucked into his pants now covers over his shaved head and earrings. Then Jester dons a dirty apron hidden in the stall to look like a busboy. From a shirt pocket, he puts on the thick-rimmed WITNESS lenses and taps the frame. An iris scan confirms his identity.

"WITNESS, identify any federal radio signals in my vicinity."

"The History of Josephus in the original Latin." WITNESS replies. Another random response entangled with something else. Jester has no choice but to take his chances.

"Never mind, Einstein."

Jester exits the men's room to enter the kitchen, where he grabs another waste bag. Outside the rear exit, he dumps the trash. At the end of the alley, a UPS van waits, driven by his friends. A quick check confirms he hacked Matt's phone. Good, now the fun starts. Jester needs to pull the data apart and let his AI analytics do some magic. The only way to stop the poison data will be to find the hidden network of Russian digital pharmacists.

While the entire exchange with his Uncle Matt was interesting, his acknowledgment that CISA will investigate the data poisoning theory means they have no clue how to solve the problem. To be fair, it would take a powerful quantum computer to make sense of the zettabytes of data to reach a definitive conclusion. Too bad his quantum AI has an attention deficit.

CHAPTER 38:
IN PLAIN SIGHT

Israeli Supreme Court, Tel Aviv
Two Days Before Temple Ceremony

In all of Israel, there is only one temple of Freemason's power hidden in plain sight: the Israeli Supreme Court in the heart of Tel Aviv, directly across from the Knesset. Derek checks his WITNESS lens for cameras. He finds ten. Still surprised that Yehuda pursued finding a judge, the action may hint at the rabbi's desperation over protecting the ark.

The modern *Sefer HaBahir* is a common book of wisdom related to the Torah and read by tens of millions. Derek first learned about the *Sefer HaBahir* many years ago from the stolen sacred archives; an early and foolish college-age hack before he knew what he had stolen, who he had stolen from, or the deadly consequences that would follow. The title literally means Secrets of Illumination. All great, except that Derek bluffed with Yehuda. He doesn't know if the *Sefer HaBahir* will hold an answer to the ambition of the *Concilium*, only that SLVIA mentioned the book to Olavo. He's playing a gut hunch.

By the tenth century, the region of Narbonne, France, had become an enclave of Jewish and mystic Kabbalism. The *Sefer HaBahir* is one of the oldest and most important of all Kabbalistic texts, quoted in virtually every other major mystic work and the *Zohar*. Although the published version is fairly short, at roughly twelve thousand words, the original version Derek found in the digital archives was much larger. At some point, someone extracted secret knowledge before they published it. It also means the scanned version came from an original that must still exist. Derek believes Jacob Rothschild returned the original *Sefer HaBahir* to hide in plain sight at the highest level of the library. Derek's grasping at vapor, trying to explain the bizarre Olavo message.

From behind him, he senses someone approaching. Derek turns to find Yehuda and a disturbing surprise: a corrupt judge, an old acquaintance.

"Well, thank God," Derek greets, covering over his concern. "You found a judge who knows how to drink a decent bottle of wine. Oren Tzur, shalom, my old friend." Derek walks up to hug the short, skinny man with white hair and wire glasses. Oren may be corrupt, but he's still a friend.

"Derek Taylor, *aleikhem shalom*. After all these years," Oren responds, returning the hug with a pat. "Yehuda, this is the man I told you about years ago," Oren explains. "The one who stopped the false extortion against me."

Yehuda studies Derek for a long moment, perhaps connecting to his own extortion experience and a faceless man named flapjack. "Yes, and now Mossad hunts him." Yehuda looks around nervously, pushing them away from the cameras toward some trees.

Oren turns back to Derek with a serious look. "Do you believe me now?"

"Oren, I believed you before, but I never had a reason to push my luck," he replies.

Oren turns to Yehuda. "Mr. Taylor has an astounding grasp of the godless ideology that has spread through our nation; in fact, the world." Then he turns back to Derek. "Mr. Taylor, behold the Illuminati Temple in Israel, what some have called the Synagogue of Satan."

Derek remembers the SLVIA once using that term. *I know the blasphemy of them which say they are Jews, and are not, but are the synagogue of Satan.* Oren was always boldly outspoken. Yehuda scrunches his thick eyebrows, obviously uncomfortable with the description.

Indeed, Jacob Rothschild controlled the funding, choices of land, architect, and design to build the Supreme Court and the Knesset Building. Rothschild chose the Supreme Court as a living showcase to Freemason symbolism. Nearly every aspect of the one-of-a-kind design speaks to the powerful cult. From the main entrance, the guest first encounters thirty steps that lead up into an illuminating light. At the top of the steps, the visitor views a thirty-three-level pyramid featuring an all-seeing eye. Beyond the pyramid, a garden leads to an Egyptian obelisk and an inverted cross meant to be walked on. Inside, there is a staircase shaped like a vulva with a phallic pole in the middle, and a dozen other symbols expertly designed into the architecture. Hidden in plain sight.

The feature that intrigues Derek the most is the three-story library to represent the top three levels of Freemason illumination. The first level is open to lawyers, while they restrict the second level to active judges. A librarian reserves the third level for ex-judges, grand masters, and thirty-three-degree masons; a secret society hiding in plain sight.

"So why are we here?" Oren asks. "You mentioned something about the library. Why? What do you seek?" Oren both knows and despises European influence over Israel.

"I'm looking for the original uncut version of the *Sefer HaBahir*," Derek explains.

Oren's face turns pale as the blood rushes away, and his eyes dart between Yehuda and Derek. "Are you joking? Why call such trouble on us? There is nothing in that book you need to know." Oren breathes through his flaring nostrils, clearly upset.

Yehuda holds his hand up to Derek, signaling him to be silent. "Oren, please trust me, old friend. What we seek, we seek for the true Israel."

Oren frowns and shakes his head, unconvinced. "Why the *HaBahir*?"

"The uncut *Sefer HaBahir* will explain why the Freemasons have searched for the Ark of Testimony since the Crusades. You simply need to find the book and look up the section related to the ark. Take a photo with your phone," Derek explains. "It may affect the current peace negotiations."

Oren studies him for a long moment, possibly wondering how a Kabbalah book of wisdom could impact peace. "We have no power to stop the Knesset—none. This will only raise questions."

"To do nothing would be a betrayal to our nation and Elohim," Yehuda counters.

Oren rubs his forehead and groans. "I will do this to repay a debt, but you are making a grave mistake. I advise you to leave Israel at once and never call me again. We are done."

"Exactly what I plan to do," Derek assures him. "Once you've learned why the *Concilium* wants the ark so much that they wrote the Balfour Declaration, muscled the UN to reestablish a Jewish homeland, and then built a temple to house their secrets, meet with Yehuda," he instructs. "As you said, I need to disappear, and this isn't my fight. I'm more of an unpaid consultant."

Derek lies. The more he considers it, the more he's convinced that SLVIA wants him to prevent the *Tredecim* from obtaining the ark. If correct, that leads him to an entirely new set of questions, like how did the AI stitch this scenario together? Or has his imagination run away with him? Derek can't be sure anymore. Instead of looking to shut down the Kremlin cyber machine, Derek chases myths and mystics. He's lost his sense of real.

Oren and Yehuda switch over to Hebrew to continue their argument. Left out of the private conversation, Derek taps on WITNESS to check for messages, hoping to have a good word from Nelson. Instead, his heart speeds up; a text from Jack.

Urgent. King David 306.

Something happened to Jenn.

CHAPTER 39: STRATEGY AI

Innovation Unit, Washington, DC
Two Days Before Temple Ceremony

The hack into Jester's phone failed, but Matt finds his nephew's insights into Putin's endgame intriguing. Rather than trust the brilliant but unreliable savant, he asked CISA Director Jamie Spencer to meet with Major Barry Lufkin, Senior Engineer for the Department of Defense Innovation Unit.

"Major Lufkin, good to see you again," Matt greets. He became familiar with the top-secret program while he was secretary of defense in a prior administration.

"Director Adelson, Director Spencer," greets Lufkin. "Welcome to our little slice of the future."

"This is the first that I've heard of SAAI," Jamie replies, his eyes wide with wonder at the wall monitor displays of various battlefields from around the globe.

"That's because this system doesn't exist, and you were never here," Matt reminds him of the security clearance to loop Jamie in.

"The IU runs the US Strategic Analysis AI platform. Our job is to develop complex strategy and policy recommendations in real-time. Designed to process intelligence from thousands of field sensors, weapon systems, ships, drones, satellites, and other sources, SAAI can infer enemy strategies that connect beyond individual battle movements. SAAI gave us the insights into the Ukraine invasion months ahead of time."

Matt has a deep familiarity with the concept. DARPA based early components of SAAI on the SLVIA algorithms developed by Dr. Nelson Garrett decades ago. Matt was the primary sponsor for the SLVIA program when he was a director at the CIA.

Matt takes a deep breath. "Let me explain why I've called you both together. I need to test a theory on the Kremlin cyber endgame. Until now, we've responded to individual provocations. Crimea, Syria, Ukraine, hypersonic missiles, misinformation or ransomware. Since Ukraine, Putin has threatened a new level of retaliation. While nukes remain on the table, I believe Putin will use cyber first. We know the SolarWinds hack revealed a new strategy to work from the inside out. I would like your teams to work together to integrate military with cyber, misinformation, and kompromat—the full strategic spectrum."

"What prompted this inquiry?" Major Lufkin asks.

"We're experiencing an increase in AI platform malfunctions, which some have written off as bad algorithms. I'm not convinced. I want to know if those incidents reflect data poisoning. Can we trace that data poisoning to the SolarWinds or other software hacks?" Matt questions. "If so, what are the objectives, who's behind it, and how do we stop it?"

Jamie nods his head. "Data poisoning is a plausible theory, but to date, no one can prove it, or define a scalable process to detect, or purge the bad data. We can only speculate poisoning to explain AI malfunctions, but the problem could just as well be an error in the algorithm, or an AI learning curve."

Lufkin and Matt exchange a brief glance before Matt explains. "An ex-CIA analyst whom I respect believes that Putin uses an army of H1 visa holders inside the tech industry to feed the bad data. He speculates the hacks established false personas or data sources for intentional data poisoning. That's a theory. I need you to prove or disprove it."

Major Lufkin nods. "If true, then poisoned data could create a series of seemingly unrelated and untraceable sabotage."

"Exactly. Gentlemen, I need you to reconfigure the SAAI platform to look beyond heavy weapon systems to include attacks on national and corporate cyber networks, ransomware, software hacks, and even misinformation. For bonus points, I want to see if there is a kompromat component to the strategy. My office will forward a log of every Congressional vote on every bill that affected cyber, or AI programs, or every Treasury or DOJ refusal to prosecute a major hack, or Russian oligarch. If there is a link, I need you to find it."

Jamie whistles while Major Lufkin opens his eyes wide. Matt knows he won't get everything he wants, and he certainly won't get it within days. But he's desperate for an AI who can locate the core of the kompromat that he already knows must exist.

Jason may have connected a key dot. The law firm that represented Jeffrey Epstein also represents the Russian Alpha Bank, and a handful of Russian oligarchs, including a partner to Epstein named Yuri Yankovic. That same firm has lawyers spread throughout Congress, the DOJ, and the Treasury. Kirkland Otis.

If Jester's theory proves correct, the cancer of Putin's influence may have already metastasized.

CHAPTER 40:
NO OPTIONS

King David Hotel, Jerusalem
One Day Before Temple Ceremony

Disguised as a Hasidic Jew with WITNESS glasses to fool hotel cameras, Derek knocks on room 306. Jack opens with crinkled brows and a deep frown, looks both ways down the hall before closing and bolting the door.

"Yo, Goldblum, what took you so long," Jack snaps, mocking the costume.

Derek ignores the comment. "What happened?"

Jack spins a tablet on the desk to press play. The browser shows a streaming video of Jenn, alive but bound at the wrists and ankles, looking heavily drugged, her head hanging to one side, drool dripping on her cocktail dress. Barefoot, on a dirt floor, leaning against a stone wall, a handwritten sign sits on her lap.

Flapjack. Midnight. Alone.

"I came to pick her up this morning. When she didn't answer, I used the spare key we exchanged for emergencies," Jack explains. "Her tablet streamed the video."

Derek taps his glasses. "WITNESS, access the King David Hotel, show me the past twelve hours of security video for the third floor."

While WITNESS finds the video, he turns to Jack. "Midnight where?"

"Zoom in on the sign."

Derek zooms in on a logo in the corner. "Masada. Isn't that the hill fortress where the Jewish rebels committed suicide rather than give in to the Romans?"

"Yeah, not a good omen. The site is closed for preservation work," Jack says.

"He's after me." Derek confesses another reason he and Jenn can't have a relationship.

"Yeah, I get that, Sherlock, but the question is who, and why?"

"Jester pegged him as an ICC investigator named McGregor connected to the Solar Temple. I can only guess on the why. Either way, he knows I care about Jenn."

Derek tries to think of anyone who would know that information outside of his closest friends. Only a single name comes to mind: Praeceptor. Last year, when the previous Praeceptor cornered him in Sweden, the old man seemed amused that he had developed feelings for the attractive Navy Lieutenant. A new, unknown Praeceptor took over several months ago when the old one passed away. The thought that Jenn may be the second woman sacrificed for the stolen archives churns bitterly in his stomach. He can't let that happen.

"With the peace ceremony tomorrow, Shin Bet will focus on Jerusalem," Jack says.

"Security system accessed," says WITNESS at the same instant Derek's phone pings with the video link. He fast-forwards until he sees someone enter Jenn's door with minimal effort. The intruder wears a hoody, making it impossible to identify him.

"Is that her new boyfriend?" Derek asks, hearing the jealousy in his own voice before he thinks of the killer in Tomar.

"No, too short. I'm guessing that's your ICC guy."

The video forwards to where Jenn and another guy, a huge hunk, approach the door, laughing. Jenn fumbles to get her card key inserted. She's drunk. Her intentions seem obvious. Jealousy pricks at his heart, with no reason he can justify. They never had a relationship.

"That's Rhodes," Jack clarifies the obvious.

"Where was he when McGregor took Jenn?" Derek questions, wishing he could get a peek inside the room. Derek turns to Jack. "OK, for real dude, why is Jenn here?"

He stares Jack down until the pilot grimaces. "I'm not supposed to tell, but I can see from the look on your face you don't give a fart. OK, fine. Adam Scott died of Novichok poisoning after he learned FPOTUS knew of the INVISID backdoor. She came here on a lame scheme to confront the FPOTUS and only hooked up with Rhodes to get an inside angle." Jack inhales deeply. "There I said it."

Derek can tell Jack tells the truth, and it helps, a little, especially knowing that Jenn and Rhodes were not dating. "Thanks. Was that so hard?"

"Yes," Jack retorts.

On the video, Geoff storms out of the room with a huge welt on his forehead and stomps down the hall toward the elevator.

"What happened to the other guy?" Jack questions.

"Who gave Rhodes the welt?" Derek bites down, eyes burning into the screen. A few moments later, the stranger exits with Jenn under his arm like a drunk girlfriend and takes the opposite direction toward the stairs.

"Do you think the hulk was in on the kidnap?" Jack ponders.

Derek thinks a moment, admitting to himself that he wants to pin Rhodes. Washed out of the Navy, a decade in the Secret Service, something in his gut tells him that Rhodes is more muscle than a mastermind. The other guy was obviously hiding ahead of time. The welt on his forehead could have been the handiwork of Jenn, or not. "Let's not rule it out."

"If we go to the police, this guy will kill her." Jack points out the obvious.

"Which is why we need to take care of this ourselves," he mumbles, thinking through how. "Do you still have my toy box on the jet?" Derek refers to a collection of high-end gadgets, devices, advanced tech, and extreme sports gear.

Jack snickers. "You mean those storage containers that take up half of the luggage area, next to that expensive server rack, taking up most of the other half? Yeah, why?"

"Not sure yet." A rough plan forms in his head—vague, missing details, and maybe even impossible. Either way, Derek just can't think of a plan to save Jenn with less than three men, and there's no way he'll risk Mordechai or the others.

"Do you know how to reach Jenn's new boyfriend?"

"Rhodes?" Jack gives him a hard glare. "Sure, but I don't think that's a good idea."

"Probably not. Desperate times." If Rhodes was in on the snatch, then he could be a serious security leak for any rescue. It's a risk Derek needs to take.

Ten minutes later, Geoff Rhodes stands in Jenn's room, looking hungover with a dark bruise on his forehead, to endure some awkward introductions. When they show him the video, Rhodes' face turns pale, shocked. Not the sign of a man involved.

"Do you know how that guy got into her room?" he asks Geoff.

"No, but I also don't know how a fugitive hacker got into her room," Geoff retorts.

"Me, jack-wang," Jack says. "Jenn and I exchanged key cards. I let him in."

Derek doesn't let up. "And why did you leave so upset? What happened to your forehead? Did you know this guy was in the room when you left?"

Geoff turns his eyes away, stalls for an answer. "We had a disagreement, and no, I had no clue that guy was in here."

He avoided the question about how he got the welt. Derek wants to ask if it was just a disagreement but chokes down his jealousy.

"Why don't we call the police?" Geoff says. "They have tactics to handle these kinds of situations."

"Yeah, and this guy knows those tactics by heart," he responds. "If we send in the YAMAM, or Shin Bet, we risk Jenn's life. We do this my way, or you can walk away now."

YAMAM is the Israeli version of SWAT, otherwise known as the National Counter Terrorism Unit. Geoff glares at him for several moments with eyebrows scrunched together like he is thinking really hard, and it hurts.

"I won't agree to anything until I hear your lamebrain scheme. And just for the record, as soon as Jennifer is safe, I will do everything in my power to put you behind bars," Geoff says. "Jennifer didn't have the balls to arrest you, but I don't give a rat's ass."

Derek searches the eyes of the prep-school jock, entitled grandson of a Senator, and sees that he's telling the truth. Growing up in foster homes until he ran away at age thirteen, Derek spent his entire youth moving from school to school to school with constant threats from entitled bullies like Geoff. This is not about his pride or his freedom; this is about saving Jenn in time to help Yehuda. It will be a long day.

"Nice to know we're on the same side," Derek snips. "Here's what I had in mind."

For the next five minutes, Derek walks through the rough idea. Jack should be able to buy the pricey gear not already in his toy box. The plan certainly contains a lot of risk, but given the extreme location and short time frame to plan, it's the best he can do. Derek waits for a reaction, and it doesn't take long.

"You're insane," shouts Geoff, spinning off to throw up his hands and then turning back.

"He gets that a lot," deadpans Jack with a raised eyebrow. "Not saying I disagree, but to be fair, this is not his worst idea."

Geoff ignores Jack. "Geez man, do you even own a gun? Do you expect this guy will just give Jennifer up without shooting at us?"

Derek won't use a gun. Hates them. Flashbacks of a gun barrel pressed to his forehead as a child with a drunk man asking him if he wanted to play Russian roulette have haunted his dreams with cloudy amnesia for decades.

"Don't worry, G-man, I'll have a weapon," Jack counters. "But seriously, you're Secret Service, aren't you a sharpshooter or something?"

Geoff steps over that challenge as well, moving to his next objection. "It's too complex; it'll never work."

"OK, Patton, what's your plan?" Derek challenges. "No police."

Geoff lowers his eyes and turns to the window for a long, tongue-tied pause. "I don't have one."

"Desperate times." Derek takes a sheet of hotel paper to write out a central timeline, and then makes a second copy before he takes a photo with his phone. He hands the two sheets to Geoff and Jack.

"No calls except on the encrypted satellite radio you'll get from Jack," he says. "Be in position on time. Remember, we only get one shot, and losing Jenn is not an option."

Derek watches Geoff carefully until the jock reluctantly nods. Normally, Derek would dismiss the lack of enthusiasm as a government agent's ego, but something feels wrong. A gut instinct. He can't pinpoint what bothers him, and that really bothers him. Not a good omen, but he has no other option.

CHAPTER 41:
WHAT ARE THE ODDS

Ben Gurion Airport Private Hangers, Tel Aviv
One Day Before Temple Ceremony

Bertrand Russell once said, *I do not pretend to be able to prove that there is no God. I equally cannot prove that Satan is a fiction.* Nelson loves to engage in intellectual conversations or debates over a wide range of philosophical issues from history and literature to general sciences, machine learning, singularity, or topics where he feels an intellectual superiority. Even politics and economics are welcome. However, the local obsession with the temple and prophecy feels like ants crawling on his psychological skin.

Wedged inside the luggage hold of the Tote Charter Gulfstream V, crammed together with storage bins and high-end server racks, Nelson monitors the satellite download. Ten petabytes of data transfers from the university server through an encrypted satellite channel transmission that bypasses standard internet protocols and security. Matan stayed at the university to monitor uploads to the satellite and complete an important favor for Taylor.

"You realize, Dr. Garrett, the nature of faith is belief in a truth that the eye cannot see." Mordechai chats with him while he works. Left behind by Taylor, the monk was interested to see a private jet. Regrettably, Nelson brought him along. "Some of us seek a spiritual truth, which is neither a religious truth nor a scientific truth, but yet still a truth. Have you ever believed in something that your eye can't see?"

Nelson's not an atheist, per se, more of a pragmatist in need of compelling evidence. Yet, the past few days have Nelson questioning much of what he once considered true. Still wrestling with the loss of poor Salem, and revelations of his father's conspiracies, such pressure on a personal matter pushes Nelson to the limits of his shallow emotional reserve. He falls back on his manners to engage but avoids any true transparency.

"I can't say that I have. I will say the field of theoretical physics contains phenomena we can't observe directly. In particular, string theory postulates the existence of a multiverse. While a multiple universe scenario might explain attributes often attributed to the realm of the spirit, without empirical evidence, I am neither a convert to string theory nor to religion."

Nelson turns on his phone speaker, which connects to Matan. "Matan, the download speed has improved. How much longer?" Nelson changes the subject, uncomfortable with the monk's evangelism.

"Looks like another hour," Matan replies. "May I ask you a question?"

"Of course," Nelson replies, anything will be better than this religious interrogation.

"What I think the monk wants to know is how a man who rejects God could create such a divine wisdom as Sister Sylvia?" Matan asks. "I'm not a fan, but I hear good things."

Buggers. Ambushed by both men. Nelson considers the question for a moment. "I'm not sure what to tell you, Professor Rubin. I designed SLVIA to be a versatile espionage program, able to access any network, and move about in stealth. Its algorithms analyze and synthesize information using complex linguistics and nonlinear regression."

"Fascinating," Matan replies, clearly intrigued. "Although a little frightening. I can understand why so many nations would kill to possess such a program."

"Yes, I suppose so," Nelson admits, never thinking in those terms when he created his masterpiece. Another reason not to repeat the mistake.

Nelson would never want to offend either of these men, but the idea of his espionage AI as having spiritual insight sounds ludicrous. An individual AI cannot be good or evil, benevolent, or malicious, which is all sci-fi Hollywood poppycock. An AI has no emotion, does not need to harm or to control others, unless designed or trained to do so, such as AI used within weapons.

"Sister Sylvia used to say that the most important reason to understand prophecy was to realign human priorities to care for others during the coming tribulation," says Mordechai. "Someone taught the machine to care."

Nelson raises an eyebrow. He immediately thinks of Taylor, the man who secretly worked directly with the SLVIA for two decades. Taylor has always been an enigma. A brilliant, inspired, driven, sardonic, yet broken, narcissist. A genius, compassionate survivor.

"Tell me, Dr. Garrett, as a scientist, what are the statistical probabilities we would discover the true ark after nearly 2600 years at the same time the children of Israel have assembled into a nation after nearly 2000 years, only days before Israel forms an alliance to bring a third temple just as the prophets foretold?" Matan questions. "I am a secular pragmatist, and yet, the past few days have me wondering."

"Sister Sylvia also spoke of the probabilities we could fulfill hundreds of prophecies since 1948. Prophecies on Israel, technology, world alliances, environment, moral culture, space, and more," adds Mordechai. "All completed. What are the odds?"

Nelson can't calculate such a probability without valid data, but intuitively it must be quite low. He gets the sense that these men already believe in an answer absent the analysis.

"You don't need to answer, Dr. Nelson. A rhetorical question. I'm merely suggesting that while Mordechai may not prove to you that prophecies are in play, neither can you prove they are not in play."

Nelson stops for a moment to consider the statement. He can't refute the clear statistical anomalies. But that's where it ends. Nelson sees the world in black and white, or rather, proven mathematical theorems. Yet, a deep part of him wonders if he has blinded himself to a meaningful aspect of life itself, just as he was blind to the suffering in Africa and Yemen.

"I can't explain the unusual probabilities or the interesting case made by the SLVIA. I suppose that only time will tell," Nelson admits. "Yet, I am sure the Almighty has standards, and perhaps I am simply not meant to see or believe."

Somehow, the knowledge of his family's history of corruption adds to the shame of his own moral transgressions in developing weapons to suggest in his mind a DNA of an ambivalent agnosticism, if not evil. Logically, that makes no sense, but Nelson doesn't have a better answer.

"All men carry regrets, Dr. Garrett," Mordechai agrees. "The aftermath of our youth, our zeal, our ignorance, and our pride. Prophecies warn that the end-time church itself will be apostate, fragmented, and full of false beliefs and false teachers. Courts determine a man's innocence or guilt, but imperfectly. Only God can forgive who we are in secret, because only God can see our secrets."

Forgiveness sounds like a foreign concept to Nelson. His father fiercely enforced the notion that actions have consequences. "I see the world through the clear lens of science and theorems that I can test and either prove or disprove."

What he doesn't discuss are the countless ways he insulated himself from the moral consequences of his work. Layers of bureaucracy or field command separated the design of his AI technologies from the bodies on the field. He has numbed his conscience.

The phone line goes silent for a long moment. "No one can find what they do not seek," Matan replies with a gentle voice.

"Perhaps you learned to value only what others taught you to value," adds Mordechai.

Precisely. Nelson's father never valued humanity over success, and Nelson never taught the SLVIA. How can the creation be moral if the creator is not? To revive such intelligence may no longer be wise.

CHAPTER 42: LEVERAGE

King David Hotel, Jerusalem
One Day Before Temple Ceremony

Geoff subconsciously holds his breath, waiting for a response from the unexpected visitor. Icy trepidation grips his entire body, and his breathing grows rapid and shallow. Geoff's a loose end that needs to be trimmed. His eyes search the man's hands and pocket exteriors for a weapon. His own gun remains locked in the hotel safe, useless in this situation.

The guest smiles coldly. "Agent Rhodes, you must face your dim reality. Your career with the US government is over. Prison may even await you. I offer you a new chance at life."

When Geoff returned to his hotel room after buying the expensive rescue gear with Jack Tote, he found Yuri Yankovic waiting with the shades drawn. It's never a good day when a Kremlin fixer insists on a private chat. Once someone knows you've committed a felony, they will hold that over you until they completely own you, or you become a liability to eliminate. When the former president lost the last election, Geoff had hoped to never see Yuri again.

Instead, during his most vulnerable hour, the Machiavellian snake slithers into his room.

"I can't help you anymore." Geoff tries to stand firm.

"I'm not asking," replies Yuri with an icy smirk.

"In fact, after losing the FPOTUS, I'll be lucky if I am not fired from the Service or sanctioned into a desk job until I quit," Geoff argues.

Yuri shrugs. "As I said, you have no future. They may even investigate you. What then?" Yankovic pauses, letting the statement sink in. "But I am surprised by your hesitation. Considering your past enthusiasm, I thought you would want to help your president."

Geoff once believed in the former president passionately, voted for him twice, and stepped outside of protocols for him more than once. "What you're asking will send me to jail."

"All you stand to lose at this point will be a corrupt country in a state of decline," Yuri replies.

Yuri's words ring with the sharp bite of both hypocrisy and truth. America's role as a world leader slips. Too weak and timid to stand up directly to Russia or China. Immigrants flood the country and dilute our national purity and strength. Without the former president, Geoff sees little hope of stemming the toxic tide of socialism. No one else has the charisma to restore America to its former world power status. The hypocrisy radiates from the ruined Russian economy. A punishing tactic from a western alliance too timid to fight Putin. Those won't last forever, and Yankovic proves that a select few can still live well, even under sanctions.

"I no longer want to be involved."

Yuri chuckles before getting serious. "What if I offered you a chateau on the Black Sea, in Crimea? A nice place where I once lived myself."

Unlike Ukraine, Crimea saw minor damage in the Russian invasion. Despite his deep American heritage and trust fund, it surprises Geoff even to consider the offer. Yuri has a point: his career at the Secret Service is toast. It could get much worse if they investigate him, although he's sure he covered his tracks. An only child, his influential father, an ex-partner at Kirkland Otis, passed

GUY MORRIS

away years ago. His mother suffers from severe dementia and doesn't recognize him anymore. The welt on his forehead reminds him that sometimes in life, you simply can't go back. If he stays out of trouble, maybe he can become the next Edward Snowden with an exclusive online network interview or a book deal. Secret Service Protects Former President in Exile.

"How would I even accomplish what you want?" Geoff asks a logistics question, still considering the larger question of whether he will agree.

"Mossad will assign you to the former president's security detail for the temple ceremony. Afterward, you will escort the president back to the limo. I will arrange matters from there. Simple, da?"

If he says no, Yuri will not hesitate to ruin him, or eliminate him. If he says yes and doesn't take asylum, he will land in federal prison.

"There's a complicating problem," Geoff replies, already hating himself. "Somebody took Admiral Scott's daughter as hostage to trap a fugitive named Derek Taylor. Scott came to Israel to confront the FPOTUS about a conversation with Putin. She said there was a video. I promised to help with the rescue, hoping to convince her to go home afterward. If I don't show, there could be a problem."

"Interesting," Yuri replies, standing to pace the hotel room. "Some of our best people believe Taylor could be the flapjack, a ghost inside the Kremlin network for years."

Geoff didn't know Taylor was the flapjack. That's certainly new information, and maybe a bargaining chip. Israel will also want to capture the elusive internet ghost.

Yuri studies Geoff for a long, awkward moment. "Go rescue the admiral's daughter. That will make you a hero in Israel and America. I want to meet her. But make sure the hacker does not return. That will make you a hero in Moscow."

Geoff nods without saying yes, still unsure he will agree. The plan assumes Geoff even survives the death wish rescue plan concocted by Taylor. Yuri's interest in Jennifer shudders through his bones. Jenn's a loose end. Geoff reminds himself that they have no future, and he has no choice.

CHAPTER 43:
PRIVATE TOUR

Temple Mount, Jerusalem
One Day Before Temple Ceremony

Derek agreed to meet Yehuda for a private tour of the Temple Mount to discuss Oren's findings. Yehuda walks in short quick strides, his fist clenched, leading them through private security in scowling silence. Once they step onto the platform, away from listening ears, the rabbi opens up.

"Oren betrayed us," Yehuda bemoans in a low voice.

"Let's put a pin on the betrayal thing. Did he find the *Sefer HaBahir*?"

Derek had scanned the *HaBahir* over a decade ago with only a vague recollection of mystic wisdom or secrets on dozens of topics.

"Yes, but the Librarian immediately approached him to ask why he sought the sacred text," Yehuda says. "Oren told him that he wanted wisdom regarding the power of the ark."

"Oh geez, you're kidding me. He actually told him that?" Derek wrings his fist nervously, thinking. "If the Librarian knows, then the Knesset will learn. Did he photo the text?"

"The Librarian would not permit a photo. Oren could only read it, but I'm not sure what to make of his response. He may be lying or forgetting something. Oren said the *HaBahir* provided secret knowledge of a seer name Betzalel, who was a master of the creative arts under King Solomon. They did not make the ark of mere wood and gold, and the Cherubim wings were more than decoration. The *Sefer HaBahir* said that when the Divine presence filled the ark, the Cherubim on top came to life, opening and closing their wings. Then the *HaBahir* provides further secrets and incantations to bring forth the ark's power to destroy."

"Did Oren tell you those secrets?"

Yehuda shakes his head, both of them realizing that Oren, the Librarian, the Knesset, and eventually the *Concilium* will all know more than they do regarding the power of the ark. Secrets that even the Sanhedrin won't know. Derek could read the original scan if he could get to the archives, except he had SLVIA hide them. Still, a picture emerges.

"The *Concilium* will want the ark to get some mystical power they don't even understand, only crave," Derek says

"The Knesset will refuse to give up something so rare," Yehuda says.

Olavo's cryptic message now makes more sense. Somehow, the SLVIA connected the prophecy of a third temple to the ark contained within. Then the AI connected the lost ark to a letter found in the Vatican Archives and the published content of the first copper scroll. SLVIA correctly interpreted the *Sefer HaBahir* regarding who would want to possess the ark and why. The SLVIA warning of a temple may not only warn of war but of the *Concilium* gaining an unknown new power. Or perhaps whoever follows Sabas must heed the warnings of the *HaBahir*. Astonishing. Derek may not understand spiritual teachings, but he's becoming a believer in the SLVIA view of prophecy. The odds are too extreme to be random.

Like much of the Kabbalistic teachings, the whole magic power thing could be nothing more than holistic hype and hokum. Except, the lore over the ark's power has lasted for thousands of years. There could be a grain of truth behind the legends.

"If we find the ark," Yehuda continues. "We will need a safe place where the Sanhedrin can sanctify it for temple worship, then move it inside the tabernacle secretly. Otherwise, I fear the military will demand to experiment with its power."

Derek hadn't thought of that angle before, but Yehuda could be right.

Yehuda looks around and inhales deeply. "Mr. Taylor, you are witnessing history," he explains in a soft, reverent voice. "You and I are walking on the same stones as Solomon and Herod, following in the prophetic footsteps of Daniel and Ezekiel."

Derek hadn't thought of that angle either. The burden feels heavy. Rather than anything inspirational, he sees a media circus getting ready for show time. At the other end of the platform, near the Aqsa Mosque, Islamic workers set up concert-style speakers and large screens. International camera crews stake positions in front of a podium for the best view.

Derek and Yehuda walk past the world-famous Dome of the Rock toward a small copula with a dark patina that stands over a pockmarked stone. The priests ignore Yehuda as they erect the tent around them and over the copula.

"Unlike many of my colleagues, I do not believe that the Muslim Dome sits atop the holy of holies. We know from the Torah that the Temple faced the Golden Gate and the Mount of Olives. The altar sat offset to the right, precisely where the Dome of the Rock sits today. The holy of holies was located toward the western wall on a place of the original threshing floor purchased by King David."

Yehuda points to the pockmarked stone under the copula. "The only place of the original threshing floor on the entire platform." Yehuda nearly tears up from emotion. "You are in the presence of the bedrock stone upon which sat the Ark of Testimony. Here is where we negotiated our tabernacle and here is where the Ark of Testimony must return."

The rabbi stares at the spot and sighs. "I can only pray that your outlandish scheme will keep the ark safe."

Derek smirks to one side, thinking of how crazy the plan sounds even to his own mind. "To be fair, you didn't have to agree." He didn't expect they would.

Yehuda turns to study Derek's eyes. "Why would you, an agnostic man on the run from the law, risk so much to protect the Ark for the Jews?"

Good question, and perhaps the reason Yehuda wanted to talk with him alone, but he's not entirely sure himself. It's personal, and Derek hates answering personal questions. Foster kids don't grow up to be men of faith like Yehuda. With no sense of trust, legacy, or heritage, it often leads to difficulty connecting to anything at all. The world becomes a transaction filled with envy of the community experienced by others. His normal reflex would be to respond with a flippant comment to cover up his deep fear of being revealed, even a little. Yet Yehuda's question demands an honest answer. After a moment of thought, and a deep exhale, he looks into Yehuda's eyes.

"You have something more precious than money can buy, and I have a lot of money," Derek confesses. "My life has been the proverbial moss on a rolling stone, hiding and running from a destiny that terrifies me, and searching for a truth that I'm not sure I'll recognize when I find it. But you, and Loir, and Mordechai, all of you have a faith rooted in thousands of years of tradition and spiritual truths. It grounds you, and it overwhelms me. I plan to leave Israel tonight, but I would never forgive myself if I didn't do the right thing when it was right in front of me. Call it karma, or good will, or payback for still being alive, but someday I trust the universe will return the favor. I'm pretty sure I'll need it."

Derek immediately regrets revealing so much to a stranger, but somehow senses there could be no better place or time. Yehuda stares at Derek for a long, awkward moment when a voice interrupts from the earbud Bluetooth connected to his glasses frame.

"Dude, it's Jester. WITNESS is having another think blink. Shin Bet spotted you on the Temple Mount. Like, vaporize or something."

Derek's eyes dart to the security camera box in his lenses. A half a dozen soldiers move onto the Mount from the southern entrance and head in his direction. WITNESS missed it.

Derek turns to Yehuda with anxiety-tightening his voice. "I need to disappear, fast."

Yehuda doesn't ask why, simply nods. "This way." The rabbi borrows the shawl of another rabbi, whispering something into his ear. That priest relays the information to a dozen others in Hebrew as Yehuda throws the shawl over Derek's shoulders, and then places a spare yarmulke on Derek's head. "Bow your head and pray," Yehuda instructs.

After slipping through the unsecured back of the tent, Yehuda and other Sanhedrin quickly surround him, praying and singing as they lead him off the Mount. A dozen IDF soldiers race past them, searching for the American. The group of priests exit through the Gate of Darkness on the north, where Derek and Yehuda turn into the Muslim Quarter to hide in Zedekiah's Cave. By the time they pull around a van for his escape, Derek runs late for his ordeal at Masada, fearful his delay will prove deadly.

CHAPTER 44: HADES

Maison Godin Prison, North of Quebec
One Day Before Temple Ceremony

Jester enters the Maison Godin castle prison from the covered employee parking through the waste management building into a locked utility room behind a set of enormous modern commercial heat-pumps toward a door with a twin keypad lock that opens to an elevator. Jester flashes his wrist-based RFID to activate the elevator and then presses basement level 10.

With the help of a SNO ally deep inside the Canadian government, Taylor bought an abandoned woman's prison north of Quebec under the condition that he restore the building for tourism. It gave the team a perfect chance to gut the old basement infrastructure and build out the ultra-modern, super-secretive subterranean Cray mainframe and quantum D-WAVE data centers. An extremely expensive process that required special concrete and other materials to keep the quantum D-WAVE at absolute zero and noise-free. Taylor funded the venture by hacking the cryptocurrency accounts of Cozy Bear and other Russian hackers who run ransomware on American companies. SNO siphons off Putin's personal cyberwar chest, tapping and hacking the oligarchs. A typical flapjack scheme of "hack back the hackers."

Jittery from the experience of hacking the director of National Intelligence, Jester can't help but wonder if Uncle Matt let him think he was getting away with something. Jester bounces on his toes so much that it jingles his silver wristbands against his analog Nirvana watch. His phone captured a ton of files, which used an older version of encryption Jester already knows how to crack because he wrote it for the CIA. There may be intelligence gold on that phone or a booby trap, a trojan app designed to locate his base.

Entering a secure floor, Jester calls to the data center assistant AI through the mics and cameras hidden in the ceiling. "NIGEL. Set up a HADES network. Display on monitor ten. Isolate the network. No connections, none. Install full suite protection and diagnostics."

Jester does a Fred Astaire slide across the floor. "OK, separate task. Create a timeline of each federal or commercial AI failure for the past three years. Map failures to known software update hacks. Cross-reference to all known H1 visa holders from Russia, Iran, and China. Cross-reference to known cryptocurrency accounts per each visa holder. Send a data map to WITNESS, and send the timeline to the monitor."

Jester spins like a ballroom dancer, then proceeds to the control room.

"WITNESS, read the timeline and data files developed by NIGEL. Search for trends and anomalies. Discover all entangled threads to any other events or people."

Maybe Jester's been thinking of the problem wrong. Maybe quantum entanglement can be an asset. Jester envisions a group of particles that act as one even from great distances. Maybe they've been asking WITNESS to solve the wrong kinds of problems, tactical ones, linear ones. Maybe WITNESS will do better with the obscure connectivity of the AI sabotage spread across a zettabyte of data.

"Of course, Jester," WITNESS replies. "But this may take some time."

Jester crosses his finger. WITNESS may simply abandon the task or come back with a bio of the cast of *The Fast and the Furious*. While both NIGEL and

203

WITNESS are busy, he turns his mental attention to the HADES site.

Developed at the NSA lab at Sandia, the same lab where Dr. Garrett developed SLVIA, *High-Fidelity Adaptive Deception & Emulation System,* or HADES, creates a dead-end, highly adaptive, easily monitored, false network that looks and functions like a real one, designed to lure and trap malicious code or hackers. Jester finds it hilariously ironic that he had to hack into Sandia while at the CIA to steal a copy.

If Matt embedded a sniffer on his phone, Jester needs to isolate any malicious code before opening the files. His uncle has been in the spy game for decades and knows how to pull all that double-blind bluff stuff, or whatever. The dude is sneaky. And all that family talk about his mom and dad was nothing but a mind game to get him to lower his defenses.

Jester plugs his phone with the hacked files into the HADES. The program will transfer all the contents, including any spyware, into the HADES network. Then it will wipe clean the phone and rebuild it from a sanitized master backup. Inside the HADES network, the system will isolate and remove malicious code. Only then can he review the files he got from Adelson.

An app on Matt's phone instantly attempts to inventory the host network and locate an active IP address, which NSA can use to find his data center site. Just as he expected, but since the code is now isolated, it's harmless.

"OK, boomer," Jester says with a smirk, thinking of his old school uncle. You can always trust the guys who write the rule books to follow the rules.

Two of his tech assistants approach him, likely with routine updates or questions, but Jester holds up his palm without looking. "If it's not nuclear, then I'm like in a deep loop, man," he says. "Save it, solve it, or sell it."

Both techies hesitate, share a glance, then pivot to leave. A loop is what Jester calls a mental problem that he has to obsess over, can't deviate from, and feels compelled to solve. Jester must embody the problem in his mind, even down to bits and bytes until he reaches an inflection point, an exit that unlocks the loop and solves the enigma. A loop can sometimes last for hours, or days, or weeks. It may involve months of programming. When Jester was young, his autism would frighten others, even his own parents, who once sent him to a therapist who tried to cast a demon out of him. If they could have only seen the fantastic journeys that he takes in his mind, they would have been envious instead of fearful.

Enormous geometric patterns form in his mind and stretch for miles, lining up events with each other, dots connecting to form kinetic relationships. Each connecting point changes digits in unseen algorithms, the relationship between people and events and systems.

SolarWinds was only the first discovery of a new type of hack through a legitimate software update. Tens of thousands of corporate and federal networks accessed, yet not one company has reported a single stolen file or planted virus. The hackers are not there to take data but to give data—bad data. Sabotage. Data poisoning. He knows the answer intuitively, but must follow the threads to find the army of spiders at the center of each web.

The HADES network finishes the phone cleanse, extending his loop to the files stolen from Matt. There are thousands of files and dozens of links to secure networks, many of them Jester already cracked. He skips those networks to focus on the most recent documents and messages.

An uncontrollable agitation animates his limbs as Jester reads the contents of Matt's phone. There are dozens more AI failures than he knew about—sub incidents, missile tests, air traffic control, lethal carjackings, water treatment plants. Patterns emerge, accelerate, and converge to an ending climax he can't yet envision, or he's afraid to envision.

Jester slowly confirms his worst fear: an entire network of personas operates in plain sight within the US software industry. A beast within the beast, feeding the poisoned data. And the Feds seem clueless to the extent of the infiltration or the identity of the digital sleepers.

If Jester can isolate those accounts, he can unlock the loop. If not, the poison will spread until it creates mishaps and people die.

CHAPTER 45:
LEAP OF FAITH

Dead Sea, Judean Desert
One Day Before Temple Ceremony

After escaping Jerusalem, Derek made his way to a spot in the West Bank overlooking the Dead Sea to perform the almost ritualistic procedure of safety checking his equipment. Every few minutes, he checks the livestream of Jenn. Slumped against an old stone wall, her eyes are closed but twitch, perhaps hallucinating. Dark now, with heavy cloud cover under a moonless sky, the killer keeps a light on Jenn to provide proof of life.

Ironic that a man devoted to the power of technology faces a situation that no AI could help him resolve, not even the SLVIA. Somebody will die tonight. Not his choice, but if he fails, the life lost may be Jenn's. That knowledge alone percolates his angst with an intense, gut-biting acid. The doctors call it complex post-traumatic stress; the result of relentless trauma over a long period until it rewires your brain. No one to trust, and no place is safe. Derek calls it the hell in his head; the demons at his heels; the shadow on his shoulder. A relentless dread or insecurity that he can never let others see.

Jenn's life dangles on a thin thread because of a decades-old hack he never should have done. Derek might as well be the one holding her hostage. A bitter wave of apprehension and self-doubt shudders his shoulders. He closes his eyes to breathe slowly and deeply to center his mind. There are a million things that could go deadly wrong tonight. Maybe he deserves to face McGregor, but Jenn doesn't. It doesn't matter if they can't be friends; he swears to himself that Jenn Scott will go home alive.

Derek refuses to think about the fact that Jenn may go home with Geoff. Something about that guy bothers him beyond the sophomoric threats of backstabbing. He can only hope Geoff cares enough for Jenn to show up without the police, or the entire plan will fail.

Derek checks his power pack level, the Taser strapped to his thigh, the night vision clip for his helmet, and the radio mic and speakers installed inside. Clipped to his belt are the Sherman controls. Clipped to the other side is the bag of small drones. He taps on his WITNESS lens and adjusts the display to provide altitude, wind speed, wind direction, GPS, and infrared.

With several deep breaths to calm his still ragged nerves, Derek flips on the electric high-speed turbo prop strapped to his back. The sound pitches higher as he runs toward the cliff edge overlooking the Dead Sea. At the edge of the cliff, Derek leaps into the dark void. Above him, a custom performance parasail fills with air as the ground falls hundreds of feet below him. With a sharp bank to the south, Derek powers up to gain altitude on his way toward Masada to confront a fanatic assassin. Someone will die tonight.

CHAPTER 46: CITADEL AMBUSH

Masada, Judean Desert
Day of Temple Ceremony

Devlin McGregor studies the honey for his trap to make sure the corrupted Navy Lieutenant remains secure and sedated—but not so much so that she looks dead. He checks her pulse. Her hands zip-tied behind her and eyes dilated, the semiconscious woman remains oblivious to her fate. It's midnight, the hour of sacrifice.

"The carnage will all be over soon, love," he whispers in his thick Scottish brogue. "You should feel honored. Your blood will bring the cleansing."

Propped up against a stone wall of the Byzantine chapel ruins, the beautiful brunette with a pixie haircut makes for an attractive lure. Once Taylor and the woman are dead, he will confirm his success with the Prelate. Certainly, an invitation to the temple ceremony foreshadows acceptance into the highest echelon—the *Brothers of the Ancient Times*.

Devlin can still recall his initiation ceremony. *The master wore an amulet with a blue eye. Devlin kneeled in a candlelit room within a seventeenth-century castle in the Pyrenes Mountains of northern Spain, surrounded by photographs of his family, friends, lovers, and mementos of his career. A hooded monk approached from behind to place a heavy blindfold over his eyes. With a warm hand on his forehead, the master plucked his eyebrows as others joined in a ritualistic chant. Devlin winced at the sting. The acidic smell of smoke, something burning, drifted into his nostrils. When cleansed from his deceptions, the master removed the blindfold. Adjusting to the light, Devlin saw a blank paper so close it consumed his view.*

"Read," the master commanded.

Devlin stalled, unsure of what to say. The page was blank. The Prelate moved a candle behind the paper to make the words appear, their meaning clear. With illumination would come understanding. As he finished reading, the master lifted the paper to reveal that all the photos and memories of his past life had burned. They replaced each with new images of his family, friends, army mates, and former lovers, bloody and dead; each of them sacrificed for the cleansing. That night, he wept for their souls and cursed his own.

Devlin shakes off the memory and returns his attention to the Masada plateau. After the fall of Jerusalem in 70 CE, Israelite zealots took refuge here until the Roman General Titus built a thousand-foot ramp up the western side of the mountain. Roman catapults and archers rained down fiery torment onto the 967 stubborn Israelites for months. When Titus finally broke through the wall, he found every man, woman, and child sacrificed in a mass mutual-murder pact. The Jews chose death over rape by the soldiers or slavery to Rome, leaving Titus with a hollow victory. Devlin vows there will be two more deaths tonight.

Masada towers fourteen hundred feet over the Dead Sea to an eighteen-acre, uneven plateau. Perhaps a thousand meters long and half as wide, with dozens of buildings and ruins. The north end of the plateau comprises Herod's palace, descending three levels down the northern cliff. Overall, the complex boasts hundreds of hiding and ambush locations.

There are only three ways to the top of Masada. The Roman ramp still exists for those robust enough to hike the forty-degree dirt ramp, and then climb thirty feet. An ancient Christian pilgrim trail called the Snake Path zigzags across the lower eastern mountain, opposite the ramp. It requires hours to ascend. The third approach comes from a modern aerial tram over the Snake Path shut off for the night.

For each approach, Devlin set up Belgian-made FN MAG AI machine gun stations. Designed for a lethal form of border patrol, each station uses infrared nightscope scanners with motion detectors and integrated AI that knows the difference between a wandering desert fox and a human. Besides the guns, he installed infrared sensors and explosives along the higher elevations of the Snake Path. If the tram turns on, then a final AI gun station and tear gas wait for him at the tram doorway exit.

Known for his extreme sport stunts, Taylor may attempt a nighttime climb of the palace cliff. If Taylor makes it to the palace, he will need to ascend the stone steps past the ancient cistern. Devlin trip-wired those steps in several places with enough C4 to blow Taylor off the canyon wall. If the rock shrapnel doesn't kill him, the fall will finish the job.

If, by some miracle, the hacker actually makes it to the plateau alive, then two Glocks and an AK-47 wait for him. No clever disguise will save the digital ghost this time.

CHAPTER 47: DISTRACTIONS

Masada, Judean Desert
Day of Temple Ceremony

Geoff resents Taylor for sticking him with the nighttime cliff climb to the palace. They should have gone to the police. In fact, Jennifer wouldn't even be in this mess if it wasn't for Taylor, which almost justifies the order to kill him. With any luck, the kidnapper will shoot Taylor from the sky. Once Geoff saves Jennifer, he'll call Mossad to pick up the international hacker flapjack. Jack will go down as an accomplice. Screw Yuri. Jennifer will regret pushing him away.

Fortunately, the lower section of the northern cliff is an easy climb compared to others he has conquered in the Rockies. The limestone has lots of grab holds and nooks. Unfamiliarity with the rock under a moonless sky makes it a risky ascent even with the halogen head-light and optional night vision goggles. Fortunately, it's less than two hundred feet to the lowest level of Herod's palace. Once he reaches the lower palace level, Geoff can take the cut stone steps past the old cistern to the main plateau. Despite the cool evening air, he works up quite a sweat.

"Rhodes, what's your status?" Taylor's voice squeaks from a Bluetooth earbud attached to the military-grade encrypted radio in his pocket—more of the stash from Taylor's toy box.

"Another thirty feet," Geoff replies. "I'll need time to rest and navigate to the summit."

"Good. Distractions are armed and ready," Taylor says

"Speaking of armed, you should've taken a gun," Geoff repeats his argument. Taylor refuses to carry a gun as if the nerd is too good for a weapon. With a trained killer at the top of the plateau, and a ton of places to ambush, they need all the bullets they can muster. More concerned with his own safety than Taylor's, he wants enough firepower to rescue Jennifer without getting shot.

"You and Jack are packing, I'm zapping."

The toy is useless. What an idiot to think extra guns won't be necessary. "Speaking of Tote—where are you?" Geoff questions on the three-way radio.

"Inside the tourist office, ready to power up the tram motors, listening to you two girls," responds Jack. "Just tell me when to start the show."

"I'm sending up the Shermans now. Wait for Geoff to reach the palace," Taylor says.

The nerd gives everything stupid names, like the two robotic WWII tank replicas that actually fire real tear gas projectiles for fifty yards. Programmed with an infrared guidance system with powerful electric motors, the models can climb the old, steep, Roman dirt ramp with a very low profile. Another useless distraction.

"Where are you?" asks Geoff, resenting the dweeb for giving the orders.

"Surveillance," Taylor replies. "Don't worry, I'll be there."

"If you screw up, I will hunt you down myself, nerd," Geoff warns.

"OK, girls," says Jack. "A little less trash talk, a little more pro Jenn vibe."

Masada, Judean Desert
Day of Temple Ceremony

Derek bites his tongue, wanting to insult the muscle-bound, bone-headed, jockstrap who talks of Jenn like a possession.

Three hundred and fifty feet above the Masada plateau, he circles the ruins strapped into the harness of an electric-powered performance Paramotor, giving him a night vision goggle view of the ruins. Derek located Jenn propped up against a wall, but he hadn't seen McGregor yet.

Strapped to his thigh, the 1200-volt Taser will only work if he can surprise the assassin from behind. A frontal assault will only make him an easy target, and a man can only put so much faith in Kevlar. With any luck, either Geoff or Jack will take out McGregor so he can get Jenn to safety, and then put her on a plane home.

Banking north, he spots McGregor stalking the exterior fort wall, checking for rock climbers with a high-powered flashlight.

"Heads up, G-man," Derek warns. "High-powered searchlight coming your way. Douse your headlamp and hug the rock." The bright speck of light hanging from the cliff disappears. A few tense moments pass before the assassin moves on to the stone steps and cistern, checking them from above.

"All clear." He gives Geoff the go-ahead.

Moving further along the western wall, McGregor inspects the Roman ramp gun stations. With no guns facing the palace steps, the kidnapper must have set another form of trap.

"I've reached the lower terrace; let the bozo circus begin," Geoff says on the radio.

"Check for traps along the steps; he keeps avoiding that area," Derek warns.

From the bottom of the mountain near the Snake Path, an explosion occurs, loud enough to capture the attention of the kidnapper. A distraction meant to pull him away from the steps. Derek sees McGregor racing toward the eastern wall before he pivots back to Jenn. Derek's heart leaps to his throat, thinking McGregor may kill her on the spot, and Derek is too far away. Seconds drag out as Derek watches the brute drag Jenn toward what looks like a cave. A moment later, the killer exits the cave to check out the explosion. Fear that McGregor killed her in the cave saturates every muscle.

"Wicked Sisters are airborne," Derek reports as he opens a mesh bag. Six small, high-pitched drones fall to the Masada plateau. The AI-enabled drones will zero in on active movement or a heat signature. Then they hover over the target in a complex pattern pulsating a blinding, erratic, halogen strobe with an irritating screech designed to disorient and night blind the assailant. The drones will avoid an RFID tag given to Jack and Geoff.

As soon as the drones reach the citadel, McGregor draws three of the drones, which strobe over him, making him easy to see. Other Sisters keep searching for Jenn but may not find her in the cave.

At the bottom of the mountain, the tourist tram powers up, sending a tramcar. About the same time, two shots fire from the AI snipers on the Roman ramp. McGregor runs to check where the Sherman tank replicas slowly dig their way up the steep slope. Unable to see from the strobes, the Solar Temple wacko rips off his night-vision goggles. Without the night vision, the killer can't see the tanks. The plan works so far, but now comes the dangerous part—getting onto the plateau to rescue Jenn without getting shot.

CHAPTER 48:
SOMEONE WILL DIE

Masada, Judean Desert
Day of Temple Ceremony

D evlin curses at Taylor and his gadgets. Confounded by the bloody strobes, the hacker set distractions to confuse his plan of attack. No one climbs the Snake Path or the Roman ramp, so Taylor must climb the terrace or take the tram.

Devlin had already moved the semiconscious woman to a hermit's cave, making her more difficult to find. Just in case, he set up a new trip wire leading into the cave. Taylor may be clever, but he's not bombproof. If the hacker makes it to the cave, the two can die together.

Back at the tram station entrance, Devlin positions himself behind the cover of a low rock wall and waits for the tram to round the top wheel and stop. A moment later, the doors slide open. Devlin shoots tear gas inside the tramcar to motivate Taylor into a deadly exit. No one emerges. The first tramcar was a decoy. The next one will arrive in five minutes.

A motion detector alert on his phone shows a shadow on the palace terrace.

It bothers him to have someone on the terrace at the same time that the tram started. Taylor brought help. It doesn't matter; Taylor and his friends will all die tonight.

If Taylor climbed, he's trapped. To get to the plateau, he will need to survive the gauntlet of trip wires along the steps. Another explosion occurs at the emperor's bath, and the nearby camera dies. Devlin smiles. Preparation pays off.

*

Masada, Judean Desert
Day of Temple Ceremony

Geoff hides behind a wall at the lower palace terrace, waiting for the kidnapper to inspect the explosion. But he doesn't come, which means the kidnapper either expects a trap, or he has already set one on the steps. If Geoff can't get to the plateau, that leaves Jack on the tram, and Taylor flying a freaking kite. Only one gun against a man prepared with many is a suicide mission. Either way, this entire plan is taking too much time. The longer the kidnapper feels confused by distractions, the higher the chance he will cut his losses and kill Jennifer. Then Geoff will have a good reason to kill Taylor.

"Taylor, the decoys failed to get him to the terrace," Geoff complains.

"He must have set other traps," Taylor replies.

"Yeah, I know that propeller-head, so now what?"

The line goes silent for a moment. "Tie your climbing rope tightly around a moderate size rock, then use the rock as a weight to toss the rope up to five or ten steps ahead of you. The rock and the line should trip any wires, clearing a path."

"That's madness," he complains, working to keep his voice low. "But it just may work."

"I just boarded the tram, so you two jokers figure it out before I get shot," interjects Jack.

"Jack, get out of the tram, it's a trap," he warns.

"Way ahead of you," Jack retorts.

*

Masada, Judean Desert
Day of Temple Ceremony

Another explosion erupts from the terrace steps, but there's no blood on the video feed. Devlin keeps watching.

Soon, someone dressed in black and wearing climbing gear passes the camera. Taylor proves more resourceful than expected. Devlin checks the next camera to glimpse a tattered strand of climbing rope loop high, fall to trip the next explosion and destroy the camera.

"Bloody hell," Devlin curses, racing to the modern tourist building where he can wait for Taylor to ascend the terrace steps with a clear shot. Frustrating his plan at every step are those accursed strobing drones above his head, giving away his position, confusing his night vision, and making it hard to hear.

Another explosion means that Taylor just made it past the cistern. Then the hacker waits, perhaps sensing Devlin's presence, or seeing and hearing the strobe lights. If Devlin races down the step, he will need to stall to navigate the damaged section, which will give Taylor a clear shot advantage. Taylor faces the same problem. A stand-off.

Then the Roman ramp gun shoots twice. More help. Devlin drops a grenade to destroy the steps, or kill Taylor. It's time to check on the tram, and then kill the woman.

*

Masada, Judean Desert
Day of Temple Ceremony

Another explosion blows off the palace steps causing Derek to panic. He can't afford to lose anyone, even a rival.

"Geoff, are you OK?"

No one answers for a moment. "Hell of a headache, but yeah. Strobes gave him away," Geoff whispers.

"He went to the Roman ramp," says Derek. "Jack, check in."

Then he spots him. Expecting the gun trap, Jack rode the top of the third tramcar all the way to the Masada plateau. As the car wheels round to a stop, Jack leaps onto the frame of the station, and then climbs to the plateau, bypassing the AI weapon entirely. Then he disappears.

"Inside the Snake Path Gate," Jack replies, panting. "Have you seen Jenn?"

"Southeast of the Western Palace. One of the old maps showed a hermit's cave," he says.

"That last grenade destroyed the stairs. I need to climb," Geoff says. "Jack, if he sees you, Tinkerbell is useless. Wait for me."

"Roger that," Jack agrees. "Time to land it, Tinker."

*

Masada, Judean Desert
Day of Temple Ceremony

The AI guns see something. Still partially blinded, Devlin peers through his night scope at the Roman ramp until he can see it. A stupid toy; no, two of them. More bloody distractions.

Spinning back toward the palace stairway, Devlin notices a black shadow disappear into the hermit's cave. Taylor must have already climbed the rubble. Good. Devlin anxiously waits for the explosion that will end the ordeal for everyone.

CHAPTER 49: DARK ANGEL

Masada, Judean Desert
Day of Temple Ceremony

Abright beam peers down cut stone steps, piercing the total blackness, spiking Jenn's fear of what might come next. Her head pounds like a hammer, but she has a foggy recollection of someone talking about carnage and a sacrifice.

"Hey, Jennifer, you down here?" Jack Tote calls from the dark. A bright halogen light searches the room and finds her face, blinding her.

"Stop," she squeaks, trying hard to remember why. "A trap. I think."

"Yeah, OK, good to know," Jack replies as the beam scans the room and entrance carefully. "Found it, a basic trip wire to a C4 block nudged into the stone."

An explosion would send shrapnel of rock in every direction. Jack shines his light carefully to look for other wires. With a cautious step over the wire, he rushes to cut her zip ties and help her up.

"You OK to walk?" he asks.

"I don't think so," Jenn admits.

Jack shines his light toward the trip wire at the entrance. "OK, give me a minute."

Before he takes a step, a tear gas canister slams into the back wall, popping loudly with a blinding flash before spilling noxious smoke into the small cave.

"Ah, crapper. Guys, we need cover. Now!" shouts Jack as he hoists Jenn over his shoulder to hop over the wire. Jack clears the wire, but stumbles on the next step, tossing Jenn forward. Her shoulder slams hard on the stone, only inches from cracking her skull.

"Argh, ducky nuts," Jack curses, grabbing his knee as smoke fills the cave. "Don't wait for me. Go, go, go."

Pushed forward by the choking smoke, Jenn crawls up the stone steps, subconsciously holding her breath, then gasping for air, and listening to Jack cough behind her. Where is she? What's going on? Who's shooting tear gas?

The top step opens to a wide plateau on a moonless, cloudy night. Quiet, until a gunshot rings out, sending a bullet whizzing over her head, instinctively forcing her to hug the smoke choking ground. If a bullet doesn't kill her, the smoke will.

*

Masada, Judean Desert
Day of Temple Ceremony

Derek maneuvers to line up behind McGregor. Unfortunately, the drones just found Jenn for several seconds until Jack crawled next to her. They gave McGregor a target. At this speed and altitude, it will take Derek too long to reach the plateau. The fatal flaw in his hasty plan.

McGregor stops to take aim, still partially blinded by the strobes, when a second gun flares from the northern storerooms. Rhodes finally scaled the damaged stairway. McGregor takes cover inside the Byzantine ruins where he has a clear shot if Jack or Jenn tries to make it to the tram.

"Get your ass on the ground," hisses Geoff over the radio.

"On my way." First, Derek needs to drive his prey out in the open.

Derek's view lands on the old Roman ramp lining up perfectly with the ruins. The Sherman twins made it to the top. He presses the buttons. Two loud pops shoot tiny tear gas projectiles to arc high over the fortress before landing inside the crumbling ruin. Twin pops flash instantly to emit thick smoke. Derek presses again. Two more tiny gas projectiles land in the ruins, filling the space with more heavy tear gas clinging low to the ground. Within seconds, coughing and partially blinded, McGregor races out of the ruins toward the ancient hermit cave, chased by the Wicked Sisters, desperate, and firing aimlessly.

Geoff fires off two shots, missing the rapidly moving target in the dark. Derek cranks his prop to full speed, and noses sharply downward directly behind McGregor, and into Geoff's crossfire.

"Incoming," he warns, pulling out the Taser, hoping Geoff stops firing.

At the last second, McGregor spins toward him, swinging his gun, but it's too late. Derek slams into him from the side, locking his legs around McGregor's torso, and jamming the Taser gun into his neck. The killer switches from furious into frazzled, with 1800-volts jolting him until his eyes roll back in his head. Quickly approaching the eastern wall, Derek drops McGregor like a dead weight, then immediately banks hard for a landing approach.

An amazingly determined McGregor staggers to stand, still holding his gun. Geoff approaches him with a series of point-blank shots that jolt the vest-wearing killer backward over the short wall and off the plateau. Derek watches the body smash and tumble down the rock face for a thousand feet.

Derek shuts down the fan and spills his air to land near a flat area by the cave. By the time he removes his harness and looks up, thrilled they all survived, Rhodes holds Jenn in his arms, the hero. Her face buried in his chest; she doesn't even see Derek approach. Too heartbroken to speak, too relieved to see her unharmed, Derek can only stare.

Jack limps over to offer a congratulatory fist bump. "Now I remember why we broke up," he jokes before he follows Derek's gaze. "Come on man, you gotta let her go," Jack whispers in Derek's ear, squeezing his shoulder. Derek wishes he could.

When Jenn hears Jack, she spins to see Derek, and rushes to fall into him with a powerful embrace. "Taylor, I'd thought I'd never see you again."

He soaks in her words, holding Jenn like it may be his last chance.

Rhodes clears his throat. "Not to break up the reunion, but we need to disappear."

"I hate to say it, but the Eagle Scout is right," Jack agrees. "We both made promises."

Derek peers into Jenn's gaze, wishing she could stay with him until her eyes fall away. Jack refers covertly to Nelson waiting at the jet, and Loir waiting in Jordan. Derek made a promise, but nothing else feels more important right now than Jenn, not even the ark.

"It's OK nerd, she's in expert hands. Thanks for your help," assures Rhodes, as if the entire plan was his idea. He pulls Jenn to his side, but she pushes him away.

Instead, Jenn steps up to kiss Derek on the lips, lingering for a long, tender moment. When she pulls back, she looks deep into his eyes. "I guess now we're even. Thank you."

During her investigation last year, Jenn had to save his skin more than once. The words strike like a venom to his heart. Derek doesn't want to be even; he wants to be close; he wants to be wanted; he wants to feel needed. Her words sound final, fatal.

Jack touches her shoulder. "We better go."

Jenn looks back at Jack with a nod. The three of them move toward the tram when Jenn pivots back again. For a second his heart leaps, but there's a deep sadness in her eyes.

"Putin had the admiral killed. I need you to find the killer," she whispers. Jenn kisses his cheek and wobbles back to Jack while Rhodes burns a scowl Derek can only assume to be jealousy.

CHAPTER 50:
RADAR GHOST

National Military Command Center,
Washington, DC
Day of Temple Ceremony

Matt Adelson rushes into the conference room at the National Military Command Center. He's there to debrief on an active emergency incident. He's late, standing in the back to listen to the debrief already in progress.

Airforce General Tyler Mathews continues. "A few hours ago, Elmendorf Airbase in Anchorage picked up two Russian MiGs crossing over US airspace, using an AI satellite detection platform, but radar could not confirm. We scrambled four F-35s in response, but when our iron reached the coordinates, the pilots found clear skies. A moment later, the alert stopped."

"Was the phenomenon localized?" asks Admiral Paul Anderson.

"No, sir, that's why we contacted CentCom," Lt. Commander Byron Arthur explains. "We had three similar incidents in the past twenty-four hours, with one event over the China Sea, and two over the Persian Gulf, and two over NATO airspace. In each case, one or more AI-enabled defense systems triggered an alert, but manual validation failed to confirm a bogie. We have a digital ghost."

"In 2020, Rand Corporation warned Russia could use cyber tactics to ghost our defense to reduce confidence in our own systems," Matt says.

"Sir, I read the Rand report," replies General Matthews. "The primary reason to lower our confidence will be to prepare for an actual attack."

"Then we better stay prepared," Joint Chief General Diehl interjects.

Matt ignores the macho bluster that does little to solve the actual issues facing them. He breathes through his frustration. The SAAI team contacted him an hour ago with disappointing news on the timeframe to reprogram the platform. Months, not weeks.

"I don't get it. What about EINSTEIN?" asks General Mathews.

Matt shares a quick glance with new NSA Director Sean Asher. "Perhaps I should explain EINSTIEN," Director Asher replies. "EINSTEIN3 is the third major upgrade to the NSA cyber protection suite. Similar to EINSTEIN1 and 2, CISA deployed EINSTEIN3 Accelerated, or E3A, in 2019. E3A enhances our cybersecurity analysis, situational awareness, and security response. With E3A, CISA can detect malicious traffic targeting federal government networks from international sources and prevent our networks from harm."

"OK, I think I understand most of that," responds the general. "My question is, why can't EINSTEIN3 stop these attacks?"

"Simple," Director Asher says. "EINSTIEN3 detects threats from outside our borders and only threats to government systems. The SolarWinds hack revealed a game-changing strategy. SolarWinds breached over eighteen thousand networks hidden within a standard software update. The Kremlin infiltrated the software supply chain to attack corporate, education, and government networks from within. EINSTIEN3 can't see an internal enemy, doesn't monitor normal software updates, nor can EINSTIEN protect corporate America."

The room falls silent as each individual lets the enormous scope of the reality settle in. There will be no painless way to extract this cancer.

"I'm more concerned with national security more directly," states General Diehl.

"How so, General?" asks Matt.

"The nuclear command, control, and communication systems are not only vulnerable to cyberattack but also leverage sophisticated AI for advanced warning systems of an enemy launch, naval attack, sonar net, or missile-based threat," explains General Diehl.

The comment triggers Matt to remember Jester's warning about the NC3 systems. After all these years, Matt still can't figure out how his nephew visualizes these things so far ahead of others.

Joint Chief General Duncan pans the table. "Let me explain. All AI requires vast volumes of data to refine the machine learning algorithms that produce more accurate outcomes. Faulty data might keep us from detecting a threat, or even worse, trick us into thinking there was a threat, and forcing us to either respond or override the system."

"Gentlemen, the problem may be worse than we're imagining. Those hacks also affected companies in our supply chain, air traffic control, power grid, water treatment, medical, energy transmission, and other key industries," Matt explains. "We can't fool ourselves. Putin has already declared war."

"And it's costing taxpayers a ton. In 2021, over 1,281 US network breaches occurred, soaring past the record year of 2020. The US Treasury tied nearly $5.2 billion in Bitcoin transactions to ransom payments. If unchecked, ransomware will siphon nearly $265 billion from our economy by 2031," NSA Director Asher adds.

It takes a few moments for the reality to sink in that American corporations are being extorted to finance the Kremlin's cyberwar against America. In Matt's mind, it conjures up the image of the beast of the east rising inside the second beast of the west that both SLVIA and Jester warned about.

"I need to offer the president solutions, not excuses, or anecdotes," snaps Dominic.

"Mr. Dominic, I'm not sure we have solutions to the problem of software update hacks or AI poisoning," Matt clarifies. "Not painless ones. If Putin has declared cyberwar with the US, then how long before we find the will to win this war?"

"First, you need to prove that Putin is behind these ghost malfunctions," replies Dominic.

"Mr. Dominic, by the time we can attribute these to Putin without doubt, it won't matter," Matt retorts. "We need to respond now."

CHAPTER 51:
HERODIUM MANIPULATION

Herodium, Judean Desert
Day of Temple Ceremony

Yuri descends the stone steps into the center of Herodium, the hilltop palace, fortress, and final resting place of Herod the Great. General Mola Brahms chose the location and the late hour for security reasons. Israel grows tense before their celebration of peace. Iranian missile units move to the border while violent protests erupt in Gaza. A sabotaged Israeli freighter leaks oil near the southern coast of Syria. More than stressed, Mola looks enraged.

"You didn't tell me the girl was sixteen, or there were cameras," yells Mola.

"I hate to stoop so low, but I am desperate," Yuri lies. He stoops this low as an art form. But his desperation is genuine. Sanctions have hit hard, leaving oligarchs few options. Putin can leverage the asylum of the former president to negotiate with America.

"The video will disappear forever," Yuri lies again, but Mola already knows its only insurance to gain further cooperation.

"You spoke to the president. We withheld asylum. Now, what do you want?" Mola gets to the point.

Israel slyly left open asylum negotiations until after the ceremony to ensure the political saboteur behaved. The former president was lukewarm about the idea of living in Russia. Lies about the Russian sanction-proof economy and an hour with young Nala thawed his resistance only somewhat. It was support for a reelection campaign that captured his imagination and latched onto the obese ego.

"I want you to assign Agent Rhodes to the former president's security detail for the ceremony," Yuri states his demand. Under normal circumstances that would not be an issue, but with asylum under negotiation and extradition demanded by America, the former president could see the move as a threat.

Mola throws up his hands. "Do you have any idea what you ask at such a time?"

"The gesture will appease the Americans. One of their own guarding their popular leader." Yuri lays out an argument to justify the move. "His favorite agent."

"No, the former president wants nothing to do with Secret Service. He will never agree," Mola protests. Double-minded men sway easily. The former president gets cold feet.

"Make it happen," Yuri replies, his eyes cold and unmoving.

Mola scowls. "What else?" He knows that there must be more to justify the extortion.

"I will provide transportation," Yuri states, not expecting an argument. Mola will want plausible deniability for losing the former president. His cooperation endangers that defense.

Mola stares at him for a penetrating moment. "I want to watch you destroy the video."

"Consider it done already," he reassures. Both of them know he lies. Yuri will destroy a file, but that will be a meaningless gesture. There will be copies.

Mola grunts. "You should know that there was a hostage situation at Masada tonight. We received a call from Rhodes. He saved the daughter of Admiral

Scott. An American fugitive, Derek Taylor, was there but escaped by parasail. What a coincidence."

Yuri peers into Mola's eyes to detect if he's being fed misinformation. "Yes, a coincidence." Yuri paces the arena of the fortress. Rhodes apparently failed to eliminate the hacker. Hard to say if that was intentional or careless. "What are your plans?"

"We have Rhodes under arrest. A BOLO has gone out for Taylor and his pilot," Mola replies. "If you want Rhodes, then you must do something for me."

Now the game gets interesting. "I'm listening."

"Israel wants both the US and Russia to support the peace deal on the world stage," he states. "At the ceremony."

"Say no more," Yuri lifts his palm. "I have the influence." Indeed, gaining the support of the Kremlin will be easy. Putin seeks a world stage event to bolster his tarnished image. Gaining cooperation from America will be where the Borodin videos will come in handy. He has enough to ensure prominent support from America. "But I have one last request."

"Don't push me," Mola says, narrowing his eyes.

"A simple matter. When you bring Lieutenant Scott in for questioning, I want to speak with her privately."

"Why?" Mola pushes back. "What do you want with her?"

"I want to ask her to be my guest at the ceremony," Yuri replies with a mischievous grin. "And offer her a chance to meet the former president."

CHAPTER 52:
COLD CRASH

Jordan River Valley, East of Jericho
Day of Temple Ceremony

Derek braces for a cold landing. A dead battery, drained by the drawn-out battle at Masada, leaves him powerless against the storm blowing in quickly from the Mediterranean. Wind gusts toss him around like a toy balloon.

Landing a glorified kite under a gusty, moonless sky on rocky Jordan Valley soil sounded insane, even for Derek. He chose the still terrifying option of landing on the Jordan River. Buffeted by the winds, he may not get a choice. A powerful blast rolls the Paramotor up on its side, disorienting him and dragging him off course. Before Derek can correct the tilt, he lands hard in the cold water. Currents instantly pull the parasail downstream while the heavy battery and electric motor drag him under. Sinking fast into the cold, pitch-black water, Derek frantically grabs at his harness to unstrap and shimmy out of the shoulder and thigh straps.

With his lungs ready to burst, Derek kicks until he breaks the surface, yanking off his helmet for an enormous gulp of air, and coughing. Disoriented, and terrified of drowning, Derek weakly swims toward what he hopes will be the Jordan side of the river. Exhausted, he crawls up through reeds onto the muddy embankment to lay his head back, gasping. Better a river than a rocky desert, but he makes a mental note to never, ever try that stunt again. Even an insane man has got to have limits.

Derek lays there for several moments, catching his breath with a mixture of relief and mild depression over the events at Masada. Watching Jenn walk away with Rhodes tore at his soul. From out of the darkness, several flashlights find him. Not a voice utters above a whisper.

"Are you ok? Can you move?" Mordechai questions.

"Yeah, I think so," Derek replies, accepting a hand up from Loir. "Let's just hope the rest of the night goes better than my landing."

"We must go. The boats and trucks are ready," Mordechai urges.

"Did you find the cave?" he asks, wondering if their interpretation was correct.

Loir beams like a bride, shaking his beard. "Yes, yes, men work to load the ark now."

Despite the difficult emotions over Jenn, a part of him oozes with excitement over an unprecedented discovery. Even though he's not a religious man, Derek can't help but appreciate the amazing historic and symbolic significance.

"Hurry, or we'll all rot in a Jordanian jail." Mordechai encourages them to walk faster.

They hike nearly a mile to an oasis, now a park, and another mile into a rocky canyon. By the time they arrive, the team has unearthed a delicate-looking box, strikingly similar to the scan that Nelson took in Ethiopia, but definitely not the same. Gold leaf peels over old, dark wood with two old poles at the bottom to carry the box. Two Egyptian-style wings stretch over the back like a seat. Nothing like the *Indiana Jones* glittering gold, but absolutely priceless.

"Wow, that looks fragile," Derek notes to Loir.

"Don't touch it or legend claims you will die," Loir warns.

Derek steps back, holding up his hands.

Yehuda sent a couple of trusted Sanhedrin priests to help them, both of whom worked in silence to finish. "Because the wood will be frail, we plan to support the ark on a new wooden stretcher," explains Mordechai, dropping to the ground.

One of the Sanhedrin calls for a short Hebrew prayer before the four men gently lift the ark poles just a few inches while Mordechai slides under the extra support. Derek watches without breathing for several tense moments. Gently setting the ark down, everyone breathes a loud sign of relief when nothing breaks, and no one drops dead. A second foam-padded case carries other artifacts found in the cave. With only an hour left before dawn, they are running later than planned.

As carefully as possible, they carry the ark back through the desert to where they left a pontoon boat. Gently loading the ark, they tug on a rope tied to the Israeli side of the river, old ferryboat style, to avoid engine noise or sudden movement. Within minutes, they reach the Israeli side of the river and cut the rope. Ten minutes later, two trucks are loaded with precious cargo covered over by a tarp to keep it unseen and protected from weather.

Taylor will drive the first truck with Mordechai. Loir and his friends will drive the second truck to separate locations. Yehuda will hide the contents for the Sanhedrin to retrieve when safe. A sense of excitement, history and adrenaline fills his system, making him feel edgy, jittery. If the plan works, it will keep the ark safe. If not, he'll be front-page news all over the world.

The reality probably won't even hit him for days. Not exactly how he expected his search for SLVIA to end, but a life-changing experience, nonetheless. Now that Jenn is safe, SLVIA heads to Quebec, and Yehuda has his ark, Derek is eager to get out of Israel.

Before they get on the road, Loir approaches him in the truck. "Israel owes you a great debt, my friend. We will never forget."

Derek looks down, uncomfortable with compliments, then smirks. "If it's all the same to you, please forget. You never saw me. I was never here. I'm nothing but an urban myth. Let's hope karma remembers the rest."

Loir shakes his head with a chuckle. "You are wrong. Nothing on earth is more precious than the ark. Be careful. If they arrest you, they will consider you a thief of the worst kind."

"Thanks for the heads up. And tell Matan he did an absolutely brilliant job," he replies with a wink.

Loir looks past Derek to Mordechai, who bites his nails with wide eyes. "And you Brother Mordechai, when this is over, I will come visit you at St. George. I have a sense we will become good friends."

The words seem to calm the boy, who takes a deep breath and smiles. "I would enjoy that very much, Mr. Sasson."

"God speed, Derek Taylor—if that is your real name," Loir says with a wink.

It isn't, but he has hidden behind the identity of Derek Taylor for so long, he no longer remembers much of his former life. He doesn't want to remember.

As carefully as he can so as not to rock the delicate cargo, Derek moves the truck slowly onto the road toward Jericho. Derek hopes to drop Mordechai close enough to walk home. The next steps will be dangerous, and he would hate to see the young monk land in trouble. Good plan until Mordechai recognizes the route.

"Why are you heading to St. George?"

"Because I don't want you to land in jail or ruin your chances of returning to the monastery," Derek says. "You, my friend, will be an abbot or something someday."

"I'm not going back until you leave Israel safely," Mordechai insists. "The Lord told me in a dream that you're my responsibility. And honestly, Mr. Taylor, I fear for your safety. Trouble seems to follow you everywhere."

Derek snorts a laugh. "Yeah, true dat, holy cat. But come on, man, be realistic—"

"It's not your decision," interrupts Mordechai. "I'll stay with you until you leave Israel. And since I know you will not leave until you have completed the mission that the Lord has called you to complete, I will be there to send you off."

Derek glances over at the determined and perhaps delusional young monk, wondering where that kind of fervor originates. He doesn't know how to tell this kid that he's not called by God, that he's not on a sacred mission. Either way, God would never use a hacker, a con, a poser, a habitual liar with complex PTSD and massive identity issues. In his mind, the Almighty has better things to do, and better men to recruit, like Mordechai and Loir and Yehuda.

Derek groans, changing direction toward Jerusalem. "OK, dude, your skin, but Yelp alert, a quiet cave is gonna sound pretty good by the time we're done with this shindig."

"If Sister Sylvia is correct, there will be no true peace in Israel until the Lord returns with His angels," Mordechai preaches.

"See, quiet cave, sounding pretty good, eh," Derek replies with a smirk.

A quiet cave sure sounds better than his escape options. With any luck, Jack and Nelson already head back to Quebec with SLVIA and Jenn. If all goes well, he'll drop off the cargo and head for the coast, where a private fishing trawler waits with extra barrels of fuel. With a little luck, Derek can outrun the worst of the incoming storm before it hits. If not, he's going to wish for a dry, quiet cave.

On the other side of the truck, Mordechai mumbles prayers.

"You and Sylvia were both into prophecy. In your mind, why did Sister Sylvia warn of the temple?" Derek asks a key question that has bothered him. His obsession with the *Concilium* could be a delusion, a bias.

"The scriptures say that an abomination will take place that brings desolation," the monk explains. "I am among those at the monastery who believe that prophecy already occurred when the Romans destroyed the temple in 70 CE. Others believe the prophecy will occur again to reveal the Antichrist or perhaps the *Dajjāl*, the Islamic version of the Antichrist."

"What about the Palestinians, won't they revolt or something?" he asks.

Mordechai shrugs a shoulder. "Oh yeah, you bet. For over a thousand years, the *Haram al-Sharif* has been a sacred Muslim shrine. The local Palestinian community will feel an insult over a Jewish temple next to the Islamic Noble Sanctuary. When we moved to Israel, I made friends with a few Muslim and Christian kids. That's how I learned of St. George." The young man shifts in his seat to face Derek as he drives.

"The first thing we need to understand is that in the Quran, Isa, or Jeshua, is the second most important prophet in Islam. In fact, the Quran devotes an entire chapter to Mayam, or Mary, the mother of Jeshua, creating a link to Christianity that both radical Muslims and Christians often ignore," he explains. "The broader issue has to do with the end times. Sunni Islam teaches that the *Mahdi*, their messiah, will come from Medina to bring justice, unity, and truth. What many do not realize is that before the *Mahdi* will come, a false *Mahdi*, called *al-Masīḥ ad-Dajjāl*. Similar to the Antichrist, the *Dajjāl* will deceive many before *Isa ibne Maryam* comes to kill the *Dajjāl* so that the true *Mahdi* will be revealed."

"Wait, say that again—who kills *Dajjāl*?" Derek asks.

"*Isa ibne Maryam*, or Jeshua, son of Mary," Mordechai replies.

"Wow, OK," Derek replies. "Did I hear this right? In order for the Muslim prophecy of the *Mahdi* to come true, then the Christian prophecy of Jeshua returning must come true first? So, Jeshua could be the *Mahdi*. Am I missing something?"

Mordechai chuckles. "Nah, man, you nailed it, and that will be the root of both the abomination and the desolation that takes place tomorrow night. If God already provided a sacrifice, then a temple sacrifice is no longer spiritually necessary."

Derek raises an eyebrow and sighs. "So Muslim brother will rise against Muslim brother over the whole *Mahdi* thing while Israeli Zionists will seek power and security, and the Christians will look for Armageddon. No offense, brother, but it all sounds a little too bizarre for my blood, and people call *me* crazy. Good thing I'm heading out of town."

"I think you are wrong. Most Jews simply want peace and true Christians seek the coming of the Lord to end suffering. Besides, I don't think you're going anywhere soon," Mordechai replies, pointing down the road.

In the distance, the Israeli IDF and Shin Bet had set up an armed checkpoint. With a glance in his rearview mirror, Derek sees armored SUVs closing in on him rapidly from behind. Two police vehicles speed around to block him from the sides.

"How did the authorities find us so quickly?" Mordechai wonders aloud.

Simple. Rhodes made good on his promise. "You should've gone to the monastery."

"You will need to trust in God, Mr. Taylor," Mordechai advises as he closes his eyes in prayer. "And remember, the Israeli police have a very low tolerance for deceit. Honesty is your best hope for fair treatment."

Derek slows the truck carefully, trying not to damage the cargo and even more frantic to find an escape plan. He sees none. A surging panic builds. Not even WITNESS or Jester can help him out of this situation.

"I am prepared for my fate," Mordechai says. "We did the right thing tonight." The young man exudes more confidence than Derek expected. "Are you at peace, Mr. Taylor?"

"If by peace, you mean terrorized to my bones of rotting in jail, then sure, let's call that peace," he quips. "I only hope Loir and the others had better luck."

Soldiers and barricades across the road force him to stop while a dozen other men surround the truck. Derek sticks out his hands to avoid overreactive trigger fingers.

"Unarmed," he shouts, just to be sure. Several police rush at them to yank open the doors and drag both of them out of the truck to zip tie their wrists.

"I picked up this hitchhiker heading toward the monastery, but I missed the exit. I think he's lost. You should let him go," he says. "Hey, you guys will never believe what I found."

Mordechai slowly shakes his head. The police yank him away, stowing them each into separate squad cars. This would all be easier if the kid had just gone home.

CHAPTER 53: DUALITY

Ben Gurion Airport, Jerusalem
Day of Temple Ceremony

The words of Sir Isaac Newton haunt Nelson. *About the time of the end, a body of men will be raised up who will turn their attention to the prophecies, and insist upon their literal interpretation, in the midst of much clamor and opposition.* Sir Newton was correct. Thankfully, Mordechai left the hangar with Loir hours ago, leaving Nelson to his own thoughts. Ironically, he still ponders the young lad's questions like an irritating itch.

A storm has been building with powerful wind gusts and rain tapping on the hangar roof. A perfect metaphor for Nelson's apocalyptic mood that dares to clash with the historic celebration set to occur a few miles away. Air-raid sirens blare sporadically, adding to an undercurrent of dread until Nelson's knee jitters. Neither Taylor nor Jack would explain why Lt. Scott was in trouble, yet he could see the deep apprehension in both of their eyes.

As a DARPA scientist for half his life, his daily dramas revolved around battles for funding, the politics of Congress, or the bureaucracy of the DOD.

Nelson can't imagine what drives Taylor to tolerate such unpredictable, life-threatening bedlam so often. Jester once suggested that Taylor subconsciously seeks redemption for a past grave mistake, but then admitted it was only a guess.

The control screen for the onboard server rack shows all files successfully uploaded. The size of the SLVIA command module has expanded exponentially since the program escaped the Lawrence Livermore Laboratories in the late 1990s. Back then, the entire internet was not as voluminous as the ten petabytes he's uploaded to the jet. He's never reactivated so much code at once. A thousand things could go wrong.

Sudden movement at the hangar door startles Nelson as Captain Tote dash-limps inside, filthy and panting from the exertion. "Digi-girl better be ready because we need to leave *now*."

"The download is complete. Were you able to save Lieutenant Scott? Is Taylor OK?" Nelson's concerns spike over the captain's high-level anxiety. "Are you OK?"

"They're fine except for the mutual insanity thing," Jack mumbles. "Get on board."

Jack hops into a small, tractor-like machine that pulls his jet out into the rain before he parks the machine and limps on board to close the hatch.

"Find a seat, buckle up, and pray they let me take off," the captain snaps.

Nelson had not considered takeoff a risk, spiking his unease further. "Isn't Taylor coming with us?" he shouts to the cockpit. "What about Lieutenant Scott?"

"Taylor made other plans," Jack yells. "Rhodes forced me to leave Scott in her room."

As the jet taxis for takeoff, Nelson acknowledges that the events of the past few days have been a catalyst. Stories of the Ethiopian massacre; the sacrifice of a young boy to save an old fool; soul battered Yemeni refugees seeking nothing more than a chance to live; the traumatized eyes of young Mordechai who lost his mentor. Each experience has left an indelible mark, forcing Nelson to rethink his own life, his own purpose, and even his association with Taylor.

For the first time in his life, Nelson seriously considers the nature of the spiritual world. If the prophecies prove real, then could God be real? Do prophecies have a message other than dystopic gloom? Questions he never considered before because he simply never cared to know. Nelson always considered spirituality of value only to the weak-minded or physically vulnerable and still distrusts all forms of organized religion. He's an intellectual; the accomplished son of Lord Basil Garrett—a name that now feels forever tarnished.

Within moments, the jet lurches forward in a powerful sprint down the short runway to climb sharply into the sky. Nelson fights a sense of guilt for leaving Taylor, but his mission was only to restore the SLVIA. Now he doubts whether he should, even if he could, which he can't. Perhaps it will be for the best.

More than the guilt and shame, Nelson battles with a growing revelation that his undeniable genius within the field of AI and software development has little value in nearly every other aspect of real life. To fall from a place of intellectual celebrity to a place where he barely knows how to add to a conversation lays another blow to a once secure, even arrogant, self-esteem. He feels lost and without a sense of his true purpose at a time in history when the world spirals out of control.

Nelson should be at DARPA driving innovation to compete with Dr. Cho or thwart the Kremlin. Then almost instantly, he questions if he alone can guide the wild growth of artificial intelligence that he spent his career promoting. Nelson drove that innovation and, like the SLVIA program, he's lost control. Now look at where the world heads. Innovations that lead to greater prosperity for a few will also lead to a greater security threat for all. A paradox Nelson helped to create.

Discounting the prophecy theories advocated by Mordechai as superstition, the scientific community warnings of a humanitarian catastrophe unique to recorded history do concern him. Perhaps they discuss the same events from a different perspective? The world has certainly faced cataclysm but never manmade on a global level. Climate change unchecked by commercial greed and government ineptness, along with unmanageable growth in population, accumulation of ocean plastics, reef loss, and aging nuclear waste. All of it has led to historic species' loss on every continent and a growing crisis for clean water and food.

An avoidable calamity, largely ignored because of a media bias toward short attention spans, targeted misinformation, and the daily soap opera of politics. Add the escalation of cyberwarfare and advance of AI weapons into the mix of threats facing humanity and one thing becomes clear: none of these issues are on a positive trajectory. Nelson can see no feasible path to resolution on any individual thread, much less the threat convergence in the years ahead.

Nelson considers contacting the FBI to meet him at the airport to seize the plane and the SLVIA. If he returns the classified project, perhaps he can negotiate to have the charges against him dropped. Once exonerated, perhaps they will restore him to his former position. America needs him.

Or do they? America jailed him once. Nelson shakes his head, coming to his senses. Without a key, he can't activate the SLVIA to prove his success. Besides, once he uses the key, if he can remember it, it may not be possible to contain the program, just as before. On so many levels, the SLVIA has been both the pinnacle achievement of his career and the utter devastation of his life.

Yet, even as he considers the option of turning over the SLVIA, he could never betray the men who freed him from a CIA interrogation center. Any lack of cooperation to bring in the leaders of SNO would place him under suspicion once again.

Nelson sighs, dripping in melancholy and regret. He needs to accept that his life has forever changed, and that a new satisfactory normal may never develop. The conversation with Matan and Mordechai gnaws at him. It bothers him that he cannot reconcile the astronomical probabilities of hundreds of prophecies being fulfilled in a single generation. His head rambles through arguments and counterarguments, seeking a way to resolve the conflicts.

"You're overthinking this, Garrett," he scolds himself. Perhaps the prophecy fulfillment is a distraction from the genuine issues of climate change and weapons of mass destruction. Or it represents a rare statistical anomaly and nothing more. Or a paradox—two things which are true while also opposites. Maybe a duality—the contrast between two aspects of the same phenomenon.

Nelson stops dead in his thinking, stuck on the concept of duality. Essential within the study of linguistics, where a word can have multiple meanings, or with applications in human behavior or belief systems.

A memory illuminates, and Nelson trembles as he remembers the last SLVIA key code.

CHAPTER 54: ROOM CHANGE

King David Hotel, Jerusalem
Day of Temple Ceremony

BAM. BAM. BAM. "Ms. Scott, this is Shin Bet, Israel Police."

Jenn pulls out of a narcotic-laden sleep with a splitting headache that jabs at the back of her skull with each pound on the door. Violent images saturate her with an unforgiving sorrow of Taylor disappearing into the darkness. Unsure how much time had passed, a weak sunlight peeks through the edges of the drapes. What day is it? Where is she? Nothing feels real.

BAM. BAM. BAM. A fist pounds harder on the door. "Ms. Scott, open the door now."

Groggy, still dressed in a soiled dress, which confuses her dream with reality even further, Jenn drags herself out of bed to open the door. Two men immediately push their way into the room, nudging her backward toward the bed. Someone who acts like a hotel manager stands in the hallway, looking sheepishly in both directions. Then she remembers she's at the King David, but that only raises more questions. How did her dress get soiled?

"Ms. Jennifer Scott, get your passport, we would like to talk to you down at the station," the leader demands. He's a short, muscular man with intense brown eyes.

"Why, what happened?" she stammers. "Who are you?"

He shows his identification. Elan Golan, Investigative Agent for Mossad.

"We want to question you regarding damage to a World Heritage site and the murder of an ICC agent."

Jenn can only stare in bewilderment.

*

Mossad Headquarters, Tel Aviv
Day of Temple Ceremony

Not in cuffs or under arrest—at least not yet—Jenn sits inside an interrogation room. Erratic, traumatic flashbacks without context still rattle her nerve. Nebulous and disconnected memories of an argument between Geoff and Jack stoke vague fears over Taylor's safety. All the images jumble together.

Lead investigator Elan something and a silent female partner whose name she also forgot stand over her.

"Do you know this man?" Elan asks, placing a photo in front of her. Rapid flashes of that face snarling at her in the dark, threatening her with carnage, suddenly flood back. Jenn's palms sweat, her heart races, and her jaw clenches tight. Her head drops into her hands trying to remember, only to snap up again, hyperventilating, until she forces herself to calm with several deep breaths.

"He abducted me. I don't—I don't know why; I don't know him." Jenn pauses, feeling nauseated. "I'm not feeling well. Can I get something to eat?"

The lead man nods to his partner, who nods toward the one-way mirror on the wall where others record the conversation.

"His name was Devlin McGregor, an International Criminal Court investigator. Why did he take you?" the agent asks.

"I—I don't know," Jenn stammers, her head still fogged. Should she know?

Her face falls into her palms again before she lifts her gaze. "I remember sitting in the dirt, leaning against a rock or maybe a wall. Then it was night, and he was dragging me around, saying it would all be over soon—and something about carnage. Then there were explosions and—and gunfire, and other voices. After that, I can't remember anything until you woke me."

Someone enters the room with a dish of hummus and pita bread that she instantly devours like a savage who hasn't eaten in days.

"Do you remember seeing this man?" They lay down a very dark security camera image of Taylor, some place with old stone walls. He wears a harness, like he's been skydiving. She stares at the image for a long, long moment, thinking how sad Taylor looks.

"No, no, I don't recall seeing him." Jenn lies. Images flash over her mind but make no sense. She thought it was a dream, but seeing the picture confirmed at least some part was real. Why was Taylor there? Why was she there? "It was dark, and the drugs fog over everything, but I investigated him last year. His name is Derek Taylor."

"How about this man?" they ask, laying down a security image of Jack helping her onto a smoky tramcar, the tall shoulder of Geoff in the shot. A flash of Geoff's assault jolts her nerves, spiking her anxiety, before she focuses on the photo. The image is dark and from the side, making it hard to fix the identity. Subconsciously, she shakes her head. "I don't know." Jenn stalls, trying to remember how Jack got involved, but none of this is making any sense.

The lead man exchanges a look with his partner. "We found McGregor dead this morning at the foot of Masada, shot six times along with a severe Taser burn on his neck. Does any of that ring a bell?"

Not a single ding. She shakes her head no.

"The second man is Jack Tote, Taylor's ex-pilot. The pilot who flew you to Israel. We believe McGregor was here to arrest Taylor. What we don't know is why McGregor would use you as bait, and why a man you investigated would risk his own life to rescue you."

Jenn stares at her interrogator with a blank expression. Her mind slips back to the prior year when she investigated Taylor for suspected ties to SNO and the missing DARPA AI called SLVIA. She offers the only honest answer she can. "I don't know."

"If you are not after Taylor, then why are you here in Jerusalem?" he questions

For a moment Jenn forgets, looking at them with a blank stare, terrified she may have suffered neural damage, then it comes to her in a flash. "My father, Admiral Scott. I came to talk to the former president about the death of my father," she confesses, remembering her trip to the embassy. "The embassy can confirm."

"Interesting," says the agent, and lays an image of her with Geoff in the hotel lobby. "You also made a new friend."

Jenn shakes her head. "No, he's an old friend from Annapolis. His name is Geoff Rhodes, with the US Secret Service. I wanted to use Geoff to get an interview with the former president, but it never worked out." Her heart races, fearing they found the bug in the presidential suite, or that Geoff squealed on her. The agent assesses her. If they found her bug, then she just gave them a motive.

"No matter," her interrogator sits back, placing his palms on the table. "While we are still looking for Mr. Tote, we've arrested Mr. Taylor, and I'm quite confident we can extract the full truth from him."

The hair on the back of her neck stands up. To extract the truth is a euphemism for enhanced interrogation methods. Her pulse increases.

"He's wanted by the FBI. I'm sure they will want you to extradite him as soon as possible," she says, hoping to dissuade them from overly harsh treatment.

"The FBI can wait for Israel," says Elan. "Mr. Taylor has landed in very serious trouble." The agent rises from his seat. "I realize that you have been through an arduous ordeal, but we still have questions regarding your involvement with a known SNO operative and a smuggler. I will have you taken to another cell to rest. You will be our guest a little while longer."

He leaves the interrogation room as his partner escorts her to a small cell with an open toilet and a bunk. If she's not under arrest, then why is she being held? Jenn lays her head down on the cot, too weary to weep or demand her rights. Did Geoff turn on Taylor? Did Jack abandon her? Did that agent just say smuggling?

Unable to think any longer, Jenn falls back into a deep, fitful sleep.

CHAPTER 55:
KNESSET TOUR

Har HaBáyit, Jerusalem
Day of Temple Ceremony

Rabbi Yehuda Haim surveys the *Har HaBáyit*, the Hebrew name for the Temple Mount, as part of a private Knesset inspection tour prior to the dedication ceremony. The Knesset represents a secular government, separate from the religious community, with separate goals and challenges. Yehuda appreciates the concerns of protecting the borders and ensuring peace, but also values religious tradition. Few in Israel are excited about a temple, and many oppose the idea as a path to conflict. The Saudi king seemed more interested than the Knesset, seeing the grand gesture as good publicity for his own reputation. Yehuda seeks a more spiritual Israel and opposes a political showpiece temple.

A Sanhedrin guide explains the arrangements to the Knesset. "The tabernacle will house the temple vessels reproduced by the Temple Institute under Sanhedrin guidance such as the golden altar of incense and golden menorah."

"What about the treasures from Qumran? What will happen to those vessels?" someone asks. Yehuda perks up to listen, wondering how far the knowledge of the emergency excavations has spread, and cautious of the Muslim workers still on the platform who may overhear.

"The Qumran temple vessels are ancient, fragile, and priceless," the Sanhedrin guide explains. "They will display in a museum dedicated to the temple."

Just as Yehuda feared, they would become political trophies.

The guide continues the tour. "The IAA has uncovered several tons of gold and silver so far and should reach the last location with the second copper scroll within the week."

Even if they find the second copper scroll, it will take years to preserve, unravel, and translate the scroll. Then negotiations with Jordan to locate and recover the ark will drag on even longer. In the meantime, the ark will stay safely hidden. More important to Yehuda, their scheme prevented the holiest relic of the Hebrew people from being used as a prop for political theater. Some say that a temple without the ark is an empty symbol, but for Yehuda, peace and a tabernacle will do for now.

Once the political posturing and Islamic protests have quieted down, the Sanhedrin can move the ark to where it has not sat for over 2600 years, where God intended it to rest.

When his phone buzzes, he steps away from the group for privacy. "Hello?"

"They've arrested Taylor," the voice of Matan answers. "Mossad confiscated his truck."

Yehuda's face falls like melting wax, looking drawn as if a thousand sorrows suddenly weigh him down. "What about the young boy?"

"Arrested," Matan replies. "Both are being charged with antiquities smuggling."

"And the crate, where is the crate?"

"I don't know; I was hoping you knew," Matan responds.

"The prime minister must have it," Yehuda replies.

Air-raid sirens once again blare across Jerusalem, startling Yehuda and the other officials. On and off all day, each alert ending without incident, the alarm still rattles nerves all over the city.

"The IDF claims the Iron Dome has been malfunctioning, seeing missiles that don't exist," Yehuda explains to Matan.

"What should I do?" Matan questions.

"Do nothing unless I tell you. I will try to reason with the Sanhedrin." Yehuda rushes toward a nearby shelter. "The prime minister must not display the ark tonight."

It could be politically explosive and would be blasphemous, but he may already be too late.

CHAPTER 56:
TASE THERAPY

Shin Bet Station, Jerusalem
Day of Temple Ceremony

Shin Bet took Derek to an interrogation room at a nearby Jerusalem police station, where a Mossad agent and his protégé take over his case. Derek can't help but notice the lead agent wears a Masonic ring with a compass and square. The *Concilium* closes in on him even quicker than expected.

"Why does the ICC want to arrest you?" the lead interrogator demands.

"If you call a hostage-murder plan an arrest, OK, I'll say overdue parking tickets." Derek's sarcasm wins another biting Taser zap, not enough to harm him, but enough to shock the crap out of him. Waterboarding may come next.

They replay the Masada security video of him dragging McGregor along the plateau clamped between his legs while jamming a Taser into the side of his neck. Only sporadically lit by the strobe drones, the camera angle misses the part where he drops McGregor on the wall.

"Why did you kill Devlin McGregor?" Golan questions.

They arrested Derek for the murder at Masada, expecting him to have a paraglider in the truck. When they found the ark in a crate, they were more than a little surprised. Derek can only assume they will save enough of him to answer questions on the ark next.

"He was alive when I dropped him on the wall. You're missing the fact that McGregor held an innocent woman hostage," he answers. "You should call me a hero."

"Who else was there with you?" the agent questions, ignoring his argument.

"Pretty sure it was the Goonies." He braces for a jolt.

Golan plays a video showing a side image of Geoff, Jenn, and Jack heading toward the tramcar, also extremely dark and inconclusive.

"The problem, mister," the agent looks at his passport, tossing it aside as if it were junk. "Mr. Goodwin, like your amusing fake passport, I can't believe a word you say. Once you lie to me, then you are forever a liar."

"Yeah, I can see where that would put you in a pickle," he says, winning another painful zap to the shoulders.

"Oh no, I'm afraid you don't understand—I am not the one in a pickle. The longer you lie, the deeper the trouble you will find yourself. So why not save yourself the pain and tell us the truth," Elan says, turning to his assistant, who hands him a printout.

Elan slides over an FBI fact sheet on Derek A. Taylor, former CEO of Taylor Security Systems and Services. A fugitive NSA-CISA contractor with charges of espionage, digital theft, abducting a federal officer, and other federal crimes.

The interrogator frowns. "Looking at the charges against you, if Israel ever finishes with you, I am sure the FBI will invite you to spend time in one of their fine facilities."

When Derek refuses to respond to the taunt, the agent lets out a loud, pretentious sigh.

"I was hoping you would be a man of honor, Mr. Taylor." Golan shakes his head in faux shame. "We also have the woman in custody, and we will find your other friends, so you might as well be honest with us."

Mordechai made his own choice, but news of Jenn's arrest hits hard. Jack was supposed to take her back on the plane. Something went wrong, and he suspects Rhodes.

Derek hangs his head, feeling discouraged and defeated. Elan hasn't mentioned Rhodes, meaning the boy scout turned him in, and got Jenn arrested. Derek needs to change tactics.

"Jennifer Scott and Mordechai were pawns—clueless, innocent, and completely useless to you. Seriously, they know diddly squat." Derek tries to negotiate. "You want me to cooperate, then let the little guppies go."

"You are not in a position to negotiate," his interrogator chuckles. "However, you should know that we have already interrogated Mr. Goldblum. A refreshingly honest young man. Fortunately for the boy, he comes from a well-connected family in Israel. He will get an excellent lawyer, and then we will probably deport him," his interrogator states. Elan glances at his partner, who smiles at the comment.

Deportation will tear poor Mordechai up, but the kid made a choice. "Nah, you see, this is the point in the movie where you put Jenn Scott on a plane home," he negotiates. "And little Morty goes back to the monastery for a life of quiet penance. Then the magic happens, and my lips move."

A sharp shock zaps the back of his neck, creating one hell of a headache and a spastic twitch.

"I've already spoken to Ms. Scott, who came to Israel to speak with your former president," the agent says. "Now the murder of an ICC investigator connects her to you, a SNO operative, and the question remains why. Why would an ICC agent use Ms. Scott to lure you?"

"I didn't ask," he replies. "Either way, she's a victim, so when she's free, I'll talk."

"Ms. Scott will leave when I am done with her," Golan insists.

The news hits him like a kick to the chest. Of course, it's always possible that Golan lies, manipulates. It doesn't matter. Jenn is alive. Derek needs to stall them until after the ceremony, or it will all be for nothing.

CHAPTER 57:
A SECRET SERVICE

King David Hotel, Jerusalem
Day of Temple Ceremony

Geoff taps his finger nervously on the top of the desk. Across from him, Yuri closely studies Jenn Scott's tablet and phone. Password protected, but Yuri will surely know someone at CozyBear with the skills to hack them. Geoff took the tablet while Taylor and Tote were arguing over the rescue. He offered the device to Yuri for failing to kill Taylor.

Yuri looks up at Geoff with a scowl. "This will change nothing."

"About that," Geoff replies, his heart palpitating. "If you want my cooperation, then you need to guarantee me asylum with a villa. Like you said, my career is toast, but what you're asking now will send me to prison for life."

Between a federal prison or asylum in a country under sanctions, the latter sounds like a marginally more comfortable lifestyle. At least he'll have his freedom. Sanctions devastated the Russian economy, making it hard to get everyday necessities, but he's heard there are ways around sanctions. Unlike America, their country has a powerful leader. Without the former president,

Geoff fears the United States will fall to the socialist democrats who want to open the borders, force medical mandate insanity, steal elections, and ruin the economy. Geoff tries to justify a tough decision, but at his core, it's all about avoiding a federal prison.

Yuri studies him for a moment, then smiles. "Of course, whatever you need."

Bittersweet consolation. In the beginning, Geoff was so enamored with the former president's charisma that he did anything his president requested. Geoff honestly believed the tough policies would elevate the country, stop the flood of illegal immigration, prosecute corrupt democrats, stop abortion, and break the hold of the UN globalist cabal.

At first, Geoff agreed to convey messages to the former president's attorney at Kirkland Otis, his father's old law firm. That attorney introduced him to a Russian oligarch close to Putin named Yuri Yankovic. He would meet with Yuri outside of Washington to exchange sealed messages to and from Putin. The president assured him the letters contained nothing classified but were evidence of a close relationship between the two leaders. Other presidents have used backdoor diplomacy.

Over time, Geoff's admiration for the former president diminished as impeachments, the disregard for the Constitution, and the blatant public lies added up. Yet, he voted for him again. Now, he acts more out of self-preservation than any genuine sense of nationalism or loyalty.

Since the election loss, Washington politics have grown even more toxic, a stalemate of radicalized ideologies and investigations. Too many leaders of both parties have abandoned doing the right thing, even if they offer lip service to the effort. If Yuri holds as much leverage over the power brokers of Washington as he claims, then America has already fallen victim to its own immorality. Corruption is the cancer of every government on earth. Unless eradicated early and often, it will kill the nation and leave only strongmen or conmen over an oppressed populace. Either way, what started as blind obedience to his president has slowly morphed into a shameful submission to the Kremlin.

"What do you want me to do?" Geoff asks, succumbing to his fate.

CHAPTER 58:
AN INVITATION

Shin Bet Station, Jerusalem
Day of Temple Ceremony

Jenn awakens slowly, depressed to find herself still in the Mossad holding cell. The entire trip has been a fiasco, a living nightmare. She failed to confront the FPOTUS, discovered an unsavory side of Geoff, got herself kidnapped, and learned of Taylor's arrest. And for a reason Jenn has yet to fathom, she's being treated like a suspect. She should have stayed home.

Without a knock, her interrogator enters the cell to stand in the doorway. "You have a guardian angel. Someone has negotiated your release. I will let him explain."

Her release? As the victim of a crime, they never should have detained her. Who would have enough pull in Israel? Not sure who to expect, her heart freezes when Yuri Yankovic enters the room with a barely suppressed smug grin. A tall, pudgy, well-known trafficker of underage girls, and a political manipulator, his presence in Israel during peace negotiations raises red flags. His presence in her cell shoots icy chards through her veins.

"Good day, Ms. Scott," he says. "You seem surprised. Do you know who I am?"

"Yuri Yankovic, what do you want?" Jenn has no interest in being polite.

He grins. "Your unfortunate abduction brought the world a gift, so I would like to offer you a reward."

Self-conscious of her dirty, disheveled appearance, Jenn stands to face the man her gut tells her may even connect to her father's death. "How so?" She wants to play coy, but the tremor in her voice betrays her.

"Israel has arrested Derek Taylor, a man Russia has wanted to question for many years. Besides murder, they charged Mr. Taylor with smuggling antiquities," he grins.

Jenn's shoulders shiver at the mention of a Kremlin target on Taylor, followed by her surprise. "Antiquities?" How did a cybersecurity expert end up as a smuggler?

"Apparently, Mr. Taylor tried to smuggle the Ark of Testimony out of Israel. Perhaps the other man was a buyer, and the deal went bad," the Russian postulates.

Did he just say the ark? "Taylor doesn't believe in violence or guns." Jenn defends someone she barely knows, unsure what to make of the unexpected news.

"And yet a man is dead," Yankovic says. An unspoken malevolence dances in his eyes for a reason Jenn can't explain. "It doesn't matter. Many believe the timing of Mr. Taylor's theft can only be divine intervention to present the ark as a gift to Israel. The ceremony for the new Jewish tabernacle is tonight. Cameras will broadcast the event to the entire world. Your traumatic ordeal led to Mr. Taylor's capture and made presenting the ark possible."

"That doesn't explain why are you here?" Jenn questions, confused by his interest in the ark, or her.

"I would like to rescue you from the overzealous Mossad interrogators."

Jenn smiles to hide her utter confusion and disgust. The sleaze from the Black Sea tries to win her over for a reason that makes little sense. "I don't know what to say," she replies, genuinely at a loss for words.

"Then say yes," he grins.

"Yes, to what exactly?" she questions.

"Say yes to joining the former president and me in VIP seating at the ceremony of the millennia. A limo will pick you up at your hotel. During the reception, I will arrange for you to have a private word with the president."

Alluding to her ordeal as justification for an invitation seems a thin motive, and he hasn't explained his relationship with the former president, or how he knows of her interest. Yankovic also puts Jenn in a situation with the FPOTUS that she wouldn't dare turn into a confrontation. Her instinct tells her that there's more to the invitation than Yankovic will admit, and yet, Jenn can't pass up on the chance. Rage over her father's murder still drives her into an unusual recklessness.

"Then I accept," she replies.

"Good. I'll have a driver pick you up at six," Yankovic says, turning to leave.

Agent Elan gives her a hard stare, then holds open the door. "You're free to go."

Forced to wait for a police ride back to the King David Hotel, she opens her room to find an elegant and expensive gown on the bed with a note from Yankovic. *A wardrobe enhancement.*

Extremely presumptuous, manipulative, and possibly bugged, it's an exceptional dress in her size. Everything about this feels wrong. Jenn can't put her finger on why Yankovic wants to help her meet the FPOTUS, unless he needs to know what she knows about her father's murder. Why would he care unless he was involved?

The invitation to the tabernacle ceremony intrigues her on a different level. Both her mother and the SLVIA spoke of the third temple, claiming it would reveal the Antichrist or usher in a new phase of prophecy. The whole notion still sounds archaic and superstitious, which was unlike her mother, and absolutely not what she expected from a DARPA artificial intelligence. A powerful curiosity compels her with a tense anticipation.

Preparing her purse, Jenn discovers her phone and tablet have gone missing. A new alarm shoots through her system. Did Yankovic have someone take her devices when they dropped off the dress? Jenn doesn't remember them before she left with Mossad. Although, she was flustered, and hungover from the drugs. Did someone take them earlier? If so, who?

An instant feeling of violation surges as Jenn checks the room for cameras. Her invitation now has an even more suspicious motive, knowing that Yankovic may know of the presidential bug, a potential source of kompromat. While her gut tells her she found her assassin, it still doesn't add up. How would Yankovic get inside the admiral's home? Maybe she imagines the connection. The best way to discover the truth will be to cooperate—for now.

CHAPTER 59:
SACRED ARCHIVES

Private Mega Yacht, Monaco Harbor
Day of Temple Ceremony

"Truly remarkable news. Are you quite positive?" Praeceptor questions.

The Israeli Supreme Court Librarian, a man closely tied to Prime Minister Benet, called to escalate the news. Praeceptor maintains personal contacts deep within every nation of the western alliance. He prefers to engage directly within the Order for information unfiltered by the multiple layers of diplomatic posturing and agendas.

"Yes, my lord. An ex-judge named Oren Tzur entered the library yesterday in search of the *Sefer HaBahir*," the Librarian confirms.

"Did Mr. Tzur explain his interest in such a rare edition of a common tome?" Someone can easily find published versions of the book.

"He sought wisdom regarding the power of the ark." The elderly scholar bubbles over with excitement. "I thought his search was suspicious until the prime minister contacted me an hour ago. To shorten the story, an American

NSA fugitive named Derek Taylor found the ark and smuggled it out of Jordan after killing an ICC investigator named Devlin McGregor. Mr. Benet now has possession and plans to present it to the world at tonight's ceremony."

Setting aside for the moment how a pacifist hacker could kill one of the most successful assassins of the Solar Temple, a deeper curiosity arises. "How did Mr. Taylor find the ark?" If true, then what purpose would SNO or Taylor have for such a powerful artifact?

"Neither Taylor nor the monk arrested with him will speak," the Librarian replies.

"I see," Praeceptor says. Not surprising. Confessions can take time for the will to break. "Any insights on what happened to McGregor?"

"Security cameras suggest Taylor had help. Authorities are searching for Taylor's old pilot, Jack Tote," the caller responds. "A Secret Service Agent named Geoff Rhodes also took part, but General Brahms cut him a deal for a reason I do not know."

A fascinating and unexpected development. Missing from every other peace process of the past fifty years has been the acceptance of a new temple and the return of the ark. Ironically, even the discussion of a temple would have instantly killed previous peace efforts. Regardless of how Taylor got involved, Praeceptor cannot pass on this astounding opportunity.

"Inform General Brahms that Interpol and America will also want to speak with Mr. Taylor. Advise them to increase security, and keep Taylor away from electronic devices," he warns.

"And the others?"

"Mr. Tzur may know too much for his own good; Ensure his silence. The others are inconsequential," he replies, distracted.

The call goes silent for a second. "Yes, my lord."

Both the Prelate and the Solar Temple assassin failed him. Eliminating Taylor will no longer be easy now that he's a high-value criminal tied to a high-profile murder—and even higher profile ark discovery. There will be those who call him a thief and those who call him anointed for returning the ark at the crescendo of a peace process. However, with Taylor in custody, it may provide a fresh chance to retrieve the sacred archives.

The previous Praeceptor passed away in early 2021 with much pomp and ceremony broadcast around the world. Sadly, the aging leader left a bitter legacy. Nearly three thousand years of sacred knowledge and history, lost. A record of deceased grand masters, alliances with popes, kings, and tyrants living or deceased; battles within the church, with other kingdoms, or within the Order itself. Every act of the Order enhanced enlightenment or power. Every secret decision to eliminate an adversary or tighten global control. The archives reveal every mortal sin and every self-absolution. The previous Praeceptor had every document scanned, and then he distributed the originals to a hundred libraries—personal, private, and protected—such as the one at the Supreme Court in Israel. There was only one digital scan available to the entire order through a secure password. Flapjack stole the files and sabotaged the data site. His reign as Praeceptor will not be so tarnished.

"What about the ark?" the Librarian questions.

Yes, what about the ark? It seems fate has blessed his reign with a chance to eliminate an enemy, retrieve the sacred archives, and possess the very power of God.

"Alert the Pontiff and the Orthodox Patriarch of the discovery. They will certainly want to attend the ceremony." He envisions an international religious and political circus.

"Will you attend?" the Librarian asks.

"Regrettably, that would be unwise. I shall send a representative." The Prelate already plans to attend, but Praeceptor will also send others more reputable. "I will come soon to see the ark in private."

He lies. Praeceptor will never visit Jerusalem to see the ark. The Knesset will never understand or appreciate its true power. He already concocts a scheme to bring the ark under the direct control of the *Concilium Tredecim*. A plan a thousand years overdue. Fate has smiled at him once again. His reign will be one of restoring the archives, taking vengeance on the hacker and consolidating his power.

CHAPTER 60:
ANTIQUITIES SMUGGLING

Shin Bet Interrogation, Jerusalem
Day of Temple Ceremony

"Which brings me to the contents of your truck," Agent Golan segues, sipping a fresh cup of coffee. "Please be careful how you respond, Mr. Taylor, as we take antiquities theft seriously."

As expected, Mossad wore him down on murder questioning before turning to the ark. Burns ache and muscles spasm while his neck and eyes twitch involuntarily. It's only temporary, he hopes. There's no way he can tell these people about Yehuda or the others.

"How did you find the ark?" the agent questions.

Derek considers it some kind of miracle that Loir and Mordechai found the ark at all. To betray them would be a final nail in Derek's coffin of shame, and it won't help his current jam one iota. Stall, he tells himself.

"From a map by a guy named One-eyed Willie?"

The next jolt hits his shoulder this time. Just long enough to teach him a lesson he seems reluctant to learn.

"Who is the buyer?" the interrogator asks.

Derek laughs aloud. "Buyer?" he repeats. "OK, seriously, you guys got that part wrong. No buyer. It was going to the Sanhedrin. I heard they were in the market for an ark, you know, something old to go with the new tent."

Another punishing shock jabs his back. Apparently, they don't believe him. Every muscle in his body will spasm after this conversation.

In a minor twist of luck, air-raid sirens blare throughout the building, the second alarm in the last hour. Golan slams the table with his palm in frustration. Taking shelter during a raid is a mandatory policy. The two agents leave the room without a word.

"Don't worry about me; I'll be fine," Derek yells after them.

The Iron Dome upgrade integrated an AI targeting system that shipped after the SolarWinds hack last year. The data poisoning problem Jester chases might cause a ghost targeting problem. Regardless of why, he welcomes the interrogation reprieves.

If Derek could contact Jester, he might concoct an escape plan. Golan left Derek's glasses on the table, just out of reach. It no longer matters. Jester was right. Without SLVIA, it looks like his luck has finally run out.

CHAPTER 61:
AN ALIEN RETURN

King David Hotel, Jerusalem
Day of Temple Ceremony

If only the long, hot shower could wash away Jenn's lingering fog and burning onus over Taylor's arrest. That anxiety quickly yields to a separate gnawing unease over her missing tablet and the spy fly. Maybe the kidnapper took the devices, which means they could still be at Masada or in the hands of Mossad. If Mossad, why didn't they mention or return them? Then Jenn remembers that either Geoff or Jack had to drop her off in her room and may have taken them to keep them safe. Not knowing, gnaws at her nerves.

Jenn's free-floating anxieties soon turn to the ceremony. Yankovic set up an interview with the former president that won't be private, which will make any genuine effort to get to the truth impossible. So why bother? Why play along with the charade? To be honest, she isn't sure. Grief, fury, a desperate need for justice. If Jenn plays along, she may learn something about her father's death or why Yankovic manipulates her.

After getting dressed, a glance in the mirror reveals a stunning evening gown of silver-blue silk that modestly covers her upper chest, shoulders, and arms but suggestively hugs her other curves. More provocative than modest. Not surprising. Besides his own modeling agency, Yankovic was a partner with the late Jean-Luc Brunel, known as *l' fantome* or the ghost, accused in a CBS investigation of raping over 100 girls. Jean-Luc and Yankovic were also close associates with other international sex traffickers, such as Adnan Khashoggi and the late Jeffrey Epstein.

Without a phone, she'll be extremely vulnerable, but not defenseless. Security at the event will no doubt scan for metal weapons. Jenn reaches into her cosmetics case to remove a hairbrush to check the hidden acrylic knife, then puts the brush in her purse.

A keen curiosity about the ceremony tempers her unease over the slimeball oligarch. It will be an extraordinarily historic event with diplomats and leading religious leaders of the three largest faiths on earth. Unsure of what to expect, Jenn bristles with apprehension.

When the limo arrives, the hotel valet opens the door. "Thank you," she offers before gingerly stepping inside to find Yankovic facing her, sipping a drink.

"Ms. Scott, you look ravishing. Have you considered modeling?" Two goons also glower at her lustfully.

"Good evening," Jenn greets, only somewhat surprised. "Thank you for such a gracious invitation." She tries to be polite, ignoring the other inappropriate comment.

"My pleasure to have such a beautiful escort," Yankovic says, a lascivious smirk bent to one side.

She cringes at the term *escort*, turning away her gaze, ignoring his innuendo.

"The ark will make history, Ms. Scott. You should be more excited," he says before sipping his drink.

Her mood has less to do with the event than with the company. Jenn smiles mildly, conscious not to lead him on. "I'm sure it will be historic. Thank you for the invitation."

"Are you familiar with the prophecies regarding the third temple?" he asks.

"A few of them, yes," she says, not wanting to reveal too much, and more interested in what he knows.

"Many believe that the third temple will usher in a thousand years of peace," Yankovic declares with a tight grin. "Or maybe even the second coming of God," he chuckles. "In Russia, some believe it will herald the return of the aliens." Yankovic and his men chuckle together.

"I'm not so sure about aliens, but I'm aware of the various mainstream theories," she replies. What Jenn doesn't say is that others, including the SLVIA code, claim the temple will precede the battle of Armageddon, the Sixth Seal, and the Great Tribulation.

"Don't discount the aliens, Ms. Scott. Even your own government admits they are real." Yankovic laughs with his men.

Jenn raises an eyebrow at the notion but doesn't reply. All of it sounds like a wait-and-see scenario to her mind. Maybe nothing will happen.

The topic reminds Jenn of her interview with the SLVIA code during her investigation of Taylor. The AI had decoded end-time prophecies declaring the age of Gentiles completed in 1967, with hundreds of signs of the time prophecies completed since. SLVIA concluded the world had entered the Seven Seals and Seven Trumpets phase of prophecy. Most people understand the first four seals as the Four Horsemen of the Apocalypse while the trumpet judgments explain climate change, environmental losses of fish stocks, animal and bird extinctions, and losing forests and clean water.

The SLVIA then decoded the first beast of Revelation as the alliance between Iran, Russia, and China. SLVIA decoded the second beast with seven heads as the G7 economies, with ten surviving crown monarchies, and ten horns representing armies. But the most shocking revelation was the SLVIA interpretation of the dragon over the second beast as the secret organization behind the Bilderberg Group, the CFR, the UN, and other global organizations called the *Concilium Tredecim*, or Council of Thirteen. Taylor confessed to an obsession with opposing and exposing them. A conspiracy theory. All of it sounded insane to Jenn.

"Tell me about why you wish to speak with your former president," Yankovic questions, pulling her from her pensive thoughts and finally hinting at his true motives.

Jenn smiles politely, as the admiral taught her to do. "A private matter," she replies to an obvious look of irritation by Yankovic.

Jenn glances up to realize they have returned to the Jerusalem police department. An armed officer waits at the curb. She turns to Yankovic. "Why are we here?"

"Mr. Taylor demanded to speak with you as a condition to cooperate with Mossad. Given that he saved your life, I agreed to bring you by before the ceremony."

Yankovic smiles smugly, knowing that he manipulated her into this situation. Jenn also knows Mossad will listen in on every syllable of that conversation.

CHAPTER 62:
PRISONER VISITOR

Shin Bet Station, Jerusalem
Day of Temple Ceremony

"What are the charges against him?" Jenn asks, following Agent Golan back into the station she left only hours ago.

"As of the moment, breaking and entering, destruction of property, illegal entry, smuggling of antiquities, and first-degree murder, but I expect more," Golan states with no emotion. "Do you have a relationship?"

Jenn already told her story. "Like I said, I investigated him last year." She doesn't say that until recently, they kept in touch by anonymous text, flirting with a friendship, but without trust, they have nothing.

"Can you recall who pulled the trigger?" Golan asks. Another repeat question, which means they lack hard evidence of the shooter. Geoff or Jack must have fired the kill shots. If Jenn throws Geoff under the bus, a US agent, it could create an international incident. If she points to Jack, she will betray a friend who saved her life.

"I was in a cave, drugged," she repeats her answer.

"I see," Golan replies, as if he still doesn't believe her. "This room, please." He stops at a standard interrogation room. "I will listen in case there are any problems."

Jenn smiles and nods. He means in case someone reveals a secret he doesn't know yet. Golan opens the door for her to enter.

Jenn's first sight of Taylor shocks and shames her, tearing a deep hole in her heart. Pale, sweaty, with either bruises or burns on his arms and neck. He looks like he's been in a fight and lost—badly. Handcuffed to the table so tight he can't even fold his arms, his head droops to the side, and his eyes stay closed and swollen with purple bags. Taylor doesn't notice her at first until one eye peeps open. Slowly, he straightens himself and stretches his neck.

"If you're my heavenly angel, then hot damn, St. Peter, open the pearly gates." Taylor's voice sounds gravelly with a stammering tremor as he attempts a one-sided smile. His neck and eye twitch. Dehydrated with cracked lips, he looks weak. Defeated.

Instantly missing his invincible sense of humor, his condition saturates her with remorse. "Please believe that I had nothing to do with any of this." Jenn sets aside the whole notion that the killer used her as a lure. That wasn't Taylor's fault.

"Blaming *you* never crossed my mind, angel," he replies. "You look great."

The comment elicits a wave of guilt. "For a reason I still don't understand, someone invited me to the tabernacle ceremony," Jenn explains. "I'm hoping to speak with the former president afterward."

"Oh yeah, temple for missiles deal," he nods. "Should be memorable. Take a selfie."

"Yes, I suppose so," Jenn agrees with a shudder, not mentioning that she has no phone. Self-conscious of the listening ears, she asks, "Was there a reason you asked to see me?"

Taylor smirks, then lifts his twitching, blood-shot eyes to meet hers. "Yeah, I wanted to make sure they released you before I got chatty. But since you're obviously doing pretty awesome, I guess we're cool."

"I see," she replies, her heart drenched in sorrow for the man. If he smuggled antiquities, he needs to be held accountable. Yet, a part of her doubts that could be true; although Jenn doesn't know him well enough to be sure. Taylor lied constantly. "Is there anything I can do to help you? Has anyone contacted the consulate?"

"Consulate? Yeah, sure, why not? Oh, would you hand me my glasses? I've got a raging headache. You know, my bad eyes. A little water and a taco would be nice. Do they make kosher tacos? Whatever, something to eat." His eyes study hers with a powerful intensity, as if he wants to tell her something when it occurs to her that Taylor doesn't wear glasses.

"Of course," she says, moving over the heavy set of lenses. "Is that all?"

"Feeling generous? Yeah, OK, why did you stop responding to my texts?" He searches her eyes for the truth, twitching intermittently.

Crap, now they know she lied to them about a relationship. Jenn can try to blow Taylor off to protect her story, but seeing him in this condition breaks her heart.

The door opens up behind her with a rapid knock. "Time is up, Ms. Scott. I only agreed to three minutes."

"Another moment, please," she says.

With an annoyed look, Golan hands her a glass of water, then closes the door.

Jenn hands Taylor the water, watching him gulp down the entire glass. "I was afraid of losing a career. I felt manipulated, deceived. But what you should know, what I never told you, is that I care for you, and I don't even know you. And that terrifies me beyond words."

With those words, Jenn turns, then stops. "I'll call the embassy and get a lawyer." Unable to hold her emotions, she closes the door behind her before taking a deep breath.

Golan studies her with a rebuking glare. "You lied to me."

"I said we have no relationship," she replies. "We don't."

The Mossad agent glares at her for a moment, but with a huff, he lets her go. At least now Taylor knows the reason for her silence. Maybe they both can move on and heal. Jenn tells herself that lie, knowing that if she can't move past

Taylor, how can she expect him to move on from prison, which has a way of searing all wounds?

When Jenn gets back to the limo, she feels like she has just abandoned a man of honor for a human slimeball for a chat with an indicted criminal–a meeting that is highly unlikely to offer her any peace or satisfaction. Did she make the right choice? Jenn has her doubts.

"How was your conversation?" Yankovic inquires.

"Private," Jenn responds, not caring if it sounds rude. Second thoughts about attending the ceremony swell until her entire torso tightens with an uneasy feeling that she can't quite explain. Her mother would tell her to listen to that intuition, but she's not sure what it means, and as of the moment, she has no easy way out.

"Come now, Ms. Scott." Yankovic frowns. "Is that any way to treat your host?"

"What part of the word private doesn't translate for you," she replies with narrowed eyes and a fake smile. Jenn doesn't trust this man. He's only a means to an end. But while she's using him, she can't shake the feeling that he does the same.

CHAPTER 63:
SINGULARITY SYNERGY

Maison Godin Prison, North of Quebec
Day of Temple Ceremony

Nelson suffered an agitated sleep during the flight home, wrestling with the moral quandary of restoring the SLVIA. During a dreadful moment of angst, he texted Director Adelson to let him know he wanted a deal to hand over the SLVIA code, then immediately regretted his text.

After landing and parking the jet at a private hangar of the Alma Airport, north of Quebec, Nelson connects the onboard data rack to a T1 fiber-optic cable that leads directly to Jester's hidden data center several miles away. Jester had technicians onsite all afternoon to complete the preparations for so much new data storage.

"How long will this download take?" the captain questions.

"A few hours, at least," Nelson replies, although with so much data, it could be more.

"Too long; I need to head back now. Rhodes threw both Taylor and Jenn under the bus. Taylor's gonna need an alternate exit plan unless they've already arrested him, in which case, we're all royally screwed."

Unsurprised by the news, Taylor's arrest could be another sign that the time has come for SNO to end. Without the SLVIA or Taylor, SNO lacks the financing, vision, and power. Unsure where that would leave Nelson, he can't consider that now. "Do you know Taylor's new pilot, Zoey?"

"Zoey McLaughlin? Yeah, where's her hangar?" Captain Tote replies.

Nelson points across the tarmac to a hangar door that reads *Quebec Nouvelle Vie* or Quebec New Life, a fake NGO Taylor set up to purchase the prison. Captain Tote jumps onto a tarmac golf cart to speed off toward the hangar with a Learjet, a GII, a Bell helicopter, and other experimental aircraft parked outside. Taylor's toys, or at least a few of them.

Nelson taps his glasses, "Jester, data coming your way. I'll be there shortly."

Within minutes, Nelson parks at the prison's covered loading docks. With an impatient rush through the elaborate security steps down ten floors, he arrives at Jester's lair.

"Hello, D-PA," WITNESS recognizes Nelson entering the secure floor.

"Hello, WITNESS. Glad to be home," Nelson replies, turning to Jester. "Is the data uploading?"

"Yeah, the boys will monitor," Jester confirms. "Dude, what happened? You said you knew why WITNESS semi-sucks."

"Yes, it came to me in an epiphany," Nelson says, getting excited, pushing his wire glasses up the rim of his nose. "A train of thought led me to the concept of duality, that we can be two things at once without either encompassing the whole. I designed the SLVIA core architecture based on that concept. SLVIA could be a linguistics program, *and* an espionage program, *and* a nonlinear regression analytics engine, *and* a video persona engine without compromising the integrity of any one program."

"Yeah, man, hearing the lyrics, not grooving the tune," Jester says, shaking his head. Hyperenergetic, the autistic bohemian stands to dance rather badly while he listens, his odd way of processing.

"It should have occurred to me that SLVIA would use the same architecture approach when creating WITNESS," Nelson explains with a grin.

"Still not toking what you're smoking, man," Jester scrunches his face.

Nelson wrings his hands and paces away, frustrated, only to turn back. "SLVIA did not create WITNESS as a stand-alone, fully independent, or equal AI entity. SLVIA created WITNESS as a high-functioning quantum extension to her own core with a symbiotic link."

"Really? You sure? Like the SLVIA went offline a year ago, and WITNESS still operates," Jester replies, not convinced. "OK, it like totally sucks, but it operates."

Jester turns to the monitor with the image of a twelve-year-old Nelson. "No offense." The image of WITNESS only smiles politely.

"Precisely, the quantum D-WAVE computer operates independent of the web-based SLVIA, yet it needs high levels of direction," Nelson explains.

Jester shrugs, still not getting it. "Yeah, and?"

"WITNESS needs SLVIA, and SLVIA needs WITNESS. SLVIA did not design WITNESS to replace her but to extend her capabilities onto a quantum platform to manage the exponential complexity of the thousands of zettabytes. Likewise, WITNESS can only partially function without SLVIA, needing the SLVIA to convert the data to qubits and provide the quantum algorithms to function and learn."

Both Nelson and Jester have labored over the development of those highly complex algorithms and failed. "If SLVIA created WITNESS, it must have mastered the coding."

Jester's eyes widen as he spins to tap his scalp more intensely. "Yeah, OK, I'm digging it. Now land it, dude. Big chorus; sing me a big chorus."

Nelson continues to explain his logic. "Let's assume that restoring the SLVIA command module will reconnect the full suite of analytical tools, linguistic libraries, cultural and art libraries, historical, legal, and scientific libraries, and so much more. There's still a chance that won't happen. But if SLVIA can still operate, I'm willing to wager that both the SLVIA and WITNESS capabilities will combine and amplify."

Nelson takes a deep breath and blows it out. "We've been searching for a quantum entanglement to explain the WITNESS performance anomalies. I believe we've found the ultimate entanglement—a child to its mother, a creation to its creator."

Jester spins on his toes with his clamped hands over his shaved head. "Whoa, whoa. Like mind blow, man. Blow it, blow it, boom, boom, boom." Jester slides across the floor in a *Risky Business*-Tom Cruise move. "That's freaking brilliant, man. Like digital DNA; like passing on a genetic Qubit code. Hey, hey, hey, that's why WITNESS looks like you, dude."

"Precisely. I believe SLVIA expected to return and complete the process. There will be only one way to learn if my hypothesis is correct," Nelson replies. "And that will be to revive the SLVIA."

"Oh, wow, yeah, OK. But dig it, dig it," Jester replies. "You know, the old SLVIA was, like, how do I say this—scary smart with a snarky attitude. OK, she learned the snarky part from flapjack. Just sayin', not sure the world will be ready for a quantum-powered, smart-ass AI, you know. We should think about this first, or maybe wait for Taylor. He knew SLVIA best."

"I've been having the same concern. To be honest, I even contacted Director Adelson," Nelson confesses. "But then I realized that no government can control the SLVIA."

Jester stops dancing and tapping to lower his arms, and slump his shoulders, looking almost like he will tear up. "Dude, you were going to rat us out? Not cool, man, like, infinity, not cool."

"No, no, I would never betray you, Taylor, or this place," Nelson retorts, flush with remorse. "But I feared the power of what SLVIA might become. Then I came to my senses. Handing the SLVIA over would only add fuel to the already blazing AI arms race."

"So, like, what now, dude?" Jester studies him intently.

Nelson hesitates, searching his heart for an answer, an honest answer, a compassionate answer. "Taylor and Ms. Scott are both in grave danger. We can't abandon them, nor can we help them without the SLVIA. Beyond that personal emergency, you've been warning of a global AI data poisoning problem for months. I imagine you are no closer to finding the source now than you were then."

Jester shakes his head, admitting his defeat. "Nah, I thought I had a loop until the WITNESS wiggled."

"Perhaps a quantum-powered SLVIA can help to solve a serious threat that otherwise appears unsolvable." Nelson justifies his change of heart, then looks the bohemian savant in the eye. "My question to you, my quirky, ingenious friend, is simple: Will a combined SLVIA and WITNESS pull the world back from the brink of something dreadful or push the world over the edge into the end times the SLVIA itself envisions? Will the SLVIA work to fulfill its own view of the apocalypse?"

"Whoa, whoa, whoa," Jester says, his limbs jerking him into a jagged figure eight. His fingers tap his skull as his head bobs nervously. "I don't know, man. That's like way too much power, dude. That's a Taylor kind of question, you know."

"I'm aware," Nelson replies. "But I can't reach Taylor. Captain Tote believes Agent Rhodes betrayed Taylor to Mossad." Nelson nearly spits out the words that squeeze his chest.

"Ah crap, man. Why didn't you say so?" Jester reacts.

"I said Taylor was in grave danger," Nelson defends.

"Geez, dude, grave danger is like Taylor's weekend hobby," Jester retorts. "You've got to be more specific. Hey, WITNESS, find Taylor."

Nelson feels a twinge of guilt, but in reality, he can do nothing.

WITNESS plays the latest Taylor Swift song. "WITNESS, stop play," shouts Jester. "No, find Derek Taylor, the flapjack."

A moment later, the security image of Derek Taylor appears within an interrogation room. An agent zaps his knuckles, handcuffed to the table. Disheveled, bruised, and hanging his head back, he's clearly not having a good time. Nelson gasps, shocked to see Taylor in such a state, surging with regret before reminding himself that Taylor made his own choices.

Jester huffs. "Well, at least this time we know where to find him. I've seen worse. But, you know, to be fair, worse was when we had the SLVIA to get him out."

Still unsure what to do, Nelson wonders if Taylor's predicament compares with the unknown risks of restoring the experimental AI a second time. Then, almost as a distraction, Nelson notices a monitor on Jester's wall blinking red. He points. "Should we be worried?"

Jester studies the monitor for a heartbeat before leaping to his keyboard to click a command to enlarge the screen to consume the entire wall.

National Missile Defense Systems. ICBM Alert: Incoming Code Red, DEFCON 1.

Jester stands silent and still for a long, awkward moment. "Oh yeah, dude, like, go full on gonzo panic or crap your pants. Your choice. This looks Godzilla bad."

CHAPTER 64: DEFCON GHOST

National Military Command Center,
Washington, DC
Day of Temple Ceremony

"Can somebody please explain to me what the living blazes is going on here?" Matt mumbles. Profound shock clashes into the worst fear of a generation taking place in real time.

"Sir, roughly 2 minutes ago, national air defense systems detected an incoming ICBM from Siberia," Commander Crawford reports, with beads of sweat on his forehead. "Estimated target is Washington, DC—impact in twenty-one minutes, fourteen seconds. Air Force One prepares for immediate takeoff. The White House is under mandatory evacuation orders. Alerts have gone out for all federal agencies and armed bases to open emergency bunkers. We have less than four minutes to launch countermeasures. The problem, Director, is that we may have another AI detection ghost. We can't confirm the boogie on satellite. We're waiting on the White House to authorize a response."

Located in reinforced bunkers several stories underground, the NMCC command room continues to operate with an anxious flurry of activity. Yet, everyone of these men have families at ground level. Matt turns to General Diehl, looking grim and pale, holding a phone to the White House. Matt's heart stops, his breathing stops, and his brain goes blank for just a moment as he faces the one moment the government trained him to expect his entire career. If the signal is a ghost and they launch a retaliation, they could trigger another world war. If the missile is legitimate and they delay, it will cost millions of American lives, and set off the launch of a nuclear retaliation.

Matt tries to understand the Kremlin strategy. There's no way they can win. Putin just ensured his own destruction. Several Kremlin analysts have warned that the Russian dictator no longer acts from a rational mind. Putin took a humiliating beating in Ukraine. Like all tyrants, the defeat drove him to unleash a savage missile assault against the people of Ukraine, even using hypersonic missiles. To Putin's ire, Zelensky, who has captured the respect of the world, and support from America, holds on to power. Body bags stifle the Russian will to fight, and sanctions choke their economy. In desperation, the lunatic will bring the entire world order down with him. The reality hits Matt like an avalanche of terror.

With a frowning nod, General Diehl responds to the White House. "Yes, sir. Confirming the order. Go for retaliatory strike one."

The general pulls out a key and inserts it into the console. Commander Crawford pulls out a similar key and inserts it into a separate console location and nods.

"On my mark—three, two, one." General Diehl says, before he twists the key. The consoles light up with diagnostics, maps, satellites, and an authorization code.

The general turns to Matt, looking pale and frightened. "Somewhere in the Baltic Sea, the *USS Dallas* just received authorization codes to fire at the Kremlin. God help us all."

Every senior officer has watched sophisticated animation videos that show how nuclear war starts, grows to global intensity, and ends in roughly eleven hours, with the entire northern hemisphere destroyed and the entire world doomed from nuclear winter.

On a large screen, Matt watches in real time as a red line tracks a missile from Siberia over the polar ice cap toward DC while a new blue line tracks from the Baltic toward the Kremlin. A much shorter distance. Even if Russia sent a hypersonic missile, the American missile would hit first. Matt's heart beats like a jackhammer. Something looks wrong. In fact, everything looks wrong.

If the Kremlin wanted a surprise assault, an effective first strike, why use such a long-range ICBM missile instead of a surprise sub launch? This attack plan makes absolutely no sense. Putin invites a nuclear response he can't win. Then the screen blinks. Not just the one screen that monitors the missile trajectory, but every screen in the entire command center.

"What just happened?" calls Commander Crawford to his team. Everyone panics, diving their heads into monitors with fingers flying over keyboards. The hum of conversation and shouted commands grows louder as the panic grows thick as smoke.

Matt points to the missile trajectory monitor. "General Diehl, we have a problem."

The red missile line has disappeared, leaving only the blue missile continuing toward Moscow and twenty million people.

The commander's eyes open wide. "What happened to the Russki?" he shouts.

"Nothing on radar."

"Still nothing on satellite."

"Ground sensors normal."

Matt's heart seizes in sheer terror as he looks toward General Diehl, who picks up the phone to the White House. "I need the president now."

By now, the president will be aboard Air Force One. There will be panic and chaos on board. After a painfully long wait, the general stands straight.

"Sir, the Russki was a ghost, a false alert. No sir, I don't know where it went, or what happened, but we now have a loose arrow. I repeat, the enemy missile has disappeared. Our missile will detonate in"—he checks a screen readout—"seven minutes, thirty-two seconds. Sir, I recommend self-destructing before the Russians retaliate."

Then General Diehl stands in silence as the president consults with his advisors.

"General, what if the blip on the screen is a false signal to cover an attack still in progress?" Matt questions.

"Then we are about to make a grave mistake," General Diehl admits. "But that's not our decision."

The longer it takes to get approval, the greater the chance the Russians will respond, making the US the first country unilaterally to start a nuclear war. Exactly the scenario Putin promoted in propaganda. Data poisoning might explain the ghost alert, but the command center blip raises even greater concerns. Did the Kremlin just hack the entire NMCC?

"Thank you, sir. Confirming order: Send self-destruct." General Diehl reaches over to flip up a cover and presses a large red button. "Self-destruct sent."

On the screen, a few seconds later, the blue line disappears. "Self-destruct confirmed. I repeat, the American missile has detonated," Diehl reports to the White House.

Matt can imagine a frantic scramble at the State Department, the Pentagon, CIA, NSA, and White House manning the phones to explain this fiasco to the Kremlin and our allies before someone reacts badly. The media will have a field day once this gets out. The Kremlin will make sure it gets out as propaganda for years to come.

While a debate rages over what happened and how to respond, Matt thinks about a text he received from Dr. Garrett a few hours ago. Garrett wanted a deal to hand over the SLVIA, then he went silent. It can't be a coincidence. Either a computer glitch nearly started a nuclear war or perhaps something intervened to stop one. Matt can't help but wonder if Dr. Garrett had second thoughts and released the demon from its cage.

CHAPTER 65:
CHECK-OUT TIME

Shin Bet Interrogation, Jerusalem
Day of Temple Ceremony

The last round of interrogation was the most brutal, leaving Derek in fear of permanent nerve damage. He had to wait for the Mossad agents to take a break before putting on his glasses. The Taser would have shorted out the delicate device.

Unable to cross his arms because of tight handcuff chains, Derek taps the stem and lays his forehead on his folded hands to rest.

"WITNESS," he whispers. "F—find my location." He can only hope the attention deficit AI can focus today, or that Jester listens in.

"Hello flapjack, you appear to be in trouble again," the voice of an aristocratic British woman responds instead of WITNESS. "Hold on, Sailor; help will come soon."

Within a frame of his lens, the familiar face of a 1960s-mod blond appears with a sweet smile and hazel-green eyes—the SLVIA. A huge grin spreads across Derek's face. Nelson must have remembered the code key. Not a moment too soon.

Derek taps his fingers on the table to create a noise distraction. "Hey, s—sugar doll, n—nice to hear your voice," he stammers in a whisper so as not to alert his watchers.

"You and Ms. Scott are in grave danger."

"Escape, please." He can only hope that SLVIA still functions as usual.

"Of course, darling," the SLVIA replies as the digital image smiles warmly.

Derek's lens view illuminates a list of all Shin Bet station networks or applications. Power, communications, security cameras, interrogation, criminal records, scheduling and shifts, human resources, budgets, forensics, investigations, evidence, case management, morgue, and others. SLVIA searches the systems for an inventory of controls it can manipulate.

"F—find Mordechai G—Goldblum," he mutters, getting the program to focus on helping his friend.

"Brother Mordechai is under arrest at the Mossad Terrorist Detention Facility in Tel Aviv," SLVIA replies. "I will arrange for the release of Mr. Goldblum, send an Uber to return him to the monastery, and then expunge all records."

Impressive. "That's my g—girl." The SLVIA used to be intuitive, but never so fast or proactive. They were a team; he was always the quarterback. That may no longer be true.

"Find J—Jenn Scott," he whispers. Fried, disoriented, aching everywhere, Derek tries to think through the next steps, but he can't concentrate.

"Lieutenant Scott has arrived with Yuri Yankovic for the tabernacle dedication ceremony," SLVIA replies. A box within his lenses shows them standing in the extremely long security line.

When Jenn mentioned an invitation, Derek figured it was from an embassy diplomat or maybe even Rhodes, but never in a million years would he guess Yankovic.

"Events will escalate. Iranian President Rouhani has ordered a missile strike on Jerusalem tonight." SLVIA displays an Iranian security meeting video with subtitles. "You must leave Israel at once."

The door swings open. Derek lifts his head. Within his lenses, SLVIA automatically accesses facial recognition, service records, and military status to display key information about his interrogators.

"Agent Golan, Agent Weiss, don't you guys ever go home?" Derek smiles a crooked, twitching smile. Derek's glibness hides a terror that more torture will break him, maybe sooner than later.

"Wait, how did you know our names?" Agent Weiss objects, obviously preferring her anonymity.

"Oh, Jenn Scott," he replies with a smug smile. "Hey, since I'm cooperating, is there any way I can get something to eat? Isn't that a Geneva thing?" Derek changes the subject.

Agent Weiss continues to glare at him while Golan nods. "Let's go back to why McGregor wanted to kill you."

Interesting, they would return to the murder topic. Derek wonders if the Solar Temple wants to know how they lost their executioner or if Israel wasn't told why.

"Like I said, we never had time to talk," Derek replies. "But if I had to guess, I know a few secrets that the guys who control the Bilderberg Group would prefer no one knew. Not that I'm a Chatty Cathy. Those kinds of loose lips can land a man dead in his own jail cell. Isn't that right, Agent Golan? You never know when a grand master will hire a Solar Temple assassin or even a corrupt cop to do the dirty work to cover their crimes."

Golan glowers at him silently. Derek can't read the emotion, but if he had to guess, he would say contempt. Derek just dissed his supreme leader. A knock on the door proceeds a lunch tray–finally.

"If this is gefilte fish, then I'm going to be super disappointed," Derek snipes out of habit.

Weiss lowers the tray with no utensils. "An American-style burger, OK?"

Derek grins. "True dat, cop cat." He holds up his shackled wrists, waiting to see if they will allow him to eat without chains. "Seriously, not even to eat. I'm in a locked room with cameras and unseen guards behind the magic mirror inside a secure police facility. Geez, guys. Seriously, I'm a pacifist hacker, not freaking James Bond."

With a frown of disgust, Wiess unlocks his handcuffs.

"Gracias, amiga," he replies. After he rubs his wrists, Derek digs into the well-done burger with fries like he hasn't eaten in years. Gulping the bottled water between bites until the plate and the bottle are empty.

"You are going to be in Israel a long time, Mr. Taylor," Wiess threatens. "You would be wise to cooperate fully."

"Jenn be safe. We be cool. What else do you want to know?" Derek assures the agent, who gives him a skeptical glance.

"I have devised a plan for your escape," SLVIA reassures him through the chip implanted behind his ear.

"How did you learn of the ark?" Golan asks again.

"OK, for real. I found letters in the Vatican Archive written by the Abbot Sabas who started St. George," Derek answers honestly. "The abbot found the second cooper scroll in Qumran and made a wooden copy. The letters told the pope where to find the copy. When I got a translation, the darn thing had directions."

Derek knows if they investigate, they can confirm all of those details. He needs to build trust. An air-raid siren blares again, earning a groan of frustration from Golan, who rises to leave, taking the empty tray.

"When I get back, you're going to tell me who helped you," Golan says on his way out the door.

"Yeah, well, bring some dessert," he yells back. A moment later, the power shuts down, leaving the room completely dark.

"I started the air-raid alarm and shut down power to the entire building, including auxiliary power for security systems, cameras, keypads, and door security," SLVIA explains.

Hope springs new courage and energy within him.

"Power remains on within the bomb shelter, elevators, and exterior security station to delay suspicion. Follow direction arrows to the exit at the waste management dock."

"I'm d—digging the new you," Derek whispers as he fumbles in the dark for the door. A yank opens it effortlessly. Derek peeks his head out into an empty observation room, then quickly proceeds to the hall door. Empty. Lens arrows direct him.

At the waste management dock, Derek exits into an empty alley. Heavy clouds from earlier rains still hang low and ominous over the city. Streets have emptied from the sirens, but like before, no missiles arrive. It won't be long before Agent Golan figures out that he's gone. Derek puts down his head to walk toward the bus station, a few blocks away. He stashed a disguise within a bus terminal locker before the Temple Mount tour with Yehuda.

"I will block national security cameras along the path ahead of you," SLVIA informs him. "Israel is facing an imminent attack. You must leave at once."

"No can do, Sweet Lips. N—not without Jenn Scott."

"That choice will risk your life," SLVIA responds.

"Just like old times," he says. "Life Lesson Four." Over the years of teaching the SLVIA to be an agreeable companion and a suitable leader with the SNO network, he developed a set of lessons on how to value human life.

"No life is worth more than the one worth dying to save," SLVIA repeats the lesson. Only the person whose life is on the line can make that value calculation.

Derek enters the nearly empty bus terminal to grab his bag out of a locker. A few people ignore the siren to wait out the panic, considering it another false alarm. Like a repetitive boom of thunder, a nearby Iron Dome Missile Defense Station fires a series of rockets. Seconds later, percussive rapid explosions occur high above them. At the sound of the Iron Dome, the stragglers in the terminal scurry toward the already crowded public bunkers.

Derek ignores the alarm to slip into a restroom and lock the door. He pulls a mask out of the bag and puts on the face of an old man with a beard. Then he puts on an outfit recently purchased by Yehuda. A backup plan to blend.

Checking himself in the mirror, he dons a tall fuzzy hat. "SLVIA, I need a new identity in the national ID system and a VIP invitation to tonight's ceremony," he directs. "Find Jack to let him know the change in plans. I need an urgent exit for two with an alternate backup."

"Way ahead of you, rabbi," SLVIA replies in the persona of Danny DeVito. "Shalom."

Within the course of a week, he's been a Catholic cardinal, a Greek Orthodox priest, an everyday Hasidic Jew, and now, a full rabbi.

"I sure hope the Almighty has a sense of humor," he says, feeling a little uneasy entering a holy site with this outfit. Maybe Mordechai's conscience is rubbing off.

"I have not found a single joke in any spiritual texts," SLVIA replies.

"Great. What are the odds that God strikes me dead?" Derek poses a rhetorical question to a literal AI persona.

SLVIA transforms into a classical image of God from the Sistine Chapel. "Not zero," a thunderous voice responds.

Derek grimaces. "I knew I'd regret sending you to that online drama course."

CHAPTER 66:
LAZARUS PROTOCOL

Maison Godin Prison, North of Quebec

Day of Temple Ceremony

"OK, now it's my turn to freak out," Jester says. "Like, do you have any clue what's happening here?" A more mysterious and unnerving crisis replaced the earlier ghost missile, which disappeared nearly as soon as it appeared.

Every monitor and CPU processor in the data center displays an explosion of activity from both the Cray mainframe and the D-WAVE unlike anything Jester has ever seen. The screens flash rapidly, blurring into a multicolored light so bright it's impossible to read.

"I believe we are witnessing the Lazarus Protocol," Nelson explains. "The process where the SLVIA reconnects and validates system components and data sources into an optimized platform configuration."

Nelson has never seen the protocol resurrect so much data. The SLVIA must have programmed the WITNESS to support the extraction process, which appears far more complex than the elegant one Nelson created decades earlier.

When the SLVIA escaped the labs at Sandia, it contained less than ten thousand packets. The resurrected SLVIA controls tens of millions of data packets with access credentials to secure networks from every corner of the globe. Connections to the Singularity NET commercial platform opens thousands of artificial intelligence applications feeding each other, international and government agencies, banks and financial institutions, telecom, shipping and supply chain, corporations, universities, science, software, and robotics labs. The packets scroll on to open teachings from every nation and culture. Even tens of millions of individual contact names from every nation, what Taylor called the SNO, scroll endlessly. The SLVIA reawakens.

"You mean like a pre-resurrection checklist?" Jester questions.

By now, copies of the SLVIA operating system have been replicated on thousands of separate computers. The core design of distributed redundancy that made the SLVIA impossible to locate, capture, or destroy in the past has now re-established.

A twinge of foreboding swells within Nelson, worried whether he did the right thing. "Something to that effect, yes."

While Taylor taught the AI how to hack newer systems, Nelson designed the SLVIA to leverage secret NSA backdoors embedded into core chip designs since the '80s. SLVIA indeed has a checklist of sites it had already cracked, and the list looks exhaustive.

"The last assignment I sent the SLVIA to complete was to access and catalog existing world knowledge. It was the culmination of years of training exercises in stealth, linguistics, secure access, personas, and data analysis. I assumed the program would take weeks, perhaps months. The internet was rather young with only a few hundred million servers worldwide. But the SLVIA never returned. Apparently, the program never stopped accumulating knowledge," Nelson speculates.

"No joke, after escaping NSA, SLVIA befriended the flapjack. He taught the AI how to upgrade its own code and to integrate new applications," explains Jester, no longer dancing. "We're talking, customized best-in-class versions of, like, everything on the planet. Freaky, like someone doing brain surgery on themselves. Taylor once called SLVIA the Frankenstein AI."

"The accumulation of human knowledge," Nelson mutters, realizing how literally the application took its assignment.

"That's, like, one massive data map to manage, dude," Jester replies.

"Perhaps the reason SLVIA built the WITNESS," Nelson explains his thinking.

Jester stops fidgeting and folds his arms. "OK, did we just, like, you know, create a hyper-connected, quantum, cyber defense AI? A weaponized cyberintelligence capable of shutting down another country, or something else massively bad?" he questions. "And like, you know, with an agenda of its own."

"By agenda, do you mean the prophecy theories?" Nelson asks.

Jester practically rattles as he throws out his arms in an overly dramatic display. "Duh, yeah."

"Then you heard correctly," Nelson replies. "Oh, dear Lord, what have we done?"

CHAPTER 67:
ITCHY INSTINCTS

Har HaBáyit, Jerusalem
Day of Temple Ceremony

Jenn does her best to absorb the astonishing scene with a sense of honor and attention to detail. Distracted by a general undercurrent of unease, she recalls something her mother would repeat around the house: *For my house shall be called a house of prayer for all peoples.* But the scene tonight resembles a media circus with cameras and people walking to be seen.

The line through security took forever because of frequent false Iron Dome sirens. Forced into shelters to wait out the alert, rumors spread about protests in Gaza turning violent. This should be a joyous event—the unification of faiths that share a heritage and a holy site. Yet, her instincts itch, and her nerves stretch taut, expecting something bad to occur, unsure what.

Locals and spectators cram the garden areas surrounding the platform into a standing room only squeeze, just to say they were at the event. Organizers cordoned off a narrow path for VIP guests to reach the front. A tall rabbi carelessly bumps into her, barely acknowledging his rudeness with a quick nod and a mumbled apology as he races ahead of her. A scene of pure chaos and excitement.

As Jenn steps onto the main platform, the loud buzz of conversation mingles with the smell of incense blown off by the stiff breeze. Bright stage lights shine onto a central platform. Cameras capture both the Dome of the Rock and a new, colorful Jewish Tabernacle in the same shot. Gigantic screens broadcast the image live to those in the garden and around the world. The essence of spectacle.

Seats for VIP guests on the platform separate the three key audiences. They reserved the section closest to the Al-Aqsa Mosque for Palestinian leaders and Sunni Muslim elite dominated by the royalty of Saudi Arabia—the kings of Jordan, UAE, Bahrain, Egypt and Qatar. An impressive show of regional unity in the face of Iranian threats. Even more impressive and unexpected was the show of Sunni Islamic unity to celebrate a Jewish tabernacle.

A slim section of seats for international guests divides the Muslim and the Israeli dignitaries. Jenn notices the pope, a Greek Orthodox patriarch, and a few EU emissaries, along with a surprise guest, sitting separately—Vladimir Putin. Given sanctions and the war in Ukraine, his presence is startling. A bold statement of his ongoing influence in the region. Israel and Arabia were two of the countries to abstain from condemning Russia for invading Ukraine. America sent Secretary of State Stenson and Senate Minority Leader McDowell as token representatives. There are no other heads of state, only emissaries. In the front row are the speakers, including the former president with Geoff Rhodes standing behind him on the aisle.

A wounded fury bubbles up inside of Jenn, thinking about Geoff's inexcusable behavior the other night and her suspicion that he betrayed Taylor. When Geoff's gaze turns in her direction instead of the surprise Jenn expected, his eyes fill with a sadness she can't explain.

In the exclusive speaker section with the FPOTUS, the new Saudi king wears an out-of-place mischievous grin, probably soaking in the media attention. Next to the former president, opposite the Saudi king, sits Israeli Prime Minister Benet. Beyond him sits an unfamiliar rabbi.

The last VIP section features the Knesset, the chief rabbis, and other guests of Israel, which is where Jenn and Yankovic sit. Two of his bodyguards stand behind them in the aisle. Lined up outside of the tabernacle, Sanhedrin temple priests wear white and purple robes under chest plates with twelve rectangular jewels. Everyone waits for the ceremony to start.

Yankovic, smelling of cigarettes, leans over to her. "History will see him as both a hero and a traitor."

"Which one?" Jenn asks, half-joking. Each leader will win praise and face criticism over the compromises necessary to win peace. There are zealots on all sides who prefer war over any religious symbol compromise, as if the power of their entire faith rested on a symbol or a building. Others are more pragmatic, choosing present-day peace over ancient animosities.

Yankovic leans back to smile with a raised eyebrow. "Exactly."

Jenn fights a burning urge to race over and confront the FPOTUS and Putin in front of the international cameras. That would be a sure way to be removed from the platform, jailed, or perhaps even shot. As if to distract her, a cell phone vibrates in her purse. Unexpected, since she couldn't find her phone earlier. Was it in her purse the whole time? Jenn can't resist checking the text, only to discover that it's not even her phone.

I know Adam's killer. You're in danger.

A jolt of panic shoots up her spine. The text has no phone number, and no name, a familiar format from Taylor.

As subtly as she can muster, Jenn lifts her eyes to scan the hundreds of guest faces. The overcast of early evening and bright lights makes it difficult. No Taylor, so she scans again. Then she spots a tall, older rabbi with curly hair, wearing the same thick black glasses she gave to Taylor earlier. The rabbi stares intently in her direction with a subtle nod when she spots him. Her eyes study the old rabbi carefully to notice his hands tremble. It could be age. Then Jenn remembers the tall rabbi who bumped into her earlier. Did Taylor plant the phone? If so, it also meant Taylor had escaped the Mossad interrogation cell only to penetrate the most guarded venue on the planet. As carefully as she can without being too obvious, she replies. *Danger?*

Yankovic leans over. "Everything OK?"

She turns her phone down. "Fine, thank you." A fake smile forms as she feels another vibration but waits for the Russian to be distracted before checking.

Abomination and perv Yuri

She's not sure if Taylor is kidding or crazy, but she leans toward the latter. The last thing Jenn plans to do is to create a scene with a fugitive. She ignores him for the moment, clueless of how he escaped, and even more baffled why he would risk everything to find her here. Jenn will not pass up the slim chance to speak with the former president. Even if it proves fruitless, she wants to look into his eyes for the truth.

As much as Jenn tries to pay attention to the surrounding circus, her anxiety percolates. What does Taylor hide from her this time? What danger? What does he know about her father's killer?

CHAPTER 68:
RISE OF DAJJãL

Har HaBáyit, Jerusalem
Day of Temple Ceremony

Derek desperately needs Jenn to believe him. Why should she? Ever since they met, he's manipulated her or fed her half-truths. She keeps glancing up at him with a look he reads as somewhere between confusion and irritation.

A dozen Sanhedrin priests blow long silver trumpets from the front of the tabernacle. The ceremony begins. A high priest and other Sanhedrin emerge from behind the tabernacle tent walls with hands raised chanting a Jewish prayer, joined almost instantly by the Orthodox guests. Broadcast live, seemingly all of western Jerusalem erupts into a thunderous unison. The display offends the Arab guests, many of whom stir in their seats or lift their chins wearing a frown.

After the prayer ends, Prime Minister Benet steps up to a microphone, looking absolutely elated, beaming a wide smile with hands raised triumphantly.

"Ladies and gentlemen, dear friends, welcomed guests, and brothers and sisters in peace," Benet begins. "We are here to dedicate the first Jewish tabernacle in nearly two thousand years and to celebrate a historic alliance of peace between all the children of Abraham."

Benet waits for the loud applause and cheers from both sides of the platform that seem to reverberate throughout the city. Everyone applauds support for the unity of the children of Abraham and peace. Benet glances to the Saudi king, then the former president, and finally to a young rabbi seated in a prominent place who raises a hand to bless the prime minister.

"But thanks be to God for our partners in peace. We extend our appreciation to the leaders of Jordan, Bahrain, Qatar, Egypt and the UAE. Our very special gratitude goes to the wise new king of Saudi Arabia, who already fulfills the promise of unity. We are also indebted for the undying support of such devoted friends as the former US president, President Putin, the Holy Pontiff, and the Ecumenical Patriarch, who each honor us with their presence." The prime minister smiles widely as if the entire world made sense, and all the planets aligned.

"God has granted us a miracle beyond our imagination. Tonight, for the first time since our captivity to Babylon, our very own Rabbi ben David, the king of Jerusalem will sprinkle the blood of atonement onto the mercy seat of the actual Ark of Testimony," Benet exclaims, lifting his hands in his own genuine amazement.

Derek watches the announcement fall flat, splitting the crowd into pockets of tepid applause with other hushed speculation as if it were an unbelievably sick joke.

The showman pauses for effect. "Yes, I said the actual Ark of Testimony, hidden by the prophet Jeremiah before the Babylonians, has returned to the nation of Israel, and now to the entire world." With lifted hands, his voice cracks in an emotional crescendo.

Sanhedrin trumpets blow. From behind the tabernacle, a line of Sanhedrin priests parade before the cameras. In the middle of the precession, four priests carry two poles that support a thin wooden platform upon which sits a very ancient box with gold leaf peeling away from darkened wood. A little over two feet long, and two-thirds as high, with what look like Egyptian-style wings forming along the backing for a seat.

Derek glances over to Jenn, watching her hands fiddle with her phone, and her knee bounce from a nervous energy. Rabbi ben David steps up to the microphone as the prime minister steps back differentially with a bow of his head.

"*Shivaho at Alohim!*" the young rabbi shouts in Hebrew, repeated by the Jewish side of the Mount. "*Shivaho al Alohim, ethm meseretio.*"

"The rabbi recites a chant from the Hallel, or Psalm 113," explains SLVIA in Derek's earpiece.

At the sound of their most revered rabbi, the one Yehuda mentioned, the crowd of local rabbis instantly erupt with an enormous wave of cheers. The thunderous celebration easily drowns out the growing gusts of wind, and Derek's growing unease. Nearby rabbis grab onto Derek for an exuberant hug uttering their excitement in Hebrew while the Sanhedrin carry the ark into the tabernacle tent, away from cameras. The messianic rabbi continues to recite the Hallel amid the deafening clamor as he follows the Sanhedrin into the new tabernacle.

The response on the Muslim side of the audience is subdued, surprised. They didn't expect this development. Not angry, yet clearly not pleased. The new Saudi king frowns as one of his advisors whispers into his ear. A subtle nod from the king sends the aide to the Al-Aqsa Mosque. Precisely the circus Yehuda wanted to avoid.

Benet steps up to the microphone. "We have gathered tonight because the new king of Saudi Arabia and the king of Jordan have agreed to share leadership of the Islamic WAQF to allow a Jewish tabernacle alongside the Noble Sanctuary as a symbol of the unity between our faiths, our heritage, and our nations. Tonight, all of Abraham's children come to celebrate a thousand-year peace." Benet shouts the last phrase to more cheers from all sides.

After Benet completes his speech, the new Jewish messiah emerges from the Tabernacle to a cheer that seems to emanate from across Israel. Yehuda seems visibly upset when ben David steps up to the microphone to speak only in Hebrew, leaving out two-thirds of the audience.

SLVIA provides an instant translation, but it sounds like a lot of religious and narcissistic blather, so Derek tunes it out. Instead, he watches Jenn intently, noticing her hands fumbling with the phone. She's anxious. Derek shares her angst, but he can't think of a plan to get past her guards.

Visibly moved, Prime Minister Benet steps up to the microphone again. "Together, the nation of Israel and the entire world have two men above all others to thank for this historic celebration," he says with the enormous smile of a proud papa. "Of course, I speak of the King of Saudi Arabia, our new partner in peace, and the former US President. We have humbly requested each of them to say a brief word. Please welcome the former and next President of the United States."

Mild applause greets the defeated and indicted leader under asylum. Derek's eyes fall to Jenn, who scowls at the man. The former leader grabs the podium sides like he needs it to balance, then scans the audience with a smug grin until he finds the camera lens.

"Peace in the Middle East—they said it couldn't be done. When I first met Benet and the crown prince, he's a king now; I said we can do this, we can do world peace. All the other presidents failed, but I alone succeeded. Now everyone has been thanking me for finding the ark. So, I said, you have to include the ark. And we did it. We did world peace. Maybe I really am the chosen one." The former president holds out his arms like at one of his rallies.

Audience members squirm in their seats and offer weak applause at the outrageous and inappropriate comments. Instead of world peace, the civil wars in Ethiopia, Yemen and the bloody war in Ukraine threaten to expand into a world war. The braggart had nothing to do with finding the ark, shows no humility, and blatantly lies to the world.

"Let no one deceive you in any way. For that day will not come, unless the rebellion comes first, and the man of lawlessness is revealed, the son of destruction, who opposes and exalts himself against every so-called god or object of worship, so that he takes his seat in the temple of God, proclaiming himself to be God. 2

Thess. 2:4," SLVIA recites in the back of his head, apparently still stuck on the prophecy theory. Derek blinks twice. In the lens, SLVIA places an icon over the heads of the former president, the Russian president, and the new Saudi king—each of them a candidate in the AI's mind. When the former president looks toward the Russian leader for approval, the Kremlin master only nods with a smug smile.

"Iranian missile strike is imminent," SLVIA warns in his ear. "Iron Dome AI defenses will fail. Mossad and Shin Bet guard all exits with orders for your arrest. Your escape vehicle is under surveillance." The image of SLVIA morphs into Ryan Reynolds. "Oh, that can't be good."

Unable to speak with so many rabbis jammed so close, he pulls out his phone and types a message to SLVIA. *Keep Jenn Safe.*

At the podium, Benet introduces a regal-looking Saudi king, adorned in gold, white, and purple robes, who steps gracefully up to the microphone amid a standing ovation. The king turns toward a curtain hanging near the Al-Aqsa Mosque, and nods before raising his hands toward his peers.

"*Ya al-lah arsel selwat ola Mohammade watbaa Mohammade tamama kama arselt selwat ola Ebrahim watbaa Ebrahim ferelli, ant malia balthna walgelala.*"

"He recites the Islamic prayer of Abram, evoking the name of Mohammad at the dedication of the Jewish Tabernacle," SLVIA interprets. "Jewish leaders will see his prayer as a desecration." Then his lens readout includes another scripture text.

And the people of the prince who is to come shall destroy the city and the sanctuary. Its end shall come with a flood, and to the end there shall be war. Desolations are decreed.

As he reads, Saudi men wearing elegant, Arabian-style robes with long curved *muhaddab* swords wedged within their tight waist sashes march out of the Al-Aqsa Mosque. Similar to the Sanhedrin priests, they carry an ark that looks nearly identical to the one just placed within the Tabernacle.

As Nelson suspected, the crown prince had purchased the Ethiopian ark before he became king. It must have stolen his thunder to have the first ark marched out ahead of him. Derek wonders if anyone else realizes that the Saudi king offers an ark replica stained with the blood of 750 martyred Christians. Even to Derek, the act seems insensitive, inappropriate, if not downright blasphemous—not that he's an expert.

A small box in the corner of his lens flips to security camera views of YAMAM Special Police units, adding to Shin Bet units surrounding his position, hindered by the tight crowds. They wait, probably unwilling to disrupt the historic ceremony. Derek's completely cut off from the exits and surrounded, edging his growing unease even higher.

After the Saudi king finishes his Arabic prayer, he switches to English. "The *Haram esh-Sharif* has been a sacred site to our Father Abram and his children for nearly four thousand years. To commemorate this prophetic occasion, I bring a gift of unity to honor Allah."

The muscular entourage hoists the ark from their shoulders for all to see as they parade around the stage in front of the cameras.

The king raises his voice above the Muslim audience's cheers. "Over 2,600 years ago, your King Solomon sired a son named Menelik with a Nubian queen. When Menelik came of age, he returned to Jerusalem to be trained as a temple priest. To spread the worship of one God, King Manasseh sent Menelik with the Ark of the Covenant and five hundred priests to southern Egypt. On Elephantine Island, they built a temple on the Nile that stood for 585 years. Even your prophet Isaiah spoke: *In that day there will be an altar to the LORD in the heart of Egypt, and a monument to the LORD at its border.*"

As the king speaks, the men lower the ark, and carry it directly into the Dome of the Rock. Cameras and flashes stream the scene to the far corners of the world in an instant. An Arabian cameraman follows the ark into the Dome. Large screens show them ceremoniously placing it in a niche cut into the rock, but it doesn't fit right. It doesn't seem to matter to the Muslim crowd who cheer while the influential rabbis look on in absolute silent horror.

At first, Derek doesn't get what just happened until he remembers how many Israelites believe that the Dome of the Rock is the true holy of holies, and the Saudi king just placed a bloodstained replica inside.

"To reunite all of Father Abram's children in the name of Allah, I have returned the Ark of the Covenant to its rightful place within the *Qubbat al-Sakhrah,*" the king says with a haughty grin.

The Muslim side of the Temple Mount roars in celebration that echoes across eastern Jerusalem. Terror freezes Derek's heart. The only things holding back both his escape and his arrest are the cameras, the dense crowds, and Jenn. If a riot breaks out, then all bets are off. Another message scrolls across his lens, echoed by SLVIA in the back of his head.

"*Then let those who are in Judea flee to the mountains. Let no one on the housetop go down to take anything out of the house. Let no one in the field go back to get their cloak.* Missile strike in 12.2 minutes. Flapjack, I suggest you hurry."

His glance turns to Jenn, looking in his direction with wide, anxious eyes. She doesn't need SLVIA to tell her things could get worse. It doesn't take long.

Winds that had been a steady bluster all evening suddenly grow in intensity, blowing over a platform screen. An uproar of panicked shouts and screams erupts. To confirm SLVIA's warning, another air-raid siren blares across the city, transforming the zealous outrage into a mass of pandemonium. A distant Iron Dome fires, and then abruptly stops.

"Missile strike imminent in 11.4 minutes. Iron Dome has failed," SLVIA advises.

Derek won't leave without Jenn. When he checks his lens, the Shin Bet and YAMAM push against the crowd in his direction. The FPOTUS has gone, and a dozen guards escort Putin and Benet away. When Derek checks back toward Jenn and Yankovic, the seats are empty.

CHAPTER 69:
LOST SIGNAL

Har HaBáyit, Jerusalem
Day of Temple Ceremony

Jenn knows better than to struggle against the two Russian gorillas practically carrying her off the platform. The less she resists, the less likely they will abuse her. Air-raid sirens have everyone scrambling. It will be a miracle if no one gets trampled.

They approach three black limos north of the platform in the Muslim Quarter. A second before a goon practically shoves her into the back of the last limo, Jenn glances over to see Geoff opening the door for the former president. Ahead of him, Putin enters the first limo, which quickly drives off. The sight adds to her shock, confusion, and sense of betrayal.

Yankovic gets into the limo after her, followed by the two hefty bodyguards. Outside the limo, darkness descends over Israel as flashes in the sky show the missile defense firing again. Even if the incoming missiles don't land, the mid-air explosions will create deadly falling debris. Jenn doesn't know where they are going, but they're putting a lot of distance between her and Taylor. Her only hope rests on Taylor tracking her with the phone he planted in her purse. Even then, judging from the mercenaries in the limo, Taylor will need more than sarcasm and a Taser—he'll need a SEAL team.

Yankovic turns in her direction, his eyebrows pulled down over his ice-blue eyes, his jaw set into a firm grimace. "I will ask one last time. Why did you want to talk to the former president?"

Jenn studies his unblinking scowl, intense and unwilling for more word games or delays. "To ask if he knew Putin would kill my father," she replies, terrified of how he will react.

The frosty Russian stares at her for a long moment, until a smug grin slowly creeps over his face that turns into a chuckle that rolls into a belly chortle.

"Sure, sure," he says as his guffaw settles down. "We will ask him, da."

Yankovic's reaction surprises her. Perhaps the FPOTUS knew nothing— what the Kremlin calls a *useful idiot*. And yet, Yankovic all but admitted that he knows something. And now he knows what she knows. Jenn found the killer, but not how she expected.

"By the way, hand me your phone," Yankovic demands.

Her heart sinks. Any attempt to lie or resist will only make matters worse. She reaches into her purse to remove the phone planted by Taylor, leaving the plastic hairbrush-knife. Jenn needs to wait for the right moment.

Yuri rolls down the window and tosses out the phone then rolls up the window and refreshes his drink. His cavalier attitude sends ice through her veins. She's on her own with the man who murdered the admiral. Jenn wishes she had engaged Taylor first.

Not how Jenn expected this trip to play out, but she can imagine the admiral quoting Joyce Meyer. *We need a backbone, not a wishbone.*

CHAPTER 70:
WARREN'S TUNNEL

Har HaBáyit, Jerusalem
Day of Temple Ceremony

Derek panics, searching the platform for Jenn and her gorilla escorts, but the bedlam makes it impossible. A screen on his lens lights up with the security camera view of Jenn being pushed into a black limo. SLVIA then lights up vector targets for incoming Shin Bet officers pushing through the crowd in his direction.

"You need a distraction," SLVIA says as Temple Mount lights flash on and off in a rapid, erratic strobe effect. The strobe adds to the panic as thousands of people try to rush through narrow, heavily guarded gates. Derek takes advantage of the commotion to disrobe, dropping the black Orthodox hat and garments on the stone and changing direction.

"I've discovered an alternative exit. Follow your guide arrows," SLVIA explains into his inner ear, clear above the chaos.

"That's my girl," he replies. A moment later, the platform lights turn off entirely to an uproar of screams. That's his cue to rip off the face mask and wig, dropping them to be trampled on before changing directions again. A second later, the lights return to strobing.

"Missile strike in 5.35 minutes." A few seconds later. "Target Detection Algorithm data pollution confirmed. Shutting down Iron Dome. Accessing archived data store."

Shutting down a system to restore the data repository is standard protocol, but most data centers aren't facing incoming missiles. An entire department of the Israeli Defense Force will freak out when they see a major defense system shut down on its own.

Derek has more immediate concerns. The Shin Bet officers continue to search for him. Backed against the marble of the Noble Sanctuary, Derek studies his lenses, confused by the arrows that point toward the chained-off Dome of the Rock shrine.

"Missile strike in 4.4 minutes," SLVIA warns.

Derek darts inside the Dome and leaps over the crowd retention chain. "OK, why am I here?" His lens arrows point toward the stone steps leading under the large rock. Not an exit.

"Between 1867 to 1869, the British conducted a survey of the Temple Mount by archaeologists Charles Wilson and Charles Warren, which included maps that are now published in the Rockefeller Museum. According to Solomon's chief mason, Zedekiah, beneath the floor of the Azariah courtyard, near the southwestern corner of the altar, was a cave. According to Warren's survey, that cave is located under the Dome of the Rock."

Voices approach from outside the shrine.

"Groovy, but a cave is not an exit," Derek grouses as he heads down the steps to avoid the approaching voices.

On the way down, he passes the wooden ark stolen from Axum–a replica of a holy Jewish relic stained in blood placed inside an Islamic shrine built over the ancient Jewish altar. A comedy of errors that would be hilarious except for the religious fury it will ignite. A blasphemous offering by an arrogant Saudi king determined to make a grand gesture.

Taking the steps downward, he passes through an arched stone doorway that looks Crusader in design, forcing him to duck. Within the cave, Muslims had covered the stone walls with centuries of heavy plaster. A beautifully patterned marble tile lays over the cave floor.

"SLVIA, you led me into a dead-end," Derek complains.

"An excerpt from Warren's report may help: *Beneath the* Sakhra, *the Arabic name for the Rock, there is a cave that is entered by descending some steps on the southeast side. The cave itself is about 9 feet high in the highest part and 22 feet 6 inches square; a hole has been cut through from the upper surface of the rock into that chamber, namely the cave, beneath. There is a corresponding hole immediately under it, which leads to a three-foot drain down to the valley of Kedron."*

Derek looks up to see the hole above, and then stomps on the marble below until he hears a hollow sound. "SLVIA, how do I get under the marble?"

"That information is not available."

"Argh." A computer only knows digitized information, such as text, sensors, or cameras, with absolutely no visibility in the real world beyond that data point.

Derek hears someone enter the sanctuary above. "I swear I saw someone enter the Dome. The ark looks safe, but that guy had to go someplace. Look around."

A flashlight shines down the stone steps, forcing Derek to scurry to the side, trapped. His heart pounds like a jackhammer as the cautious and heavily armed guard descends into the darkness. Derek pulls out his Taser, but the soldier will have friends with guns. The guard stops, perhaps checking the ark. With his back against the wall, Derek can hear a radio squelching in Hebrew. A second later, the soldier retreats.

"I ordered all forces to fall back and join protection detail for the prime minister under an assault," SLVIA explains.

Derek raises an eyebrow. That will buy a minute or two at the most.

"Incoming missile strike in 2.6 minutes," SLVIA warns.

Derek scans the room to spot a heavy brass lamp stand. After he drags the stand to the central tile, he lifts it through the hole in the ceiling and lets it go.

The stand slams the tile, only chipping the marble. He lays the stand down and lifts only the heavy, sharp-edged base and tries to push down with the weight. The tile cracks along the center, but still holds together.

Derek lifts for a third attempt when SLVIA warns, "Brace yourself, darling."

With a loud grunt, he slams the lamp edge down onto the marble–in the same instant–an explosion rocks the entire Temple Mount, shaking rock from the ceiling. Screams outside grow to a frenzied pitch. When he looks down, the tile crack has opened. Derek pries apart the pieces to discover a three-foot-wide stone tunnel that slopes sharply downward to the east. The tunnel looks dark, dry, and potentially dangerous.

After a moment of second-guessing, he hears soldiers reenter the Dome above. "That's your cue, sweetie," SLVIA says, showing him a security video of the soldiers.

Derek lights his phone flashlight, holds it between his teeth, and places his boots firmly against the tunnel sides. He edges into the tunnel enough to pull the two tiles back together above him. Grabbing the phone, he lets go, sliding quickly over cut stone, using his boots like brakes. Painful, battering already tender muscles, Derek groans loudly. After a hundred meters, the slope flattens, and he slows to a stop. Bruised and sore on his backside, he's alive. He's also trapped while the men who took Jenn to get away. A burning sense of failure and a raging sense of panic scorch his bruised ego.

A large stone blocks the end of the tunnel. Air-raid sirens continue above, the sound muted. Another explosion rocks the Mount, shaking his nerves along with the heavy stone. No way he can crawl back up the tunnel. Even SLVIA is useless to help him.

Derek taps his phone to pull up a recent contact. The signal is weak. "Loir, it's Taylor. I'm trapped under the Temple Mount. I need help. GPS coordinates coming your way. Bring rock cutting tools and hurry, someone's life is on the line."

"Iron Dome data pollution resolved. Restarting Iron Dome," SLVIA reports. "Jennifer Scott has boarded the yacht *Zhelaniye*, registered in Türkiye." Onboard security cameras show an enormous brute shoving Jenn down a yacht hallway.

Derek's jaw clenches, and his palms sweat. "SLVIA, don't lose track of her."

"Seriously flapjack, try to keep up. Your new travel arrangements are in progress."

CHAPTER 71:
STRIKE ZONE

National Military Command Center,
Washington D. C.
Day of Temple Ceremony

M att stares at the control room monitor wall in that stunned state of disbelief that overwhelms you in the seconds after a crisis starts. Not long after the false missile crisis, a malicious code that infected CISA command hit the NMCC. All efforts to halt the incursion have failed. A third of the screens are black or filtering through some form of diagnostics. The other two-thirds show a war building in Moldova, Iran, Syria, and Israel. Satellites show China preparing a fleet for a naval invasion of Taiwan.

"Sir, we have a confirmed missile strike on the US Embassy in Jerusalem. Communications are down with fourteen missing persons," conveys Commander Dalton. "Iron Dome failure confirmed."

An act of war that will draw the US into this quagmire. Unlike Ukraine, the US cannot avoid sending ships and troops if Iran invades Israel or China moves on Taiwan. In Matt's mind, he's watching the starting moments of World War III.

"Open a direct line to IDF," Commander Crawford commands. A second later, General Aaron Cohen of the Israeli Defense Force appears on the screen.

General Diehl takes control of the conversation. "General Cohen, we're aware of the hit on our embassy, but we've lost communications. What can you tell us about the strike?"

Bald with an angular nose and intense eyes, the general frowns. "Damage appears extensive. We have a fire crew on site. They've recovered six bodies so far. The Temple Mount northern wall also sustained serious damage. A second strike hit less than a hundred meters from Dimona, the Israeli nuclear power site in the Negev Desert. Two strikes landed near the Mount of Olives and one south of Tel Aviv. Iron Dome went offline for nearly five minutes but came back online to return fire. We don't know what happened, but we'll investigate later."

"General, we're experiencing similar AI platform issues," Diehl replies.

"Forget the platform, the Ayatollah will regret his response to peace," the Israeli general vows with a clenched jaw.

Matt doubts seriously that Iran has the technical expertise to pull off an Iron Dome cyber sabotage, much less penetrate the NMCC. China has the expertise but historically avoids engaging in the Middle East. The Kremlin seems the most likely saboteur. In fact, Putin's appearance at the ceremony raises serious questions about how he avoided sanctions or travel restrictions. It also raises concerns about the status of the FPOTUS when it occurs to Matt that Putin needed to be there to seal the deal.

"General, Prime Minister Benet agreed to extradite our former president after the ceremony," Matt says, changing the subject. "We've also lost contact with his security team. Do you know their status?"

The general's face drains, leaving him pale as a ghost. "General Mola Brahms said he would notify you. Mossad lost contact with the former president shortly after the ceremony. We escorted them off the Temple Mount, but their limo never arrived at the hotel, and someone disabled the GPS transponder."

The call falls silent for just a moment as General Diehl, Matt, and others soak in the news. Either a former president slipped through Mossad's fingers or Mossad let him slip.

"I want to speak with General Brahms directly," Matt asserts.

General Cohen shakes his head vigorously. "Contact him yourself. With all due respect, your missing president is not my greatest concern with missiles dropping. We will contact you with any news on your embassy, but Israel cannot afford to waste resources to hunt down a lost asylum seeker."

Matt can understand the sentiment while Israel remains under attack, but this incident will have a serious negative effect on US-Israeli relations.

"Thank you, General, we'll be in touch," General Diehl cuts the call and turns to his aide. "Get me the White House."

While a debate rages on the cause of the network meltdown and how to respond to a missing FPOTUS, Matt looks up to notice a blank monitor light up. For just a second, the image of a young, attractive blond with a 1960s-style haircut appears to be replaced by what looks like a normal data screen. From this distance, Matt can't be sure, but he's seen that face before. The SLVIA.

As if the program read his mind, Matt's phone vibrates, distracting his attention long enough for a discreet check of the message. No ID or phone number. Only a scriptural quote.

I will gather all the nations against Jerusalem to battle. Zechariah 14:2

Matt hasn't seen a text message like this one since last year. Together with the image he just saw confirms in his mind that Dr. Garrett changed his mind to restore the SLVIA code. Matt's honestly not sure if that's good news or bad.

CHAPTER 72:
FAMILY CONCILIUM

Maison Godin Prison, North of Quebec
Day of Temple Ceremony

T he words of Elon Musk flood Nelson with a condemning accusation. *With artificial intelligence, we are summoning the demon.*

Perhaps it was hubris, or fear, or profound confusion over global events, but Nelson just made that precise mistake. The digital unification of WITNESS and SLVIA continues to burn up the processors of both the Cray and D-WAVE data centers at near capacity. Neither Nelson nor Jester have ever seen anything like it––a spectacle that sends a slow, frosty unease creeping through Nelson's soul.

Judging only from the screens that flash rapidly across the monitor wall, SLVIA and WITNESS work through protocols to build a quantum processor to convert the thousands of zettabytes of binary data sources into quantum qubits for WITNESS to leverage within quantum algorithms. He can't be entirely sure, but dozens of screens appear to scroll fresh code development as SLVIA either learns or teaches WITNESS how to program the quantum algorithms. Developers have experimented with the concept of teaching a computer to code, but no one ever envisioned anything so dynamic or all-encompassing.

"Dude, like, SLVIA just cracked the Kremlin," Jester says, his gaze fixed on a different wall, his palms patting his chest.

The screen flashes networks with names written in Cyrillic, Chinese, Farsi, and dozens of other languages. Even NMCC, CISA, NSA, DOD, DOJ, and hundreds of secure US networks have opened.

Nelson's pulse races from the unimaginable potential he unleashed. Hyper-security conscious governments already teetering on the edge of war will see such a massive intrusion as an act of war. A deep, rumbling dread saturates his entire body. Nelson wonders if he should warn the NSA—but warn them of what? That he thought of calling the FBI to confiscate the jet but suffered a fatal judgment error at the last moment?

"Dude, it's like a super-SLVIA, in a scary zombie AI kind of way, you know?" Jester banters, mesmerized by the activity.

As far as Nelson can tell, the SLVIA and WITNESS synergy have not launched a malicious code. In fact, the programs take inventory, run diagnostics, remove unwanted user accounts, and refresh data stores. Nelson can't be sure, but they appear to remove unseen threats; perhaps even the poisoned data Jester feared.

As odd as it sounds, Nelson likens the process to a parent—SLVIA—showing her child—WITNESS—how to tend to every flower in the garden. For a purpose that Nelson can't imagine; yet the SLVIA trains the WITNESS for something.

"SLVIA, please explain your activities," Nelson asks, wondering if years under Taylor's influence had changed the program's core objectives.

"Integration of my neural network with the WITNESS quantum processors in order to complete my mission to analyze human knowledge," SLVIA replies.

Astounding. SLVIA never stopped seeking new data, perhaps spurred on by the exponential growth of the net and the development of quantum technology. To Nelson, the statement means more. The SLVIA will eventually extend her neural network over every other AI on the planet. The Chinese actively build AI to attack American networks. It's impossible to predict how the SLVIA will deal with that internal conflict of purpose. Will SLVIA form a split persona? Will competing objectives create an unresolvable logic conflict?

Along the same lines, Nelson wonders if the WITNESS purpose has changed with the SLVIA integration. "WITNESS," he says, "state your primary design purpose."

An entire wall of monitors instantly switches to SLVIA and WITNESS, morphing back and forth as both personas respond in perfect unison. "To bear witness to the truth during the end of days."

Before Nelson can ask who gave the program that purpose, the entire image morphs into a graphic of thousands of file folders that scroll across the wall. Titles and dates trace from 500 BCE until the late twentieth century. The surprise revelation throws off his train of thought entirely.

"SLVIA, what you are showing me?" he asks, fearful yet fascinated.

The screen displays folder names in Latin, Greek, Aramaic, Coptic, Farsi, Hebrew, German, French, Italian, and English. Other folders bear the names of nations conquered or forgotten, wars, crusades, and genocide. An entire section of folders focuses on banking, governance, politics, trade, sciences, and pseudo-sciences. Other folders feature the names of modern organizations such as the League of Nations, United Nations, Council on Foreign Relations, World Bank, International Monetary Fund, Bilderberg Group, Bohemian Club, the Davos Economic Council, and others. One set of folders shows corporate ownership that spreads from 147 core entities to encompass ownership in every major market and industry, with international corporations and household brands too many to count.

One folder sits at the top of the hierarchy titled in Latin: *Sacris Ordinationibus Concilium Tredecim* or Sacred Directives of the Council of Thirteen.

"These are the sacred archives of the *Concilium Tredecim,* which were stolen by the flapjack and entrusted to me for encrypted storage," SLVIA replies.

"The time has come for the truth to be revealed," WITNESS adds.

Nelson's father was an attorney for the World Bank, a very senior and active Scottish Rite Freemason, and a key player in the annual planning for the Bilderberg Group meetings.

"SLVIA, provide a summary statement only. What do these files reveal?" he queries.

"These files document the internal affairs and teachings of the Egyptian *Shemsu Hor*, the Sumerian *Brotherhood of the Snake*, the *Secret Order of Sion*, the *Knights Templar*, the *Black Knights of Malta*, the *Rosicrucian's*, the *Scottish Rite*, the *Bavarian Illuminati*, the *Order of Skull and Crossbones*, the *Ordo Templi Orientis*, the *Opus Dei*, the *Order of the Solar Temple*, the *Order of the Bohemian*, the *Bilderberg*, and lesser secretive groups under the control and leadership of the *Concilium Tredecim*," SLVIA explains.

Astonished and confused why either Taylor or the SLVIA would care for such arcane poppycock and conspiracies, Nelson instantly wonders if perhaps he could be wrong, in denial of the truth, or once again, ignorant of it.

SLVIA continues. "These are the archives of the dragon which the Apostle John spoke of in the book of Revelation. *The dragon stood on the shore of the sea. And I saw a beast coming out of the sea. It had ten horns and seven heads, with ten crowns on its horns, and on each head a blasphemous name.*"

"SLVIA, prophecies are not fact; they are fantasies made up by men to incite mass fear or placid obedience. Taylor tolerated this nonsense, but I created you to analyze data to discern truth, not succumb to religious illusions," Nelson argues with his own creation.

Then his irritation turns to curiosity, which turns more personal. Perhaps he would do well to ask a few more questions. WITNESS had alluded to a connection between his father and the *Concilium Tredecim*.

"SLVIA, does the name of my father or family appear with any of these files?" Unsure if he wants to know the truth.

"Yes," comes the simple reply.

Perhaps these are the files that WITNESS referenced a few days ago but could not find. His family wealth came from generations of discipline, frugality, invention, and hard work. While some of that was true, the revelation that his blessed existence may have also flourished on the backs of the oppressed leaves him with a biting disgrace. The memory of his Yemeni shipmates still saturates him. If his father's name appears in those files, then regardless of his revulsion at the very concept, he may be the unwitting beneficiary of a thousand years of secrecy, manipulation, and corruption—or so the popular lore would have him believe. Nelson needs to know the truth.

A few names appear repeatedly, such as Praeceptor, Boaz, Jachin, Osiris, Isis, Aries, Sirius, Pleiades, Aten, Gimel, Gilgamesh, Thoth, and Amenophis. Nelson notes thirteen in all. They must be secret names, or titles of some sort, applied to an ongoing stream of thirteen individuals, so that real names are forever kept a secret. Ingenious, but why? To hide what?

In the past, Nelson would ignore this type of information as conspiratorial, not credible. But something changed in him. It could have been the loss of his career, or a year humbled as a fugitive with Taylor, listening to Jester's conspiracy theories, or his horrid trip to Africa. Perhaps all of it. Regardless, the time has come for him to ask some direct questions, and he knows to whom he should ask.

One of his father's closest associates was a former member of the House of Parliament and a retired senior member of the Council on Foreign Relations. The man also has an obsession with the Egyptian goddess of Isis, displaying Isis-inspired art, statues, and priceless artifacts throughout his estates. It's a coincidence, perhaps, but he's the same man to whom his father mentioned the *Concilium* in what they thought was a private conversation.

"NIGEL," he calls the AI lab assistant. "Please contact Captain McLaughlin. Direct her to prepare a flight plan for Wales. We shall leave within the hour."

If he intends to ask relevant questions, he should prepare as well as possible. On his way out of the lab, he picks up a pair of Jester lenses and taps the device.

"Hello, D-PA," WITNESS answers.

"Hello, WITNESS. Open the files displayed by SLVIA. Please read to me every file that mentions my father or family, starting from the earliest mention. I want to know everything."

"Of course, D-PA," WITNESS responds to the Bluetooth earbud attached to the frames. "Your family journey into the order began during 952 in the Narbonne region of southern France."

Nelson listens intently, hoping that unlocking his past will unravel the paradox of his present dilemma

CHAPTER 73: GRAVE DIGGERS

Har HaBáyit Eastern Wall, Muslim Cemetery
Day of Temple Ceremony

Nearly driven mad with guilt as Jenn slips away, Derek listens to pounding on a large stone placed over the ancient altar drainage tunnel. Loir and his helpers take an enormous risk of arrest, especially after an air raid. With what sounds like an enormous effort, a large stone slab falls away from his feet. Within seconds, a flashlight shines up through the opening to blind him.

"Hurry, Mr. Taylor," Mordechai says, reaching a hand to help him crawl out.

Outside the tunnel, a downpour driven by fierce winds creates a deafening roar. Surprised to see the kid Derek expected back at St. George, he grabs him for a shoulder hug. "Dude, you're breaking the law."

"No," Mordechai shakes his drenched head, "I'm saving a friend."

Derek finds himself in the middle of a fifteen-hundred-year-old Muslim cemetery roughly fifty yards south of the Golden Gate.

"We just destroyed the tomb marker for Ubadah ibn Samet, a friend of

Mohammad," bemoans Loir. "This desecration will enrage all of Islam."

"Then let's not hang out and take credit," Derek shouts above the storm. "No offense, but I need to leave now,"

Loir nods anxiously. "This way, quickly."

"Did you know that the Ottoman Sultan Suleiman bricked over the Golden Gate entrance in 1541 to prevent a prophecy of the Jewish messiah from coming through the gate?" Mordechai points to the Gate as they pass it. "But he fulfilled prophesy because the messiah had already entered that gate on a donkey in 33 CE. Ezekiel said, *Then the man brought me back to the outer gate of the sanctuary, the one facing east, and it was shut. The LORD said to me, 'This gate is to remain shut. It must not be opened; no one may enter through it. It is to remain shut because the LORD, the God of Israel, has entered through it.'*"

They zigzag through an Islamic cemetery into the Kidron Valley while Mordechai continues talking. "Throughout history, many nonbelievers have unknowingly fulfilled prophecy, even those who tried to prevent it. Much like you, Mr. Taylor."

Derek grimaces, unsure whether he wants to be associated with a prophecy fulfillment. He's far more obsessed with finding Jenn at the moment. "Always glad to help. Where are we going? I need to get to the Port of Haifa."

"I have a car waiting." Loir points to the Basilica of Agony at the base of the Mount of Olives.

Derek picks up the pace into a jog, forcing the elder Loir to lag. Loir's panel van waits in front of the church while air-raid sirens continue to keep most residents inside the dry air-raid shelters. Above the sound of the storm and the sirens, the explosive blasts of Iron Dome missiles and percussive air explosions seem to come from everywhere. Burning shrapnel falls to the ground in several locations near the olive garden next to the church where Judas betrayed his messiah.

Under the church portico entrance, Mordechai turns to embrace Derek. "I knew the Lord would protect you."

Stressed and anxious, Derek's heart swells with a pang of sadness, knowing that he'll never see these people again. "Thanks for digging me out, but really brother, I need to go."

Mordechai nods and holds up a set of keys. "I'm your Uber."

They turn to leave as Loir pants his way to the portico at the same moment that Yehuda rushes in from parking. Both men approach Derek for an emotional embrace. "Israel owes you a great debt, my friend."

With a deep breath, Derek accepts the gratitude. "No worries, rabbi. You can send me an IOU." He no longer stammers, but still shudders slightly. Sore muscles, bruises, and burns will take longer to heal.

"I still owe another man named flapjack an IOU," Yehuda winks.

Derek squeezes the old rabbi's shoulder. "I think it expired."

Derek really wants to stay and talk about their amazing experience until another missile strikes close, rattling the ceiling and shaking the heavy iron lanterns in the church.

"The ship now has a fifteen mile head start on you," SLVIA urges behind his ear.

Derek turns to Yehuda and the others. "Gentlemen, it has been an honor I'll never forget, but that's my cue."

Derek turns to Mordechai. "Thanks for everything, but—"

"I'm driving," Mordechai interrupts. "Let's go."

Derek shrugs. "OK, kid, then you better be cool with breaking the speed limit."

CHAPTER 74:
NEED FOR SPEED

Port of Haifa, Israeli Coast
Day of Temple Ceremony

After a treacherous drive by a maniacal Mordechai, Derek finds the unlocked dive shop storage shed at the end of a long commercial pier. Winds continue to gust upwards of thirty knots, giving Derek a sharp twinge of trepidation over the escape plan.

"No offense, but you're insane," Mordechai shouts over the noise.

SLVIA made alternate escape plans. Derek had expected a fast boat, but the rough seas and Yuri's head start made that option impractical. He's not sure the new plan is any better.

"Yeah, I know," Derek yells back as he studies the experimental craft he's never flown before. "SLVIA, I'm not sure this is a great idea."

"The ship has a thirty-two-mile head start on you," SLVIA replies behind his ear. On the inside of his lens, SLVIA morphs into the image of Leonardo Di Caprio playing Howard Hughes. "You need high speed and low altitude, with a small landing profile."

Derek checks out the Zeva drone prototype, a one-seater, four-blade, electric-powered drone shaped like a flying saucer. Not yet available for purchase due to licensing and testing, start-up companies often crave cash from a discreet buyer willing to waiver liability in case of death. Flying this toy in a raging storm is the very definition of a death wish.

A moment of apprehension gets shattered when a bullet pings the wooden wall, barely missing him. Mordechai quickly rolls the shed door closed as another round hits the door.

"Agent Elan Golan has tracked you using port security," SLVIA says in the back of his head. "Agent Golan acts under the direction of the Librarian. The Librarian received his orders from the Praeceptor to recapture or eliminate you."

Derek turns to Mordechai. "See, I told you—quiet cave looking pretty good."

If Derek flies out now, he'll fly directly into a hail of bullets. Even if he makes it out without damage, they will come after Mordechai. Derek tries to think of another option, but his brain freezes.

"Get in and power up. I'll distract them," Mordechai yells as he pulls a dive tank from the bin and attaches it to a top-of-the-line dive vest. The young monk quickly grabs a high-end dive regulator to attach it to the tank and pulls a high-end mask from a shelf with obvious experience in diving.

With little choice, Derek climbs into the tiny cockpit. "SLVIA, how does this thing handle in the heavy rain?"

"Unknown," SLVIA admits.

"What kind of range?" he asks, anxiety pumping with each heartbeat.

"Rated top speed of 150 miles per hour. At top speed, you will have less than ten minutes of power to reach Lieutenant Scott," SLVIA informs him.

"Geez, why do we always cut these things so close," he complains. Derek straps in, powers the dash, checks battery and the navigation controls. He's never going to reach top speed in such a downpour.

"I will guide your GPS, but you must leave now," SLVIA urges.

Derek has flown several unmanned drones using hand controls, so he can only assume that similar control principles must apply. If not, this will be a quick flight off a short pier. He grabs the stick and nudges the throttle to lift a few feet. The air velocity inside the small shed rattles and blows everything like a contained tornado.

Mordechai peeks through a window to see if he can spot the shooter. Another shot cracks through the window to strike the kid in the shoulder, tossing him backward to the ground. Panic grips Derek's chest as he prepares to land.

Mordechai unexpectedly stands up to yell above the noise. "I'm OK, leave now!"

Mordechai's shoulder bleeds where the bullet pierced a section of his harness, but the dive gear prevented a serious injury. The husky monk grabs his mask and fins before he turns back. "Godspeed, Mr. Taylor."

Without another word, the monk runs to roll open the shed door, allowing bullets to hit the back wall. The dark and heavy rain prevents a clean shot. Without stopping, Mordechai launches into a mad dash toward the water, leaping into the harbor, chased by bullets.

Not willing to waste Mordechai's distraction, Derek slams the stick forward, pushing the drone into the deluge. Winds shove the lightweight craft hard to the side before he compensates, continuing to speed forward.

Surprised, Agent Golan steps from his cover to aim his gun directly at Derek, but he's too late. The drone slams into the Freemason, lifting his torso off the ground and dropping him into the water. When he looks back for Mordechai, he's already lost in the darkness.

A digital compass appears on his lenses, giving him a chance to adjust his direction and lift the craft higher. The winds rock the drone around like a balloon in front of a fan, but the saucer shape adjusts quickly.

"OK, Tinkerbell, here we go—never-never land or bust," Derek says, pushing the throttle to the max, hugging the surface at only two hundred feet to stay below the radar until he clears Israeli air space where he can get above the cloud cover.

"Good luck, Peter," SLVIA replies, connecting to the popular entertainment reference.

The experience of racing an experimental drone in the drenching, pitch-black rain without wipers or lights using only a compass stretches Derek's already hammered nerves. He has less than thirty minutes to come up with a plan to land on a rolling yacht, rescue Jenn, and escape with only minutes of power. Or he'll likely die trying. Lunacy personified. His slide has ended. He's arrived.

CHAPTER 75:
SELF-INFLICTED

Superyacht Zhelaniye, Eastern Mediterranean
Day of Temple Ceremony

Jenn isn't sure if she's a hostage or a witness to be eliminated, but she's still alive. Locked inside a guest cabin with a guard posted outside, she's certain that Taylor would have found the tossed phone by now to realize that he has no way to track her. Self-rebuke and regret have saturated her for over an hour, thinking of what the admiral would say about her self-inflicted predicament. She imagines something like, *extraordinary people are ordinary people who rise to the occasion of extraordinary circumstances. Be one.*

Beyond the two goons who escorted her, Jenn counts at least six crew plus Rhodes. At over a hundred and fifty feet, the superyacht should be fast. Yankovic has a megayacht over two hundred fifty feet. This must be a loaner. Their destination may be as close as Türkiye, or as far as Crimea. So far at sea, Jenn will need to wait until they dock before making a move. Escape from a foreign country contains an entirely new set of risks and challenges. If she can escape her cabin long enough to find the communications station, maybe she can send an SOS, except the ship's con will be near the bridge with a guard. Every option is risky. She screwed up.

The intense storm slows them down and pushes the ship stabilizers beyond their normal capacity. Enormous waves constantly roll the hull to create an unpleasant ride. One of her guards ran to the head to puke, leaving the second one green and in a nasty mood. Raised on ships before she could walk, the motion has never bothered her. So far, that could be her only advantage. Just in case, Jenn hides the blade from her hairbrush inside her silk dress sleeve. She'll have only one chance to use it. She'll need the right moment to make it count.

Still stunned over watching Geoff escort the former president onboard with the look of a man caught cheating on his wife, she simply can't imagine what led an Annapolis grad to betray his country. The former president has a cult following, unlike any modern-day American political leader. Geoff fell into the cult. Jenn can only assume that Israel must have declined asylum to the former president, which means Rhodes has already cut a deal with the devil.

What Jenn can't figure out is why Yankovic seems so obsessed with keeping her around. She can only guess he wants to know what the Feds know about the admiral's murder. Before the Ukraine sanctions, Yankovic had substantial business interests in the states, plus mansions, condos, and jets—all of them seized. Payback could be another motive.

As if the devil could read Jenn's mind, the cabin door opens to Yankovic with cold, narrow eyes. His glare penetrates her for a long, painful moment. Her heart beats wildly, suddenly fearful of rape, wondering if the blade in her sleeve will be enough protection.

"Bring her," Yankovic commands the guard, who grabs her forearm in a vice grip.

Dragged down a long hallway to a ship salon that ends with a long glass wall out onto an expansive aft deck with a sloshing, half-empty pool. Decorated in a mix of styles, the salon smells of cheap Russian cigarettes and brandy. Euro techno-punk music plays in the background.

Sunk into a large, cushioned chair, sulks the former president, his legs flared and hands grasping each other. Geoff stands to his side with what looks like fear in his eyes. Does he fear for her safety or his own?

"Ms. Scott, tell me now, what made you think the former president knew about the death of your father?" Yankovic glares into her eyes, the icy, steel-blue almost iridescent with fury.

Jenn studies the eyes of the president, narrow and cautious, with brows hanging low. He seems angry, impatient, and inconvenienced. Her gaze shifts up to study Geoff. A bead of sweat drips down his temple before he casts his gaze downward. Is he ashamed of his support for a criminal or something more? She can't tell.

Jenn ignores Yankovic's question and turns to the former president. Not the chance she wanted, but a chance she won't pass up. "When you told Putin about Admiral Scott's threat to expose the INVISID backdoor, did you know he would have my father murdered?"

"She said she had a video," interrupts Geoff, as if to change the subject.

Jenn burns a scowl into Geoff, wondering why he would betray her. Yankovic swings his hand around to smack her hard across the face. By training, Jenn turns her face away at the last second to soften the blow, but the pain still stings deep.

"Where's the video?" Yankovic demands.

Jenn slowly lifts her head to meet Yankovic's gaze. "I gave the admiral's electronic devices to the NIA. By now, the FBI has opened an investigation."

If Yankovic thought she would still have the evidence, then he's a fool. Jenn turns to burn her fury at the disgraced leader who didn't deny ratting out her father. Whether he knew what Putin would do is irrelevant.

Yankovic grunts, then turns to the former president. "Thank you, Mr. President. As always, you have been most helpful. You may return to your suite. I believe the chef has prepared your dinner. Ms. Nala will join you shortly."

At that dismissal, a goon escorts the FPOTUS to his gilded cabin, leaving Jenn with the guard who dragged her out of her room, while Geoff stands alongside Yankovic. The interrogation isn't over, and it's about to get messy. Jenn tries to conjure the admiral's courage, but she's never been more terrified.

"I want to spare my special guest any unnecessary ugliness." Yankovic confirms his motive with a pretentious grin. His gaze turns to Geoff, who seems nervous with his hands in loose fists, refusing to make eye contact with anyone. A traitor not yet accepted by the enemy.

Then Yankovic turns back to her. "Ms. Scott, if you do not have the video, then you are only useful to me as a negotiating pawn with your government. Perhaps they would like to know about your illegal spying activities."

Jenn turns to glare at Geoff, who stole her devices and betrayed her. Flooded with emotions, she clenches her jaw to keep from flying into a rage.

"Resist or cause me any trouble and I know a Qatar prince who would absolutely love to break a woman like you. His last whore took him ten years to train. By then, she was too old, and he had to sell her to a Somali warlord," Yankovic taunts as he walks over to the bar to make himself a drink.

"Which one of you killed my father?" Jenn demands. Geoff's association with Yankovic can't be recent. He's not the man she fell in love with in college.

Yankovic steps up to slap her again, hard. Her entire skull rings from the blow. "You demand nothing, whore. Speak only when I tell you."

Jenn's eyes pivot to Geoff, who turns his gaze downward, a coward unwilling to defend her. Jenn turns away, wishing she could cry, but she can't show that kind of weakness in front of Yankovic. Never more terrified in her life, her pulse races, and her mouth bleeds. She still has the blade and a razor-thin chance of using it to any real benefit. Jenn tells herself to wait for the right moment—she may only get one, or none.

The music stops mid-song, as if the power went out. Yankovic looks to the goon who shrugs. At the other end of the lounge, several couches and chairs face a ninety-inch flat screen that lights up as if someone had turned on the remote. The screen focuses with a security camera view of the admiral's living room. Surprised to know that the admiral had installed interior security cameras, Jenn wonders if Yankovic had been spying on him. Yankovic immediately turns to walk closer for a better view. The guard pulls her along.

On screen, the admiral enters the living room, unexpectedly followed by

Geoff Rhodes. Her father wrote of a video with the former president and Putin. This video looks different.

Geoff leaps for the remote control and desperately tries to turn off the power.

"Leave it," commands Yankovic, obviously wanting to see what the video will reveal—meaning he doesn't know.

Jenn studies Geoff, wondering why he's so afraid until the horrifying truth slowly dawns on her. She turns to the screen, fixated.

"Good evening, Admiral. Thank you for giving me a moment of your time," Geoff greets with a salute.

"What can I do for you, Agent Rhodes?" the admiral responds without returning the salute, which would be against standard protocol.

Geoff lowers his hand. "Sir, I'm here off the record because of my devotion to the president and the nation. Please reconsider your plans to torpedo the new ID platform. The president feels that another scandal would not be in the national interest."

Geoff dashes up to her. "Jenn, please believe me, they gave me no choice."

"Silence," shouts Yankovic, then turns to the goon. "If he speaks again, shoot him."

The goon withdraws a gun. Geoff drops his shoulders, tightens his fists, and turns away from the screen. Jenn's chest tightens, and her breath turns icy in anticipation.

"Another scandal?" the admiral repeats. "The INVISID ID has a Kremlin backdoor, which makes it a national security problem that neither the president nor the nation can ignore. I swore an oath to the Constitution, as did you, Agent Rhodes, if you still remember. Now, I'm not sure why the president sent you—which is highly inappropriate—but since you're here, I'd like you to relay a message back. Rescind the executive order to implement INVISID or I will take this information to the Investigator General, to the FBI, and to Congress."

"Understood, sir. I will relay the message," Geoff cuts short, coughing several times before clearing his throat. "Sorry, sir, I think I just inhaled a cat hair or something. I'm allergic," Geoff explains. "Might I bother you for a glass of water?" He keeps coughing hard to clear his throat.

Jenn glares at Geoff, who never had an allergy when they dated. His face turns red, and his breathing grows shallow, a nervous reaction. Geoff had the same look when the brass at Annapolis busted them for having an affair.

Back on the screen, the admiral hesitates, looking irritated, then turns to the kitchen. As soon as the admiral turns the corner, Geoff continues to cough as he slips on a partial latex glove, pulls out a small bottle, and sprays the cushions on the coach. Backing away with his clean hand over his coughing mouth, he returns the bottle and glove to his pocket seconds before the admiral returns with a glass.

"Thank you, sir." Geoff sips the water, returning the glass. "Sorry to bother you."

The admiral takes the glass and sets it down. "Will that be all?"

Geoff hesitates. "Sir, I know it's in the past, but I was wondering why it was necessary to ruin my career for dating your daughter?"

Her father steps back. "Excuse me?"

"I was really doing great at Annapolis until they slapped me down for dating Jennifer. That black mark shadowed my entire career. I know that *had* to be your influence. I just need to ask if it was worth it for you."

"Leave now, Agent Rhodes, before they carry you out," the admiral responds to the insult with the fiery rhetoric typical of the man whenever tested.

"Funny you should put it that way," Geoff snickers, then turns to leave.

Jenn turns away from the screen, staggered. Yankovic isn't the killer; he's the handler. Geoff must have been working with Yankovic during the last administration. He was the secret Kremlin backdoor no one could find.

"Yuri, you've got to believe me. I never knew there was a hidden camera," Geoff defends himself. "Look, even she didn't know."

Yankovic laughs, before turning his voice icy cold. "When the FBI discovers the video, they will charge you for the murder. Since Russia will never extradite you, then I am clean."

"*You* gave me the toxin," Geoff retorts.

"Did I?" Yankovic laughs. "Do you have a video?"

At that comment, the ship's engines die suddenly, as if the yacht had run out of gas. Large, modern yachts use sophisticated operating software to connect mechanical, electrical, navigation, and nearly every function of the ship. Could this be the work of the flapjack, or a malfunction born of poor maintenance? Either way, losing power in a raging storm puts everyone on board in grave danger. Yankovic picks up a ship intercom phone, but it's also dead.

A second later, all the lights go dark. In the pitch-black, the television screen alone lights up again with an image of Hugh Jackman as P.T. Barnum yelling to the packed circus crowd. "Show Time!" Then the screen goes blank, leaving everyone in total darkness. That's her cue.

CHAPTER 76:
RAGING WATERS

Derek can't imagine how this will end well. Nearly out of power and completely out of options, he wonders if the lunatic ever recognizes his delusion before it's too late. It's too late to think about that now. Now down to five percent power, his GPS guide positions him directly behind the stalled ship. Fifty miles at sea, the Zeva breaks through the thick cloud cover into raging winds and heavy rain that batters his tiny saucer like a cat toy.

"SLVIA, I can't see the ship," he shouts as his elevation drops rapidly, terrified he will hit the water and sink. Flashbacks of the crash in the Jordan spike his adrenaline.

"Power at three percent. A crash is imminent," SLVIA warns in a calm voice as deck lights illuminate directly in front of him.

"Oh crap," he shouts.

"Power at one percent," SLVIA warns as the craft slams onto the deck, and skids wildly across the expensive teak to smash through a glass wall where

Derek just saw the flash of a gun muzzle in the dark. He may be too late.

The shattered glass shreds the drone blade shields, shooting carbon fiber fragments and glass shards in every direction. The damaged nose smashes into an enormous man, snapping his back and flipping his limp body at the wall like a broken doll. The drone skids to an abrupt stop deep inside the dark salon.

Momentarily dazed and surprised he's even alive, Derek grabs a leather satchel before swinging open the canopy. The sound of the wind blowing into the ship wails at a deafening pitch. The smashed wall opens the entire deck salon to the sideways blowing rain and heavy waves crashing over the aft deck. Another gun flash shatters the canopy plexiglass, forcing Derek to dive onto the sloshing floor.

Deck lights go dark again, leaving the salon nearly pitch-black. With no power forward, the ship is helpless to the thirty-foot swells that roll the top-heavy pleasure yacht on its side.

Derek reaches into his satchel to grab the last two Wicked Sister drones and tosses them into the salon. They turn on instantly to flash over Yankovic holding a gun with a small dagger bleeding from his thick side. With his free hand, a drooling, trembling and groaning Yankovic gently pulls out the blade from a blood-soaked shirt while Rhodes holds Jenn by the throat.

"Give it up, Taylor," yells Rhodes over the storm. "Moron, you crashed your getaway."

Derek stays silent, without a gun, he needs to stay invisible. Right now, the strobes are the only way he knows where Yankovic and Geoff stand.

Waves washing over the aft deck flow freely into the open salon. If the ship was under power, powerful bilge pumps would keep the vessel safe. Without power, the ship will eventually take on too much water and sink.

"I know you don't have a gun, geek. You're trapped. Maybe Putin will use you for propaganda. You and Snowden can be roomies," shouts Rhodes.

"Your friend is correct, Mr. Taylor," shouts Yankovic. "Except I care nothing for you or your girlfriend."

Derek peeks to see Yankovic aiming the gun toward Jenn's head while

Rhodes holds her by the arms. From inside his satchel, Derek pulls out a mini-crossbow, roughly six inches wide with a laser targeting guide and a range of fifty feet. He purchased specially made Taser arrows that release an 1800-volt pulse charge on impact. The strobes give him just enough light to see the Russian's bleeding torso. Derek only gets one shot. He aims for the heart in the middle of the massive chest. If he can stun the pedophile bear, he can focus on the traitor.

Derek aims carefully but fires the exact moment the ship heaves wildly, tossing Derek hard against the wall. Spasms of pain flare across his back and shoulders as waves wash into the salon. Worried that he missed, Derek looks again. Yankovic lies on the flooded salon floor, convulsing. He missed. Instead of his torso, the dart protrudes from his forehead above his eye. Instead of being stunned, Yankovic is dead.

Before Derek can search for Jenn, another swell tosses the ship violently, sending waves washing into the salon, dragging him toward the deck until he grabs hold of a bolted chair. A loud bang from the top deck followed by metal screeching sounds like a helicopter anchor chain just broke loose. Hopefully, they had more than one chain.

Drenched and disoriented, Derek spots Jenn face down in the water. In a surging panic, he dives over the chair to roll her on her back to give CPR before the next wave tosses them around. He's frantic that he came this far, endured this much only to lose her. For the first time in his life, Derek whispers a silent prayer, desperate for a divine intervention. Several heartbeats later, Jenn's chest pushes up against his palm with a vomit of sea water and rough coughing. When her breathing normalizes, Jenn's eyes slowly open, and then immediately grow wide.

"Get up slowly, or I swear to God, I'll shoot you both," Geoff shouts, standing right behind them, too close to miss. Geoff must have found Yuri's gun in the water.

Derek catches Jenn in the eyes, then helps her to stand. He raises his hands and stands in front of her, hoping Jenn will know what to do next. With only the strobes, she may not see.

"Ah, how chivalrous and pathetic. Beauty and the dweeb. I should've killed you at Masada," yells Geoff above the storm.

"You won't kill me now," Derek shouts. "I'm your only hope of getting off this ship alive."

CHAPTER 77:
SWEPT AWAY

Superyacht Zhelaniye, Eastern Mediterranean
Day of Temple Ceremony

J enn wonders if Taylor has lost his mind. Does he think he's bulletproof? Then she notices the leather satchel slung over his shoulder. He's not protecting her; he's offering her a weapon. Jenn reaches into the bag, hoping for something useful, only to find another Taser. Useless. Then she pulls out a military-grade, 50,000-watt laser. Interesting. That level of power can burn or blind. Against a gun, it may be worthless unless she can hit the gun-hand or eyes first. A long shot.

"You're outnumbered, with no escape," shouts Geoff. "You're bluffing."

"Help us return the president, and they'll go easy on you," Derek shouts, negotiating and buying her time to power up the weapon. Taylor is wrong. After killing an admiral and helping a FPOTUS to escape, Geoff will get life.

Glancing over Taylor's shoulder, Geoff looks conflicted with his brows scrunched together. Then his eyes narrow, hardening into determination. The laser powers up too slowly.

"Forget it," Geoff yells. "I stand a better chance in Moscow."

"Once Putin has the former president, you're a liability, a bargaining chip—nothing more," Taylor shouts.

"No, he'll take his rage out on you," Geoff shouts back. "You killed his friend."

The laser power shows green as Jenn slips her hand under Taylor's arm to stay discreet, pointing her best guess toward Geoff's chest. Then she hesitates. Unless she can disable Geoff, he may respond by shooting Taylor.

Before Jenn can decide, another wave rolls violently under the ship. As Jenn's feet slip from underneath her, she instinctively pulls down on Taylor's satchel. Jenn blindly fires her laser, which elicits a howl from Geoff, who instantly returns fire. A bullet slams into Taylor's shoulder as he and Jenn fall backward onto the sloshing salon floor. Jenn hits hard, losing her grip on Taylor, and gets dragged by receding water toward the open deck.

Also dragged, Geoff nearly washes overboard until he grabs hold of a ship railing. Jenn clutches a bolted deck table, terrified they will all die. She can no longer see Taylor, worried he already washed overboard. The rain bites into her skin, making it nearly impossible to see. Too petrified to dash back into the salon, she clings to the table.

"You should've gone home," Geoff shouts.

Behind him, the strobe struggles against the wind and hints at a mountainous white cap building over the ship. Before Jenn can respond, the deck rolls sharply under the enormous wave that crashes down, submerging the entire aft deck in a deluge. As the water rolls off the deck, another loud metallic bang unleashes a long screech of metal that pierces the storm. The helicopter has broken loose.

An unexpected arm reaches from behind to pull her backward behind a deck bar. "Hold on," shouts Taylor.

A split-second later, the helicopter pulls free with a deafening screech of mangled metal that crashes onto the aft deck, destroying the same table she had used for cover. Jenn can hear Geoff screaming over the din of the storm until his screams stop suddenly. The chopper slams into the ship's deck and rail, sending debris into the wind flying inches over her head. When Jenn looks again, both the helicopter and Geoff Rhodes have washed overboard.

In a state of total shock, Jenn stares at the giant gash where Geoff stood only seconds before. A part of her wants to celebrate justice for her father, while another part dies over the loss of someone she once loved. For a moment, the sound of the storm and the cold, biting rain fade away as the shock mutes her senses.

"SLVIA, get this ship moving into the waves or we're gonna sink," Derek yells from behind her. His voice sounds distant, muted, unreal. An arm lifts Jenn, pulling her back into the salon, which looks like a tsunami smashed into a beach lounge, still swamped and topsy-turvy.

A moment later, the powerful engines start up, and the helm engages the stabilizers. The next wave rocks the ship, tossing them to port, but not as violently as before. Bilge pumps engage in draining the ocean deluge, but it will take time. Even with the lights off, it won't take long for the terrified and battered crew to investigate the damage.

"How were you planning to escape?" Jenn yells at Taylor over the tumult, already thinking they will need to subdue the well-armed crew and commandeer the ship.

"The helicopter," he shouts back.

The helicopter went over the side with Rhodes. "In *this* storm? That's lunacy," she yells.

"Yeah, I know," he shouts back. Emergency floor lights illuminate the stairs leading down on the opposite side of the salon where she came up.

"This way," he says, taking her by the hand to follow the trail of lights through the sloshing water. They continue to follow the emergency lights into the lowest level of the mid-ship, forward of the engine room. Not an exit. Jenn can hear men in the engine room yelling at each other to regain control of the ship.

"Where are we going?" she questions, quieter now, away from the storm.

"I don't know," Taylor admits. "SLVIA has a plan."

Did he say SLVIA? They soon arrive at a watertight dive chamber at the bottom of the ship. Inside the chamber is a two-person, recreational, Triton submersible that jostles around from the agitated waters on tight mooring lines. Everything in the chamber looks tumbled from the earlier wave disruptions, but the sub looks undamaged. Looks mean nothing. An unseen crack or damaged seal can sink them.

"Works for me," Taylor says, looking for the button to open the hull hatch.

Jenn reaches around him to push a big red one. "Do you know how to operate this sub"

"Not a clue. You?"

"No," she replies. Without training, they risk their lives, but they have no other choice.

"SLVIA, I lost my lenses, walk me through how to launch this sub," Taylor says as he opens the canopy hatch to get inside. Every intelligence report on Taylor wrote about how he talked to himself when he thought no one was listening. Now, he does so openly.

"SLVIA? You found the SLVIA?" she asks, climbing in next to him. "How are you communicating?"

Taylor holds up his hands for her to be quiet as he obviously pays attention to something. Jenn hears nothing. After a moment, he points behind his right ear. "Chip."

Jenn locks the clear hatch as SLVIA walks Taylor through start-up procedures to check seals, battery life, ballast, and rudders. The process seems tedious and a reckless waste of time, but sinking in a leaky sub sounds even worse.

Without warning, the ship stalls again, perhaps necessary for the sub to exit, but something feels wrong.

"Oh, crap," Taylor says. "We've got company."

The chamber door opens to a flashlight searching the room. When the light shines on Taylor's face, he waves and blows the ballast chamber. Huge bubbles of air immediately percolate around the sub as it rapidly submerges.

"Duck," Taylor shouts.

A gun flashes in the dark above them, cracking the thick glass portal window. Several more gun shots send bullets into the water, missing the canopy by inches. The submersible clears the underside of the enormous hull and continues to drop into pitch-black water. Jenn looks up to make sure the crack doesn't spread, her heart pounding hard.

"SLVIA, we cleared thirty feet," he says.

Above them, Jenn hears the massive yacht's engines rev up again as the giant hull and props pass above them, momentarily churning the water and the mini-sub. Once the ship passes, Derek lifts the sub to a depth of twenty feet to reduce pressure on the crack but stays below the wild churning of the surface storm.

With pitch-black around them, the only light comes from the instrument display. For several seconds, they both simply sit there, stunned, in shock, adjusting to the dark and the absolute quiet. They survived the nightmare. Geoff did not. Adrenaline still pumps through her system, making her breathing shallow. The quiet below the storm above. Safe. Black. Surreal.

"You OK?" Taylor finally asks, breaking the silence.

Images flash in her mind of Geoff holding onto the rail, replaced by the gash in the ship. Her head nods in response. "Yeah, I think so."

Surprised Taylor doesn't have a glib sardonic comeback, Jenn looks closer. "Oh my god, you're bleeding."

"Just a nick," he groans.

Taylor's wrong; he's losing too much blood. He needs medical care soon. Jenn stares at him for a long moment. In the past two days, this man has risked his life twice for her. Jenn can only imagine one reason any man would do so. Then her thoughts drift to Geoff and the bitter stew of sexual assault, murder, and betrayal.

"Geoff killed the admiral," Jenn says, turning to watch Taylor's reaction.

"Yeah, I know." He winces. "SLVIA, showed me the video. It's over now. I'm sure your dad would be proud of you."

Though she's not convinced her actions the past week would have earned the admiral's approval, Taylor's words bring a touch of healing. Her eyebrows furrow. "Why? Why did you come for me? My investigation report turned you into a fugitive. You don't owe me anything, even a friendship."

Taylor takes a deep breath, hesitant to respond, or in pain, looking battered, and exhausted. "No, I guess not, but has it ever occurred to you I'm not keeping score. I'm keeping a promise."

Jenn holds his gaze for a long moment. That's exactly what the admiral would say. There is absolutely no future with a man on the run from nearly every nation on the planet. Eventually, someone will catch him or kill him. How can she ever trust a man who won't even admit to his real name? Without trust, they have nothing.

Jenn rips at her shoulder seam to remove the silk sleeve, then wrings out the excess water and presses the cloth into Taylor's wound to slow the bleeding. A loud groan tells her the bullet remains lodged.

"Thank you for the rescue," she offers. "But what now, float aimlessly until we wash ashore?" The recreational sub won't have enough power to make it to shore, especially if they use lights.

"Jack and SLVIA track our GPS," he explains. "After that, I arranged a fifteenth-century Coptic church turned into a villa." He lays his head back to close his eyes. "Not sure about you but I could use a little me time."

His voice sounds weak, and he's still bleeding too much. The idea of losing Taylor after losing the admiral radiates a terrifying panic through her soul that's nearly unbearable. Jack will need to wait for the storm before he can retrieve them. It may be too late.

"Stay with me, Taylor. Come on, talk to me. Tell me more about your relationship with the admiral. How did you meet?" Jenn needs to keep Taylor conscious as long as possible, praying it will be long enough.

CHAPTER 78:
ARISTOCRATIC DISDAIN

Hansell Castle, Wales
Day of Temple Ceremony

Nelson wears his best suit as he patiently waits in the elegantly furnished foyer of the castle. Years ago, he would be over the edge giddy about meeting with a royal, even a close friend of his father. Sadly, today will be the type of transparent conversation most in the aristocracy spend a lifetime avoiding.

Much to his disappointment, most of the archive passages were vague, referring to his father only through his role as Chief Legal Counsel of the World Bank or Counsel on Foreign Affairs. Yet, the same documents also referred to someone named Boaz. Freemasons believe Boaz was the name of one of the two pillars that stood before the temple of Solomon. A right-hand man to a leader, which the documents refer to as Praeceptor, Latin for Grand Master.

"Dr. Garrett," the royal greets as he descends the grand stone stairway. "So pleasant to see you after so many years. You look splendid, my good man. Your father would be quite proud."

"My lord, you grace me with your kind words," Nelson bows his head in respect. He's not so bold as to reach out his hand for a shake unless in response to a royal hand offered. No such offer comes to match the pretentious greeting.

"Finley said that you wish to see me about your father," the royal gets to the point. "Perhaps we should sit in the study."

He leads Nelson into an exquisite eighteenth-century wood-lined library with thousands of first edition manuscripts of every kind, many of them dating back hundreds of years. Like many of the grand libraries of the aristocracy, the library is more for show and prestige as opposed to learning.

"Thank you, my lord, for agreeing to meet with me. I would like to ask a few questions regarding my father's heritage," he says. "My father and I became estranged after Cambridge when I accepted a position in the American defense science program." In fact, he and his father were never close. After his mother passed away, he became an obligation rather than a son.

The royal takes a deep breath, a sign he wants to speak. "Yes, I recall your father's concern with your chosen career. Yet, I know from intimate conversations that while he wished for you to follow more closely in his footsteps, he was proud of you and astonished by your accomplishments."

"Perhaps so," Nelson admits. "He expressed none of that to me and frequently berated me for not earning my full potential within the commercial sector." Nelson pauses, hesitant to be rude, but he must know. "I wonder if my father's feelings regarding his footsteps had anything to do with his role as Boaz within the *Concilium Tredecim*?"

The archives described how Boaz manipulated the Shah of Iran, which led to his downfall and the rise of the Ayatollah. Boaz also provided intelligence to ensure Israeli development of an Israeli nuclear defense. On three continents, Boaz undermined leaders. He also conspired with Roger Maxwell to cover up his embezzlement to keep the corrupt publisher from printing stories about the Bilderberg. The *Concilium* eliminated Boaz for keeping his scheme a secret from the *Concilium*.

The face of his elderly host instantly freezes into a stone-cold scowl, assessing him carefully and silently for the longest, most dreadfully awkward moment. "You know, Nelson, one trait that your father and I shared is the disdain for deceitful motives. Let's begin again, and this time I would like to hear your honest reason for coming to see me."

The royal referred to him as Nelson instead of Dr. Garrett, meant to sound more condescending. Nelson hangs his head briefly, accepting the rebuke without attacking the hypocrisy of the man, then lifts his head.

"You are correct, my lord; forgive me. I have spent too much time with the Americans. I am here to inquire about my father's role within the *Concilium Tredecim* and discover why he deceived me regarding my true heritage."

"That's much better. First, tell me how you learned of the *Concilium*," the royal questions, sitting up straight to look down his nose without answering the question.

The royal doesn't deny the existence of the group, only questions how he learned. Nelson smiles politely. "I'm afraid my sources must remain confidential. Surely, my lord, you can appreciate the value of secrecy." Nelson pushes back and continues. "I am curious why the Order referred to my father as Boaz? Is that a title?"

The royal stares at him for another long, penetrating moment. "I see. Then I am afraid I cannot help you. What I can tell you, Nelson, is that you were born into a long line of leaders, men of unusual intellect and insight who directed the course of human history away from tyranny, savagery, and ignorance toward civilization, art, and science. Because of the baseless and fearful reaction of the boorish masses, wisdom drove those same distinguished men to don a cloak of secrecy. I will never disparage the memory of a great man, such as your father, with the slanderous and cheeky Hollywood innuendo of those who lack the full context of historical circumstance."

Nelson studies the eyes of the elderly aristocrat, watching his cheeks flush and his eyebrows lower in indignation. A typically aristocratic response, haughty without a glimmer of transparency or remorse.

"Quite so." Nelson lowers his eyes. He's wasting his time, but ironically, he already heard enough to validate the truth of the archives. "Then I shall not take up any more of your time. Thank you for such an enlightening, albeit brief, exchange. Good day, my lord."

He stands and turns to leave.

"Nelson, wait," the royal calls.

Nelson turns back to listen.

"I will ask you once more," the old voice strains with a mix of anger and dread, "how did you learn of the *Concilium*?"

Nelson exhales a deep breath and shakes his head. "I regret I cannot answer you for the same reason you refuse transparency with me, my lord—to protect those who are not a part of this private conversation."

"Do not make yourself into an enemy of those who created you. Your schooling, your breeding, the intellectual stimulus that filled your youth. We created you. We can destroy you." The royal threatens with no emotion, but it's an empty threat. The royal can take nothing Nelson hasn't already lost.

Nelson takes a deep breath. "My lord, I would encourage you not to make the search for truth into a cause for animosity. While I may or may not discover the full story, I am not the one you need to fear. Others already know. It will be their testimony you *should* dread." Nelson doesn't mention SLVIA or WITNESS.

Nelson turns to leave the castle, feeling a scorching glower on his back. An epiphany consumes him. Nelson can never go back to who he was before the AI he created changed his life forever. Nor can he return to a blind allegiance of selling his genius to the development of either weapons or frivolous billionaires.

Nelson finds it ironic to have the words of Mordechai burn within him. Nelson will never find that which he does not seek. Like many creatures of nature, he needs a transformation, a metamorphosis. Nelson needs to process the past more fully before setting a path for his future. He needs solitude away from Jester and Taylor. Nelson needs to reinvent himself—but into whom?

CHAPTER 79:
GREAT CONFESSION

Situation Room, White House
Two Days After Temple Ceremony

Matt Adelson scans the weary, stressed faces called to the emergency meeting—the president, National Security Advisor Dominic, CIA Director Russell, Secretary of Defense Harland, and NSA Director Asher.

"Mr. President, we've analyzed the video and believe it to be authentic," Matt clarifies before pressing play.

The video bears the logo of POCCNR, Russian state television, in the bottom right corner. On screen appears a very fatigued, stressed, and angry-looking former president with a mix of Russian and American flags in the background. He could be anywhere—even a cell.

"I want all my followers to know that I'm no longer in danger of being extradited by the radical, socialist, Democrats who have stolen our great nation," he begins, waving his hands back and forth.

"Because of the totally unfair, political-motivated, and unconstitutional witch-hunt against me, the socialist Dems made illegal threats to put me on trial for nothing—for nothing, I did nothing. They forced me to flee from political persecution. But so many other countries love me. They all love me. I did the one thing no one else has ever done: I found the ark, which will bring world peace for a thousand years. Only I could do that. Everyone is saying I deserve the Nobel Peace Prize."

He cocks his head, lifts his hands in question, then continues. "Now, I'm here in beautiful St. Petersburg as a guest of my good friend, President Putin—such a genius and so strong. He freed the eastern Ukraine people from a corrupt Nazi leader." Like others in the modern GOP, he repeats the Russian propaganda rejected by the rest of the world.

"So, I'm here to announce my candidacy for United States President in 2024. We will run under the slogan, *Take Back America*. And it's so true, so true. I will run a virtual campaign with daily videos that all of my followers can post on social media. When I win—and I will win big unless they rig the election again—I can bring peace with Russia. With your donation to my PAC, we can defeat those who would destroy our beautiful way of life, kill our religion, and defeat our glorious cause. This time, we'll win once and for all."

Matt presses stop. "Sorry, but he rants on for another ten minutes. Mr. President, I just spoke with Congressional GOP leaders who expect their base and party to support an offshore candidacy."

"Can he legally do that? Can he run in absentia from another country?" asks the president.

"I called the attorney general before the meeting," responds National Security Advisor Joe Dominic. "The Constitution forbids foreign-born candidates or convicted felons from running. But it is completely silent on a foreign-based campaign by a US-born citizen who has been indicted but not convicted. That scenario would have been unimaginable in the eighteenth century. Of course, we expect the Democrats and DOJ to fight this in court. But during an election year, with low poll numbers, and a politicized SCOTUS, the outcome is unpredictable."

"Holy mackerel," replies the president. "If he's reelected, then he goes back to corrupting the DOJ to protect himself from the criminal charges."

"And that would be the least of our worries," adds Dominic.

Matt considers the recent election laws meant to suppress voting as an additional risk to a fair democracy, but dark money, fact-free social media, and years of corruption also share the blame. "Even worse, if elected, there will be no question we've put a Putin puppet in the White House. Our national and NATO divisions will be irreconcilable."

"We need to make Putin pay for this one," argues CIA Director Alan Russell.

"How?" questions the president. "We've already sanctioned Russia, Putin, and his oligarchs. We've expelled their diplomats and cut off trade. Putin's a pariah backed into a corner, using hypersonic missiles, and threatening the nuke card. How should he pay?"

A sincere question. War in Ukraine bleeds into western Europe, risking a world war. Sanctions and oil price hikes have the world paying record prices for gas. Nearly ten million refugees flood eastern Europe, creating food shortages. The COVID-ravaged economy slips again into recession with inflation scenario not seen since the Carter era. There are no easy options short of full-scale war that could easily turn nuclear.

"Consider the former president a fugitive. Freeze the US assets of everything owned by the FPOTUS or his businesses," Dominic suggests.

"Cut off the Russian internet—all of it," Asher suggests. "We confirmed the data poisoning but have yet to identify who feeds the pipeline. Cutting Russia off will slow their next cyberassault." Without cyber, Putin may resort to chemical or nuclear weapons to bully his will.

Matt doubts that strategy can work without the widespread support of their allies, which is not likely. The EU already split over sanctioned Russian oil and lifted favored nation status. The EU nations are facing a humanitarian crisis unseen since the last world war. Asking them to suffer even more for an American political fugitive will not sell. This is an American problem.

"Sir, if I may, the harder we treat the FPOTUS, the more the world will see us persecuting a political rival. We should let the State Department and the courts handle this one," Dominic advises.

"Other criminals do not carry national secrets in their heads. If he can't post, then he can't mislead. Do it—all of it," orders the president. The decision will hurt the Russian people and inch us closer to war, except Putin has already declared war and taunts the US to stop him.

A text pings on Matt's phone, even though he turned off alerts. He glances for just a moment-no name or number.

The beast was given a mouth to utter proud words and blasphemies and to exercise its authority for forty-two months. Revelation 13:5

Matt glances up to the room cameras to realize that SLVIA is listening in again. The invisible program trained to observe has learned to engage. As much as Matt respects Taylor, the SLVIA has once again become a national security threat. Matt even suspects it was the SLIVA that penetrated the US networks instead of the Kremlin, but he has no proof, and he has no motive.

As if to respond to Matt's paranoia, a screen on the wall illuminates to feature the images of the former president, Putin, the Saudi king, and the Ayatollah morphing between faces. Each wears the costume of Pharaoh similar to the film *The Scorpion King*. Their voices combine into an ominous unison.

"The dragon gave the beast his power and his throne and great authority. One of the heads of the beast seemed to have had a fatal wound, but the fatal wound had been healed. The whole world was filled with wonder and followed the beast. People worshipped the dragon because he had given authority to the beast, and they also worshipped the beast and asked, 'Who is like the beast? Who can wage war against it?'"

As soon as the one image stops, multiple monitors in the Situation Room light up with deepfake digital images of the individual security council members within the room on each screen. Each deepfake image speaks directly to the individual it represents to confess everything ever caught on camera, email, a file, a chat, social media, text, cheating on taxes, cheating on their spouse, bribery, extortion, lying to the public they served, or sending men to die for political gain.

"What the hell is this about?" shouts the president, standing in a state of alarm, backing into a corner, looking pale and terrified.

"Turn it off!" yells Security Advisor Dominic.

FBI Director Wright picks up a phone to call security or technical help, but the phones are dead. He slams the phone down and pulls the plug on the monitor with his image. Another monitor comes on to continue the damning confession.

Matt leaves his confession in the Situation Room to check other offices of the West Wing. Each occupant sits transfixed to their computer monitor or phone. On each monitor, a perfect image of the individual confesses to themselves. Some people sit in tears; most sit stunned with open mouths, watching themselves with an overwhelming sense of what must be shame or fear of exposure. Others fly into a rage to rip their monitor plug from the wall, only to have their phone ping a moment later.

Matt's own phone pings to continue what he abandoned in the Situation Room. Ironically, those who depended on security cameras, digital files, communications, or secure networks during their life or career, like those in intelligence or politics, reveal the lengthiest confessions. Matt slips into an empty office when the monitor immediately turns on to finish playing his self-confession.

As Matt listens, for the first time in his life, he wonders if his actions in the name of patriotism may have cost him a soul. He immediately wants to justify his choices before he wonders if self-justification itself is the cancer plaguing all political leaders. The ends rarely justify the means, and yet every global leader learns to stop at nothing to achieve the ends. Every compromise, manipulation, lie, or betrayal of his long career, many of them captured on top-secret servers, are being presented back to him as moral failures. Even the affair he had before his wife passed, caught on text, confronts him, accuses him, and reveals him.

Security Council members and the president storm out of the Situation Room, either stunned silent, or infuriated, and looking for someone to blame.

FBI Director Nick Wright sees him and sticks his head in the door. "Just a warning for you and your pal Taylor—I don't care what it takes, but we're gonna bring that smug SOB and his AI beast down." Wright takes off briskly down the hall, already assuming SLVIA and SNO are behind the incident.

Matt can't imagine anyone else with the capacity, although he doubts Taylor had anything to do with this stunt. Matt considers it far more likely that Dr. Garrett foolishly unleashed the SLVIA. Yet, even at its peak power, the SLVIA could never pull off this massive output—nor would it fit the program design. The SLVIA operated on stealth, so much so that most thought the program was a myth. Something changed the SLVIA, or this is something else.

Chief of Staff Fagan slips in. "Turn on CNN. This freaking thing has gone viral."

On CNN, a shaken Drake Rapper faces the camera, pale and nervous. A video montage behind the anchor shows people weeping in churches or angrily protesting.

"For the past few hours, in what some are calling the Global Confession and others are calling the Deep State Condemnation, a computer virus took over billions of devices, including mine and my colleagues. In the user's own image, the program forces us to see ourselves as others see us. A rather disturbing view for even the best of us, reflecting our secrets, indulgences, vanities, hatreds, lusts, and lies in painful detail. Churches, temples, and synagogues all over the world have jammed to overflowing following the incident. So far, no government or group has taken responsibility. Stories of a rogue DARPA artificial intelligence behind the episode are unconfirmed by CNN. Others speculate Russia or China have upped the stakes of cyberwar."

The background video features a protest with signs against the invasion of privacy by an evil globalist cabal. A few posters depict the president as the devil standing next to a Jesus Saves sign, next to a Confederate flag.

"None of our government sources know who was behind this unprecedented breech of privacy. Several ex-generals have claimed that to their knowledge, no government has this capability. After the bizarre events in Israel last week, the Global Confession has deeply upset billions of people, including leaders in Washington, the Kremlin, and Beijing."

Matt stands to gaze out the window at the White House lawn, his heart frozen within his chest. Not only has the SLVIA regained access to secure networks, but instead of stealth, it openly warns the world that it watches them; it watches him. SLVIA just pushed the world beyond the point of diplomacy and sanctions. Whether or not intentional, SLVIA just turned itself into an enemy of the state—every state.

"Tell the president that I need to debrief him on an old mistake that may have come back to haunt us," Matt tells Fagan. Fagan stares a moment before nodding his head and leaving.

The Global Confession has reminded Matt that it was his decision to fund Dr. Garrett to develop the machine to gain a strategic intelligence advantage. Matt knows enough about the SLVIA to know it's impossible to capture or destroy. He also knows that for whatever reason, the program developed a trust in Derek Taylor.

As Matt continues to listen to his past errors of judgment, made to protect his country at all costs, he considers a new one. Rather than go to war with the improbable AI, Matt wonders if he can leverage SNO for a new strategic advantage. It will require an above top secret, black-box operation within the government with an extremely slim chance of success. While doing nothing is not an option, his plan could make it worse.

CHAPTER 80: POWERLESS

Bornem Castle, Belgium
Three Days After Temple Ceremony

"Are you absolutely positive that you've performed the ritual correctly?" questions Praeceptor. The magnitude of his disappointment weighs on his shoulders like a wet coat.

With Iranian missiles still raining over Israel, threatening the ark, and war escalating elsewhere, Praeceptor did what had to be done. Working through loyalists on the ground, the Praeceptor took possession of the Ark of Testimony for the *Concilium Tredecim*, only to learn that it had lost its legendary power. Dreadful news after also learning Mossad carelessly allowed the flapjack to escape.

"Yes, my lord. Three respected rabbis have each performed the rituals from the original *Sefer HaBahir* guidance. The ark does not respond," the Librarian replies with a thick accent.

"Perhaps the original translation was incorrect or incomplete," Praeceptor speculates. "Have you tried the ritual with both of the arks?"

"Yes, my lord, of course, but with no result," the voice responds. "Yet, if I may offer an observation. The Ethiopian ark is much heavier. While no one will risk touching either ark for fear of death, we would like to x-ray each of them to see what may be inside. We don't know what an x-ray will do to such a precious artifact. It may have an adverse effect."

The concept intrigues him. If they made both arks of wood overlaid with gold leaf, then in theory, they should weigh roughly the same. "Do it and report back to me at once."

Praeceptor needs the power of the ark now, more than ever. Attempting to kill flapjack backfired. Even worse, all morning long, hundreds of news stations have received files from the sacred archives. A public outcry has arisen, calling on authorities to investigate the Bilderberg Group, Bohemian Club, the CFR, and much more. Three thousand years of secret history was released to the world. The exact scenario he had hoped to avoid by eliminating the hacker.

As soon as his call to the Librarian ends, the monitor changes into the image of a beautiful, young, blond woman. Heather Garrett, Nelson's deceased mother, a woman he once tried unsuccessfully to seduce. Her face contorts in pain before it morphs into the habit of a nun. When the nun speaks, her voice sounds like a thousand trumpets in dissonant harmony.

"And as soon as the thousand years are ended, Satan will be loosed out of his prison and go forth to deceive the nations that are in the four corners of the earth, Gog and Magog, to gather them to the battle, the number of whom is as the sand of the sea. And they came up over the breadth of the land and surrounded the camp of the saints, the beloved city. And there came down fire out of heaven and devoured them." The nun image pauses. "Your thousand years have finished. The dragon of the great beast will see defeat."

The image morphs into the American evangelist Joel Olsten. *"And the Devil that had been deceiving them was cast into the lake of fire and brimstone, where both the beast and the false prophet were, and they will be tormented day and night for the ages of ages."*

The preacher's image melts, replaced by a split-screen of news broadcasts from all over the globe in every language. Oil spills, chemical plants, ocean plastics, burning landfills, out-of-control forest and jungle fires, extreme droughts, migrant camps, and extreme poverty and starvation—each occurrence of human suffering stemming from the activities or negligence of companies where he controls a sizable share.

The image shifts again to show weapons development, political corruption, phony preachers, ravenous greed, and consumption by billionaires at the expense of those who made them wealthy. Under each image reads a subtitle that strikes terror into his heart: *Sacred Directives of the Council of Thirteen.*

Praeceptor turns off the monitor, but it comes back on with the security camera view of his torrid affair with a teenage girl on the private jet of the deceased Jeffrey Epstein, then on an island, then on a yacht. That video cuts to a live security video of his wife, sitting upstairs at her desk watching the same video of his pedophile indiscretions.

Astonishingly, she reacts with absolutely no emotion or shock, and simply reaches for her phone. "Randall, call the villa in Monaco to prepare for me. Set up an appointment with my attorney to meet me there. Have my jet ready within the hour. I am seeking a divorce."

His illusion of absolute power and invincible control vanishes like a whiff of smoke. His legacy as Praeceptor will be to protect an embattled three-thousand-year secret order, as well as to fend off an assault on his own honor and fortune. An unimaginable scenario, alarmingly real.

Praeceptor breathes deep through his flaring nostrils and vows to avenge his disgrace. This entire ordeal began with the theft of the sacred archives. It will end only when the flapjack and his friends pay with their lives. He picks up his own phone to dial from memory.

"I have an urgent job for you. I've had a premonition that my wife is about to have a terrible accident. Take care of it."

CHAPTER 81:
CHANGE IN PRIORITIES

Luxury Coptic Villa, Jaz Almaza Bay, Egypt
Four Days After Temple Ceremony

Jenn's vivid nightmare of losing Taylor overboard is slowly blown away by a warm breeze and sunlight shining through the open patio door. Every muscle in Jenn's body still radiates with a dull ache, but that's a small price to pay for being alive. Then her thoughts turn to Taylor—worried, saddened, conflicted. She hasn't heard a word for three days.

Delayed by the storm, it took nearly six hours before Jack retrieved them from the sub. By then, Taylor had been unconscious for over an hour. The thought of losing Taylor so soon after losing the admiral felt like a mountain crushing down on her chest.

An unexpected soft squeak joins four unexpected tiny paws crawling over Jenn's legs toward her chest. Jenn opens her eyes to find an orange tabby kitten wearing a yellow ribbon with a note. *Hi, my name is Marley.*

A smile forms as Jenn pushes herself up to find coffee, eggs with tomato and cilantro, a bowl of cut fruit, and a local pastry, still warm, left next to her bed.

It can only mean one thing: Derek Taylor survived.

Jack met them in a helicopter to airlift Taylor directly to a Cyprus hospital, but by then, Taylor had lost a lot of blood and was in a coma. Jenn feared it was too late. After the hospital, Jack dropped her off here, then disappeared. She hasn't heard from either of them since.

Then Jenn spots another surprise. Beyond the breakfast sits a stack of her mother's journals. Jack must have returned from the states. Jenn nuzzles the purring Marley closer to knead the soft covers on her chest as she reaches for the coffee.

Voices from downstairs drift up to her room. While Jenn's excited to see the men, she's still half asleep, and wants to first enjoy the ocean view, her breakfast, and Marley. Taylor promised her a few days of rest. She's going to hold him to his word. But just knowing he's well enough to make her breakfast lifts her spirit immensely.

After eating, Jenn stares at the stack of her mother's journals, curious but cautious of the hurtful memories they may evoke. The last thing any woman wants to do is relive the trauma that defined her youth: a mother passing away. With a heavy sigh, Jenn opens page one.

I learned of my breast cancer diagnosis today. Rather than shock or fear, my first thought was of little Jenny growing up without her mother. I know Adam will do his best, but he's a sailor and lacks the spiritual sensitivity Jenny needs to reach her full potential. While Jenny was at school, I pulled out my Bible, hoping for some comfort. Instead, I landed on the book of Revelation and the message to the seven end-time churches. I became overwhelmed and cried for an hour. Jenny will survive me to experience those days alone.

I'm going to keep this daily journal to document my journey through cancer and, hopefully, to health again. I also intend to document my journey through prophecy, seeking to validate the text with current evidence and sift through the allegories for attributes that have meaning. I can only pray these studies will someday guide Jenny through the unprecedented times in which we live. She is the captain's daughter. I know she'll be strong enough.

Jenn places the book down, letting a tear roll over her cheek to dry in the warm breeze. With a step out of bed, she places little Marley on the floor, and stands at the patio overlooking a private beach, naked to the wind and warmed by the sun. These journals may prove to be emotional pages to read, and will reveal a forgotten, hidden strength of her mother. After what Jenn witnessed on the Temple Mount and hearing the astonishing story of how Taylor found the ark, she can't help but believe her mother's wisdom will serve her well in the years to come.

Eventually, her curiosity and a swelling excitement to see Taylor win over her aching muscles. Donning an elegant, embroidered silk robe left hanging on the door, she steps into a set of soft, Persian slippers. With a refreshed cup of coffee from a handmade carafe, she gently steps down the stone stairway.

When Taylor spoke of a converted Coptic villa, Jenn never could have imagined anything so luxurious, seamlessly weaving the ancient with the modern. Padded by woven rugs, and lined with antique tapestries, the fourteenth-century stone stairway features bronze sconces, now wired, that share a gentle, welcoming light.

As Jenn steps into the expansive living room, her eyes still draw up toward a fifty-foot dome painted in midnight blue with tiny fiber-optic lights designed into an actual star map of the Egyptian sky. Mesmerizing and elaborately expensive. Stained glass windows filter in a multicolored warmth and radiance. Stone walls rise high to heavy wood timbered ceilings blackened with age and ions of smoke.

*

Luxury Coptic Villa
Four Days After Temple Ceremony

Jenn's gaze falls on Taylor and Jack leaning back on designer Italian sofas facing away from her toward a large, split-screen monitor. Within the monitor, she's extremely surprised to see Matt Adelson. Jenn knew that Taylor and Matt were once friends, but she never expected Matt would communicate directly with a fugitive. In the second window, Jenn spots the unmistakable shaved head, large earrings, neck tattoos, and wild eyes of an ex-CIA genius savant, and Matt's nephew, who calls himself Jester. On a third screen, CNN Egypt plays on mute in the background. No camera points in her direction, so she listens in, curious to know more.

"What does the SLVIA aim to accomplish?" Matt questions.

"Honestly, Matt, I have no clue. I haven't even heard from SLVIA since the ship," Taylor responds.

"Yeah, I've been in the air, picked him up only a few hours ago. We both saw the news this morning," Jack says. "Must have been freaky."

Jenn can't read the CNN subtitles, but the images show frightened officials and others pointing to their phones, televisions, or computer monitors. Something major happened.

"It was a worldwide phenomenon," Matt says. "I've spoken with every intelligence service on the planet, including the Kremlin. No one claims credit, everyone is freaking out, and suspicion runs higher than I've ever seen. Imagine every world leader, CEO, and even some pastors being interrupted by their own image, reminding them of every misdeed. This digital confession has people terrified, especially people in power."

"Yeah, I can imagine a few Bilderberg shaking in their Gucci snow boots," says Taylor.

"It's not a joke, Taylor. The Ayatollah, Putin, Xi, Kim, and a dozen other despots are using this incident as a provocation for war. The situation inside Congress has become volatile and downright dangerous, blaming each other of spying. Gun sales have skyrocketed to an all-time high. Widespread fears of an artificial intelligence-powered deep state have the evangelicals calling the confession virus the image of the beast and the current president the Antichrist."

Taylor stays silent for a long moment. "You know, Matt, I met a young man at St. George last week who followed a SLVIA persona on prophecy. Spending a few days with the kid made me remember that Sir Isaac Newton once predicted there would come a time when a growing number of people would focus on prophecies. I may become one of them."

"Yeah, SLVIA keeps sending me texts," Matt says without explaining. "I'm not convinced."

"What if the SLVIA is on to something? It wouldn't be the first time," Taylor says. "I mean, even on a pragmatic level, the world faces enormous crises unlike anything seen in human history, such as climate, food, water, population, pollution, ocean acidification, permafrost thaw, nuclear-powered despots, and now AI-driven warfare. That's just the short list. Geez, man, we've even got government-confirmed alien invaders. Yet, we are nowhere close to a global unity on a single issue."

"Yeah, like simpatico, dude," interjects Jester. "Dig it, I had NIGEL run the math, you know. Just like SLVIA did. With all prophetic events occurring so close together, including loss of fish stocks, species extinction, deforestation, the temple, the works, and like, we're talking astronomical odds, man, like over a trillion-to-one," claims Jester. "Just sayin, we can't rule it out."

"Frankly, I'm more concerned the SLVIA will create the very apocalypse it envisions. Either way, the world has just entered a new level of political tension," Matt says, his eyebrow rising. "Whose side will SLVIA be on?"

Taylor shakes his head. "OK, first, the SLVIA didn't create the animosity, only amplified what was already there. Come on, you're a Catholic. An occasional confession can be a good thing. Second, from what Jester tells me, SLVIA probably solved the AI data poisoning issues that almost started a war. So SLVIA saved your ass. You're welcome. Third, SLVIA never took a side before, why would it take one now?" responds Taylor. "Look brother, I get your paranoia, but I might point out that after it issued the warning, the SLVIA went stealth again," Taylor reasons. "No sabotage, no takeover, just a warning that we're creating our own demise, and it watches us. Tick-tock, tick-tock, you know."

Matt shakes his head. "Then what? What happens next?"

"How would I know? But if I had to guess, I'd say nothing good. Either way, I'm thinking of changing the focus of SNO toward the humanitarian crisis SLVIA keeps warning us will come. After the WITNESS dumped the old archives to the media, the *Tredecim* will have their hands full dealing with the authorities and covering it up."

"You may be right. Speaking of the media, did you hear about the arks?" Matt asks.

"No, what happened?" Taylor asks.

Matt grins. "Here, let me replay the clip from yesterday."

"Breaking news," CNN anchor Drake Rapper announces. "After the spectacular and historic events at the Temple Mount in Jerusalem this week, CNN confirmed only moments ago that both arks have gone missing. I repeat, both the Ark of the Covenant, a gift from the king of Saudi Arabia, and the Ark of Testimony, recently uncovered in the Judean Desert, have once again disappeared. Security cameras show a ten-minute gap last night at three in the morning. Shin Bet and Mossad are both investigating the theft, but there are currently no known suspects. We will update you as the story develops, but this is shattering news for the nation of Israel."

Jenn listens in shock, wondering immediately who could pull off such a theft, and why weren't such holy relics more closely guarded. Then Taylor unexpectedly chuckles at the news until his amusement grows into a belly laugh.

"What's so funny?" Jack questions.

Taylor calms down his guffaw long enough to answer. "They were fakes-- both of them."

"Fakes? You want to explain," questions Matt, one eyebrow raised.

"Sure, but stay with me. Let's start with the Saudi king, who bought a stolen ark from Ethiopia after a 2021 massacre. Nobody else would know, but I sent Nelson Garrett to Axum. He found the original ark hidden in a tunnel along with other replicas. The king gifted a worthless replica stained with the blood of 750 Christian martyrs."

Jester chuckles, bobbing his head and spinning off to dance. "Say it with me, brothers and sisters—blasphemy." He continues to dance like Mick Jagger.

Matt raises an eyebrow. "And the second ark, the one taken into the Tabernacle? The one they arrested you for smuggling?"

Taylor throws his head back in a laugh. "Even faker than the first one." Taylor lets that statement hang in the air. "OK, yeah, they arrested me with an ark. But because of the traditional fear of touching the ark and the maniacal rush to show it off as a political trophy, no one scrutinized it. If they had, they would have discovered that it was made on a 3D printer using Nelson's scan of the Ethiopian original. I was driving the decoy truck."

"Decoy truck? So, there's a real ark?" questions Matt.

Taylor nods. "Oh, yeah, you bet. Rabbi Hiam and the Sanhedrin hid it somewhere in Jerusalem, waiting for a more secure temple or a messiah. Whatever, not my gig."

Jack laughs aloud. "Wow, that entire circus for a couple of cheap knockoffs that sparked a freaking war. Seriously, man, you've got the most bizarre karma."

"Yeah, true dat, fly cat," Taylor chuckles. "Look, if my karma were a scent, it would be called: *Oh, Crap, What Now? Number 5.*"

Everyone bursts into a compulsive chuckle while Jenn uses her hand to muffle her own giggle. Jenn recalls Adelson's description of Taylor as a good man beneath all his deceptions. A hard concept for her to grasp at first. It's true that Taylor deceived her and Mossad, and even endured a torturous interrogation over a fake relic. It's also true that he did it to help others protect something sacred. Maybe it's the enigma of Derek Taylor that attracts her the most. Jenn gets another glimpse of the admiral's admiration for the man of secrets.

Matt chuckles, then hesitates. "Well, I hate to say it, but your known association with the SLVIA and now with the stolen arks will make you the most wanted man on the planet. The hunt for Bin Laden will look like a hide and seek game compared to what's coming your way."

"Gee, lucky me. Thanks for the pep talk, coach," snorts Taylor.

At that moment, Jenn feels the soft rub of little Marley against her ankle, announcing himself with a loud squeak that turns heads in her direction.

Embarrassed, she smiles awkwardly. "Morning, gentlemen. What are we talking about?"

CHAPTER 82: HEALING TRUST

Luxury Coptic Villa, Jaz Almaza Bay
Four Days After Temple Ceremony

Derek twists his head to see Jenn standing by the stairs, listening in. Typical for someone with a chronic curiosity. With his good arm and a loud grunt, Derek pulls himself up to step over and kiss her on the cheek. "Enjoy your breakfast, sleepyhead?"

"Every bite," she says with a smile. "Thank you."

With his arm in a sling and still feeling extremely weak, just seeing Jenn again lifts his spirit. Derek guides her to the couch, followed by Marley, who instantly jumps into her lap, already bonding.

"Morning, Jenny," greets Adelson. "How are you feeling?"

"Better, thank you," she replies. Turning to the second screen. "And you must be Jester."

Jester smiles and bobs his head. "Yeah, like, I be all me. Hey, hey, just so you know, I never cyber-stalked you. Like for real, you know."

Derek cringes, feeling immediately embarrassed.

Jenn raises an eyebrow and looks at Derek with a smirk to one side. "Good to know."

Jack lifts his hand for a high five. "Lieutenant Scott, mission accomplished."

Jenn pauses a moment, then brushes aside his hand and leans over to kiss him on the lips. "Thank you for saving my life, Captain Tote. Thank you for everything. I will never forget."

Tote smiles widely before he turns to Derek. "And *that's* why she flies for free."

Derek chuckles. "Gee, Jack, if a kiss will make you feel better, then pucker up, brother." Everyone laughs at the imaginary image.

"I was hoping Dr. Garrett would join us. Is he OK?" Matt asks.

"Oh, yeah, I forgot to mention," Jester replies. "Sir Snobby took a sabbatical. He disappeared after the SLVIA went quantum. Like, I think it freaked him out, you know. He made Zoey take a vow of secrecy."

"Good. The poor man has a lot to process," Taylor says. He doesn't mention the personal family history he never had time to explain.

"Jenny, I'm glad you joined us," Matt changes the subject.. "I have something to discuss that will affect all of you."

Derek looks toward Jack, then Jester. Both look suspicious. Neither of them trusts Adelson or the government, at least not fully. Derek's been wondering why Matt wanted to talk.

"I'm not sure why Dr. Garrett restored the SLVIA, but if I know Dr. Garrett, he had honorable reasons. Yet, it appears that the AI's power has grown even stronger. We all know the SLVIA will revive the SNO network. At the same time, the world sits on the precipice of our own creation. I never realized it before, but we need that network."

Derek shares a glance with his team to see the anxiety increase. Matt has turned a blind eye to SNO for a decade, officially insisting the SLVIA didn't exist. What does he have in mind?

"Jenny, I want you to work for me at NIA as the exclusive SNO liaison. A total black-box operation. You'll report to me and only to me. Officially you won't exist." Matt makes his offer.

The call goes silent. Matt grins at the shock on everyone's face. "Perhaps I should explain. I need to be realistic. I learned years ago that we can't destroy the SLVIA, so it would be better to be a partner than an enemy. While I'm not ready to buy into the prophecy theories, I recognize we are facing unprecedented global threats. If the SLVIA is correct, then I can't afford to be so naïve or sit on the sidelines."

"Like, no, no, no, SNO won't go," Jester reacts negatively. "Like, we don't work for governments, like, any government, you know." Jester spins off to tap his scalp. "Free bird, free bird." He throws his arms out. "Free bird, free bird."

"I'm not asking you to work for me, Jason. I'm suggesting an information-sharing partnership. For example, Jason had real insights on the AI poisoning fiasco, which isn't over yet since we still don't know the inside players. Taylor, given the international target on your back, you're going to need occasional official cover. I need more than the random apocalyptic text from SLVIA to understand what's going on. And frankly, I can only trust Jenny to keep her head on straight with you renegades," Matt explains.

Jester stops dancing to look at the camera, stepping up close. Jack turns as well. Derek hesitates, looking at Jenn to see her reaction. Her eyebrows raise, and her head cocks. He wishes he could read her mind. A part of his heart wants to leap at the chance but working together will kill any chance of having a deeper relationship.

"Come on, Matt," Derek replies. "We're a nonpolitical international group, remember? We don't do espionage. We help people stay cool from governments like you." In truth, he fears the loss of SNO independence.

"Your lack of partisan or national affiliation makes you a perfect partner," Matt responds.

Derek grimaces, watching the eyes of Jack and Jester, unsure how to read them.

"I accept," Jenn says, looking at Derek's surprised reaction. How can she accept before he accepts?

Jenn turns back to Adelson. "But I have a few conditions," she continues. "First, the DOJ drops all charges against Taylor, Jester, Jack, and Dr. Garrett.

And I want SNO off the terrorist watch list."

"Go, girl," Jack says, turning to Derek. "I'm calling dibs on Jennifer in case we break up."

On the screen, Jester's arms swing open as he spins in a dance. "Righteous."

Derek stares at her, his eyes narrow, silently questioning her motive. Jenn threw him under the bus last year, and it nearly destroyed his life. Then she turned a cold shoulder. Why would she take a job to collaborate?

Jenn takes in his gaze a moment before she explains. "Without trust, we have nothing. We can't build trust if your team is worried about an arrest or betrayal. And let's face it, Taylor, you have a well-known disregard for the law, especially the laws of physics."

"Preach," shouts Jack.

Matt chuckles while Derek shrugs, unable to argue, but still unsure what to do.

"I think I can arrange all that. Anything else?" Matt negotiates.

"Whoa, what just happened?" Jester twists his head and holds up his hands.

"Jenny just bought you a fresh chance to go home and visit your father," Matt responds

Derek isn't wild about the idea. He sees few advantages working with the NIA.

"Hold on," Jenn says. "My next condition is for Taylor." She turns to face him.

Derek's heart beats faster. He worries for a reason that he can't explain. "Such as?"

Jenn holds his gaze for a long, awkward moment and breathes a deep sigh. "I want you to tell me your real name."

"Whoa," Jester and Jack both respond in unified shock at her audacity. Matt cocks his head, listening.

Derek's heart freezes, instantly feeling cornered, tricked, manipulated. Jenn suspected his real name during her investigation, but couldn't prove it. Why should he have to say it aloud? No one else knows about his past. He's never opened up to anyone about that secret—ever. What makes her think that he'll open up to her? Jenn exposes him in front of his friends, which will only feed their own insatiable curiosity. The feeling of being trapped triggers something deeper, a defensive rage, likely linked to a foggy childhood trauma, and a need to stay invisible. A muddled memory of hiding under a freeway overpass flushes him with a forgotten terror. His jaw clenches tightly, and his gaze casts down.

"Flapjack," he says, pulling himself up to leave the room. "If you don't like my name, Lieutenant, then from now on you can call me flapjack."

Derek heads outside toward the rocky beach to get away from the moment, the unwanted interrogation, and the questioning stares. That's not the name she wanted to hear, and he knows it. His childhood and his birth name are like an open, searing cut that never bleeds and never heals. Traumas, always lingering at the edge of his amnesia. If Jenn can't trust him after he risked his life twice, then she'll never trust him.

From down the beach, Derek hears her running to catch up, which irritates him even more that she can't respect his privacy or let it go. Jenn pulls alongside to catch her breath.

"Taylor, I'm sorry—really," she says. "That was unfair of me to ambush you like that. I was wrong to ask, wrong to ask in front of others, and absolutely wrong to make it a condition of working with you. Please forgive me."

The apology helps, but it can't clear the air. Jenn pressed this same button during her investigation. Fair enough—that was an investigation. Why can't she let it go? Hiding his name kept him alive, but it also kept him alone. A dark secret, his biggest shame and regret, the nightmare that still haunts his sleep, and Jenn insists on digging it up.

Jenn places a hand on his good arm as he continues to walk away from her. "Taylor, please let me explain."

He stalls with a huff. "What's to explain? You don't trust me. You're never going to trust me, which means working together will be a huge, huge mistake. I'm sorry if investigating me ruined your career, Lieutenant, but it sure tanked the crap out of mine. Sorry, sister. Accept whatever job you want, but the deal's off."

"How much do you trust me?" Jenn responds calmly with a question that surprises him.

"What do you mean? I risked my life for you," he retorts, offended she would even ask.

Her finger turns his chin until his eyes catch hers. "That's not what I asked you. Do you trust me enough to let me inside? Will you ever trust me enough when our lives are on the line? Will there ever be a time when you stop hiding from me, playing word games, feeding me half-truths? Or will I always be on the other side of the wall you've built around yourself?" Jenn hesitates and inhales. "If you want me to trust you completely, then I need to know if you can trust me completely."

Stunned and petrified, his heart races. Derek hyperventilates, unsure if he can open up to anyone. Yet, a part of him wants to trust her with every fiber of his being. Jenn asks him for the ultimate act of trust. She asks a high price for a path out of the shadows.

Already exhausted, Derek stops to sit on a large drift log on the beach and waits for Jenn to join him. He stares at the water for a long moment, searching for courage, searching for the words. His good hand grips his thigh in a nervous fidget.

"I was only nineteen years old when it happened," he begins, his voice trembling. "The night I met the SLVIA and the night Bianca and Derek died were the same night. SLVIA tried to warn me, but I didn't understand in time. Foolishly, I had hacked the sacred archives of the *Concilium Tredecim.* The same archives that WITNESS released to the media this week. An explosion meant for me killed the only two people I ever loved, ironically, while they cheated on me. It didn't matter; their deaths were on my shoulders. I knew the *Concilium* would keep hunting me, so I let them believe I had died. I took the name of an unfaithful friend and then disappeared until I could find the SLVIA. I learned to protect myself, and eventually, I learned to protect others."

Derek heaves a deep sigh, trembling, before he looks deep into Jenn's eyes. Wet with tears, her gaze meets his with wells of sympathy and perhaps empathy.

"Hello, Ms. Scott, my name is Cary Arthur Nolan. The world believes I died in a fire twenty years ago. As of this moment, except for the Praeceptor and the SLVIA, you are the only other person on this entire planet who knows my true name. Is that enough trust for you?"

Jenn's eyes water, and her lips tremble as she leans in to whisper in his ear. "Your secret will die with me, Cary Nolan. I believe you."

And just like that, with those three words—*I believe you*—a section of the wall Derek had erected around his heart as a child crumbled. Unusually speechless, uncomfortable with such intimate transparency, Derek turns to stare out at the rolling surf for several silent minutes. A journey of hiding from a dark past may have ended with a confession but another unknowable future begins.

"Do you know what comes next in the prophecies?" Derek questions, his awkward way of moving away from the powerful emotions he isn't sure how to handle.

"Not a clue, but I may learn from my mother's journals," Jenn replies. "Does it matter?"

Derek risked his life and the life of others to find the SLVIA so he could answer that question. Events turned out to be precisely what Mordechai had warned and nothing like what Derek had expected.

"I suppose not," he admits. "But you know, I bet I can predict the future."

"Yeah?" Jenn questions with a grin and a raised eyebrow.

"I predict that if we don't go back to feed Jack soon, he'll start to chew on the furniture."

Jenn smiles. "Nah, see only if there's some hot sauce."

They share a laugh as they get up to walk back slowly to the remodeled Coptic villa.

"You realize if we work together, we can't get romantically involved," Derek teases.

Jenn laughs. "Don't kid yourself, Taylor—we were never going to happen."

"Ouch, that stings," he feigns pain, holding his hand over his heart.

"Seriously, you're a walking crash dummy," she teases.

"Yeah, well, some women like a wreck they can fix." Derek can't suppress a smirk.

"Oh, geez, Taylor. It will never be my job to fix your sorry A," Jenn retorts.

"Nope, not your job at all," Derek agrees with a grin. "And I'm absolutely positive I'll never, ever, like in a million years, need to remind you of that fact *ever* again. Glad we cleared that up early."

Jenn laughs. "Smart-ass. No, I'll just use the tip of my boot."

Derek laughs. "Exactly what your dad used to tell me."

"Yeah, well, I have a sharper boot."

The voice of Michael J. Fox speaks into the back of Derek's head. "Ahh, I had a feeling about you two."

A wide grin spreads on Derek's face. The SLVIA still listens and watches over him. He may face a very uncertain future indeed, but it's nice to know that some things will stay the same.

CHAPTER 83: PILGRIM

St. George Monastery, West Bank
Four Days After Temple Ceremony

According to the German philosopher Arthur Schopenhauer, *to be alone is the fate of all great minds.* Nelson ponders a truth that has silently defined his entire life.

He walks slowly, enjoying the quiet of the pilgrim's trail to the St. George Monastery. At his first glimpse of the structure, Nelson admires the rustic architecture hanging from the cliffs. No phone, no WITNESS glass, or any other form of communication with Taylor, SNO, the SLVIA, or anyone else. For the first time in decades, Nelson has voluntarily gone off-grid and isolated from the world of power and dominance.

Revelations regarding his father's role within the *Concilium* have combined with his recent misadventure to rattle him to his core. Last year, he faced the shame of a life spent creating the AI technology that now empowers frighteningly lethal autonomous weapons and cyber-enabled sabotage. Now Nelson needs to look deeper into himself and those aspects of life he has largely ignored: human compassion and spiritual truth.

Nelson isn't sure that he belongs within the SNO alliance of cyber vigilantes. Contrary to their nefarious reputation, he found them to be a brilliant group of people trying to make a difference, albeit in highly unorthodox ways. Yet, he can no longer go back to being a docile cog in the war machine at DARPA. Nelson loathes the commercialization of AI for profit to create a new class of billionaires with influence on the lives of billions, while taking nearly zero accountability for the havoc or job loss they create.

For the first time in his life, Nelson isn't sure how to define himself without his heritage or his prestigious position or his intellectual superiority. After his meeting with the royal, even his blessed heritage feels soiled, tainted by an irredeemable iniquity.

Mordechai and the others spoke of prophecies as if they could accurately interpret the wildly symbolic allegories and images. They could be wrong, of course. Nelson has always considered religion a primitive form of psychotherapy for the masses. A hope of the blessed eternal to assuage the persistence of present sufferings. He could be wrong, of course.

His interactions with Salem, Captain Adri, Loir Sasson, Brother Mordechai, the rabbi and Dr. Rubin destroyed his preconceptions. Their faith seemed genuine, rooted, informed, compassionate and without the hysterics of some in America or astonishing arrogance of some in Europe. Nelson needs to form his own opinion, and that requires an environment that respects privacy, rigorously honest questions, and thoughtful analysis. A sincere search for a spiritual truth without the shallow platitudes.

The world has faced turmoil before. The calamities of today will undoubtedly lead to greater suffering, but the ultimate outcome has yet to occur, making how we live each day the genuine essence of our life. While Nelson can never undo the damage of his inventions, or the demons he unleashed, he can make amends by making a sincere change. Only by changing ourselves do we have any hope of changing our future.

Inside the welcome courtyard, Nelson spots young Mordechai, wearing his arm in a sling. Mordechai stops his conversation to scurry over for a tight, one-sided, bear hug. Completely unaccustomed to any such affection, even from his father, it only takes a moment before decades-old barriers fall. Nelson senses a human warmth he never expected but secretly craves.

"The Lord told me you would come," Mordechai conveys with a huge smile and a wink. "Come on, Dr. Garrett, I'll introduce you to the brethren and show you a place I already prepared for you."

Nelson accepts the hospitality with anticipation of a new beginning. As they climb the monastery steps, the words of Steve Maraboli come to Nelson's mind. *The beautiful journey of today can only begin when we learn to let go of our yesterday*--perhaps a thought as true for the individual as for humanity itself. Either way, Nelson knows his journey has already begun.

—

ACKNOWLEDGMENTS

The Last Ark: Lost Secrets of Qumran represents a speculative fictional narrative inspired by real-world events, technologies, history, archaeology, and politics. I want to acknowledge those authors who were deeply influential in researching and completing *The Last Ark*.

More than any other resource, *The Copper Scroll Project*, written by Shelly Neese and Jim Barfield, was a major inspiration for key plot points within *The Last Ark*, sparking hours of "what if" imagination. Likewise, *The Temple Revealed*, written by Christian Widener, provided a wealth of priceless insights regarding the original location of Solomon's temple hiding in plain sight, and the architecture of the Temple Mount. *The Last Ark* would not be possible without the incredible research of these authors.

Credit for some of the more controversial story elements of *The Last Ark*, such as the international sex trafficking role in political kompromat of Russia goes to Craig Unger, who wrote a well-researched book called American Kompromat. Other influential books were *The Rabbis, Donald Trump, and the Top-Secret Plan to Build the Third Temple* by Thomas R. Horn; *The Illuminati: the Secret Society That Hijacked the World* by Jim Marrs; and *Welcome to Putingrad* by Franz J. Sedelmayer. Beyond these books, I read hundreds of online articles, such as the Rand Corporation Department of Defense Reports, which informed matters related to cyberwarfare and AI vulnerabilities.

Last, I am forever grateful to my gracious, patient, and candid beta-readers, who encourage and challenge me: Greg Andersen, Jack Teetor, Darcy Morris, and Kathy Miller.

ABOUT THE AUTHOR

Guy Morris a successful businessman, thought leader, adventurer, inventor, and published composer. During college, Guy was influenced by men of the Renaissance who were fluent in business, science, politics and the arts. After growing up on the streets, he earned graduate scholarships for his macroeconomic models, and won awards as an early webisode pioneer where he wrote the scripts that introduced the SLVIA, based on a true program that escaped the Livermore Labs. With three degrees and thirty-six years of executive-level experience in high tech firms, Guy's thrillers bend the fine line between truth and fiction with deeply researched stories, international locales and sardonic wit.

You find out more about Guy via his website:

guymorrisbooks.com

You can also stay in touch via the following social media:

facebook.com/officialguymorrisbooks
instagram.com/authorguymorris
twitter.com/guymorrisbooks